BLOOD
OF THE
WATER

JAMIE MALTMAN

ARTS REBORN: BOOK II

TESTUDO

PRESS

Library and Archives Canada Cataloguing in Publication

Maltman, Jamie, author
    Brush With Darkness/Jamie Maltman.

Issued in Print and Electronic Formats.

ISBN 978-0-9921474-3-3 (bound).-- ISBN 978-0-9921474-2-6 (epub)

    I.Title.

This is a work of fiction. Names, character, places and incidents are either the product of the author's imagination or are used fictitiously, and any resemblance to actual persons, living or dead, business establishments, events or locales is entirely coincidental.

Cover Design by Keri Knutsen, Alchemy Book Covers

Maps © 2013 Jamie Maltman

Published in 2014 by Testudo Press

To Alex

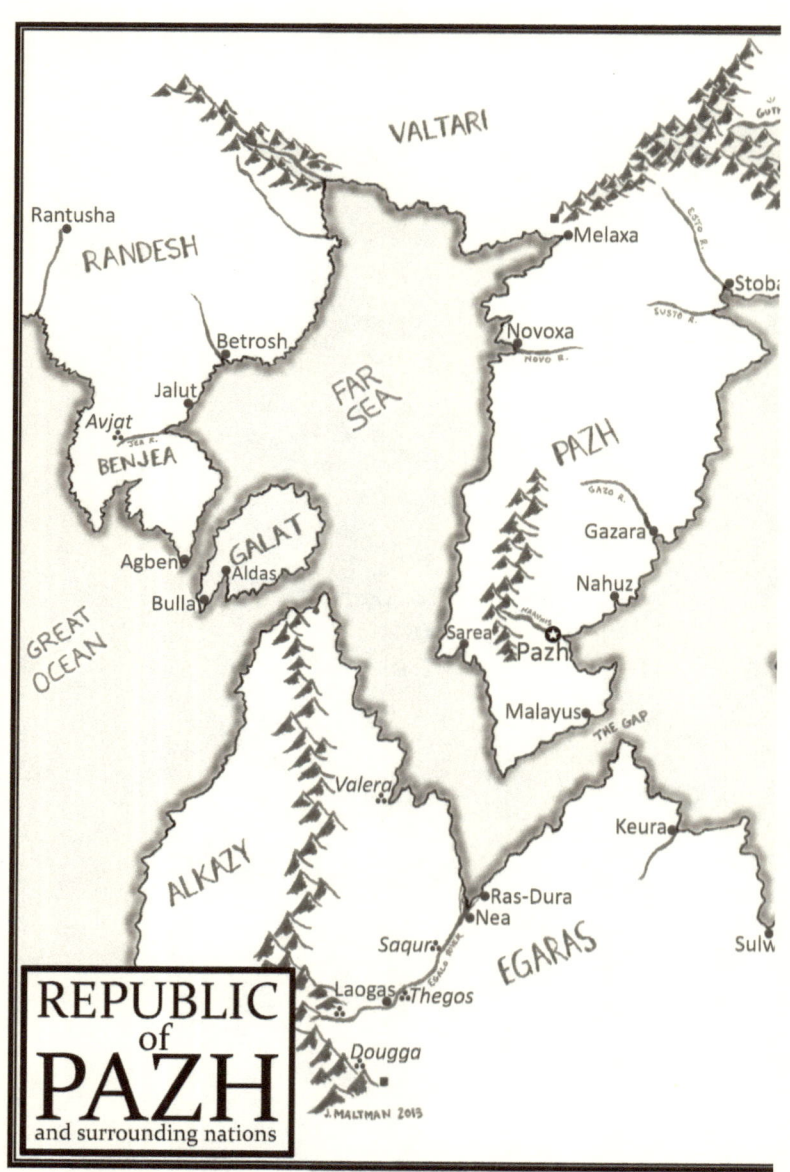

I

ᏮᏌᏮᏌᏮᏌᏮ

Vengeance

Waves crashed against the weathered fishing boat; spray like icy daggers stabbed at Glebric's thin face. He pulled the hood of his heavy woolen cloak down tight, shutting out the starry night. His stomach rocked with every lurching stroke as the fisherman rowed them across the bay.

Glebric had hired the boat to take him to Corus, to his mother. She was all he had left, and now he meant to set her free. How would he deal with Ventus? He still wasn't sure. But he couldn't think of any other way. Not now that Xelos was dead.

He didn't mourn his former employer. No, he mourned the passing of his duty. His duty to his mother, to keep her alive. *That bastard Ventus.* Holding his mother's safety over him, forcing him into this role, all because they had been born slaves.

Why did Ventus care about Xelos anyway? The old man was rich, too interested in the arts, and Simon was the first unusual visitor worthy of reporting. Well, Elysia was very interesting, but for other reasons. But she was just a local girl. Simon had been there less than a month, not even long enough for Glebric to make his next report. His first real report. The one he was supposed to give to Ventus tomorrow. But what now? The attack had put everything in jeopardy. *Will Ventus have any use for me now that Xelos is dead? Will he do terrible things to Mother?*

Glebric was putting it all on the line, making his own way to Corus, while Ventus would be in Attarsus for their meeting. He would sneak into Ventus' house, rescue his mother, and then... *what then?*

"Glebric..." whispered a voice, blowing on the night breeze. His head snapped around, searching out the source in the darkness. The fisherman kept rowing, seemingly oblivious.

"Come… Glebric…" said the voice, louder this time. *A woman?* From the rocks ahead to the right.

"What are those?" Glebric asked, pointing at the rocks.

The fisherman followed his gesture, and his eyes opened wide, startled. "I swear they weren't there before." The man looked around, skittish, and increased the pace of his rowing.

Glebric stared at the rocks, trying to make out details in the dim starlight. As they came alongside, the formation looked almost like… a natural doorway?

"Take me there," he said.

"I don't think—"

"Another silver if you don't think, just do." Glebric produced the coin from his pouch, and it glinted, reflecting the man's greed.

When Glebric had returned to the house, he'd been rewarded. It was full of death, but also riches, since he knew where to look. Xelos kept a lot of coin on hand, out of sight. With his former employer dead, Glebric needed money to fend for himself. Whoever was Xelos' heir wouldn't miss a few bags of gold. Sure, Glebric had felt a little guilty, but he'd served the man well for the past three years.

With his hands quivering, the fisherman directed the boat toward the rocky gate. Glebric flipped the coin to the man when they pulled up beside the rocks. He fumbled it and swore as he bent over to pick it up.

"Wait here," Glebric said.

"Attarso himself couldn't make me go in there." The fisherman dropped the anchor.

"Glebric… I'm here…" came the voice again, rising and falling with the waves. From between the rocks. Glebric lit a torch, illuminating the rough doorway of irregular natural stone, covered in slimy vegetation and with edges worn smooth as if it had been underwater. Maybe covered at high tide?

Glebric walked through into the passageway beyond, curiosity and desperation driving him forward. His quest to save his mother was already folly, so nothing held him back.

"Who are you?" Glebric called out into the yawning darkness. "How do you know my name?"

"Come to me, Glebric…"

More tendrils of slick weeds criss-crossed the floor, and the faint sound of water trickling down the walls fed several small

2

pools. The strange stone underneath his feet was more smooth, but still irregular, and sloped gently down, below the surface of the sea.

The tunnel opened into a kind of grotto, his torchlight illuminating the organic rounded walls. His feet splashed through inches then feet of water as he went forward into the gloom.

"Welcome, Glebric," said the voice, resonant, strong, and very feminine. Right in front of him. But there was nobody there. Goosebumps rose on his arms.

He waved the torch around, but still no figure. Just a protrusion of blue coral in the middle, growing out of the floor into the shape of a table. But this table must have been perfectly formed by the hands of man.

"Closer, Glebric... come closer..." A ghostly blue light rippled under the surface of the table with each word. "Let us talk of the future. Of rescuing your mother..."

How could it know? He shuddered, feeling naked, vulnerable. But his curiosity kept him rooted to the spot. "What are you?"

"Your deliverance. Bring me the one you fear. Tell him you have found something that he needs to see."

"Ventus?"

"Bring him to me, and save your mother."

"But how?"

"Do you wish to remain a slave?"

"I am no slave!" But it was a lie. His hands shook. A slave to Ventus and the control he had over his mother. Even though Xelos and his staff had treated him as a servant, a valued employee. Especially Elysia...

"Do you wish to make Ventus pay?"

Tears streamed down his face. "Yes!"

"Bring him to me, and you will have vengeance. And power. To do what you think is right."

Glebric's head swam. This table, speaking to him, in his mind? Reading his thoughts? Promising him power? It was crazy.

"Is it?" the voice asked. Glebric snapped to attention. "Or is it madness to reject such an offer, and submit yourself as a worm to this life you hate? A life owned by others?"

He clenched his teeth. He hated this life. He hated himself. Powerless. Out of control.

"Yes, Glebric. That is the choice before you."

Mother, I do it for you.

3

"I will bring him to you."

⟨⟨⟨⟨⟨⟨⟨

The first light of the sun streamed over the mountains in the east onto Simon's sleeping face, which shone like polished bronze. Elysia loved watching him at peace. She breathed in the crisp, clear air, tinged with the smell of her two companions. Simon smelled like a man, her man. And Zeno? He smelled like a horse, but a clean one. They'd bathed in the cold mountain stream last night and then slept like the dead, curled up together in the foothills on the edge of the Boraki range.

She'd wanted to see mountains—real mountains. Her native Attarsus was a hilly island, but nothing came close to these majestic pillars of stone. The towering range was the far eastern frontier of the province of Myrak—wild, unspoiled lands that also met Simon's desire to get away from civilization.

Was it a week since they'd left Tamar? Leaving behind war and death and the problems of the Republic. They had soared over the fertile plains of Pelusia in a single day, flying high above the land on Zeno's wings. Simon had wanted to stay away from the cities so they flew around Sal Pratta. He was worried that too much was still afoot with remnants of the Scentari invaders and the Pazian legions rooting them out. They didn't know the route Shadush had taken to come to Tamar, so they gave the whole province a pass.

They'd camped that first night in the wilds between Pelusia and Myrak, but in the morning her curiosity had urged them onward. Myrak, the provincial capital, beckoned with new people, customs, and food. Away from the perils of war, they were a new couple playing at being tourists. Tourists with a flying horse. Didn't they deserve a vacation?

Simon stirred, and Zeno withdrew the wing he'd laid over the two of them as a blanket. Elysia touched Simon's cheek and the two days of prickly growth since his shave at the barber in Myrak. She'd have to help him shave again; she far preferred his smooth face to the beards of the men in her native Attarsus. And she was getting good at it.

"Good morning, my love," he said, blinking sleep from his eyes. She kissed him lightly on the lips, not lingering long enough for Zeno's reproach.

"It's so beautiful—look at the sun over the mountains. Thank you for bringing me here."

"I could get used to it. I've never been anywhere so quiet, so peaceful."

They rose together, but his foot caught on her long dress and they stumbled, falling together in a heap.

"Be careful!" she said, checking to make sure he hadn't fallen on the wood she was carving.

"I'm not used to these new clothes," he said, tugging the long sleeves of his flowing robe before helping her up. They'd bought clothes in the local style in Myrak, again at her urging to try something new. They were very comfortable, so much softer and lighter than the wool she'd always worn, if not practical up here in the foothills. He hadn't wanted to buy them, but she'd convinced him with his own argument. He still worried that someone might be following them, even so far away from everything that had happened in Tamar. The clothes would help them blend in.

He examined her work, his face lit up with curiosity. "What are you working on?"

"I was hoping to finish it before you woke." She handed him the delicate butterfly, almost ready to be brought to life.

In his hands it looked so small, and he turned it over reverently. "How can you make it so thin, without breaking? Your Talent is truly remarkable."

"So is yours! And you can paint whatever you want."

"But it's still flat. To be able to bring something to life like this... can I watch you finish it?"

She smiled and sat back down to where she was using a large flat rock as a table. With her knives and chisels, she pared away the excess to expose the pure form underneath. A form only she could see. Each scratch brought it closer to freedom, from being trapped inside the wood.

When every detail was perfect, she closed her eyes and held it in her hand, connecting with the intense feelings of love, peace and wonder. They swirled up from her heart, through her arm, and into the wood. It became warm to the touch, and just as she opened her eyes, the fluttering wings tickled her hand as it flew into the air.

"Oh!" she said. "I was going to have you paint it." The light brown wood looked dull like a moth.

"It's still beautiful," he said, following its path as it flitted around their heads. He put his arm around her. "How does it feel? Bringing them to life?"

"It's incredible. I don't know what it's like to be a mother. I... I never spoke to Mother of such things before she passed away. I wish now that I did. But it must be similar. They're like my little babies, and I want to protect them, keep them safe."

Zeno snorted. She walked over to stroke his mane.

"Yes, I know you keep me safe too. And I appreciate it."

Simon looked thoughtful.

"What is it?" she asked.

"How will you bring your new little friend with us? I'm afraid it won't be able to follow us like the birds did."

She frowned. The birds had flown along with them at first, but when they'd entered the city of Myrak, she had to set them free. They were living creatures and couldn't be held in a saddlebag, nor could they follow them around inside the city. She'd brought them to life outside Tamar, to save Simon from the riders, but had never considered what would happen to them next. Were they able to fend for themselves in the wild on their own?

"Well, we're not moving on yet, are we?" She couldn't bear to lose another one of her babies, not yet.

Simon put his arms around her. "I can't think of a reason. I only want to be where you are." He leaned in to kiss her, but the butterfly tickled his nose on its way to landing on his shoulder. She laughed while he twitched in his attempt to shoo it away without causing it any harm.

"Good. Then I'll have plenty of time to find a home for this little guy before we move on."

ᏳᏋᏳᏋᏳᏋᏳ

Legate Persei Lokuta lifted a cup of wine from the platter, letting his eyes linger on Mirasha's cleavage for a few delicious moments before meeting her eyes. He felt his need rising again, and her eyes smiled back before she bowed with appropriate deference. She brought the tray to the others on their dining couches.

Persei watched the other guests over his cup, taking note of the length of their stares. His brother, General Daymar Lokuta, barely acknowledged her—ever the noble host—while Tribune Kyso Scribora, so cold and bookish, looked down at his cup. Harron,

Daymar's new aide, was brazen in his leer. With another woman, Persei might have given him a night with the girl to bind him closer. But not with this girl. She was his. Drinking deep did little to cool the fires of jealousy.

She'd been beautiful when clad in barbarian furs, but dressed like a proper Pazian lady she was breathtaking. Dark hair framed her tanned face; the flowing blue dress clasped at slender shoulders and flowed down over her chest; ties crossed below her breasts to hug the form of her slender waist before caressing her hips on the way to the floor. He wanted to take her again, right there. And knowing she wanted him too drove him wild with desire.

But this wasn't that kind of party. This was their small council, housed in the commandeered home of a Pazian merchant who'd fled Tamar to escape the Scentari. Comfortable and better than the garrison mess hall, yet still a far cry from the comforts of home. In the absence of sufficient slaves, Mirasha had been pressed into duty as a cup-bearer.

Daymar had invited them to discuss their imminent and victorious return to Pazh. The campaign had been over almost before it started. His 7th legion had cut through the leaderless Scentari on the streets of Tamar, turning the tide with their numbers boiling in from the harbor. And Persei himself leading the charge. That had won him a crown of honor, as the first officer over the wall. Technically he hadn't crossed any wall, but was the first one to set foot in the occupied city, even if they'd come by sea. He'd wear it as a badge of honor in any parade or special occasion. Which brought greater satisfaction: the pride in achieving one of the greatest honors possible in the legion, or Daymar being forced to publicly recognize his greatness?

The honor was warranted, for it had been the turning point for the city, and saved so many lives. Once they'd seized the wagon train in the morning, the remaining barbarian riders had fled, likely all the way back to Scentar. Genaro Morichea was mopping up any remnants in the northeast of the province of Pelusia.

Persei had initially bristled at Genaro being the one sent to finish things off, but any thoughts of furthering his own name were drowned in the earthly delights of exploring his prize. He'd found her, Mirasha, the Scentari princess, in one of the biggest tents of the wagon train. *His* tent. Shadush, the fallen Scentari grand thane. By rights she should have been common legion property, shipped

7

back for the triumphal parade and then sold at auction. But officially he'd labeled her as one of the camp followers, which meant she was free to go as she pleased. Only he knew her true identity.

In reality, she was already so much more.

When he discovered her after the battle, he burned with anger. She'd branded him when they'd first met, before sparing him from the pyre and setting him free to report back with word of her father's power. Mixing in with that anger was his frustration at being denied the opportunity to kill her father himself, and the desire that had filled him since he'd first set eyes on her. He'd been prepared to force himself on her, as the conquering hero.

But he had no need to force her. He could see it in her eyes. Women always loved him, and she wanted him even more. She had willingly offered her tender lips, and guided his hands down to remove the furs and reveal the delights underneath. He shivered at the thought of that first time. He'd had a lifetime of women already at the age of twenty, but she captivated him like no other.

The week that followed had been filled with nightly passion, and she was learning Pazian with remarkable speed. He found himself enjoying the conversation nearly as much as her body. He couldn't wait for her to learn more; he had so much still to ask her about the source of her father's power. What a woman, and still so young.

"Persei!" Daymar called to him.

"Sorry, what?"

His brother shook his head, rolling his eyes. "Get your mind off your little pet, and back to the matters at hand. Did you get the report from Genaro?"

Persei bristled at his brother's tone—always so superior. He longed to break that haughty jaw. He was bigger, stronger now. But his brother was the General of the East, and his direct superior.

"Yes, Genaro reported that there are no organized Scentari left anywhere in Pelusia. Any of the dogs that remain have gone back to their homeland, tails beneath their legs. He will be back here in two days."

"Excellent," Daymar said. "And Kyso, how go the plans for the triumph?"

Kyso sat up on the couch and drew out several sheets of papyrus lined with figures. "General, we have cataloged everything we found, including the prisoners. We won't be adding much to the

Senate's coffers directly, but through the sale of the slaves the men should do reasonably well."

"It was never expected to be a profitable campaign, other than preserving Pelusian trade. Harron, is the fleet in order? How soon will they be ready to return us to Pazh?"

The ambitious young officer puffed up when addressed. Persei didn't like him. He was lowborn—*mundati*—and a sycophant. But Daymar had retained him as useful. Persei considered it a little too convenient that Harron had fallen and hit his head early in the battle and managed to survive while the acting General Garas Numeno had fallen with the rest of his men.

"It will be ready before Morichea returns from the border. The 7th will return with you to Pazh for the triumph, the 3rd will stay here, while the 8th returns to Melaxa and the 9th to Egaras, correct?"

Daymar nodded, satisfied. "Then with the province pacified, the campaign is over. Persei and I will return to Pazh first. We have some unfinished business to take care of in Attarsus." Daymar looked down his long nose at Persei, who flinched.

He never fails to remind me of every mistake. Even after I did so well here.

"Kyso, I'll leave you in charge."

Harron frowned. At least the rat won't be able to feed from my brother's plate any longer.

"Do you require us to attend to any further details?" Kyso asked.

Daymar thought for a moment. "Kyso, did you or Garas ever hear anything from Persei's fellow messenger? Simon Baroba?"

"Simon—"

Harron cut him off. "His special defenses sure didn't do much."

Persei spluttered. "His defenses? You mean Simon was here?" He and Daymar exchanged a glance, and Persei shrank into the couch. Damn that Aktar!

Kyso was sweating. "He… he was at my side when we fought Shadush, outside the city walls. There were riders after the grand thane fell. We… were separated. I have not seen him since, nor any sign of his body, but most were beyond recognition. Why do you ask?"

"I only remembered him now, since he and Persei spent time in Attarsus. That will be all. I will see you two in the morning."

Kyso and Harron stood, saluted, and made their way out.

9

Daymar motioned for Mirasha to refill his glass. "She is a beauty, Persei." The girl blushed. "And learning so quickly." Daymar put his arm around her waist, drawing her close to him.

She looked at Persei, her face pleading. Persei yearned to strike his brother; the raging fire burned inside him.

"Why should I let you have such a prize," Daymar asked, "when you cannot even track a fugitive?"

Persei clenched his fists and sat up. "Aktar had everything—"

"Aktar failed. Obviously. And you must own that failure. It seems likely that your friend Simon died in the battle before you turned the tide. But I would prefer to see a body. Do you trust that Kyso never saw him again?"

"That one isn't capable of lying, though he and Simon were friends."

"We are not getting anything more from him. But Aktar owes us an explanation. We will stop to see him in Attarsus. Who knows what loose ends your blundering have left for us to deal with." He kissed Mirasha on the cheek. "Well, if the results are too dire, I will keep this one as compensation."

Over my dead body.

⊖⊖⊖⊖⊖⊖⊖

Elysia woke up from a bad dream. All she remembered was Persei Lokuta's leering wink, as he stood over the dead bodies of Xelos and her father. Her jaw hurt from gnashing her teeth, and her hands shook. Simon and Zeno were fast asleep, so she rose without disturbing them.

It wasn't the first time she'd had that kind of dream, and wouldn't be the last. Not while the murderer was still loose, and the arrogant noble who ordered the killing. She rubbed at her chest, imagining a hole in her heart where Xelos and her father had lived.

The moon was still hours from setting, and along with the sky full of stars it gave her enough light to walk. She needed to carve, to try to work through these painful emotions. She scanned the ground at the edge of the glade, searching for good-sized pieces of wood. Some wind-felled branches caught her eye. What would her Talent reveal inside?

The first held a handful of spiders, and she shuddered. She'd never cared for bugs. A larger one held a rat, but the eyes and teeth looked vicious and deadly.

This wasn't helping her forget murder and death.

Inside a stump she could make out tusks and bristles of .. a snarling boar, ready to charge. *Is some dark force inhabiting this wood?* The shadows seemed suddenly deeper, more forbidding.

She turned to run back to Simon and tripped, landing painfully on her elbow. Rubbing the bruise, she inspected the oak branch at her feet. It was wider than her arm, with a charred end that looked like it had been struck by lightning. But it was the figure beneath the bark that called to her. She couldn't see the whole thing. The angry head resembled the little lizards that lived on the beach, but the body was indistinct, hazy, which only intrigued her more. *I'll figure you out.* She set down to work.

"What happened to your arm?" Simon asked. It was fully light, and she'd been working for hours.

"What?" She looked down and saw dried blood. She hadn't even noticed. She'd been fighting with the wood, trying to unearth the creature inside. But while she'd worked it down to the shape of the head, the rest still eluded her. "Oh, that. I tripped. It's nothing."

"What are you working on now?"

"I... I don't know. I... I think it's another kind of weapon."

"Weapon? A creature as a weapon? Like the birds? Elysia, what's wrong?"

"I... I feel guilty. Being out here in such beauty, such wonder. Enjoying ourselves... exploring cities and temples and trying new foods... when they're dead. Yet *Persei* still lives."

"Elysia, look around you. Master Xelos and your father would want you to appreciate all this. All this life. Put Persei out of your mind. Don't let him back inside."

"Easy for you to say!" She surprised herself with the outburst. "You were able to save your father." She felt a stab of regret when she saw how she'd wounded him. It wasn't fair of her. He'd tried his best to save her father and their beloved mentor. Why did she have to make him suffer? To share her pain? But she wanted a life with him, with no secrets.

He broke away from her, gazing far downstream. Toward the sea, civilization, and the past.

"I... I'm so sorry that I failed you, Elysia. But can't we leave that all behind? There's so much world to see, and I want to go with you." He reached out his hand to her, hopeful. "And you're doing amazing things with your Talent. I haven't even begun to test mine. Out here, we're free to try anything, together, without anyone after us, or scared of our power.

"Persei probably thinks we're dead. He and Daymar will turn our victory into their own, and return as heroes. They'll be showered with promotions, and success."

She crossed her arms. "Exactly. They don't deserve it. You're the real hero, but you have to live in hiding? How could you have loved a nation that would let this happen?"

He pursed his lips. "I... I know. It is the nation of my father, and your mother. But it's my nation no longer." His face softened. "But I promise you, Elysia. We will find a new home. These provinces are still part of Pazh. Maybe some far off corner or provincial town? Or beyond the borders of the Republic. Yalath or one of Master Xelos' other contacts will have a better idea. I still think we should go to Jeppo."

"I just wish there was something we could do against Persei. If I could just get close enough, and I had the right weapon... one of my creations..."

Simon took her hands, holding them steady. "No, Elysia. You're not a killer. You don't know how it feels. Remember what Xelos taught you: our Talent is meant for creation. For good."

"I killed those riders." And she'd felt no remorse doing it. Instead she'd felt powerful. Something she still hadn't shared with Simon. There just hadn't been the right time. The riders had threatened not just him, but also her and Zeno. She'd been justified in protecting them.

"Only as a last resort. What you're talking about is... premeditated. It's murder."

"Like you seeking out Shadush to destroy him?"

His face belied the struggle she was causing him. "It's not the same."

"Isn't it?" She wrenched her hands away. "It is right to seek someone out for revenge on what they did to your nation, to your legion, and to remove the danger that they might kill again?"

"Yes, exactly."

"Then why isn't it right to do the same when you know someone is horrible, and sanctions the murder of innocent families—

your family! We should go after him!"

"It's… it's… I… I can't argue with you." Simon let his arms fall, and looked so sad, so defeated. "I'm going for a walk. I need to think. Maybe I'll come up with something. I'm sorry Elysia, but if that's what you want me to be…" He let his words trail off as he turned and walked away.

She wanted to follow, but froze, consumed by her own thoughts. *It hurts to ask you. But it hurts more to leave this hole in my heart.*

II

꘎꘎꘎꘎꘎꘎꘎

Kashaka

Glebric's hands shook as he pointed. "Do you see it?" His triumph loomed so close.

"Those rocks?" Ventus asked. He turned to the captain of his small ship. "The boy says those rocks over there."

The captain looked surprised. "I've been through here a thousand times, and I've never seen those rocks."

"Most intriguing," Ventus said. "You have done well, boy." He lowered his voice and leaned in to Glebric. "*They* will be pleased with your discovery. Maybe even enough to set you free."

Glebric's eyes gleamed in the starry night. To make sure the tide was right, he'd tried for the same time as last night's trip. "And my mother?"

Ventus' lip curled in amusement. "Not *that* pleased."

The ship couldn't get too near the rocks, so two of Ventus' guards rowed them to the rocky doorway.

"Watch your step," Glebric said.

Ventus reached out his arm for a guard to assist him, and gingerly stepped onto the rocks.

"You two, tie up the boat and stay here. I'll call to you if I need anything. If you don't hear from me in thirty minutes, come in and kill the boy."

Glebric fought the urge to grin. This one had it coming. He listened carefully, but so far, no whisper.

Ventus lit an oil lamp. The flickering light made his narrow face look even longer, more forbidding. Glebric hated that face, and what it represented.

Mother, you will never have to touch that greasy hair again.

"Lead on, boy."

The pools of water on the floor seemed bigger this time. Or

maybe it was just the different light. And the tunnel seemed some-how... alive. Glebric held his head high, not wanting the Pazian to call him a coward.

Down, down, down they walked with splashing steps. Ventus breathed heavily behind him.

"This had better be good, boy."

It had been easy to convince Ventus to examine the grotto. Explaining what had happened to Xelos, and the disappearance of Simon and Elysia... that had been much harder. Ventus had been very angry. All this since Glebric's last monthly report? But news of the grotto had settled Ventus down, and they'd left that very night to investigate.

"We're here." The corridor opened up in front of Glebric, and he stood to the side so Ventus could see.

The middle-aged Pazian's eyes opened in wonder as he took in the grotto, culminating in an exultant smile when he saw the altar.

Altar. Not table. But how to get him to touch it? How do I even know that's what I need to do? But Glebric *knew.*

Words leaped into his mouth. "Did I tell you... if you touch it, it glows!"

"You did not. This is an incredible find, Glebric! Well done!"

"Is it a place of great power?"

Ventus' eyes narrowed. "That is not for you to ask. But... perhaps I should test it."

"Shouldn't you leave that for your superiors?"

Glebric winced under Ventus' withering glare.

"*I* will say what is appropriate for my investigation." A few long strides and Ventus reached the altar, with Glebric following close behind.

After a furtive glance back at Glebric, Ventus touched the altar with his right hand. A glow radiated out from the contact, a green-ish-blue that made Glebric think of the sea.

Ventus grunted with delight.

"Hold this, boy." He handed Glebric the lamp. He rubbed both hands together and placed them on the altar. The coral glowed brighter this time, lighting up the room. "Mmmm...." Ventus moaned with pleasure.

He didn't see Glebric draw the knife from his sleeve.

"How does it feel?" Glebric asked. "To pay for your crimes?" He tried to slash Ventus' throat, but his hand shook so violently that he only nicked him. Ventus' head lolled to the side, eyes rolling back in rapture. A few drops of blood dripped out, collecting in the basin in the top of the altar.

Glebric stepped back, dropping the knife from shaking hands.

The basin was filling up. But not with blood, with a metallic liquid seeping out from the stone, shimmering as the level rose.

"Give him to me!" said the voice.

Glebric grabbed Ventus by the hair and dunked his head into the liquid. There was no struggle as the face went under, just streams of bubbles escaping with every breath, slower and slower until they ceased entirely and the body went limp.

What have I done? Glebric stood transfixed, unable to will his legs to flee.

The pool rippled once, twice, beginning to swirl around the head. The streak of red disappeared into the dominant silver, and the entire pool gleamed in the ghostly light from the altar.

The liquid began to drain. But not down into some unseen space below, no, it was pouring in through the mouth and the nostrils. Into Ventus.

Ventus' lips moved, but it was a different voice that rushed forth. "Thank you, Glebric. I accept your sacrifice."

"What is happening?" Glebric backed off, holding the lamp before him to ward off this strange apparition. "This is impossible!"

Ventus stood up. His expression was now calm, even serene. The liquid and wound were both gone without a trace.

Glebric shook his head in disbelief.

"We will do great things together."

"Who are you?"

"Not who, what. Look at your hands."

Bluish-green water oozed out from his skin, puddling in his palms. He rubbed his fingers rapidly, trying to shake it off, but he felt something very different... like liquid power. For the first time in his life, he felt strong. The sensation was intoxicating.

"I will teach you to control it. Power, Glebric. That is my second gift to you. Power to do whatever you want. But first... let's go find your mother."

ᏯᎬᏯᎬᏯᎬᏯ

Simon put the finishing touches on a window portrait of his father, with Elysia sitting behind one shoulder, enjoying the show. It hadn't taken long to settle into his painting, which was easier with a table than it had been out in the wild. It was a welcome release, and allowed him to channel his worries into checking in on his father.

"I never get tired of watching you work."

He turned and kissed her without fear of interruption. Zenc was safe and dry in the stables beside the inn, which meant they were very alone in their room, and had made good use of the privacy. He hoped that the intimacy and his work got her mind off the constant thoughts of revenge.

The city of Bor was an intriguing respite from the winter rains that inundated the eastern provinces, and had driven them out of their mountain idyll. After four delightful days in secluded paradise, the rain had started light. They tried to wait it out for a day, but were forced to beat a retreat and decided to strike south into the province of Bor, and the capital of the same name.

Although a province of the Pazian Republic, Bor was like a different world. From the top down through all strata of society, the roles of men and women were completely different from anywhere else. It showed in every aspect of society, including fashion. The female governor was locally elected in their traditional fashion, by a majority of adult women, rather than appointed by the Senate in Pazh. The province had voluntarily joined the Republic in return for aid in the 2nd Marassani War, and that was the major concession. The Borathi were defiant in their defense of the rights of women, and all major elected and appointed positions in the bureaucracy and religion went to women, while men had a monopoly on physical trades.

Elysia was intrigued by the differences, and suggested that it might be the best place for them to settle. Simon hoped he could convince her otherwise, rather than have her adopt the local customs, like shearing off her long hair to match the local style. They'd already changed to the rather utilitarian unisex tunics that were prevalent. They might not flatter Elysia much, but at least they weren't awkward like the Myraki robes.

Confined to their room that night, driving rain outside, he'd decided to contact his father. Another test of the limits of his Talent.

"From how you described him, I thought he'd look mean."

There was truth to that, and Simon felt guilty. How long had he pictured his father that way? Had that been the truth, or just his perception? But this time, his father was wearing a proud smile.

"I think I see him clearly for the first time that I can remember."

With the painting of the window and portrait complete, Simon closed his eyes to better focus his Talent. His hand leaped to life, and when his eyes opened, the brush was filling in sand around his father's feet, and clear blue sea behind him. His father looked ten years younger.

"Sarea must be treating him well," Simon said.

"The sand looks beautiful! You could write him a message!"

Simon nodded, and took back control of his hand from his Talent, drawing words in the sand.

Father, it's Simon. I'm safe. You can write to me.

He reconnected with his Talent to await his father's response. Yet nothing changed.

"Something's wrong," Simon said.

Elysia pushed his shoulder. "Nothing is wrong, he just didn't see it yet! He's still looking at the sea."

Simon chewed his lip until he thought of an idea. He painted a little crab between his father's bare foot and the message, and had the pincers nip the big toe. Though it was tiny, the exertion required to effect the change left him sweating and drained.

"That should do it."

The Talent took over, and his father's momentary pain changed to surprised relief as he looked down at the message. A response appeared, wiping out Simon's message.

Simon? Thank Salar! You see me?

It began a strange two-way conversation of Simon's hand painting and repainting questions and responses in the sand.

Yes. Far away.

Success?

Pazh is safe. But I had to leave.

Alone?

No. Elysia is with me. I love you.

I love you, Simon. Am I safe here?

Yes. I think so.

Bring her to see me?

Simon looked to Elysia and squeezed her hand. She nodded.

Someday. She would like that.
Tell her to take care of you.
She nodded and laid her head down on his shoulder.
She said she will.
Lokuta still after you?
Likely think I'm dead. But might come after you.
I'll be careful. Thank you.
How is Sarea?
Beautiful. Sea air is good for me.
We've traveled across the east.
I'm happy you have someone. Must go. Cousin.
I love you, Father.
I love you too, son.

His father cupped his hands and washed away their messages. Simon rolled up the parchment.

"He's so nice," Elysia said, wiping a tear away from Simon's eye. He sighed.

"It's a welcome change. I'm so happy for him, and for the first time in my life... I miss him."

She tensed up.

"I'm so sorry." He hugged her tight and she buried her face in his chest.

"It's just... I want to meet him. He's the closest to a father I have left now "

In that moment, somehow it all connected together.

"Elysia, I want to make this right for you."

ᏬᏋᏬᏋᏬᏋᏬ

The sea voyage didn't treat Mirasha very well, but that suited Persei just fine. She felt somewhat better in their well-appointed cabin, and that's where he spent most of the day and night. Daymar had commandeered a fast merchant ship that was used to transporting important passengers, and had the accommodations to satisfy that discerning clientele.

She was lying on top of him, her perfect breasts pressing against his naked chest. He couldn't get enough of them. Of her. Of their lovemaking. And she could keep up with him! He'd found his perfect match.

And when they weren't in bed together, asleep or otherwise, she was pushing him linguistically. She seemed to burn with an equal passion for knowledge. That was new to him. Sure, his sister Lokilla loved to read the great poets, but he'd never met a woman so hungry to learn. About everything. Those horse-riding bastards didn't seem to know much about the wider world, and if they ever read books they didn't share them with the women.

But she kept him motivated with that incredible body of hers. For one so young, and so inexperienced—a virgin, now that she knew the word for it—she was a natural. Athletic, acrobatic... she was even coming up with new positions to experiment. Even minutes after his last climax, his loins begin to stir again. He let his hands slip down from her waist, meaning to pull her against him.

She propped herself up on her elbows and shook her head playfully. "You promised me another story first." Even her accent was improving. And he rarely had to correct her twice.

He feigned innocence. "Did I? I'm sure the story could wait..."

She pulled the silk sheet over her body. "No story?" She yawned. "Maybe I go to sleep again?"

"Go *back* to sleep?" He scowled, but began thinking of how to please her. This was new for him too. He'd never been concerned about the happiness of his many, many lovers.

Which story? She loved history, and myths even more. He'd already shared tales of the founding of Pazh, its great generals and leaders, and their campaigns to conquer most of the world. He covered the uniting the cities of the peninsula, the fall of the tyrant kings, and the wars that brought each new province into the fold. She'd laughed when he told her of the strange Borathi, with women in charge and their own elected governor. She was excited to see the island city-states of the Izar peninsula in the middle of the Near Sea. Previously independent, they had all ultimately submitted to become protectorates of the growing Republic. All she brought to the table was the story of the submission of her people, and how they conceded Pelusia a few years before she was born.

Perhaps another myth? She loved stories of the gods, and their wars with the Damoz.

"Did I tell you how the Tynos the Izari stopped the flood?"

She shook her head and clapped her hands with girlish delight, but the dropped sheets drew his eye to her more womanly charms. Catching his gaze, she shook her finger with a sly smile before

BLOOD OF THE WATER

covering herself again. After laying her head down on his chest, she waited for him to begin.

"When the city of Pazh was still young and ruled by tyrant kings, the Izari cities dominated trade in the entire Near Sea. Their artists were acclaimed as the best in the world, and it was said that even the commoners ate the best foods the world had to offer.

"Of course there were others that were jealous. Especially the Maruthans. The New Maruthan Empire had just been established by Emperor Uru-Maru, with a new capital at Uraka. After centuries of drought and poor harvest that had fractured the country and brought down their great First Empire, he blamed the proliferation of a thousand gods for diverting their attention and their faith. He put in his lot with the river goddess Kashaka, banning all the others." Her eyes lit up at the name of the goddess.

"He built many temples in her honor, including the greatest of all in his capital. And the river began to flow at a steady pace, under control. Harvests increased ten times and the population boomed. They began to export, and the Izari merchants quickly saw an opportunity to dominate trade. With their puny navy, the Maruthans were powerless to stop them.

"So it is said that Uru-Maru communed with Kashaka herself and she answered his prayers, granting him and his priests great power. The power to control water itself." Persei's eyes blazed. He'd loved this particular story and wished for his own chance at such greatness. To wield such power.

"So what did they do?" she asked, rapt.

"They began to slaughter the Izari, without even touching them. They would point at one of the fat merchants," Persei said, mimicking the motion, "and when they clenched their fist, it was if the water of life flowed out of their target's body, through the air into the hand of the priests."

Mirasha gasped, covering her mouth. He stroked her hair, enjoying how she hung on his every word. His storytelling was improving, with all the practice.

"It killed them?"

He laughed. "Not just killed them, they were left a dried out husk, like a raisin left in the desert sun. It is said that if you struck the body, it would crumble to dust."

"Such power…"

"Yes. And then they decided to wipe Izar off the face of the

21

map. Did you know that the islands used to be long strips of connected land, like snakes entwined?"

She shook her head.

"All the priests, including the Emperor as high priest, stood at the mouth of the Vanusa River Delta, linking hands and chanting. The sky turned dark and it began to rain... and rain... and rain. The sea rose before them, day after day. And even they were forced to retreat, since the water claimed much of their most fertile ground, as Kashaka's price for their demand."

"But what happened to the islands? To the Izari?"

"The waters swept them away in their ports in Marutha. Battered the coasts of their homeland. But one of their merchants escaped and fled back to Attarsus and went before the council of elders. Shocked at what evil the Maruthans were willing to do upon them, the Izari banded together, and some of their number had a plan. They had to capture Kashaka, to contain her power."

"Capture a god?"

"Not a true god. Not like Salar, or Choron. Or even your Mija."

She scowled at the mention. "I'm no heathen. There are greater powers than Mija in this world."

"You will come to love my gods." *Is it so hard to civilize these barbarians? At least the women know what's good for them.*

She smiled, nodding. "So how did they catch her?"

"Their greatest artisans fashioned a golden throne. It was elevated on bars to raise it above the floor, above the common man. Some say they imbued it with magic, but that's just an old wives' tale." He paused, considering. "Although with what we've seen, I wonder."

She crossed her arms, impatient.

"Sorry, you make me think." His smile was genuine. She really did push him in new and exciting ways. To hell with what Daymar thought, Persei would keep her as his favorite. "So they sent it on their fastest ship, which soared over the biggest waves the world had ever seen. When it left, the waters were already swelling the rivers of Izar, drowning the people who didn't heed the call to hide in the highlands.

"When the delegation arrived, they hid a hundred warriors below the decks, and sent the council out to offer Kashaka their gift and their plea that she spare them. Tynos, the lead artisan and one of the elders of the council, presented the gift. When she

22

accepted, he took her hand to raise her up on the gilded throne, accepting her as the new queen of their gods.

"Except it was a trap. When she sat down, bars sprung up, enclosing the pair of them in a cage. The council members shouted to summon the soldiers who had slipped into the city one at a time. They rushed the palace, killed the shocked and powerless Emperor, and fought their way back to the ship, carrying off Tynos and the screaming Kashaka in her gilded cage.

"It must have been magic. Even a woman could break out from behind gold bars."

Mirasha swatted at him, pouting.

"What happened to Tynos?"

"They say she first threatened to kill him, but he told his people that he would give his life many times over to save them, so they left him. She had her revenge on him, draining his life's water with her mouth.. sucking him dry. His screams destroyed the minds of many of the soldiers."

"What did they do with her?" Mirasha's eyes were intent on him.

"Imprisoned her in a temple, under the water."

"Where?"

"No one knows for sure. The waters rose permanently, leaving the coasts as we see them today. Could be anywhere in the Near Sea."

"So the story is true?"

"Well, there was some kind of flood. Divers in Izar are always trying to find old relics from the cities underwater, even today. But the rest of it? I don't think so."

"I thought you were teaching me history?"

"No, today it was myth. I wish it were true."

She narrowed her eyes. "Why?"

"Can you imagine what I could do with such power? I'd give anything…"

"Even me?" She pouted again. So beautiful. How did she make him want to give in?

"Surely you wouldn't be the price?" Now seemed like the perfect time to ask her the question at the forefront of his mind. He'd been waiting until they got closer, and until her words caught up with his questions. He was tentative, a feeling foreign to him. "Mirasha… there's something I want to ask you."

She narrowed her eyes, suspicious. "What? You *do* want to sacrifice me?"

He took her hands, and kept his eyes locked on hers. "I wanted to ask you about your father. I know you miss him."

A tear formed in the corner of her eye, and he kissed it tenderly away.

"How did he find his power? Did he tell you?"

She looked distant, haunted. She nodded reluctantly. "Once."

He squeezed her hands. "What did he tell you?"

"You'd probably think it's just one of your *myths*."

He shook his head. "You can tell me."

"You want power like that." Words laced with accusation.

"Of course I do! Wouldn't you?"

She threw his hands back at him. "You only want me as a *slave*, so you can get power! I hate you!" Turning away, she covered her face in the sheet and began bawling.

He had no idea what to do. But had to make things right.

"I... no... Mirasha, I'm sorry."

"And to think... I was... I thought I..." Her eyes betrayed her. "You men are all the same. You lust for power, and for... this." She pointed at her body. "And what do we get? We get to be your slaves."

"No, Mirasha... I... I care about you." And he did. Yes, he cared about power... how he lusted for it. With power like her father, or like these men in the myths, he could own Pazh... the world.

Bitterness poked through between sobs. "Then what would you do? If I showed you this power?"

The words leaped off his tongue. "I would make you my queen. We would rule together."

She opened her eyes wide, questioning. "Do you mean it?"

He nodded, both to her, and to himself.

"Then let us seek out this power together." She reached back for his hands, her eyes full of passion. "Your myth might contain more history than you think."

Now his eyes went wide. "Why?"

"Because my father found a temple like that, in the wilds of northern Scentar. A temple that granted him his power."

"So you think..."

"He believed there were others like it. Where other beings of

24

great power were imprisoned. Teach me more myths. Give me more books. Let us find this Kashaka together."

"And bend her to our will."

Mirasha held her head up high, and in that moment, he pictured her as his exultant queen. *No, empress. Emperor Lokuta.* Between the heady thoughts of power and her regal beauty before him, his manhood stirred to life again. She looked down at him and bit her lip. He shivered with anticipation.

"But first I bend my king to *my* will."

III

ᎶᎾᎶᎾᎶᎾᎶ
Inheritance

Ever since the night of the attack, the city had taken over stewardship of Xelos' house. With no heir to be found, ownership would revert to the state within the month if no claim was made. So Glebric decided to make one.

He'd been granted access as one of the few surviving servants, after answering a few questions from the city watch.

Where was he during the attack? He'd been sent to the market that morning, and granted leave to stay with friends overnight.

Was that a bit suspicious? Not really. The visitor he was serving was out for the day; naturally he had the day off.

Was there anything strange leading up to the attack? Xelos had been worried that someone was watching them, some sort of threat. He'd brought in more guards than usual, but all had died in the attack. That's all he knew.

Before he was assigned to Simon, he'd often helped Ycastros with the accounts and records for the house and Xelos' businesses. It took him only a few minutes to find a suitable document and Xelos' seal.

He took them to the small house Ventus used when he spent the night in Attarsus. Ventus was waiting for him, while his mother slept in the other room. She'd been ill on the sea voyage over from Corus, but so happy to see Glebric, after three years apart. He was a man now, seventeen, but she'd held him like a child. When Ventus told her that Glebric had paid to set her free, her shock and elation sent Glebric soaring. They hadn't told her why they were in Attarsus, and though she fought the idea of coming, he had insisted she come see his surprise.

Glebric could hardly contain his excitement. *If this works, I give her the life she deserves!*

26

Ventus showed him to a table with the other materials he needed: sealing wax, fine vellum, and ink. He spread out the stolen letter next to a blank page.

"Do it," Ventus said.

Glebric breathed in to focus his emotions. What right had Xelos and others like him to own so much, while Glebric was a slave, forced to do things against his will? He was fueled by the injustice of a system that made this possible. *I want more.* Clenching his teeth together, he connected his mind with the ink. Drops rose out of the inkwell, becoming a steady stream floating through the air toward the page. He set the words in his mind, while looking at Xelos' handwriting on the other page, and willed the ink forward. Drop by drop it settled onto the blank page, composing a perfect facsimile of the message he wanted: a will leaving everything to his favorite servant, Glebric. Last came the signature, and that of Ventus as witness.

"Child's play," Ventus said. "You can do so much more."

If the authorities accepted his claim, not only was he no longer a slave, he was rich.

They accepted it, especially with Ventus at his side as the official witness. They were surprised, but Xelos was a known eccentric, and childless. Only one council member raised a question. He'd been a friend of Xelos, and asked why the will didn't mention Elysia, since Xelos had treated her like a daughter. Glebric shed a tear, real emotion. He feared she was dead, but if she ever returned, he would make sure she was given her due.

Glebric sat in Xelos' study—now his study—and imagined Elysia working there. Xelos always made him stand at the door, looking out and waiting for them to be finished, but he'd sneak a peek whenever he could. For a glimpse of hair, or her hand working the beautiful marble. If only she were here, now. He'd have her create for him.

The house was his, and it had been almost too easy. Thanks to his new power. But this was only the beginning.

ᏤᏋᏎᏋᏎᏋᏎᏤ

Persei knocked gingerly on the stained door at the address Aktar had given him. Daymar stood behind him in full general's regalia, glowering, with four guards flanking each side. Pazh made sure its generals were protected. Persei wouldn't normally be caught dead in a place like this, but his agent had needed to blend in for his mission. His evidently failed mission. Now Persei would get some answers.

The door opened a crack, and bloodshot eyes widened at the sight of him.

"My lord!" Aktar said, opening the door wider. Aktar's mouth dropped open when he took in Daymar and the guards. The stink of cheap wine assaulted Persei's nose. His agent's eyes narrowed, shifting around like he was looking for the best escape route.

"We wish to speak in private. Are you alone in there?" Persei asked.

Aktar nodded and tried to stand up straighter.

Daymar addressed his guards. "Keep watch from outside, we will be quite safe here." The guards saluted and set up a perimeter. He turned back to Aktar, his face laced with scorn. "Aktar, good to see you."

Aktar was sweating profusely as he led them in to a dirty sitting room. He lived like a pig. Aktar offered chairs to the two brothers, and stood at attention before them.

It made Persei's blood boil, seeing a hard man, a trusted operative like Aktar, looking so worried. The cloying stench of failure had a life of its own, trying to grab hold of Persei as well.

He was glad Mirasha didn't have to see this.

Daymar looked bored, but nodded for Persei to begin.

"Aktar," Persei said, "please give us your report. We've just returned from Pelusia and have heard nothing of your success in recovering Simon and the girl."

"My lords," Aktar said, rubbing his hands on his dirty tunic, "we had them penned in the house of the wealthy local, Xelos. Or so we thought. The attack was a success, we breached the entrance and cornered the old man, who died in the battle. But—"

Persei's eyes held fury. "But?"

"Neither Simon nor the girl were there."

Persei clenched his teeth. "They escaped out a back door?"

Aktar shook his head vociferously. "No. There was no other way out but over the walls, and we had that covered. We were watching the place for days, and we knew they were in there... but

28

that night, somehow, they were gone."

Daymar's voice betrayed no emotion. "How did you let this happen?"

"They… I think they knew we were coming. Suspected something. They sent out several people that morning, I think to draw us off."

"And then our targets escaped out the front door?" Persei was incredulous.

Daymar shook his head. "So you failed us. Did you at least cover your tracks?"

Aktar nodded with equal vehemence. "We killed all the guards, and any staff who were present."

"So nobody can link you, or more importantly us, to the scene?" Daymar's eyes had come to life.

Aktar's mouth twitched.

Daymar pounded his hand on the table. "What? Out with it!"

"Something strange happened at the door. An old man came calling, and the girl's father, who we'd brought as a bargaining chip, called out to him. When our men went out to find the caller, one was killed and the other hobbled. He said it was an old man with a gray beard, but who fought like a much younger man. And ran like one—my men gave chase and lost him at the docks."

"But he never saw you?" Persei's anger and shame were boiling over.

"No. Only the two men he fought. And we were proactive. We pinned the whole thing on the old man. Said we were chasing him after seeing him leave Xelos' house. The city watch is still searching for him."

That settled Persei slightly.

"But that meant we had to leave the house before the watch came. A shame too…" He paused and looked straight at Daymar. "You would have paid dearly for the sculpture we found."

Daymar leaned forward. "Quality pieces?"

Persei shook his head. *You're going to speak of art, when you failed? And Daymar could be so easily distracted?*

"Worthy of the great masters, or as close as I've seen."

"Are the pieces still there?"

"The city had locked down the house, with apparently no heir to the fortune. But that changed two days ago. A claim was approved."

"I would like to see these pieces. You will take me there to see these works, and potentially make an offer to the new owner." Daymar was softening, while Persei still seethed.

"There was something strange... maybe you can make sense of it? When I confronted Xelos in his workshop, surrounded by great works... he was destroying some of the pieces."

"Destroying them? To stop you from getting them?"

"Yes. Curious, isn't it? Armed men break into your house, and the first thing you do is smash some statues?"

"What were they?"

"Faces on a wall, as far as we can tell. They were smashed beyond all recognition. I dispatched him personally."

Persei couldn't take any more discussion of art, not with things still unsettled. "What about Simon? Or the girl? Any leads?"

Aktar's renewed confidence shattered. "None. We watched the port and her father's house, and nothing. It's like they disappeared."

"Apparently Simon made it to Tamar before we did," Persei said, barely able to contain his fury.

"What?" Aktar looked genuinely shocked.

"And then he disappeared again. Presumed dead, with no body."

"What do you wish me to do, my lord? Keep searching?"

"You failed me, Aktar. Why shouldn't I have you strung up in this room?"

Daymar held up a hand. "Because he is going to show me the way to this house of Xelos. I want to see the artwork with my own eyes. Your failure is unacceptable, but you have served our family for years, and have done some good yet. Clean yourself up. I want to be back to the ship by nightfall."

"I'll meet you back here." Persei stormed out to get Mirasha from the ship. He'd had enough of these two. If he had to go to see art at some stupid house, at least he could enjoy her company.

Even Persei had to admit that the entrance to the house was impressive. The sculptor knew his trade. Daymar and Aktar gushed over the designs like gossiping women as they waited to be shown the artwork inside.

Mirasha tugged at Persei's sleeve. She pointed out one scene with a hero slaying a many-headed lizard. "More myths?"

"Izari myths, yes. Looks like the owner enjoyed them as much as you do."

"Do you think he'll have books about them?"

"I'll ask. I'd rather take you to look at books than gaggle over more artwork with those two."

"Your brother is a dedicated collector."

Persei rolled his eyes. "I'd rather collect—"

"Collect what?"

"Collect... books for you." His days of collecting experiences with young women seemed to be at an end. Or at least focused on one young woman. And the thought was disturbingly comfortable. *What is she doing to me?* At least his words elicited a smile. She took his arm and they followed the others inside.

The steward stumbled over his introduction of the young master, who looked barely Mirasha's age. "Master Glebric, this is the General of the Pazian Legions of the East, Daymar Lokuta, and his brother Tribune Persei Lokuta."

The boy shifted on his feet, uncomfortable. "Welcome, General. I understand you would like to buy some of the late Master's art? You are a collector?"

Daymar was his usual smooth self. "Yes, Master Glebric. Were you also involved in his business?"

"No. I don't have skill in that area. He... he would have been happy for someone who appreciates such things to take a look at them." The boy looked like he might cry. Persei rolled his eyes again.

"Please, take me to them," Daymar said, putting his hand on the boy's shoulder like an older brother.

Mirasha elbowed Persei in the ribs. "Master Glebric," he said, "do you happen to have a well-appointed library? The young lady here was wondering if you have any books about history, or local myths."

Glebric's eyes flicked over her face, and he broke out in a shy smile. He took her hand and kissed it awkwardly. Persei bristled, but didn't make any move to stop him, though he wanted to strike down the precocious little prig.

"I could not stop such a beauty from looking at anything." He spoke to the steward in Izari, who nodded. "He'll show you to the study. If you see anything you like, take it, as a gift." His eyes traced the curves of her chest, all that was visible under her traveling cloak. "General Lokuta, please follow me."

Persei and Mirasha followed the steward into a large study where floor to ceiling shelves were filled with books, scrolls and loose papers.

"But can you read Izari?" Persei asked her.

"I can learn," she said, her voice defiant. With anyone else he'd think she was crazy, but her progress in reading Pazian had been remarkable. "Will you teach me?"

Persei gulped. Like any well-educated *digniti* son, he'd learned Izari in school so he could read the great poets, playwrights and engineers... but it had always been a struggle. At least he could sound out the titles for her. "I'll hire you a tutor when we get back to our home in Pazh."

She smiled at him. "So, see anything I'd like?"

He traced the spines with his fingers. Half the library looked to be on topics she'd be interested in. "You're in luck. There's so many here for you that we may have to pay the young master for his trouble."

ᏮᏮᏮᏮᏮᏮᏮ

Glebric showed the general and his more scruffy companion into the workshop. They'd cleaned up Xelos' body, but everything else lay undisturbed, including the shattered remains of those statues on the wall. That used to be part of the wall. He'd always wondered what had been there, behind those curtains, but the master never showed him, and this was the one room that he couldn't freely access.

Now it was all his, and it seemed that this general would be willing to pay dearly to take much of the clutter away. Glebric needed gold and silver, and lots of it, for his plans. And after finding that Xelos kept much of his wealth in land, businesses, and art... an additional source of funds would be welcome.

He was giddy. A general in his house! Xelos' guests were always more of an artistic bent. Local officials sometimes, but they weren't interesting. War had seemed like something far away and exciting, and now he hosted someone with direct experience. And according to his steward, from one of the great families of Pazh! The man must be wealthy beyond even Xelos' dreams, and powerful.

This general, who carried himself like he owned the world, who was he? Why did he deserve this greatness? By virtue of his noble parentage? At home did he relax in pampered splendor while an army of slaves catered to his every whim? While Glebric, conceived through the rape of a slave, was doomed to a life of servitude? Bitter anger churned inside him, like a raging whirlpool in a stormy sea. Moisture formed on his palms.

I could strike a blow for justice. For equality.

He looked at the two men as they puttered around from piece to piece, obviously enjoying themselves. *One of the most powerful men in the world, and here he is fawning over trinkets?* Glebric clenched his fists and began to focus on the blood, the life's water in the two men. *I have the power in my hands. I can—*

He was startled by a hand on his shoulder.

"I hear you have visitors, Master Glebric," Ventus said. His eyes were hard, intense, and the grip firm.

A dam formed around his anger, penning it up, restraining it.

His voice came out a strangled gurgle. "Yes."

"Please introduce me to these esteemed figures."

Glebric nodded with restraint and took Ventus to meet the general.

Glebric was disappointed that he didn't get to see the girl off, she and the tribune had left before he had finished settling the sale with the general. The steward said they'd left him a few gold and thanked him for the books. If ever he were in the city of Pazh, they would take care of him.

The guards had needed a large wagon to take away all the statuary. 20,000 gold paz! The letter of credit he held in his hands brightened his mood considerably. He'd make that trade any day. Art and a life, for the gold he needed. Now he could start the next phase of his plan.

IV
☾☾☾☾☾☾☾
Triumph

After contacting his father, Simon had thrown himself back into exploration of his Talent, and Elysia settled into her own routine. They'd acquired more materials for their art, and set themselves up in a large, pleasant room in Bor, with a storeroom as a stable for Zeno.

She would start each day with Zeno on a morning ride. It let her mind wander to ideas for new projects. She loved the fresh air and open spaces. The flat grasslands dotted with farms trailed off in every direction. It was like living in a sea of green, rather than the rocky island she grew up on. The climate was milder and crops still grew. Even in the middle of winter, a light cloak was sufficient.

On that morning she'd cut her ride short because of excitement over her new project. Yesterday she'd bought a new kind of local stone, and she'd seen more butterflies inside. At least a dozen waiting to be released. She could see them so clearly, alive and circling around her in the air, telling her what they'd seen. She chuckled to herself as she climbed the stairs to their second floor room. *They'd make good spies!*

When she opened the door, Simon started, and stood in front of the panel he was working on, obscuring it. Hiding something.

"You're back early," he said.

"I'm excited to start on my new project." She craned her neck to see his picture. *Was that a woman's hair?* "What are *you* working on?"

He blushed. "I... uh... it's a test. Part of my idea... I wanted to try it out first before telling you."

"Then show me."

Reluctantly he stepped aside, revealing a window portrait of a foreign looking woman with dark hair. Beautiful. Dressed in simple

Pazian dress, but with the curves especially accentuated by the cut.

Elysia bit her lip, flooded with unfamiliar emotions. She'd felt so special when Simon had painted her, like she was the only woman in the world to him. But seeing this picture... this beauty he so obviously appreciated...

His face told her a different story: flushed, concerned, but not guilty... no, it showed concern for her, not this other woman.

"So, who is she?"

"Mysena."

"The Lokutan slave? Why are you painting her?" Did he really reject her advances? Or was that a lie? But he looked so earnest...

"It's... it's for a test. For you."

Now she was totally confused.

"Why would I want to see her? To see how pretty she is? Do you like the way she dresses?"

"What? No. Nothing like that. Let me explain."

He took her hands and led her back to the picture. "I've had some ideas, some theories I wanted to test. About what I can do with my Talent through one of these window paintings."

"And it involves her?"

The hurt in his face gave her pause. "Elysia. I love you. It's not about her. But she lives at House Lokuta."

A rush of excitement made her smile. "Are you spying on Persei?"

He held up a hand. "First, I wanted to get a view of what's going on at their house. Whether Persei is back and what he's doing. I wanted to try to locate him, without focusing on him in particular."

"You're looking for him... for me?"

He breathed a sigh of relief and held her hands intently. "That's just the start."

"You could have just told me. Instead of painting beauties in secret." He winced. "So what's your plan?"

"I didn't want to paint Persei himself for a test, because I'm worried that he might notice."

She nodded. "I didn't feel it the first time you painted me, but in the studio the second time..." They shared a knowing smile. "And then when you were watching me in Tamar, sending me the message... I felt a kind of presence."

"Right, that's what I'm worried about. Without a distraction, he

35

might realize we're watching him."

"That makes sense. But what else do you want to do? Find him so we can go after him?" Every time she even thought of his name, or her father or Xelos, it added kindling to the fire that burned for revenge. She looked over to the other table, where her unfinished lizard sculpture lay.

"So far, we know that I can do little things to communicate with the subject in the picture, like nudge Father to draw his attention." His infectious excitement carried her along with him, like it always did when he got a new idea for using their Talent.

"What if you could make something more significant happen through the window?" she asked.

"That's what I wanted to test. It was tiring, what I did with the crab. But what if instead of creating something there, I send something through. I'm almost ready to try. Would you like to watch?"

"You think I'm going to let you do things to that woman while I'm not watching?" She angled herself so she could see both his painting and his face. She trusted him, but would it hurt to watch his reaction, just this once?

He closed his eyes, going into a trance-like state. His hand flowed across the page, filling in the background—a very simple room containing a table with a small bronze mirror and an array of makeup.

The woman became even more beautiful with every stroke, the red accentuating her lips, and a delicate green around her eyes.

"Do even the slaves in Pazh know how to beautify themselves? I hope you don't expect me to do that."

"What? You? No. And... no... well, some of the Lokutan slaves did. But not Mysena... at least, I didn't think so."

"Then she must be going somewhere special. I wonder where."

"I think it's ready for the test."

"How about this?" She took out a silver one zal coin.

Simon shook his head. "We need to watch our money. I was going to try this." He held up a curled shaving of wood that looked like it came from her carving.

"If this works," she said, "can you imagine the possibilities?"

"I've only just started thinking about it."

He focused his attention and moved the piece of wood slowly toward the picture. The entire image shimmered at the point of contact, like a pebble being dropped into a pool. The muscles in his arm tensed as he pushed it through, flicking it the rest of the way before his hand touched the painted surface. Simon's other hand resumed its painting.

Mysena jumped, staring in confusion at the wood sticking out of her makeup jar.

"It worked!" Elysia said, grabbing his clammy arm. "What now?"

"A message," he said, picking up a small square of parchment from a pile of several.

"Would have been easier with your father. What does it say?"

"*Is Persei here?*"

Elysia nodded, and Simon repeated the process. His arm shook with the exertion and she feared he might faint.

The note settled on the desk. The woman looked around, startled, before reading the message. When she finished, she checked the door, her eyes wide.

"I'll write another one," Elysia said.

Don't worry, you're safe. Don't tell him.

He passed it through the window and Mysena mouthed something in response, looked around and wrote on the note. She held it up to the air.

Who are you?

Simon scrawled a final response. *A god watching over you. Goodbye.*

In the picture, Mysena held the notes over a candle, setting them alight. Was she crying? It touched Elysia's heart. Here she had been jealous of this other woman, but he'd only thought of being kind once he got his question answered.

Elysia couldn't imagine living a life where someone actually owned her. Especially when that someone was Persei Lokuta. Even forming the words in her mind made her clench her teeth.

"So what do you think?" Simon asked her.

"That was beautiful. She's a slave, with a hard life. And you gave her some small measure of joy." She held his sweaty and shaking hand. "Is it hard?"

He nodded. "I had to really focus every time to send something through. And it was harder with a distraction here…" He smiled at her, and she enjoyed the attention. "It might be based on the size of the item, or the distance it travels. I'll have to do more tests." He sighed, and looked ready to fall asleep on his feet.

Her mind raced over the possibilities. One in particular. Her voice turned hard. "We could strike at him."

"No, that's not what I meant. I thought we could get some other kind of revenge—"

"He deserves to die. I would do it myself if I could. You want to keep us safe? This is the best way."

"Elysia, self defense is one thing, but that would be cold-blooded murder. Would your gods condone this?"

"My gods? You know the stories. They're no strangers to killing."

He looked so conflicted. She could see the love in his eyes, but also the desperation. This really did bother him. His heart was so good. It was almost enough to soften her stance. Almost.

"If I do this, I feel like I'm wronging the gods somehow. Using my Talent for evil. It makes me like Shadush. Is that the man you want to be with?"

She had to have her revenge. He was her best chance. Even if it hurt him. It was for their own good.

"Simon, do this, to protect me."

ᏮᏋᏮᏋᏮᏋᏮ

Persei had never felt so alive, so powerful, with the clear winter sun shining on his face and setting his golden crown ablaze. Battlements of gold rimmed the siege crown, and all eyes in the crowd stared in awe and wonder. The roars of adulation bathed his ears from all directions. This was his due, returning home as the conquering hero. Surrounded by a million people, he was the center of attention as the triumphal parade wound its way through the streets of Pazh.

Or almost the center. That would be Daymar, like a god in his gleaming golden toga, riding the general's gilded four horse chariot. A slave held the crown of triumph, delicate gold oak leaves, over Daymar's carefully styled hair. The tradition was for the slave to keep whispering to him: "You are not a king. You are not a god." Even if the people now considered him close to one.

Persei and the other officers were mounted and rode on Daymar's flanks. *Always a step below.* The thought twisted like a knife in Persei's gut. Daymar's victory came in the Senate house, but it was Persei who had won the real battle. One day he would seize the glory for himself.

But first, Daymar would be the one reaching even greater heights of glory. The entire Senate fawned over him, and at the end of the parade route he would be announcing his candidacy for the upcoming Presidential election. Heir to one of the oldest families, supported by one of the main factions, and returning a victorious general after a lightning-quick campaign? Why would anyone waste money running against him? Not after he won the crowd today.

Everyone in Pazh was there to watch the triumph, whether slave, Senator or somewhere in between. A triumph meant a public holiday, and it had been twenty years since the last of this size.

Slaves flanked the procession, tossing coins with Daymar's likeness out into the crowd. Men, women and children scrambled for them. Fights even broke out. For a single silver zal! The poor were like dogs, begging for scraps from their rightful masters. But so many of them, and falling in love with the name Lokuta. That brought a smile to Persei's face.

The captured Scentari slaves and booty stretched out in front of them, on display as part of the pageant. With no enemy leader in chains, they'd mocked up one of the captured warriors with Scentari armor and Shadush's bearskin cape to lead the procession.

The pace was so slow that Persei could look at every gathered face if he wished, but they melted together into one adoring crowd.

Well, most of them. Off to the right twin blonde beauties waved to him, batting their eyes while competing to bend forward to offer a more enticing view. And enticing it was. For a moment his mind fell back into old familiar patterns. With the slightest wave they broke out in delighted tittering. His hand was already raised to call one of the slaves over to approach them on his behalf when another face rushed into his mind.

Mirasha.

Clapping his mouth shut, he jerked his gaze to the other side of the street. It was still a struggle, getting used to this new version of himself. Where once the flood of nubile women throwing their bodies at him would have filled his nights for weeks, now his eyes sought out just one woman, his Mirasha. But it would be hours before he'd see her again. His sister Lokilla would be in her rightful place as one of the *digniti*, with a spot much closer to the Great Forum and the end of their route. Mirasha would be there, with the other slaves.

The adulation had long since worn thin when he finally caught sight of his sister waving. *To him? Daymar?* He followed her gaze. *Kyso?* He strutted like a peacock with the golden sword he'd won by stealing Persei's rightful kill of Shadush. But no, it wasn't him, she was mooning over an embarrassed Genaro Morichea, riding to Daymar's right. Lokilla's heaving chest looked ready to burst out of her dress and greet him personally. He didn't look away. Genaro might be married, but he was still a man.

And so was Persei. There, a few deferential steps behind Lokilla stood his target. He couldn't help but grin. Mirasha looked ravishing in the sky blue silk gown he'd bought her, with hair arranged as elegantly as his sister's. She looked like she belonged with all the *digniti* women lining this section of the parade. She was waving to him. And she was worth it.

Lokilla had been livid when she'd seen the money Persei was spending on the girl.

"On some foreign whore?"

His hand had come too close to her face. He'd wanted to strike her, but self-preservation held. Only Daymar, as head of the household, had power over Lokilla. And him.

Persei had seen his sister's sentiment reflected on the faces of the other women in the household. Women with the temerity to believe themselves slighted by his preference for Mirasha. And it didn't help that he'd set her up in better quarters, Or that she was the only women he took to his bed. *That's what they miss. I almost feel bad for them.*

Mirasha wasn't making any friends either. She and Mysena had almost come to blows just yesterday, and he'd had to intervene.

Right on cue he spotted Mysena, standing at the back of the box, and when her eyes met his they flashed with some undecipherable emotion. She looked down, fidgeting. *Probably jealous like the others.* Mirasha pursed her lips; she'd seen the exchange.

He swore under his breath. *I have to get out of here. Get her away from their claws. I'm not sure I can survive the battles.*

I need to get right back into the field. To forge a name for myself. But where?

V

ᎶᏋᎶᏋᎶᏋᎶ

Freedom

Simon walked alone through the cobbled streets of Bor. His steps were deliberate, slower than most on the street. Man, woman or child, they looked the same with their short hair and formless tunics. Not a place for the arts, and he'd be happy to move on.

But am I ready for that next step?

Ready as I'll ever be. If I'm doing this for her, I have to do it right.

He'd delayed several days already, wanting more practice, better materials, better ideas. What would be the perfect plan for this attempt on Persei's life, this... *assassination*, through a picture? What would provide the least possibility of failure, and be versatile enough to deal with the inevitable challenges? The conundrum had plagued his restless sleep for a week.

And could he even go through with it? He knew how desperately Elysia wanted this, and she was justified. Persei was vile. Xelos and her father had been killed without a second thought, when Simon was the real target. To allow someone like that to be free...

But it was still murder.

A creeping darkness invaded Simon's thoughts, whispering to him, dragging them down into evil places. If he could do this, why not other dark deeds? With justification, of course. Once you play at being one of the gods, how can you resist doing it again?

It terrified him.

But he loved her so dearly, and wanted to fill that hole in her heart. And she believed *this* was the answer.

One act, then a life of freedom, together.

That final argument tipped Simon over the brink into action.

He channeled his creative energy into planning the perfect fail-proof attack. He sketched and painted ideas through the daylight hours, working at a feverish pace. But at night his mind found new obstacles, gaps and holes he couldn't overcome. Each tired morning he had to start afresh.

But last night, it had come to him in a dark dream.

The picture of Persei was a perfect likeness, right down to the signature arrogant smirk. The one he'd show to a fawning admirer before taking her to bed.

The women of Pazh would be better off with this one dead.

Simon's hand brought the background to life. Persei strutted through the streets of Pazh, head held high and guards at his flanks, feeling like a master of the world.

The brush flicked out in the space behind his back, and a legionary javelin appeared in the air. Long, sleek, and perfectly balanced, with the tip coated in poison.

Perfection.

In a flash, it launched through Persei's back. With accusing eyes, he reached to his shocked guards, one hand clutching at the slick red tip protruding from his chest.

He sank to his knees, coughing his life's blood onto the streets of Pazh.

And Simon whooped in elated vindication.

His cry had woken Elysia, and he'd settled her back to sleep, saying it was just a nightmare. But he'd started the day early, with very clear goals in mind.

First he'd gone to the barracks, not to go inside, but to get a good look at the javelins carried by the guards. He hadn't held one since before Garas had enlisted him into his Prefectural retinue, and he wanted it to be perfect, just like in the dream. When the guard left his post to approach him, he'd stopped staring and hurried away. *Great, now I look like I'm planning an attack on the local Pazian forces.*

Well maybe not here in Bor, but in the city of Pazh itself. Killing a superior officer in the legion was treason, and carried the death sentence. By crucifixion no less. Simon shuddered at the thought.

With his plan firmly in his mind, he'd gone out for more supplies. Was it procrastination again? Trying to make things too perfect?

And that brought into focus another looming problem. They were running out of money. Their costs were burning through

Xelos' parting gift: Simon's paints and boards and her marble, along with lodgings for them and Zeno. They could keep eating simply for a while yet, but their days of staying in the city were numbered.

He hadn't told Elysia yet, as much as he wanted to. Her work kept her busy, and her mind off revenge for at least part of the day. By leaving these stresses to him. Once he did this—this vile act— then he'd tell her about the money. And they'd head south again. Now midwinter, the nights dipped close to freezing and he didn't relish the thought of camping for weeks on end.

Might Yalath be as charitable as Xelos, and treat them like brothers and sisters with Talent? He hoped so. Otherwise they'd have to find some kind of work just to survive. Sometimes Simon wished he hadn't been exposed to all these logistical realities through his father's business and his role in the legions. It was another layer of worry intruding on his creativity, stifling his Talent. At least if he shielded Elysia from some of the worries, she could continue to create. He wanted her to keep that joy.

So south, toward Jeppo. Marutha was supposed to be warmer than Bor, so it seemed like a good option. The vacation had been nice, but real life needed to start, and soon.

We'll leave tomorrow morning. After I do this.

He opened the door to their room.

ᏫᎬᏫᎬᏫᎬᏫ

The house of Glebric was filling up nicely. For the past week he'd been putting the money to good use, clearing out every slave auction and market. Ventus had been doing the same on the island of Corus. It galled Glebric to pay this money, more than he'd ever seen, to take control of the lives of other people. Men who didn't deserve such a fate. People shouldn't be sold like cattle. It was wrong.

His neighbors likely thought it quite reasonable that the new master of the house would be repopulating his staff. More than a few were happy that he was once again employing slaves; Xelos' eccentricity in only hiring servants had been ill-received. *It shone a light on their oppression, and they must have hated him for that.* That set off a chain of mixed emotions inside Glebric. On one hand he resented the wealth and power Xelos had enjoyed, but on the other he did employ many, was benevolent, and didn't abuse his position. There were things to emulate there, now that Glebric was the one controlling the wealth.

He had gathered fifty of the strongest, healthiest and smartest slaves today for a banquet, after making sure they were clothed and washed. They'd pulled every couch and chair out in the central atrium, and his array of cooks had laid out a hearty but simple meal of meat, fish and vegetables. Some of the bigger slaves were drooling.

Glebric beamed. This was only the beginning.

He pitched his voice to carry, like Ventus had taught him. The former object of his loathing had become a mentor, teaching him much in the ways of the wealthy of Pazh and Izar. He had to act the part. Today he was dressed in a simple but well-fitted tunic of soft wool. It didn't scratch and chafe like the cheaper ones he'd always worn.

"Welcome, all of you." The fifty slaves stood before him, none daring to take a seat on a chair or recline on a couch. "You're probably wondering who is coming for dinner? Or is it just my mother?" he said, pointing to her on the seat to his left, "Master Ventus and myself?"

A few of the slaves exchanged glances. They were every race and color: the midnight of a proud and rangy Alkazy, the deep mahogany of a Benjish cook, the rich copper of a pair of well-muscled Egarasi, a handful of tawny Kawanians with their slit-like eyes, golden Maruthans, swarthy Myraki, pale Valtari, olive-skinned Izari like himself, and others he couldn't place. He'd been learning his geography with Ventus to place these people; most so far from home. If they would join him, he'd give them a new one.

He stretched out his hands. "Please be seated," he said in Pazian, trying to reach the maximum audience.

Most complied automatically, taking his words as an order. *Longtime slaves, no doubt.* Others stood defiant, narrowing their eyes at the perceived trick. A few appeared confused, as if they'd heard him wrong, or didn't understand.

He forced a laugh, trying to make it genuine. "I mean it. Sit as my guests, as equals. It is my invitation. I don't give orders."

That seemed to convince a few more, but the Kawanians and Maruthans still looked mistrustful.

"Let me settle your fears. I was born a slave." He heard the word echoed in all the languages of the Republic, and beyond. "A month ago, I was still a slave." Whispers broke out.

"Why then should we serve you?" called out the Alkazy in heavily accented Pazian.

A few gasped at his challenge.

Glebric nodded. "A good question. And one I'm here to answer. You shouldn't. No man should have to bend his head as slave to another. No woman or child either."

"Why did you buy us?" the Alkazy asked.

"To set you free."

Cries of joy and surprise erupted throughout the crowd. Except from the Kawanians. One of them stepped forward. "Why?"

"Because I was born a slave. And I think it's wrong. But I'm just one man—"

"One boy—" one of the Maruthans said.

Glebric nodded again, conceding the point. "In some lands I am a man, in others a boy. Here, I am old enough to own slaves. But I choose to set you free."

He addressed Hector, his steward and friend, the first one he'd freed. "Did you bring them?"

Hector nodded.

"Thank you. So to all of you, enjoy yourselves tonight, and at the end of the meal he will give you your manumission documents. You will walk out of here freedmen and women. If you choose to leave."

The Kawanians rose and started to walk to the steward.

Glebric's voice broke for the first time. He hadn't expected that. "Wait!" The three men turned back. "Don't leave yet. Please hear me out." Their eyes narrowed to tight slits, but they returned to stand behind empty chairs. "I brought you here to make you an offer."

He stood up.

"Have you all suffered injustices at the hands of your former masters?"

Nods and shouts rang out in the affirmative.

"So are you with me, that slavery is wrong? A blight on the face of our world?"

Stronger agreement.

"Well, I am just one *boy*," he said, nodding to the Maruthan, "but I want to do something about it. I started with what I could afford, today. I have other businesses. I offer employment to any of you who will stay with me, according to your talent. I would rather pay people like yourselves for your honest labor, and grow our collective wealth.

"Why? So that we can buy and free more slaves. And more. And start a chain. And when we have enough of us, working together... then we will rise up. And free all the slaves of the Izari Archipelago."

A chorus of cheers rang out, from all but the Kawanians.

"The people of Pazh are dependent on slaves for their everyday life. Without them, things will fall. We will go province by province to the gates of Pazh herself, and free them all. And then we can be masters of this world!"

"Fine words from a boy," called out the vocal Kawanian. "But you would need an army. The legions will crush you."

Glebric nodded again, but this time his eyes were defiant. "Would you fight with me? Your people love freedom."

The three of them looked at each other, and then stamped their feet in unison. "Yes, we would always fight. We would die. But do you have a plan to do better?"

Glebric felt a trickle of sweat escape down the back of his neck. He willed it away, and it disappeared—the tiniest possible display of his power, and effortless. He'd been practicing, and this was another reason he brought them to the huge atrium. He walked over to the large fountain carved from leaping marble dolphins. He touched the highest one.

"Here we sit, in the middle of the Near Sea. The water surrounding us. What if... our water god Nydos smiled upon us?"

The Alkazy spat. "Don't speak to us of your pagan gods."

"All nations honor water and the power of the sea in some way. Here in Izar, we call him Nydos. Azzam, you might have a different name. Even you," he said, indicating the Benjish woman. "Your solitary god draws power from water and the sea. No matter the name you use, water has power. This power has spoken to me. And supports this vision; of all slaves set free from their bondage. And I mean to do it with all the power in my hands."

He raised up his hands for them to see, and the bluish-green water began to drip from his palms. He pointed them at the fountain, and drew his fingers up, focusing his full willpower. The water in the fountain began to bubble and churn, turning the same bluish-green. He willed it to rise, and it floated out of the basin and around in the air, to the gasps of the audience. None screamed or ran, they all sat rapt, impressed by the display. The water danced in circles, streaking past them and around his head like ribbons in the air. When he willed it back into the pool, it splashed down and returned to its original clarity.

All eyes were on him.

"Who is with me, to wash away the bonds that tie down our fellows across this rotten Republic?"

They all rose to their feet and cheered. Even those who had challenged him. His mother was crying happy tears. Even Ventus smiled.

VI

ᎣᏋᏋᏋᏋᏋᏋ
Javelin

Elysia was already awake when Simon walked through the door.

"You were up early. More shopping?"

He smiled. It was the first time in Bor that he'd gone outside before her. He held up the paints and treated panel. She nodded, and went back to her carving.

"The butterflies aren't done yet?" he asked, walking over to put his hands on her shoulders.

"Hey!" She recoiled from his cold touch and glowered at him.

"Sorry, I was just trying to…" He rubbed his hands together to try to warm them up. "Turn around, I meant to do this…" He massaged out some of the knots she built up in her daily carving, and she purred her thanks. When his hand strayed down, she flicked it away playfully.

"I'm working. In the flow. What do you think?"

She wasn't working on the butterflies, which sat off to the side. Instead there was a stone knife that looked almost sharp enough to cut, and beside it, that half-finished *thing*. It had a head like some mythical serpent, with vicious teeth. Why she'd want to carve something so horrendous was beyond him, but she never mentioned it and usually kept it out of sight.

"To defend yourself?"

"Only if Persei intrudes on us." She put her arms around him. "Any progress on your plan?"

He gulped, and instinctively pushed away the idea one more time.

"Do you ever miss your other pieces?" he asked.

"The ones I set free?"

"Yes, or those we left with Xelos? Or in your workshop?"

"Yes. I was just thinking about them. About going back to get

48

them. Or just making new and better ones."

"About that…" The words slipped out.

Her brow knotted. "What is it?"

Now he had to tell her. "We're… running low on gold."

She pursed her lips. "Will we have to move? I was just starting to like it here."

"But…"

"Does this mean I can't get any more stone?"

He didn't answer.

There was hurt in her face. "Simon, why didn't you tell me sooner. Is this my fault?"

"No, Elysia… it's… it's just… we need money to live. Things were easy when we had a place to stay… but now we have to pay for the room for us, for Zeno, food, supplies… it adds up. And I don't know if I can find work here."

"What kind of work?"

"I'd rather do something with my art… even as a draftsman? But if I had to, I could work for a merchant? It might be tougher here… since they expect men mostly to do the… heavy lifting."

She was silent for a time, staring out the window. When she finally spoke, excitement had returned to her voice: "Do you think my father, or Xelos would have left something for us? Money? Or we could sell my other pieces. That would be a start, wouldn't it?"

"But it's not safe! Not Attarsus. Not unless we're certain Persei's agents have stopped looking for us. And he has the money to keep them looking forever."

"We should have faked your death."

He frowned. "Don't even joke about that."

"Why not? With our Talent we might have been able to pull it off. It's just an idea. Unless you have a better one?"

He breathed deep.

"I'm going to do it."

"Do what?"

He took her hands, and her eyes lit up in recognition.

"It's what you want, more than anything else, right?"

Her grip tightened, quivering. She nodded slowly. "You would do this for me?"

He gulped. "For you. For us."

Now she looked unsure. "Are you ready?"

"Ready as I'll ever be."

He explained the idea from his dream. "No matter where we find him, alone or in a group, I think I can do it. And quickly. Even if he's wearing armor, I can go for a weak spot."

"Simon, I know this is hard for you, that you think it's wrong. But it's the only way. When he's gone…"

"Then nothing will stop me from spending my life with you. Starting a family someday. I'll do this, and then let's get married." He tried not to make it sound conditional. It wasn't.

She turned her head slightly to the side, tears forming in her eyes. "I would marry you one hundred times, Simon Baroba. But I won't make you do something evil. Not even for me. Not unless you think it's right."

Why was she making this harder? He'd already convinced himself.

"No, you're right. This is the best way. I do this for our future children." He tried to smile away his nerves.

"So… now?"

He nodded and laid out his new materials.

He started with a sketch of the javelin, to get the form out of his head, to make sure it was perfectly balanced and a suitable weapon for the mission. *The execution.*

"So you'll paint it into existence, then launch it fast enough to spear him?"

"We'll get one shot."

She chewed at her lip and glanced over to the corner, to a pile of wood. "What if… you can draw me a good plan, right?"

"For what?"

"For the javelin. If I make one, you can launch it through the painting. Wouldn't that be better?"

It was a good idea. Probably better than his. "But what about the head? Wood might harm him, but not like hard iron."

"What if you painted it that way? Made it change like the scales you put on Zeno? I can make it sharp, but you could make it harder."

He nodded along with her growing excitement.

"We're stronger when we work together," she said, holding his hands and sealing it with a kiss. He felt himself stir, and kissed her back, but she pulled away. "Let's get our work done first, and there will be time for that later."

The sun had already set, with the shorter winter days, when he put the finishing touches on the portrait. He worked slowly, checking and double-checking everything, while her javelin waited for him to paint the tip.

Elysia scowled at the image of Persei, in profile so he wouldn't be looking right at them. "I'd punch him in the face just to wipe off that smirk. It's unmistakably him."

Painting the javelin head an iron gray seemed trivial after the painstaking detail of the portrait, but touching it with his Talent still drained him. He tapped on the tip with one of her chisels, and it responded with a metallic clang.

"Incredible!" she said. "What else could you…"

"Transmute? There were stories about wise men who turned lead into gold… maybe they were some of us? There are so many ideas I want to try. But I'm feeling a bit weak. Are you hungry?"

They ate a cold dinner in silence, oppressed by the weight of what they were about to attempt. He thought of the poison he had seen in his dream, and it turned his stomach. But since he was going to throw the javelin instead, he figured he could strike a killing blow without resorting to such despicable means.

"Are you sure you want to watch?" he asked. "It might be… messy."

Her eyes turned dark with a terrible intensity. "I wouldn't miss it for anything."

He shuddered and cracked his knuckles.

Painting the window took no time at all. Everything was ready for him to let his Talent loose.

He turned to her one last time. "Last chance to back out."

How could she look sad and furious at the same time? Yet he felt the same way. Except with the added dread of this darkness creeping into him like a stain on his soul. If this worked, a man would die on the other side of the sea, at his hand. The magnitude pressed on him, as if he were being buried alive. Sweat trickled down his brow, into his mouth. Would the taste of victory be salty? Or even bitter?

Closing his eyes, he took five deep breaths to center himself, and forced his hand to begin again.

Colors swirled onto the page stroke by stroke, filling in the background first. A bedroom ten times as lavish as the Lokuta guest quarters. Persei on a bed, covered in silk. At home, in the site of too many conquests, so many women violated.

With a rush of righteous anger, Simon picked up the javelin with his off-hand while the other kept painting in the details. Persei was kneeling, his shoulders covered only by a light sheet, his chest naked and heaving and…

"He's…" Elysia broke the silence. "He's with a…"

Who was this in his bed? *Mysena? I don't know if I can…* Simon couldn't risk killing an innocent. Not someone who had been kind to him.

"Do it now," Elysia said. "He's distracted, and you have a clear shot!"

"But who is she?"

"Just throw!"

Simon handed Elysia the brush and gripped the javelin in his right. He channeled all the fear, loathing and pain into his connection with the smooth wood, focusing on his target: the exposed neck. After one last breath he reared back and threw with all his strength. The javelin stabbed through the page, which rippled as the shaft passed through.

Simon felt suddenly weak, like his breath had been stolen.

Elysia pressed the brush back into his hand, but he could barely grip it. Gritting his teeth, he dipped it in paint and let his Talent show them what they'd done.

Persei's face contorted with rage as his hands wrestled with the shaft, trying to pull it out of his shoulder.

"I missed." The life went out of Simon, but his hand continued to paint more of the aftermath.

Filled in… darkness. First he thought it was the flowing hair or skin of the woman, but the black took on a life of its own. Shifting, swirling, writhing like…

The horror of recognition washed over Simon. Dark flames, entwined around Persei in the throes of passion, in the shape of a woman. His hand fell to his side, but the flames kept moving, the head turning to look at them. Two points of absolute black boring into his mind.

The fiery form pointed at them. Panic surged through Simon as he backed away.

Elysia screamed.

ᎶᏋᎶᏋᎶᏋᎶ

"Salar's blood!" Persei shouted, pain lancing through his shoulder. A smooth wooden shaft protruded from his naked flesh, and his head spun with the shock. He clutched at it, mustering the strength to pull it out.

Mirasha screamed—and not the kind Persei liked. She sat bolt upright, pushing him off with surprising strength, and pointed to the left. No assailant? The room was empty. Yet she stared at something.

"Who is that?" she asked.

Persei grunted as he pulled out the weapon. The wound wasn't deep, but painful and bloody.

"The man?" she said again, more insistent. "And woman next to him?"

Persei strained his eyes in the dark, but still nothing.

"Can you help me bind this?" Sticky blood poured from the wound, and he clawed at the sheets to use as a bandage.

Mirasha clung to him, terrified, still staring at nothing.

"Help me, woman!" She finally recognized his injury and used the javelin tip to cut strips of cloth before expertly binding the wound. He moved his arm around, and while the pain was bad, he still had his mobility. *Could have been much worse.*

"Who did this?" he asked, through gritted teeth. "How did they get in and out so quickly?" *And miss from such close range?*

"Did you see them?" Mirasha's eyes brimmed with tears, crying out for validation that she wasn't crazy.

"Only the javelin. But how did it get here? Did you see someone throw it?"

"It was like it came through a window in the air. To our side. But behind the window... two people, in a fully lit room."

"Magic?" Persei's head spun. From the injury... or the impossibility?

"It looked like an inn. He was tall. Your age? Dark hair and skin like bronze."

Persei felt like he'd been punched in the gut. *Simon? How?* The words came out strangled. "Simon is alive? And tried to kill me? With magic?" Persei's heart blazed with rage, but his arm was starting to feel cold.

"And there was a girl. Dark curly hair, features looked... Izari? But dressed strangely. Plain tunics—both of them. Mannish. Didn't you feel something?"

"All I felt was you," Persei said, "and then this." He pressed his hand against the wound, which still throbbed. The pain somehow focused his thoughts.

"Simon and Elysia. Together. And targeting me."

"Are you sure?"

"Their dress sounds Borathi."

"South of Pelusia?" Since they arrived back in Pazh she had been devouring not just books of history and myths, but maps as well. Her knowledge grew day by day, though not as quickly as her command of the Pazian language.

He nodded. "Why could you see him, and I couldn't?"

She broke down crying into his chest. His words had been harsher than he intended.

"No, don't cry. It's not your fault."

"Why would they try to kill you?" she asked.

They must know about Aktar. Damn him!

"Or do you think they were after me? After killing my father?"

He put his arm around her to try to drive away the terror in her voice.

"Don't worry, I'll protect you."

She turned her face up to his, clasping her hands behind his neck. It pressed her breasts against his chest again, releasing a surging torrent of heat through his body. The pain of the wound lost its urgency. "You would do that for me? Hunt down these... witches that would seek to harm us?"

Witches? Simon, a warlock like Shadush! In my own house! Which infuriated Persei more—Simon betraying him, or having access to power that he didn't?

"I would fly around the Near Sea to get our vengeance. I want him dead. We can follow them to Bor..."

"But to go after someone with power... you need power of your own." She nibbled at his ear. "We need to find her. Kashaka. And claim her for you."

"I thought you said the libraries here were useless, with nothing more than what I already told you?"

She nodded. "But what about the other provinces? Some of them are the descendants of formerly great nations. There must be better clues there. Scholars who might know something?"

Her fingers traced delicate circles along his spine, working their way down to further inflame his desire.

Through the sensuous haze, a single thought rose up into clarity.

"Marutha."

She breathed on his neck, kissing her way down, down... but his mind was fully engaged.

"Their country is old. If we're going to find records of what happened, it won't be in Pazh. But it could be there." He looked thoughtful. "They only joined the Republic under our boot. They're restive. We always need a good legion there. I will get the 7th transferred."

She jerked her head back up with an accusing look.

He put one finger on her soft, moist lips. "And you will come with me. To find our answers. And I'll send someone to Bor, to seek out those two."

A glorious smile broke out on her face. "I heard there are ruins there. Probably full of clues. This is so exciting! Shall we leave now?"

His mind empty of ideas, he let his body take over, and she giggled as he pushed her back onto the bed.

"There's something I need to finish first..."

ᏀᏋᏮᏋᏮᏋᏮᏋ

"That's not just the power, that's her!" Simon said in a strangled voice, transfixed by the moving flames in the picture. His mind screamed out to run, but he had to act. *Could she come through the portal?* He flipped the picture over onto the floor. The connection to the darkness shattered and the room brightened back to normal.

Elysia melted into him, shaking, while he scrambled to make sense of the apparition.

"Persei is with... with the Damoz herself. What did Xelos say her name was?"

"Zaliakara," Elysia mouthed, barely a whisper. It was like she didn't dare say it aloud for fear of drawing attention back on them. "She was looking right at us... but that's not possible, is it? For her to see us from the other side?"

"We don't even know what's possible. But I felt it too. She must have sensed the contact." Alarm rang out in his mind. "What if she can do even more?" He ran over to the lamp and poured burning oil on the back of the board, setting it alight. Relief washed

55

over him as the wood curled in fiery red tendrils before turning black.

"What if she can control the fire?" Elysia asked.

But the fire looked ordinary as it consumed the picture. Warm, natural flames. He breathed a sigh of relief. "I don't think she can do anything with this. And they won't know where we are."

Elysia tugged at his formless Borathi tunic, shaking her head.

"Our clothes. Us. She saw us. What if she can place us here in Bor? She... when she tells him..."

Simon's heart sank. "Persei will know I'm still alive."

He paced around the room, wringing his hands. "I've failed you, Elysia. He lives, and now he knows about us, and my Talent. And knows I tried to..." The walls felt like they were crashing in on him.

A different burning smell interrupted his self-flagellation. *The floor!* He grabbed a pitcher of water and poured it on the charred remains of the painting before the fire spread further. *There's another few silver wasted...* He chastised himself for thinking of the practicalities, but it was too natural. And that left them with even less for food.

"We have to leave, right away," he said.

"Tonight?"

"It will cost us more than a few nights' coin for the damage to the floor. They may kick us out. We're already low on money. And with Persei coming after us..."

"But they're two weeks away by ship."

His voice was short. "What if he can use her power to get here faster? Like us? Or send something after us?"

Elysia's face fell. "But where will we go?"

"Jeppo. We've put this off too long. We need to seek out Yalath. He's our closest option, and maybe he'll know something about what we can do?"

With Elysia on the verge of tears, Simon felt like his heart would burst. "What is it?"

"It's all my fault. I shouldn't have made you do this. You knew no good would come of this."

He breathed in. *She was right, but what use was that?* He tried to keep his voice level, comforting. He had to be her hope. "We know Persei is working with Zal... Zaliakara. Kyso always told me that the first rule of war is to know where your enemies are."

"So this is a war?"

"Yes. And we don't even know what Zaliakara wants. But it can't be good. After sleeping so many centuries, she must be angry."

Elysia sat down. "We've already failed Xelos."

"What do you mean?"

"He said that even more important than defeating Shadush was to find the source of his power. To shut it down."

"Right, the source is Zaliakara."

"Yet we're no closer to stopping her."

Simon started packing his art supplies. "No, we're not. Not yet. But hopefully Yalath can give us advice. These Damoz were suppressed somehow, or they would be wreaking havoc on the world. They don't seem like the types to just sit at home in idle leisure."

Somehow that brought out a chuckle from Elysia. "Indeed. I wouldn't call what she was doing idle."

That served to drive the point home. Persei was literally sleeping with this ancient enemy. *Did he have any idea? Was he to be the next Shadush?* He was ambitious and bitter, but would he work with darkness to get what he desired? The sinking in Simon's gut gave him his answer.

"She... should we even call her a she?"

"Seems like Persei is." Elysia wrinkled her nose, and then carefully packed away her unfinished carvings, rolling the more delicate ones in spare clothes.

"Well, she's very close to the heart of Pazh. When she was supplying Shadush with magic, that was a danger... but this is a disaster. And it brings wealth, political power, and military might all within her grasp."

"Then we'll stop her, again." Elysia said, defiant in her confidence. "And destroy her accomplice." The last words dripped off her tongue like she was tasting poison.

He nodded in grim resignation. Their world had changed again, and not likely for the better.

"Ready to go? Zero should have us in Jeppo by morning."

VII

ᏬᏬᏬᏬᏬᏬᏬ
Yalath

Did the air even feel different in Marutha? They'd only been flying for a few hours southeast from the capital of Bor, but Elysia would swear it was warmer.

Was it the excitement overwhelming her fear? Another desperate flight into the unknown, but this one to an exotic place of legend. *Marutha!* While Myrak, Bor and Pelusia were interesting in their differences, she hadn't heard much about them because there wasn't that much to tell. But Marutha? Home of two of the greatest empires the world had ever seen? Their artists were legendary for massive temples and iconic sculpture. And the marble from the Jeppo area was the very best. She hoped they could find the time to visit some of the ruins, since the current province was but a shadow of the nation's former greatness.

Was she selfish to think of such things when she'd put them in danger? Simon was quieter than usual on their flight. Deeply troubled by the disastrous assassination attempt, or was he just tired? They hadn't slept yet, and the sun's first glow peeked over the eastern horizon, across the empty plains. Plains where she could imagine the famed Marassani horsemen riding free, beyond the reach of the Republic.

The Republic that might become their enemy, with Zaliakara allied to Persei.

Simon disturbed her thoughts. "See that up ahead?" He pointed to a larger speck on the horizon, beyond the endless waves of wheat fields, beside the sparkling azure sea. "We're here."

Jeppo bore little similarity to the other cities Elysia had visited. As large as Attarsus, but far older, it was surrounded by thick, towering walls that made Tamar look puny by comparison. As the former frontier of an empire, the stones bore mottled scars to prove the city had seen its share of conflict.

The moment they passed through the gates and joined the crowd, the stares began. The local women's skin and long unbound hair closely matched the color of the wheat fields surrounding the city. They looked so cool in their pale linen dresses, with thin straps that exposed bare shoulders. Elysia had to stop herself from staring at the way it hugged a mother's curves after weeks surrounded by the drab asexuality of Bor.

Everything about her marked her as an outsider: her dark hair and pale skin, and especially her formless Borath tunic. Even that light wool was already sweaty in the morning sun. Simon had said something about different wind patterns blowing the air in from the Gandari desert, but until they landed she hadn't made much of it. Now she recognized the hot bite to the breeze.

Would their tight budget support another change of clothes? And would Simon accept the unusual garb? The men wore linen skirts to their knees, and no shirts, with a few sporting vests that left their chests visible. She wouldn't mind seeing how that would suit him.

"Where do we go now?" she asked as they rode through the streets toward a small open-air market.

He frowned. "We don't know much about Yalath. Just the shape of his face, and his voice. No profession or address. I've only got one good board left for painting, so I'll have to make it count."

"Can we get a room so you have a place to work?"

"We can, but it will mean giving up meat and fish until we can find a new source of money."

Elysia's stomach rumbled. She hadn't eaten since before their attempt on Persei's life. Exotic spices filled her nostrils: sweet, spicy and pungent. A vendor proffered seared fish with a sauce so rich that she nearly fainted. She thought of father's olive bread and her mouth watered while her heart felt heavy.

Simon read her mind, counting out a few of their precious remaining copper coins to buy two plates of simple flatbread and a handful of fresh dates. She offered Zeno one of the sweet fruits first and stroked his head, thanking him for carrying them all night. He poked at it suspiciously before taking a bite. He wasn't impressed, but was hungry enough not to reject it.

"It's warm and dry," Simon said, "and I wouldn't mind doing

my work outside. I'll only be working in one color, so I don't even need much space. We only saw Yalath as a statue, so I couldn't even guess at the real colors. But we're only trying to locate him, not contact him, so I might not need the same level of accuracy. At least that's my hope."

The thought of Simon working out in the open brought back the memory of the first time she'd laid eyes on him, in the agora of Attarsus with his bronze skin shining in the late afternoon sun. He'd almost looked like a statue himself, with his glow. She had very nearly walked away, but the subtle draw of his Talent had entranced her. And that decision had changed her life.

"That sounds wonderful. By the sea?"

He nodded, and after getting directions they found their way to a quiet jetty at the edge of the harbor.

"I think this shelters the other piers so they last longer," he said, as he sat down on a pile of rocks. She was always amazed at how he understood the function of different things, asking questions she would never even consider. To her, everything was about the form—of what something could become. Even clothes really only interested her in how they could be depicted on a statue.

"I hope the picture gives us something we can recognize," she said. "I think it's best if we draw as little attention to ourselves as possible."

"New clothes, again?"

She put her hands on her hips. "I'm just being practical." She brushed her hand against his hairline. "You're sweating too. Did you see how different the clothes are here? Sensible in this heat."

"I hope Yalath can help us with that. I hope he can help us with a lot of things. But first, we have to find him."

Elysia watched the boats come and go as Simon worked. Many were the typical galleys and merchant ships common in Attarsus, but flitting between them were smaller craft with single triangular sails. Their trade took them south, toward the great Vanusa River of Marutha. With so many kinds of goods and people coming and going from every corner of the Republic, maybe they could find related work?

"Ready?" Simon said. He'd made quick work of drawing in Yalath's tall nose with its distinctive hook, and his bald head. He looked as surly as when she'd witnessed Master Xelos communicating with his statue.

"Looks good to me," she said.

Simon's gaze softened, becoming distant and unfocused, until his brush leaped into action filling in the background.

Was it a trick of the sunlight on the water? Or did his hand and brush glow ever so slightly as he added each stroke? Talent in action? She never tired of watching him work—the most beautiful act imaginable.

"Look!" she said. "That's the same market we walked through! He's buying dates from the same woman!"

Simon was already packing his materials back in the saddlebag. "We'd better hurry then, before he's done."

The streets were busy, but allowed them a brisk pace as they rode back to the market. They spotted the date seller, but Yalath was nowhere to be seen.

"You ask her if she knows him," Simon said, "and I'll search the rest of the market."

"Hello again," Elysia said to the round-faced matron.

"Back for more already?" The woman's Pazian was excellent. "I told your husband that these were the best. Better than anything you'll find in... where are you from?" She looked over the tunic. "Bor? But such lovely hair. You didn't hack it off like those crazy women. They trade beauty for power, not realizing that the former has its uses too!"

"No, I'm from... Pelusia," Elysia said.

"A long way from home then. Do you even have dates up there?"

"No." The woman smiled. "Actually, I wanted to ask you if you saw where my friend went."

"He's not your husband then? You should get on that. I saw the way he looks at you. And I wouldn't let that one go!"

Elysia blushed. "No, not him. Another friend of the family. From a distance I saw him buying from you. He's local. Bald? A little older? He was just here."

"Yalath?" She snorted. "That curmudgeon? He's probably back to his dusty old scrolls with that boy of his." She raised an eyebrow. "There's something strange about the boy. But don't tell him I said that. Yalath is a good customer."

"Which way?"

The woman described the route to a house a few streets away.

"Thank you so much. I'll get my... husband to come back and

buy more from you later. He has the money."

The woman clucked her tongue. "Let me give you some advice young lady. Don't leave the money up to him. That will bring you nothing but trouble. You have to watch out for yourself, or you'll find yourself destitute like my sister. Too trusting, that one."

Elysia had never even thought of that. Her mother had managed the household, so she'd never had to deal with money, and Alexander had taken over after her death... but she could figure that out later. She turned and waved Simon over.

"No luck," he said when he got close.

"Give me a coin to buy more dates."

Simon handed over the copper with a pained expression. Elysia passed it on to the date seller.

"Thanks again," she said, as the woman gave her a knowing nod.

"What was that about?" Simon asked as Elysia led him away.

"Just wanted to thank her for pointing us to Yalath. She knows him... and his boy?"

"A son?"

"No idea. Xelos never mentioned anything."

They left the market and followed the woman's directions, which led to a warren of mud-brick apartments several stories high.

"She said it was that one, at the end of the block."

"Would it be safer for me to go alone?"

"I'd rather stay together. He knows both of us."

Zeno snorted.

"And we'll introduce you, don't worry." She stroked him under the chin.

Simon knocked on the door, which was answered by a handsome man who wore his blond hair long. *Boy? I don't think so...* Muscular and nearly as tall as Simon, his bare chest was smooth and shone like it had been oiled. He appeared surprised when he saw Elysia, but he brightened considerably when he caught sight of Simon. There was something odd, almost controlled in that perfect smile.

The man's voice was like silk, even in a language Elysia didn't understand.

"We're here to see Yalath," Simon said in Pazian.

"And who do I have the pleasure of saying is calling on him?" The man switched over effortlessly, his accent impeccable.

"Do you know Xelos?" Elysia asked.

The eyes narrowed, as the young man shrewdly reassessed them. *This is no servant.* But he didn't resemble Yalath at all.

"Wait here a moment."

Elysia turned to Simon, who was smiling. "Good idea," he said, "mentioning Xelos before our own names. We can't be too careful. Even if he's our only hope right now."

She took his hand and squeezed it. "I—"

"Where are my manners," the young man said, interrupting her. "I'm Remeth. I work with Yalath. He will see you now." He looked down at her hand, and she released Simon's, somehow feeling embarrassed.

"Our horse?" Elysia asked.

Remeth pursed his lips. "Hmm… it's not a good idea to leave him alone out there. Would he come inside?"

Elysia nodded, grateful. "He'll stay just inside the door, won't you, Zeno?"

Zeno whickered in response, and Remeth raised an eyebrow. *Perceptive, this one.* Elysia intended to keep a close eye on him.

Remeth led them into a small room with a simple wooden table and four chairs. A bald man that exactly matched Simon's painting stood up when they entered. He scowled at Simon, and the hooked nose made him look like an eagle about to strike its prey.

"What happened to Xelos? You're endangering all of us by coming to my home." His voice was laced with venom, or was it just the heavy accent?

"I'm Simon—"

"Obviously. I asked you a question."

Elysia's control was fading. Who was Yalath to be rude to them after all they'd gone through?

Simon kept calm, his tone flat. "He's dead."

Yalath's scowl deepened. "I suspected as much. His foolish plan was the death of him."

"Foolish plan?" Elysia shouted.

Yalath was livid. "Silence, *girl!*"

Without Simon's hand on her shoulder she would have charged the old man. His eyes implored her to calm down. She tried to slow her breathing.

"His plan worked," Simon said.

Yalath was taken aback.

"*You* imprisoned Zaliakara?"

"Uh... no," Simon responded. "I killed Shadush, the warlock of the Scentari. I never faced Zaliakara."

"So where is she now?"

"Pazh."

Yalath's eyes bugged out. "The Damoz of Flame is in Pazh? You stupid, stupid boy. How could you let her get away?" He clucked his tongue. "I told Xelos he was a fool, thinking he could train you. Now instead of containing her in the provinces, she has access to the center of power. How do you even know she's there?"

As angry as she was, Elysia accepted the truth in his words.

"I... saw her in my painting."

Yalath bent forward, shouting something that sounded like Maruthan curse words while furiously rubbing his scalp. "She knows about you? Your Talent? Are you trying to destroy the world?"

"Master Yalath," Simon said, his jaw tight, "my Talent was able to save whole legions, and the people of Pelusia."

Elysia couldn't hold back any longer. "If it weren't for Simon, Shadush and his army would be laying waste to the entire East, and heading for your homes here!"

Yalath stabbed a finger in her direction, hissing. "So you think he saved us? This undisciplined boy will be the death of us all." Yalath sat down and wiped sweat from his bald head. He poured himself a cup of wine, making no offer for them to join him.

They stood in silence until Yalath finally looked Simon in the eye. "So, what is your plan now?"

Simon shuffled uncomfortably.

"Let me guess," Yalath said, rolling his eyes, "that's where I come in? See, Remeth? *This* is why I won't let you go out and use your Talent without mastering it first. You'll get yourself killed."

"But Master, Simon has done some good. He killed a warlock, and used his Talent to find this Damoz, and now you." Remeth smiled at Simon. It bothered Elysia. Why did that smile set her on edge? He was too charming. Too attractive. She forced herself to look away.

By the time Yalath drained the cup of wine, he'd calmed down.

"So you're staying here in Jeppo now, looking for me... do you have any ideas at all?"

Simon looked down and again Elysia stepped in. "We were hoping you understood more about the Damoz, and might know better how to stop her."

"We... we don't have a place to stay," Simon said. "We can do work for you. Whatever you need, if you can help us out."

"Does this place look like I have room for you, and a horse?"

It was smaller than Elysia's family's modest house.

"Master," Simon said, "we need your help. Now she is looking for us, but likely in Bor. When I saw her, she was all dark flames, in bed with a Pazian noble. Persei Lokuta, younger brother of the general who fought back against the Scentari. She must be seeking something out. But what?"

Sitting a little straighter, Yalath changed his tone. "I have devoted my life to learning about our ancient enemies. That's what they are, you know. We, the Talented, are here to keep the world safe from these creatures of elemental destruction. The battle has raged on for as long as man has walked this world. Or so the myths seem to indicate. While Xelos had little luck finding anything in Pazh or Izar about this, Marutha is a different story."

Elysia breathed a sigh of relief. They had come to the right place, after all. There were so many things she wanted to ask, but she let Simon speak for her, since this boor of a man didn't seem to have any use for women.

"What can you tell us of Zaliakara?" Simon asked.

"Not a single reference from the past thousand years. Zaliakara is the Izari name for her, but here in Marutha we call her Zalikko. It's old Maruthan for 'Fiery Destroyer'. In the time of the empire they saw her as a rampaging demon, bent on destroying the nation and its people. Prophecies from the New Empire period claimed that when the people turned their backs on Kashaka, that Zalikko would come again for vengeance. But I believe that was just propaganda from the priesthood." Playing the part of the lecturing scholar made Yalath surprisingly pleasant, and he even gestured for them to take a seat. Simon and Remeth sat across from him, while Elysia pulled her chair away from the table, to keep her distance.

"Who is Kashaka?" Simon asked, drawing another scowl.

"The main goddess of Marutha? The giver of life? Queen of the river? Did Xelos teach you nothing?"

Simon answered with an embarrassed shrug.

"But let me tell you what I've found." Yalath grinned. "With

65

the help of Remeth here, I was able to locate several interesting ruins in Uraka. I bought the houses that sit on top of the old sites, and we're just starting exploratory excavation. And through a scholar friend of mine, I have access to several other digs in the ruined New Empire city of Gardisha. In all of them there are references not just to Kashaka, but leads on Zalikko as well. We're close to a breakthrough, learning more about our enemy. And not a moment too soon."

Ancient ruins and sculpture might have answers for them? She lived for the chance to explore such treasures.

"Can we see them?" Simon asked for her, correctly reading her excitement.

"It's no place for a woman," Yalath snapped. "This is a man's work."

She wanted to punch him in the face, but Simon's pained plea kept her quiet and in her seat.

He was more diplomatic. "I understand you have different... customs here. But Elysia's Talent is in sculpture. She would be invaluable in examining the relics."

With pursed lips and only after trading a long look with Remeth, Yalath reluctantly nodded. "And I suppose your Talent would be a boon as well. On second thought, I'd rather keep you with me, rather than traipsing around causing more mischief. But do not use your Talent unless I instruct you to. If you're going to be staying in my house, you live under my rules. And I'll expect you to do your share of the chores."

Simon nodded, relief obvious in his face. Remeth looked happy as well. *Less chores for him?*

"Remeth, let's get a meal together here. And maybe find a stable for their horse?"

"Um..." Elysia started, but Yalath shot her daggers again.

"What Elysia was going to say," Simon said, "was that this is no ordinary horse. He's her greatest achievement." He gestured to Elysia to bring Zeno in through the doorway.

Normally obedient, Zeno glared at Yalath, sniffing disdainfully. "Zeno," she whispered in Izari, "I don't like them either, but they're going to help us." That seemed to do it, and the winged horse entered the room. She pulled back the saddle blanket, and he stretched out his gleaming white wings.

Remeth clapped his hand over his mouth to cover his gasp,

while Yalath approached cautiously, but couldn't hide a glimmer of curiosity.

"Very fine work. Xelos helped you with this?" He turned to her and expected a response.

Oh, now I get to talk? She almost wanted to stay quiet just to spite him and his misogyny.

"No. Zeno is my pride and joy. Simon added the finishing touches of color. Zeno flew us from Attarsus, across the islands of Izar, to Pelusia and now down here."

Remeth whistled appreciatively. "You can control him?"

Right on cue, Zeno shook his head. "Control? Do you control a friend? You're a good friend, aren't you Zeno?" He leaned into her as she stroked his mane. "But he generally agrees to our requests."

Yalath nodded with grudging respect. "This is impressive. I see you might yet be of use in our archaeological expedition. Remeth, clear out this room and they can all stay in here." He actually looked apologetic. "I live simply. My money goes to books or purchasing sites and supplies for my research. I'm afraid I don't have beds for you."

"That's quite all right," Simon said, "we've been staying in the wilderness for much of the past month."

Remeth was more genial. "You two... three must be tired. Why don't you rest now, and I'll get us some food from the market for an early dinner?"

Maybe he wasn't so bad after all. But Elysia wasn't looking forward to sleeping on the hard floor.

"Good thinking, Remeth," Yalath said. "I will need at least two days of preparation before we're ready to leave for Uraka."

VIII

⚍⚍⚍⚍⚍⚍

Talents

Between Glebric and Ventus, they now had over five hundred freed slaves in their growing force. It wasn't yet an army, but they were working to change that. The biggest slave auction in weeks was in Attarsus today, and Glebric wanted to secure the best prospects.

His businesses were booming, bolstered by the diligent work ethic of grateful freedmen, and he'd sold off three more, resulting in a significant war chest.

After his fifth successful bid, a scowling ball of muscle stormed over to him. Even with Azzam, the dark Alkazy, at his back, Glebric shrank from the approach, his anxiety coalescing as water in his closed hands. The swarthy man's bald head and face alike bore the evidence of battles barely survived. He could crush Glebric with one meaty hand.

"Your school must be well funded," the man said.

"School?"

"You've bought the best fighting men this auction has to offer." He pointed them out. "That one is quick, the other one strong, and him... I doubt he even feels pain. Who is your trainer?"

"I don't have one. But I'm not starting a school. My name is Glebric, who are you?"

"Zustar, but I doubt you would have heard of me here."

Glebric allowed his eyes to flash to Zustar's scars. One ran across his forehead like a jagged worry line. "You were... a gladiator?"

"Won my freedom ten years ago. Trainer ever since. Finally saved up enough to go home and start my own school."

"Where is home?"

"Bor."

Glebric held up his hand to bid for a tall Kawanian on the block. "You're here to buy more slaves?"

Zustar grunted his assent.

"Well you're right about one thing. I'm well funded. I'll be taking all the best today."

More creases formed on the man's forehead, and the scar puckered into a frown.

"Tell me, Zustar, how did you come to be a slave?"

"My village was taken in a raid by the Marassani. They sold me to Maruthan slavers, who eventually brought me back to Pazh."

"And now that you're a freedman, you buy slaves of your own?"

The man stayed silent.

"Let me guess. You want to give them the opportunity you had? To win their freedom? But how many will die along the way? How many were sacrificed to give you your chance at redemption?"

One of Glebric's servants took a pouch of coins to the merchant to complete his latest purchase.

Zustar averted his eyes.

"You know I speak true. But what if there was another way?'

The spark of interest was undeniable.

"I was born a slave," Glebric said.

"You? But so much wealth… and so young? Who is your backer?"

"I am my own man. Free. And I believe it is everyone's right. Tell me, Zustar… if you had the chance to eradicate slavery, would you?"

"How?" *This man doesn't waste any time, good.*

Glebric leaned in close. He might be thin as a rail, but he had a few inches on the old gladiator. "There will be a reckoning. I am freeing all the slaves I buy. Giving them work. Giving them hope. And we're working together to make things right." He paused to let it sink in. "But money can only take us so far. Muscle can take us further, and faster. And you know the Pazians aren't going to like this."

"All the provinces keep slaves. How can you move an ocean?"

"One drop at a time. Leave that to me. But I need someone with talent to train my army. Someone who understands what freedom means, and is willing to die for it. Are you that man?"

Zustar stuck out his arm, his eyes blazing, and Glebric took it.

"You can stay at my house until we get a more suitable training ground. Bring your slaves. My mother won't like it, but I wish to train with you too."

He turned Zustar around to look at the next slave on the block. "Help me choose. I want the very best for our venture."

ᏧᎦᏧᎦᏧᎦᏧ

The ride to Uraka gave Simon his first real opportunity to get the measure of his new allies. Yalath and Remeth had left Simon and Elysia alone for the two days they needed to prepare for their journey, with strict instructions not to touch anything, practice their Talent, or leave the house. It had driven Elysia crazy, being cooped up like that, but Simon didn't mind the rest. Or the free room and board. But it left little time to learn much about the difference between Yalath's mentorship of Remeth, and what they'd experienced with Xelos.

Traveling together cramped in a bumpy cart, Simon decided talking would help pass the time. Elysia slept instead. She hadn't been very friendly to any of them, not even him, and chose to ride Zeno when she was awake, so Simon left her to brood by herself. At least she looked good while she did it, with the light Maruthan dress much more flattering on her slender frame than the baggy Borathi tunic.

He shifted uncomfortably in the new clothes Remeth had bought for him. The skirt felt awkward, and with the heat even the light vest made him sweat. Next to the golden and muscular Remeth, Simon felt so dark and lean, but at least the clothes fit, thanks to Remeth's good eye.

Despite the heat, Yalath wore his vest buttoned up, which was probably doing them all a favor. Yalath was a strange one, so different from Xelos. Yalath's reaction to their news had shocked Simon, and at first he'd thought they were at the end of their road.

But discussion of his nation's history brought out the best in the crotchety old man. He told them more about his exploration of Maruthan ruins, and their destination, the former capital of Uraka. With a history stretching back through two periods of empire and the chaos and fractured kingdoms in between, most of the major cities were built on successive layers of ruins. Digging for relics was practically the national pastime in the province, especially when times were tough. Few of their people possessed Yalath's respect for history, and tunneled through floors and basements to see what treasures they could unearth to supplement their income.

Yalath worked with old maps to locate houses that might lead to old temples or tombs, and they were headed to one such place.

As much as Simon enjoyed learning about the new and old, there was a much more burning question he wanted answered.

"So you're both Talented?" he asked. Elysia peeked out, suddenly interested and very much awake.

"Of course," said Yalath. "And we've been practicing our Talent much longer than you have. Decades longer, in my case."

"So what are your Talents?"

Yalath produced a small reed flute from inside his vest and wiggled the instrument in the air.

"Music?" Simon asked. "How does it work? You play a song and... your enemies dance?"

Remeth laughed with Simon, while Yalath scowled. The old man put the flute to his lips and began to play a lively and enchanting melody. As it sped up, the warm wind on Simon's face blew faster. Sitting up straighter, he looked over the edge of the cart and watched in wonder as the road raced by, with Zeno and the oxen moving along as if at a gallop. But...

Yalath abruptly stopped, and the animals slowed to their regular pace as if nothing had happened.

Simon nodded. "Impressive. What else can it do?"

Yalath laughed. "It's more powerful than your unrefined scribbling."

"Scribbling? My scribbling defeated the most powerful warlock this world has seen in hundreds of years."

"You think you can come in and wave your brush around, and suddenly you're a hero? You're nothing, Simon. I was wielding more powerful magic when you were suckling at your mother's breast. Did she applaud your little doodles?"

Elysia sat bolt upright, his anger reflected in her face. Simon's neck grew tense. "Why you arrogant—"

Yalath held up a hand, and started to play again. The melody was delicately soft and gentle in Simon's ears, like a mother's soothing kiss. The anger drained away, and his lids grew heavy and...

When Simon woke, it was morning, and he had a stiff neck from sleeping so awkwardly. Elysia was still asleep, and Yalath too, while Remeth drove the oxen.

"Good morning, Simon," Remeth said and smiled broadly. As awkward as things were with Yalath, Remeth was a pleasure to be around.

Simon rubbed his ears. "Did... did Yalath put us to sleep?"

A knowing nod. "Nice little trick, isn't it?"

"Did he say those things just to anger me, so he could—"

"Yes and no. He wanted to demonstrate his power, but I'm afraid he'll never use honey to cover what he really feels. And he's getting worse as he gets older." Remeth's laugh was musical.

"How do you put up with it?"

"How could I not? How did it feel when you first met someone who could understand you?"

"Incredible. Like I'd been incomplete all my life."

Remeth nodded. "He appreciates Talent. He treasures it. It's his life's work to understand it better, to nurture and protect it. It's been a whole new world since I started working with him."

"How did you... find him? Find your Talent?"

"Hold the reins for me." Remeth passed a hand over his face, and Simon did a double take at what he saw.

A trick of the morning light?

The genial smile was replaced by an incredible duplicate of Yalath's scowl. "Simon," Remeth said in an eerily perfect imitation of Yalath's voice, "I was wielding more powerful magic when you were suckling at your mother's breast! Close your mouth, or the bugs will fly in." Simon burst out laughing before clamping his hand over his mouth so he wouldn't disturb the others. "You should see your face! Wait..." Remeth passed his hand over his face again. Now the expression looked like... Simon himself? And in Simon's own voice Remeth said: "What do you think?"

"How? Your Talent?"

Remeth's ear-to-ear smile put him at ease. "My father is an actor in the comedies. Ever since I was little, I'd go to watch him rehearse with the others. When they're practicing they don't use the masks. I'd copy their expressions, mannerisms, and voices."

"You'd be the star of the show if you pursued it."

"I was a child prodigy, already taking on roles at twelve. That's when I first met Yalath. He loves the theater. Of course, he's usually focused on the music, but he keeps track of the artists, the players, everyone. Always looking for Talent. He came to congratulate me after my second show. I could see from that very first moment that he was different. Can you see it too?"

"What do you mean?"

"See the Talent radiating out of someone, like a glow. I see it on both of you, when I'm looking for it. But only when I focus. Yalath just looked different. And his praise meant more. He would always congratulate me, every day of the show—we have a month of shows to celebrate the New Year in Uraka."

"So you're from there?"

"Yes. After a month he took me aside and asked me how I practiced, how I honed my skill. I told him, and then he asked me to watch the others and figure out what was different. Said he'd be back for the next festival, but if I was ever in Jeppo to look for him."

"So what did you see?"

"The others *were* different. They could be... themselves, their own style. But they weren't as versatile. Even my father... I realized then just how different I was. When Yalath came back I asked him why. That's when he told me about Talent, and how I was blessed with it. And that it was my destiny to explore how to use it for good. He showed me a few of his tricks and I was hooked. To be told you have magic inside you... once you recognize that, things are never the same again. But you know that, don't you?"

Simon absolutely understood, and it brought him a new feeling of connection, of shared experience.

"So after another week the festival was done, and I asked Yalath if I could come with him, learn with him."

"How did your parents take it?"

Remeth's face betrayed the pain. "Father said he never wanted to see me again. Mother just cried. They didn't understand. Yalath told me not to explain about the Talent. That it was dangerous. But I couldn't just stay with the players... not when this new road beckoned."

"So that's it, you gave up your career on stage?"

"No, I still go back and do a few shows each year. Helps me pay my own way. But in between, I work with Yalath, exploring my Talent, and assist with his research."

"So how does it work, you can copy anyone?"

"What do you mean, women shouldn't speak?" Remeth said in Elysia's voice. Simon's eyes nearly jumped out of their sockets.

"You'd make an incredible spy," Simon said.

"Spy, hmm? Never thought of that. You have some pretty creative ideas, Simon. I'd consider it, if it would help our cause."

"Have you ever met the others—like Xelos?"

Remeth nodded. "Yes, but only when he came here to Marutha. Mainly in Jeppo. I would love to see the world, with all its different people. Would you take me with you, Simon?" His eyes were full of longing.

"For now, it seems we'll be staying in Marutha."

"I'm sure you'll love it here." He looked over to where Yalath was snoring loudly. "And I for one am glad you are."

IX

⊙⊙⊙⊙⊙⊙⊙
Sukko

Elysia wasn't sure where to step in the old house in Uraka. Between the filthy floors and the rank smell, it officially signaled the end of their vacation. Her workshop was far from tidy, but it was never disgusting. Simon must have noticed her wrinkled nose and squeezed her hand in silent reassurance. *The old temple can't be any worse.*

"How did you get this house?" Simon asked.

"The owner died. I haven't had a chance to get it cleaned yet."

Thanks for the obvious.

"The body might still be here."

Elysia recoiled, thinking of her brother's body lying dead in their home. *There's no way I'm staying up here alone while you guys explore the temple.* Simon nodded, seeming to understand.

A pile of rubble surrounded a hole in the main room's floor. When they got closer, Elysia saw a ladder stretching down into the darkness.

"Remeth," Yalath said, "bring the lamps."

"Can I try something?" Simon asked.

Yalath raised an eyebrow. "What?"

"Using my Talent for better light. Won't the lamps get pretty smoky down there without any ventilation?"

Yalath scowled. "Such frivolous use of great power. Did Xelos teach you nothing?"

Remeth stepped between them, his face apologetic. "Master, it would make the work a lot more comfortable. And what if we can get better light? We have to hope the inscriptions are in acceptable condition as it is."

"Don't you start with me, Remeth. Know your place. We have to be careful." Yalath breathed deeply. "But the smoke *could*

75

damage things. What do you have in mind, boy?"

Elysia smiled to herself. *Small victories.*

Simon was earnest in his explanation. "One time I painted light onto a figure, remotely. It should be a simple matter to paint the light onto something like a torch or a lantern, so that it shines but without heat or smoke, and is still easy to carry."

Elysia couldn't help herself. "What if you wore it on your head? Kept your hands free?"

Yalath's withering look did nothing to stifle the respect showing on both Remeth and Simon's faces.

Simon nodded. "That's a great idea. But since all four of us are going down there, we should have enough hands. But I'll paint it on something we could tie on if space is tight."

Yalath made to protest.

"She's coming, Master," Remeth said. "She knows stone better than any of us, remember?"

"Then she will be *your* responsibility. Work of this magnitude is no place for a woman."

Elysia bit back a curse word she'd only ever heard her father use.

"Hurry it up then," Yalath said.

Simon searched through their pack for something suitable. He pulled out her Borathi tunic. "You're not going to wear this again, are you?"

She wrinkled her nose.

"It should come out with a wash, but... I'm not even sure of that."

He set to work painting the chest of the tunic with a burst of light radiating beams outward toward the edges. When he had the pattern blocked in, he closed his eyes and focused. Yalath and Remeth stood, rapt. *Now you'll see how Talented he is, you old curmudgeon!*

Without opening his eyes, Simon touched his brush to the center. The air crackled to life with a warm glow that spread as he swirled around and out along the rays. The room was suddenly as light as midday in the desert.

Remeth grinned and put his arm around Simon. "I wish I could do that!"

Elysia took his other arm. "You don't want me to wear it, do you? Won't it be hot down there?" Even inside the house, the

76

midday heat was stifling. Their winter was warmer than summer in Attarsus.

"You'll be able to direct the light if you carry it in front of you, and you could close it if..." He looked around. "If for some reason we wanted to put it out?"

Yalath sniffed. "Never hurts to prepare. Who knows what we might find down there. Could you... do that again on my lantern? I'd prefer to have another light source."

"How about a coin?" Remeth asked.

Simon nodded. "Much more portable."

When Simon finished painting it, Yalath held the glowing coin with childlike awe.

Simon bundled up his paints again. "Ready?"

"I'll go first," said Yalath. "Everything down here is of great historical significance. Be extremely careful. The relics are priceless, and anything might contain a clue about Zalikko."

"What temple is this?" Elysia asked.

"A shrine to Sukko," Remeth said.

"Who?" Simon asked Yalath.

"A minor fire goddess who had some support in the New Empire period when Uraka was at its height. I believe it's another guise of Zalikko set up to dodge official censorship."

"So why start here?"

"It's the closest, and the least significant. Gives me a chance to show you reckless kids how to properly explore a site like this without destroying it."

Elysia's heart sunk a little, wondering if they could afford the time for Yalath's painstakingly meticulous approach. *Zaliakara is loose, and... after us.*

She perched over the hole, shining her light down as Yalath descended, followed by Simon and Remeth. She came down last, while the others looked away modestly.

The hole went down around twenty feet before the walls changed from a mixture of dark soil and rubble to dressed stone. It must have been hard work to cut through the roof of the old shrine.

"How did it get covered like this?" Simon asked.

Yalath took on his scholarly tone once again. "Alternating periods of flooding and drought ended the New Empire. Uraka was devastated at that time, sitting where the Vanusa opens up into the delta. Huge portions of the city were abandoned to the deluge. But a map I found in one of our digs last year led me to this and a few other finds. My agents are constantly on the lookout for sales in any of my key areas, and we pounced on this one." He beamed. "The crew just finished clearing out the soil last week. It was an even worse mess than the house up top."

"So where do we start?"

And what are we even looking for? And how much longer can I hold my tongue?

Elysia scanned the surrounding walls, which were covered in carvings. Dark soil filled in the details, and the effect was eerie.

Yalath approached a raised platform, surrounded by semi-circle of thick columns. "This was the central room for worship. I would imagine..." He took out one of his many brushes and wiped away some of the mess, revealing a rough patch on the floor. "Hmm... the altar itself was either destroyed, or was wood.

"I was hoping to inspect any engravings. If you see anything that resembles an altar, let me know. And look for pictures on the wall, or references—" He huffed. "Of course, none of you can read any of this, but I can."

Elysia reached up to touch one of the dirt-filled inscriptions. Yalath waved frantically.

"Gods, girl! Don't you dare touch anything! Use a brush!"

Elysia had never dealt well with being told what to do, and by this insufferable old fool...

Simon held her hand. "Sorry Yalath. This is all new to us, and very exciting."

She shot Simon an angry glance and pulled her hand away. "You should—"

He touched her mouth and whispered: "I know, I know. But he's the only one who can make any sense of this."

Scrunching up her mouth, she breathed deep and nearly choked on the faint smell of decay. *Hundreds of years since anyone had been in here?* At least that was exciting. *And maybe some statues?*

"Fine. Maybe we can find the altar?"

Simon nodded.

Elysia walked over for a closer look at the floor Yalath had been inspecting. "Can I use one of your brushes, Master?" Remeth brought one to her. She brushed away the dirt to reveal the stone underneath. It wasn't one continuous space, but four closely set circles where the stone might have been sheared off. One was more jagged. "It looks like the intricate base of some kind of statue. Do you know how they depicted Sukko?"

Yalath shook his head. "I've only read references. The cult fell out of favor long before the end of the New Empire."

Remeth drew his attention over to some wall carvings.

"Do you think the priests came through here?" Elysia asked Simon, pointing to one of the doorways.

Yalath shot them a glance. "Priestesses." He was listening. "That might lead to some kind of preparation room. Worth checking out, but *please* don't touch anything."

Elysia walked through the door with Simon on her arm and the light shining from her tunic in the other hand. At least the light was warm, steady, and inviting. In the flickering glow of a lamp, the place would be alive with terrifying shadows.

As soon as they turned the corner, Simon snuck a kiss and she welcomed his lips. She mouthed thanks, happier than at any time since the failed attack on Persei. The passageway turned to the left and opened into a larger space, where the opposite and right walls were filled with alcoves. A stone bench sat in the middle of the room, and a strange mottled pattern decorated the left wall.

"Nothing in here," Simon said and turned to leave.

Something didn't fit—a light gray line on the far wall. The room was all stone, not brick like the other one. She walked over to the line, shining her light back and forth. She reached out to touch it.

"Yalath said—"

Elysia could only imagine the look she shot Simon, because he swallowed his words.

She ran her fingers along the line, feeling the stone, finding a gap where the wall wasn't flush.

"Look at this," she said.

Simon ran his hand along the line, which came away dirty. He rubbed his fingers together and looked at her, perplexed. "It's... uneven stone?"

She pursed her lips. "But it shouldn't be. The rest of the stonework is perfectly smooth. Look at these alcoves. Flawless. They wouldn't have left it jagged like this. But see how it only comes up to a little above your height?"

He nodded. "It looks like—"

"A door. This might sound a little crazy, but... I can see that this wall is supposed to move. That's what it's made for."

"I don't see it... but I believe you." He tried pushing and pulling the overhanging lip, but to no avail. "But how do we open it? Should we ask Yalath?"

"Well, he certainly doesn't want to hear anything come out of *my* mouth."

"It's pretty bad."

Elysia huffed. "That's an understatement. I thought Izari men, my father excepted, were bad enough to women. But if he's an example of the attitude of Maruthan men..."

"Remeth seems nice enough."

"To you. He's cordial to me, but..."

"But what?"

"He... doesn't look at me like a man would."

Simon laughed. "It's not enough that I love how you look, you want other men... appreciating you? I thought it made you mad when Persei did that."

"It does. That's not what I mean. But even nice men, they will sneak a glance at... you know."

Simon looked thoughtful, conceding the point.

"Hey, that does not give you permission to look at other women like that. Especially that Mysena."

Simon threw up his hands. "Is that what this is about?"

"No, and keep it down. I don't want them to hear us. What I mean is... Remeth doesn't look at me like a woman."

She almost laughed at his bewildered expression. "So he looks at you like a man?"

"No, he looks at *you* like that."

"Me? What—" Realization shot through him. "You think he... oh. I... just thought he was nice. Curious about my Talent."

"Wasn't that how Mysena looked at you?" She deserved at least a little revenge for his painting.

"I..." He shook his hands in front of her. "Well, you know I only have eyes for you—"

"For women anyway, and hopefully mostly for me. But just be aware of that. He knows you care for me, but I'm not sure he realizes that there's no room in your heart for him too. Just be careful."

Simon exhaled slowly. "Thanks for telling me. Any ideas for getting this open?"

"I was thinking of asking the stone."

He raised a quizzical eyebrow. "You can talk to it?"

"Not exactly. But it already showed us that there is a door. My guess is the answer is in one of these alcoves."

She felt along the insides of the alcoves carved into the door shape. *Such fine work, perfectly smooth limestone.* Nothing special about the first three, but in the fourth she found an irregularity.

"Hold this." She gave Simon the glowing tunic.

"What is it?"

She blew into the space, and choked on the dust that billowed out. A rectangular shape was incised into the bottom of the shallow alcove, as tall as her thumb and wide as her hand. She turned back to Simon, and before he could protest, pushed it down. It moved, just like she knew it would, revealing a space inside wide enough for a finger.

"Watch this," she said.

"Do you think you need help?"

"No, they were priestesses, remember?"

Curling her fingers into the space, she felt for something, anything, found a catch, and pulled. With a groan, it shifted outward. She grinned at Simon and pulled again. The door swung out to the right, exposing a dark void behind.

"What are you doing?" Yalath shouted as he ran into the room, Remeth trailing behind him. "This could be dangerous—" He gaped into the opening.

"What is it?" Elysia asked, straining to look.

Illuminated by the magical light, a skeleton lay contorted behind the doorway, hands clawing at the ground in a doomed attempt to escape. The musty smell of centuries of pent-up decay assaulted Elysia's nostrils. Yalath covered his mouth, gagging.

Simon stepped around the doorway to look inside as well but came away nonplussed. "You haven't been around many battles, have you? The bones are nothing compared to what I've seen. Or was she a friend of yours, Yalath?" Remeth stifled a giggle, but Yalath growled.

Elysia shone her light deeper into the secret compartment. "It's the statue!" The shiny black stone reflected the magical light, or she wouldn't have been able to see it at all. "One of the priestesses must have brought it in here for safety... but got trapped here? What a horrible way to die, alone in the dark." She turned to

Yalath, hands on hips. "Do you want to bring it out, or can we help?"

Yalath waved them on, turning away.

With Elysia holding the light steady, Simon aimed one tentative sandal toward the floor around the twisted skeleton, trying to avoid stepping on any part.

A loud hiss shattered the silence as a sheet of dark flame shot up from the ground. Simon flew backward with a yelp, landing in a heap. He untied the burning sandal and threw it to the floor.

"How can we put it out?" Remeth asked.

"Rain!" Elysia shouted, drawing a puzzled expression. "I mean water!" Remeth ran back to the main room to fetch a skin from their cache of supplies. She shone her light on Simon's scorched sole.

He winced. "It's not that bad. I got it off quick enough. We have to put that out! Shadush used it to burn stone!"

Remeth ran back in, frantically waving the waterskin. "What do I do?"

Elysia grabbed the skin and poured carefully over the remains of the sandal. The dark fire fought back in a cloud of angry steam before hissing out. The front half of the sandal was black ash sitting in a small depression where the floor had melted away.

Yalath was deathly pale. "Magical traps? But there is no record of—"

"Good thing we were here to take care of you," Elysia said. "Now about getting into that secret room..."

"What?" Yalath said. "It's not safe! If this whole temple catches fire, we lose so many relics, so much history—"

"Elysia is right," Simon said. "Whatever is in there is important. They went to great lengths to protect that statue. We have to find a way in."

"Could there be a way to deactivate it?" Remeth asked.

Elysia smiled at him. "In one of these other alcoves?"

Testing his foot successfully, Simon stood up. "What if it's simpler than that?"

"What do you mean?" Yalath asked.

"Maybe it's a one shot trap." He gingerly picked up what was left of his sandal. "Not much good anymore." Lying down on his belly, scant inches from the threshold of the secret room, he stretched out the sandal toward the invisible line.

"Be careful!" Elysia said, her stomach in knots.

Simon's cautious expression calmed her. He was brave, but certainly not stupid. He inched the sandal forward until it touched the skeleton. Nothing. Elysia exhaled.

Simon popped up and looked to Remeth. "Shall we?"

The two of them carefully stepped around the skeleton to pick up the statue. Elysia remained on edge, but nobody caught fire.

They carried the statue like it was nothing. It was smooth and dusty, in a simpler style, less realistic than the classical Izari sculpture Elysia had grown up admiring. The life-sized figure depicted a woman whose clothes and hair were rippling flames, dancing atop a blazing fire. The ordinary stone base was broken, but two of the four fiery tendrils Elysia had spotted on the altar were still attached. The body was adorned with the same kind of wedge-shaped script that covered the walls of the main shrine.

"Hopefully the inscription tells us something," Remeth said. "Definitely Middle Maruthan. We're in luck."

Having recovered from his earlier shock, Yalath directed them back to the main room. "There will be more space to inspect this. Just be careful! Obsidian... a piece this big would be exceedingly rare, and valuable. Imported."

Curious, Elysia looked closer at the fallen priestess. Everything had rotted away, leaving just the perfect skeleton, something she'd never seen before. It was fascinating, imagining how the bones served to support the human structure, yet capable of contorting into so many shapes. It gave her ideas for techniques she could try with human forms—something she hadn't had much success with in her sculpture. *It's a shame we can't bring it with us.* She banished the thought as too macabre, not to mention disrespectful.

Instead, Elysia tried to commit every detail to memory, inspecting each joint and bone. *How the fingers could grasp—* Clutched in the left hand was a dark object. Steeling herself, Elysia slowly lifted two fingers to withdraw the small metal tablet before setting them back down with the utmost care. *Sorry to disturb you, but this could be the clue we need!* Suddenly feeling very alone, she hurried after the others.

"So what does it say?" she asked when she saw Yalath huddled over the statue, now lying on its back.

"This takes time—" He snorted when he remembered who was asking.

Remeth was more forthcoming. "There's some damage to the inscription, which makes it difficult. Middle Maruthan was already significantly abstracted from the former pictograms. One missing stroke completely changes the meaning."

"You can read it?" Simon asked.

"Only a little, some of the more common words. Or words Yalath wants me to keep an eye out for."

Yalath huffed and slapped his thigh. "Useless. Just a dedication. *Sukko, take this offering into your flame. Burn our enemies. Burn for us.*"

Simon paled. It sounded far too similar to the Scentari pyre.

"Maybe you'd like to take a look at this?" Elysia said, holding out the small tablet in the palm of her hand.

Yalath was on her in a flash. "What did I say, girl?"

"It was in the hand of the... priestess. Some kind of charm?"

Yalath daintily laid it on the altar. His light illuminated a tiny inscription, different from the carvings on the walls and sculpture. "No. It's freehand. An order. And in perfect condition. Let me... *Sisters of Sukko, you must keep our lady...* warm? No, *dry. Our cousins aim to destroy us. Bring her to safety in Gardisha.*"

"What does that mean?" Simon asked. "Cousins? Is this a family affair? The priestesses were all one family... with their enemies?"

Yalath was sweating. "I... I'm not sure. It could refer to the Maruthan pantheon. Most of the gods are related through birth or marriage. But Sukko... Zalikko is not... this is most strange."

"Gardisha?" Elysia asked. "Is that where you said you found other useful sites?"

Yalath nodded, but still glared at her. *Small victories.*

"Is there a more major temple to Zalikko there?"

"If my records are correct, it was the heart of the faith."

"Then that's our best chance at finding out more. When do we leave?" Simon asked.

ᎶᏋᎶᏋᎶᏋᎶ

Persei stood alone at the bow of the legionary transport as it sailed into the sheltered harbor of Jeppo. An impressively large city, more like Attarsus than that backwater Tamar.

Mirasha was down below, violently ill after her longest sea voyage yet. She claimed that her people were meant to ride horses, not boats, and he was inclined to agree with her.

The Near Sea was notoriously unpredictable in the winter, and the storms off the island of Aktiri had challenged the stomachs of even the most seasoned sailors, but had made the trip shorter than usual. Persei spent most of the trip consoling Mirasha, who stayed with him in his Legate's quarters, but with the sun finally shining, he wanted to be seen by the men as they sailed into their new post. Or the gateway, at least.

They were stopping briefly in Jeppo before marching on to Uraka. Incessant flooding in the delta had silted up the ports further up the river, so larger ships diverted to Jeppo.

Mirasha was excited about the stop. A friend of Persei's late father owned a sizable library of ancient texts here in the city. They were to visit him before heading on with the legion.

Relief was painted clear across the faces of every one of his legionaries as they entered the port. The foul weather had humbled these veterans of his victory against the Scentari. They'd all be happier with solid ground beneath their feet.

Whispers had come to Persei's ear that a few were blaming Mirasha's presence on the ship for the storms. The ship's captain had paled when he found out Persei was bringing her along. Women on ships being bad luck was a well-known superstition. But to hell with them. Persei was in charge and he wasn't going anywhere without Mirasha. At least it had helped that she'd been stowed away, sick the entire voyage. Persei's aching loins hoped she'd feel much better once they got settled onshore.

He'd provided final instructions to one of his guards that he'd snuck aboard the ship, doctoring the manifest to have him listed as a legionary. The guard would be heading north to Bor by boat or horse, whichever was faster, to search for any sign of Simon and Elysia. A long-shot, but damned if Persei was going to let that half-breed Benjai live in peace after the attempt on his life. He'd even brought the javelin with him as a reminder. Well-made. Magical.

Simon, we're coming for you. I will find my power here, and then I will destroy you.

X

ᏮᏋᏮᏋᏮᏋᏮ
Numerius

Numerius Ontillus knocked on the door of the large estate. Corus was always one of his favorite stops in his rounds, and he and Ventus went way back. He'd recruited Ventus to be his main Izari informant. Ventus was one small node in the web of information that flowed back to Pazh through the work of people like Numerius. But Ventus was a good one, and always served excellent wine and local delicacies. Like those little crabs that only came out in the winter. Numerius licked his lips and patted his paunch. Tonight would be a good night. He deserved it after weathering the mess in Pelusia. Food shortages! And talk of dark magic. He shuddered. No, he much preferred being here in the civilized part of his itinerary. With a good friend. And then on to Pazh with all the news he'd collected.

A letter had been waiting for him at the port when he got in, from the higher-ups in Pazh. They were especially curious about the situation here in Attarsus, and one from Ventus' special watch list. *That suspected artist... what was his name? Xel...* Izari names always gave Numerius a headache.

It took far longer than usual for the door to open. *Service is slipping? Not like Ventus.*

An unfamiliar Izari face looked out. Numerius heard the sound of metal ringing on metal in the background. *What in Salar's name?*

"Yes?"

"Ventus is expecting me."

"And you are?"

"Numerius Ontillus. You must be new here. I meet with Ventus regularly—"

"Well, he's not here."

That was very unlike his friend. He was always so conscientious.

"There must be some misunderstanding, when will he return?"

"He's off the island. I don't know. Good day."

"Wait... where is he?"

"Attarsus, of course, with Master Glebric and the others."

"Others? And what's going on in there? Fighting?"

The man looked skittish. "I've said too much. Good day." He shut the door unceremoniously in the shocked face of Numerius, whose spirits turned dark.

I'll have to report this back to the superiors. At least the food should be good in Attarsus. He scowled. *Ventus had better not let me down...*

⊖⊇⊖⊇⊖⊇⊖

Persei had never seen so many books in his life. Ilson Vanatri's library was extensive. The Vanatri were an esteemed and wealthy family, but rather than make a name for himself in the Senate and military like his second cousin Daras, the decorated general, Ilson spent his life and money on books. At one time Persei would have scoffed at such a notion, but now it served his purpose, and Mirasha's quest for knowledge was infectious.

She really was incredible. How could the daughter of a barbarian chief house such an intellect? She challenged Persei to grow in so many ways, and he was enjoying it. With her at his side, it was only a matter of time before he seized the power he was due.

Of course, Persei could only read a fraction of the books and scrolls, with the majority in various forms of Maruthan. Lucky that Ilson could. And Mirasha would probably become his equal with just a few weeks of study under his tutelage. He continued flipping through one of the few Pazian books they'd found, but his eyes were firmly focused on Mirasha and Ilson chattering over another book.

No matter what she wore, she looked good, but the thin linen of the white Maruthan dress he'd bought her that morning left little to obstruct his view. It hugged her curves and the short length accentuated her long, firm legs. Persei felt the heat rising again. The color was back in her cheeks after almost two weeks of seasickness, and he longed to get her back to their room now that she had recovered.

Ilson certainly appreciated spending time with her beauty. And no wonder—he probably hadn't seen a live woman in years. Few would be so entranced by his dusty collection, especially among the locals. Persei had always thought the gold on gold Maruthan coloration to be attractive, and between the heat and local styles, they wore less and showed off that skin perfectly. But the women were forbidden to study outside of the home and few were literate. Mirasha would be quite enchanting to a Pazian who had lived here so many years in pursuit of his eclectic interests.

Was the old lecher putting his arm around her? Persei bounced out of his chair and walked over to them.

"What have you found?" he asked.

Mirasha looked apologetic, shaking her head slightly at what must have been anger or jealousy in his eyes. "Ilson has been keeping abreast of the latest research about all the ancient gods of Marutha. Did you know there have been many recent finds unearthed in both Uraka and the ruined city of Gardisha?"

At least this is proving useful. "So you're an expert?" he asked Ilson.

Ilson removed his hand from Mirasha's shoulder, shaking it to ward off the compliment. "No, no, no. I am more passionate about the history of the New Empire period, and the intermediate period that followed. But here in Marutha history and myth are inextricably linked."

"So are there others we should be seeing instead?"

Mirasha was trying to stop him, but he couldn't let them dally. They were leaving for Uraka tomorrow and he needed the best information they could glean. And there was no way he would allow Mirasha to stay back without him.

After a thoughtful pause, Ilson responded: "For your particular line of inquiry, your best option here in Jeppo is Yalath." He frowned. "But he tends to be terribly prickly."

Nothing a little money wouldn't solve.

"A friend of yours?"

"Not exactly. But we have collaborated on a few expeditions, including the excavation of the great temple of Kashaka in Uraka. What a wonderful site, full of history. You'll definitely want to spend time there, Mirasha. Actually, you're in luck, I believe Yalath has gone that way himself."

"To the temple?"

"No, but he's working on several other sites in Uraka. I'm not sure of the specifics."

"Well, that is good luck. Would you know where to locate him there?"

"I can connect you to friends who would."

"Excellent. Well, Mirasha, did you get everything you needed?"

"Oh, I was hoping she could—"

"No, I'll need her with me when we meet this Yalath."

"Persei," Mirasha said, "there are still a few more references Master Ilson was going to walk me through. And a map of several of the sites in Gardisha. He's been ever so helpful."

Is the old man blushing? Persei gritted his teeth. He wasn't used to having to cater to others to get what he wanted, but it seemed to come naturally to Mirasha. With a sigh, he resigned himself to spending the rest of the afternoon among the musty books. At least he could enjoy the view and daydream about getting even with her in bed that night. Could she read his smile? Her wicked wink made him shiver with anticipation.

"Thank you, Persei, for the opportunity to work with such an esteemed scholar."

Maybe I can do something useful as well. "I'd like to see those maps. And do you have anything about Gardisha in Pazian?" Moving his legion to the capital was one thing, but to a ruined city? If it warranted it, maybe he could send an agent to scout ahead? He needed to better understand the situation in the province while keeping Mirasha close to him, where he could enjoy her ideas... and that body.

૭ළ૭ළ૭ළ૭

Glebric was interrupted by a knock on his study door, where he and Ventus were planning their next steps.

"Sorry to disturb you, Master Glebric," said Hector. "There is a man here to see Ventus. He says his name is Numerius Ontillus."

"Do you know him?" Glebric asked.

Irritation flashed across Ventus' face. "Give us a moment," he said to the steward, who nodded, stepped out and shut the door. "We have to do something about him. I missed giving him my report."

"Your report?" Glebric knew Ventus was keeping track of Xelos through him, and he'd been meaning to ask why. The time had come. "Who did you report to?"

89

"Numerius was the one who recruited me. He was part of a web of investigation. He referred to them as the Keepers. They wanted to know about anything strange happening here in Izar. It was just a sideline for me, and paid well. Numerius became a friend—he was always good company." He exhaled sharply. "It was an oversight on my part. I should have met with him, just to keep him out of our business. If he's here now…"

"Then what?" Glebric didn't like where this was headed.

"Don't worry yourself. I'll deal with him."

"But if you meet with him now, won't he be suspicious?"

Ventus nodded, his eyes cold.

"I won't let you kill him."

"Let me? I didn't realize you were my Master?" Darkness swirled in Ventus' irises, unnatural and terrifyingly deep. Glebric enjoyed the taste of power, but when Ventus looked at him like that, he felt like he was teetering on the edge of a deep abyss, at risk of falling in to be lost forever. His conscience fought with his desire for more power, which meant maintaining this relationship with the one who granted it.

"I am your faithful ally, Ventus. But if these Keepers wanted to know about Xelos, maybe we can learn from them? From Numerius? What if we kept him here?"

Ventus considered for a moment. "That is acceptable. Would you like to be present when I see him?"

Glebric didn't hesitate. "Yes." He still didn't understand what was going on, and resented the implications of years of being a pawn in some larger web.

Ventus nodded, and opened the door.

"Hector," Glebric said, "bring wine and snacks, we will receive this Numerius Ontillus here in my study. And once you see him in, have the Alkazy wait outside, to enter if I call." The steward nodded and rushed off to fulfill the request.

"Is he dangerous, this Ontillus?"

Ventus laughed. "He's a good man. Enjoys the perks of his role. I always kept him well fed. He is no direct danger. But I don't know enough about these Keepers, and if they were trying to watch for signs of magic around Xelos, then we can't let him know anything about your powers. Or even what we have going on here."

Glebric's heart sank. "Then by seeing him, I've effectively forced him to be our prisoner." Glebric swore under his breath.

Even when I try to take control, things move on their own.

There was a knock at the door.

"Come in."

"Ah, Numerius, good to see you!" Ventus said, rushing over to the pasty Pazian man. His head reminded Glebric of a potato, misshapen in places and plagued by several large moles each sprouting a growth of wiry black hair. Sunken eyes peered out at Glebric as the man opened his mouth.

"I missed you in Corus, my good friend," Numerius said, but his voice belied caution. He addressed Glebric. "You must be Glebric, Master of the house?"

One of the servant girls entered with a pitcher of wine, three glasses, and sweet cakes.

"Welcome Numerius, be my guest." Glebric pointed to the chair opposite him.

"Ah, well... Ventus and I have business to discuss. If you could pardon us—"

"You can speak freely with Master Glebric."

Visibly shaken, Numerius let his mouth fall shut and poured himself a glass of wine.

"I... I don't believe it would be..." Numerius said, looking sideways at Glebric, "prudent... to speak of such things."

"No, it wouldn't," Ventus said, "but we're going to do it anyway."

Glebric leaned forward, elbows on the big desk and hands clasped together. "Numerius, I know you're with the Keepers."

Numerius choked on his wine, spitting droplets on his toga and the table in front of him. After a fit of coughing, he glared at Ventus.

"Did they have any special instructions for you?" Ventus asked.

Numerius coughed again, and his voice came out rasping. "I... I don't know what you mean. I don't..."

"Numerius, old friend," Ventus said, taking a sip of his wine, "do you think we're stupid? If you've followed me all the way here to Attarsus, there must have been something in particular you were checking for."

Numerius glanced around and stood up. "I'm afraid I must decline your hospitality, Glebric. I will be going now."

"Sit," Glebric said, keeping his eyes hard. Now he really wanted to understand what was going on. "I have a guard outside. If I say the word, he'll slit you like a pig." The threat sounded so vile as it escaped his lips. *When did I become capable of such a thing?*

It had the desired effect. Numerius sat down and began whimpering.

"Here, have some more wine," Ventus offered. "Then let us know what they asked of you."

Numerius took the cup as if it were filled with poison. But he drank it. *Glutton. These nobles enjoying the fruits of our labors.* The man looked up to the heavens, as if beseeching a higher power to save him.

"Xelos. They specifically wanted an update on Xelos." He looked around. "This is his house, so I can see why."

"Did they say any more?" Ventus asked, his eyes like steel.

"No. That is all. And for this you threaten me? After all I've done for you?"

"Who do *you* report to?" Glebric asked.

"I... I..." Potato head looked like he was going to throw up.

Ventus stepped in. "Did you already send word to them? That you missed your meeting with me?"

The man nodded meekly.

"Then I'm afraid you won't be leaving here... alive," Ventus said. "If you tell us more about your Keeper friends, then we might let you live."

"I... they don't show me their faces! I don't know! That's all I can tell you."

"Men?"

"Yes."

"And you only meet them in Pazh?"

"Yes, and only once each year. The rest of the time I send letters..."

"And who do you send them to? Give me the name!" Glebric said.

Eyes shut tight, the man's jowls rippled as he shook his head. Ventus slapped him, and the sunken eyes peered out in abject terror. The stink of urine suffused the room and Glebric gagged. Without a thought, he clenched his fist, focused on the source of the smell, and it disappeared.

Glebric reached across the desk for the jug of wine and slowly poured it onto the table in front of Numerius, who looked on in terrified confusion.

"Imagine this is your blood," Glebric said.

The man fainted. Ventus had to slap him again to bring him around.

"Why are you doing this to me?" he asked, blubbering.

"Why were you spying on me all these years?"

No response, and none expected.

Glebric pointed to the wine. "Your blood." He channeled his anger, disgust, and violation at having his life controlled at a distance by this man and his Keepers. *No, by the Keepers through this worm.* Curling one finger up for effect, he imposed his will on the liquid. The surface began to rise, like a finger pushing through fabric. Already pale, Numerius drained of any remaining color. His lip quivered. Glebric raised his hand and the finger broke free of the pool with a ripple, undulating as it formed itself into a ball. It looked so very much like blood. As Glebric rotated his hand, it danced through the air, zooming in close to Numerius' face, and he flinched.

"Can you imagine how it would feel, if your blood were to do this? To leave your body and dance around the room?" The thought excited Glebric, almost more than he could bear.

Numerius squeezed his eyes shut again, dropping his head in defeat. "Tullus! His name is Tullus!"

Glebric took out a blank page. He willed the blood to form letters, spelling out the name Tullus. "Address?"

Sounding utterly broken, Numerius dictated the location.

"Now was that so hard?" Glebric asked. He snapped his fingers and the rest of the puddle of wine leaped into Numerius' cup. Glebric offered it to him. "You look like you could use a drink."

∞∞∞∞∞∞

The click of the key in the lock somehow made the nightmare real. Numerius was alone, in the dark, in some kind of storeroom. After what he'd seen today, and Ventus' betrayal, the solidity of the darkness was somehow welcome.

Ventus a traitor to the Keepers? He still couldn't believe it. He'd known the man for a decade, and this was not at all in character. *He even threatened me!*

Glebric, a warlock? There was no fact in all the Near Sea of more interest to the Keepers, yet here he was, unable to get them word.

93

How did they know something strange was taking place here in Attarsus? *And what happened to Xelos? And this Simon he was supposed to check on?*

As terrified as he'd been when faced with the reality of this dark magic, he was still alive. At least he'd had the foresight to send word of Ventus' failure to check in. *It's the standard protocol, after all.* But why didn't he tell them where he was going? At least then they would come to Attarsus, and with Xelos the only clue they had to work from, they might even find him. Well, they might remember Elysia from Ventus' previous reports. But there was no sign of her either.

As long as you breathe, there's a chance of escape. Though the guards around here look like gladiators. He shuddered again at the vision of the tall Alkazy who'd escorted him to the little prison. He wouldn't want to be on the wrong end of his sword.

Well, it could be worse. At least the wine was good…

XI
ᎶᏋᎶᏋᎶᏋᎶ
Gardisha

Gardisha lay a full day south of Uraka by barge, but it seemed a world away. The slow-moving river cut a green swathe through the golden desert, with the land on either shore devoted to intensive grain cultivation. But where the boat let them off, there were no farms, just desolation. Yalath said the river used to run alongside the edge of the city, but had found a permanently lower level in the past millennium.

With blowing sand filling his mouth, the resulting slow trudge up the dusty incline left Simon in a foul mood. And the view from the crest of the hill was equally unimpressive. While the streets of Uraka teemed with lively commerce, Gardisha was populated mainly by sand blowing in from the desert, with the flowing dunes broken up by irregular protrusions of dark stone, like rotting teeth.

"This is it?" he asked a sweating Yalath, who nodded. Away from the coast the climate was much drier and hotter. And it was only mid-morning; the midday sun would be deadly. Even Zeno was complaining, especially with extra blankets to hide his wings.

Gardisha was a protected site, so as soon as they disembarked they had been assigned an aide from the office of the Prefect of Antiquities.

The aide, Jukaro, was an unremarkable man whose hair and skin were such a perfect match for the desert sand that Simon didn't think he'd be able to see him if he laid down naked. He was to accompany them everywhere they went, so opportunities to use their Talent would be severely limited. Simon hoped that wouldn't inhibit their progress.

In a few places Simon could make out patches of pale blue, almost like... cloth?

"So are we going to that set of tents over there?" Elysia asked, recognizing the forms just before Simon. "Or the bigger one over there?" Jukaro pointed to a third group between the two.

Since locating Shadush half-buried in murky water, the scene had repeatedly haunted Simon's dreams. He always woke up before being buried alive, but it was terrifying. These tent villages surrounded by shifting sand were a little too close to the mark. "When you say excavation, you mean it's covered in sand? How do you keep it out?"

Jukaro answered: "There are alternating layers of sand and silt. The area was flooded many times after the city was abandoned. The tents keep out the sun, and we build embankments with the soil to keep the sand from pouring in."

Simon only relaxed a little.

When they got closer, Simon realized he'd underestimated the size of the dig. Few of the tents were blue; the rest blended in with the surroundings.

Two guards nodded to Jukaro as he led them in past two armed guards. Under the segmented canopy, a miniature town thrived away from the hot sun, in the strange muted light that filtered through the tarp. Dozens of workers were busy at various tasks; repairing tents, shoveling sand, building more embankments or carefully transporting chests that Simon guessed contained recovered artifacts.

They followed Jukaro to a large blue tent, where again two guards let him pass and he announced them. "Supervisor Eppeth, Yalath and his crew are here to see you. They have a permit for site seven."

Behind a desk covered in fragments of stone and pottery, a wizened old man with a scrunched up face squinted at them. Irregular tufts of white hair erupted from the golden wrinkles of his bald head, bearing a remarkable resemblance to the tents sticking up out of the desert. Two middle-aged men stood with him, poring over the materials. They didn't look up.

"Yalath? I hadn't expected to see you again so soon. And with such a large crew."

Smiling for the first time Simon could remember, Yalath approached the old man. "Good to see you, Eppeth. How is the work going in site seven?"

"We've cleared out the whole wing. Some very interesting finds." His eyes darted to Simon and Elysia. "I can tell you later."

"They're part of my crew, and trusted."

Elysia's eyes bugged out, so Simon nudged her in the ribs.

"A woman in your crew? You know that's an affront to the gods. And she's not even…"

"She's a visiting expert on statuary. I was hoping to show her some of the finds. And I don't believe this particular god would have any issue with a woman in her temple."

The old man considered his words, and then nodded. "It's on you. You'll be on your own, I don't think any of my men will go down there with a woman. It's just not done. And especially after… there was an accident." He looked very tired. And older if it was even possible. "One of the men was trying to bring out a statue he found. Of a woman. Should never have attempted it by himself, but that one was hoping for glory. The body was charred beyond recognition. Must have fumbled his lantern and set himself on fire, trapping himself in where nobody could hear him calling for help. Careless. Avoidable."

Yalath's interest perked up. "Where did it happen? Can you direct me there?"

Eppeth led them to another table with a map, which detailed every foot of the site with remarkable precision. Simon would be proud to produce such quality, and attempted to commit it to memory.

"The statue was found… here." Eppeth pointed to a small room connected to a large hall. It looked like a larger version of what they had found in Uraka.

"Out in the open?"

"No. Hidden away in a secret compartment. The man opened it by accident. The others won't go in there. I was worried to do so myself. He was working alone, so we don't know exactly what happened. Some of the men believe the goddess is angry that we disturbed her. That the statue might somehow actually *be* her."

"Zalikko?" Simon asked.

The heads of Eppeth and his men snapped on him in shocked unison. Yalath grabbed Simon's shoulder. "Do not say the name of The Devourer. Not here."

Simon bowed his head in apology, and so they wouldn't see him rolling his eyes. *I wonder what they'd do if they knew she was walking free in Pazh right now? The fright would be enough to stop Eppeth's old heart.*

"Pazian?" asked one of Eppeth's men, his eyes full of suspicion.

Simon nodded. The man exchanged a glance with his counterpart. "You must be even more careful. There is a reason they call her The Devourer. You do not understand. Yalath, keep your *outsiders* in line."

Chastened, Simon bowed again. "I will follow Master Yalath's lead." It seemed to satisfy them.

Yalath snorted. "The boy thinks he knows more than he does. He needs to learn humility. Seeing the magnificence of ancient Marutha will show him his place."

Simon burned inside. He thought he'd left this kind of treatment behind when he got away from Persei. But he had to keep calm. Especially since Elysia was ready to strike Yalath at any further provocation.

Eppeth addressed Yalath. "If you have everything you need, Jukaro will show you to your quarters. You can go to that site whenever you wish."

"Thank you, Eppeth. We'll head down after lunch."

Their quarters consisted of bedrolls in a crumbling ancient mud-brick house. Dark, dusty, and dry, but at least it kept out the heat. Simon licked his lips. The place did seem forsaken by water, whether that was some goddess or Damoz or just nature.

Carrying ordinary lamps, the five of them descended a recently constructed stairway into the subterranean world. Whole streets had been emptied out into impossibly large tunnels.

"This way," Yalath said, and the path matched the route Simon had memorized from the map. "The temple was housed inside a large villa."

"So even in their largest temple, they met in secret?" Simon asked.

"Yes. Officially, all worship of Zalikko was banned. Still is."

Elysia nudged Simon and whispered, "They probably didn't like women being involved in religion." Simon nodded ruefully.

It was hard to tell the size of the villa from the tunnel, but the doorway was larger than even the nicer houses of Pazh.

"Were there nobles involved?" Simon asked. "And their cousins, perhaps?" Jukaro looked confused, but Yalath looked angry enough to spit. Simon held up his hands in silent apology. That reference to cousins still confused him. He had hoped Jukaro might at least know something.

"We enter through the storeroom," Yalath said.

"They must have entertained a lot of visitors," Simon said. "I wonder what the neighbors thought? Do you know much about the kind of women who were involved in the sect?" Yalath's scowl indicated that it wasn't much. *Perhaps prostitutes or slaves? Or just friends of the family?*

They followed Yalath's lead into the storeroom. As they made their way down the ancient stairs, Simon felt a strange prickling on the back of his neck. He looked to Elysia, and could tell she felt it too. Remeth and Yalath also looked uncertain, while Jukaro's eyes darted from shadow to shadow. *Am I becoming more attuned to the dark power? Something is... or was... here.*

"Maybe... I'll just stay here," Jukaro said, "and you can fill me in on the details."

Yalath raised an eyebrow. "Aren't you supposed to keep track of everything we do?"

"I... I'm sure we can trust you. With all your... experience." Jukaro managed a weak smile.

"I'm sure you can," Yalath said. Their erstwhile minder climbed three quarters of the way back up the stairs before sitting down, lamp in hand. Elysia rolled her eyes as they continued into the ancient temple.

"Good riddance," she said. "I don't trust him."

Simon agreed. Especially if they needed their Talent, which seemed increasingly likely.

A long corridor led to a heavy door, which Simon and Remeth opened without much difficulty. The air beyond was heavier, oppressive, and tinged with the smell of stale smoke. Yalath gulped audibly, looking unsteady on his feet.

"Don't worry, Master," Elysia said. "There won't be much left of the body." The old man was too queasy to bother with silencing her.

Their lamps illuminated a layout similar to what they'd seen in Uraka: a roughly circular room, multiple pillars supporting the ceiling, and a large raised dais opposite them. Once again, the statue was missing. Elysia immediately made her way over to investigate the base.

"Definitely larger," she said. "I don't think one woman carried this by herself."

Simon pointed to the doorway along that same wall. "The smell comes from over there, so that's probably where they hid it." He motioned for the others to follow, but Yalath was distracted by large relief carvings on the wall behind where the statute had been. "What?"

"It's a shame these are so damaged," Yalath said. He pointed to the images of a beautiful woman wreathed in flames, and a group of worshipers before her. "This is definitely Zalikko. These would be her followers. And these…" The next panel was badly damaged, showing part of a figure next to a river. "That's curious… This is a man, and see that flower? That's the water lily of Kashaka. Why would they be showing them here?" He screwed up his face, squinting at a particularly damaged part that would be the next scene in the sequence. "I wish we could see the rest, and the text. The image doesn't make sense."

"Not much we can do about that," Simon said. "Why don't we take a look at the statue?" Remeth and Elysia followed quickly, while Yalath dragged his feet.

As he would have guessed, the passage turned to the left before opening up into a larger room with alcoves lining the walls. The charred smell was much stronger, but not unbearable. A large pile of ash sat on the threshold of a dark opening in the wall, surrounded by scorch marks on the stone.

Yalath actually looked relieved.

"So, it's just bodies that bother you?" Elysia asked. "What about blood?"

He seemed to ignore her barb. "Simon, can you… see about getting that statute out?" He pointed inside at the dark shape, barely visible in the secret space behind the doorway.

This time Simon came prepared. After a check to make sure Jukaro hadn't snuck up on them, he took out his glowing coin and a strip of leather he'd cut from his former sandal. Kneeling carefully on the floor at the edge of the scorch marks, he set up the coin to light his way, and started sliding the little leather strip toward the threshold.

He looked back nervously, and Elysia nodded.

When it came level with the pile of ash, Simon yelped, violently jerking his hand back to cover the coin. Someone screamed like a young girl. Yalath cowered behind Remeth, quivering and on the verge of fainting. Remeth burst out laughing, followed closely by Elysia. She'd suggested the trick to Simon, if they found themselves in a similar situation to the trap in Uraka.

Was Yalath turning purple? Simon couldn't tell in the dim light, but his eyes blazed with fury.

"This is no time for childish tricks!" Yalath said in a shrill voice. "This is dark and powerful magic!"

Chastened, Simon carefully pushed the leather probe the rest of the way into the secret room, without it bursting into flame. "Just like the other one, a one-shot trap."

Remeth hadn't stopped grinning when he joined Simon inside the secret room. The statue was cast bronze, which somehow made the curves even more voluptuous. It held the same pose as the statue of Sukko, except almost naked, with just stylized flames covering the intimate regions. Simon had to adjust his hands twice to avoid gripping anything unseemly. Remeth showed no such inhibitions and shared a knowing smile with Simon. *Maybe Elysia had been wrong about him?*

"Bring it all the way out to the main temple," Yalath said, his voice stern. "And be careful of the inscription."

"This would've taken three or four women," Remeth said, with a grunt, and Simon nodded. They carefully set it down on the dais in front of the frieze.

Yalath set to inspecting the inscription on the back. "I wish I had better light." When Simon offered the coin, Yalath waved him off. "No, we can't risk it. Our friend," he said, indicating the passageway where they'd entered, "can't be trusted."

Simon and Elysia inspected the frieze on the wall. "Pretty impressive, for the time," Elysia said, "but not to Xelos' standard."

The carvings were barely more than two dimensions, not carved as deep as those that adorned the great temples of Attarsus.

"It's such a different style," Simon said. "Such a contrast from the statue. It looks so real, while these look more like what we drew as children in my school. Actually, some of them were much better."

"Like you, I'm sure," Remeth said.

"Was this the typical style?" Elysia asked Yalath.

"Hmmm? Typical? Yes. You would find similar decoration in all the major temples of that era."

"Wouldn't the supporters of Kashaka have opposed them? If this temple was forced underground? Water and fire opposing each other?"

Yalath was flustered. "Well… Yes, that's what is generally assumed."

"Then why do they look friendly here?" Elysia asked. "Almost like they're coming to visit."

"I don't know," Yalath said. "Stop pestering me. I've almost deciphered this inscription…" He sighed, disappointment etched on his face. "Just another prayer, this time to Zalikko. More burning… purifying flame… nothing useful."

"How is everything?" came the voice of Jukaro from down the hall.

"So much for his meddling stopping at the stairs," Elysia said.

"Should I go give him a report?" Remeth asked.

Yalath waved him on, nodding. "Nothing too accurate."

Elysia had a curious look on her face as she ran her hand over the rough parts where the frieze was damaged. She closed her eyes as she communed with her Talent.

"What is it?" Simon asked when she opened them again.

"I… It's hazy… I can almost see… what they were trying to do. Some of these missing pieces are large. Did they take them out, catalog them?"

"Yalath," Simon said, "where do they keep any relics or items of archaeological interest that they remove from sites?"

"Eppeth and his team painstakingly organize them in a few of the buildings that they have dedicated for that purpose. Why?"

Elysia looked at him expectantly until he nodded for her to speak. "I think I might be able to piece this together, if I can get more to work with. With my Talent, I can feel their intention for each of the stones, but with the missing portions it's hazy, indistinct."

Remeth returned. "Sorry to interrupt, but Jukaro is asking if we'll be able to bring the statue out. I told him we might, but would need more men to help carry it, so he ran off to ask Eppeth where to take it. It would be the most significant find yet in this dig."

Yalath nodded. "Good work, that should get him off our backs for at least a little while. And when he returns, I suggest we see if my old colleague would show us around some of the findings, to get Elysia a look at more of those fragments."

"Should we just leave the statue here then?" Remeth asked.

"Yes. And besides, it's not likely to yield us any additional clues.

I'd like us to spend the time until Jukaro returns to thoroughly map out the figures from on the walls here, to uncover any other useful lines of inquiry."

XII

ᕯᕯᕯᕯᕯ

Suspicion

Elysia wrapped the scarf tightly around her face to ward off the blowing sand and harsh sun. Jukaro was leading them to one of the larger camps, to where they housed the recent finds. Yalath thought it unusual; they normally performed those tasks at the source site. Perhaps because of the accident? Elysia was uncomfortable leaving Zeno at the stables, surrounded by the strange creatures they called camels, but Simon reminded her they had done the same when they entered the temples underground.

The sand was blowing harder now, mixing with sweat from the oppressive sun, hot even this late in the afternoon. She turned back, so at least the sun wouldn't be in her eyes as she tried to blink away the grit. *Was it a trick of the light? Or were those—*

"Riders!" she screamed.

Camel-riding men in flowing sand-colored robes reached them in moments, their curved swords glinting in the late afternoon sun. Ten men surrounded them, circling slowly, sizing them up. But none said a word through the scarves that shielded all but their impassive eyes.

Jukaro threw himself down on the sand, looking up at them in terror. He started babbling something she didn't understand in the flowing Maruthan language.

"What is he saying?" she whispered to Remeth on her left.

"To spare him, that he has nothing to do with us," he said without expression.

One of the riders barked a command to Jukaro, silencing him. His accent changed, becoming harsher. He called out a question and Remeth raised his hand. The man nodded and Remeth spoke carefully, in a different, more erudite voice, like an academic. The man grunted and gave another command to the riders. Five

104

dismounted, approaching Elysia and the others.

One man walked toward her, rope in hand. "What are they doing?"

"Just cooperate," Remeth said, putting a finger to his lips before holding up his own hands to be bound. "If you say anything, they'll beat you."

The riders searched the men for weapons, taking Simon's knife and all their bags, but thankfully only bound her hands.

After mounting their camels, they led Elysia and the others back toward the largest camp, at a pace slow enough that the captives could follow on foot, pulled along by the ropes. When they reached the entrance, marked by a black tent, her captor dismounted again. He held a rough sack, and terror welled up inside Elysia. Simon's expression called out to her with silent comfort, and the world went dark.

Elysia lost count of the steps and turns as she was led blindly through the camp. At least it was cooler out of the sun, but the gritty sand remained in her mouth; the bag made it impossible to spit out.

With the noises of the campsite all around her, she couldn't determine how many sets of footsteps were with them. It brought a fresh wave of panic—*what if I'm separated from the others?* She began to struggle against her bonds, until a sharp slap across her backside made her yelp, more with surprise than pain.

"Elysia?" came Simon's unmistakable voice, laced with concern. Another smack.

"I'm all right," she said, resulting in another slap. She smiled despite the sting. At least Simon was still with her. Hopefully the others too. But none dared speak for the rest of the walk.

She heard the jangle of keys, the creaking of a door, and their footfalls began to echo. Another set of steps, more keys, another door, and a rough shove.

A flash of light stung her eyes when the sack was suddenly lifted, before the door slammed again and she was thrust into total darkness. Her hands were still bound.

"Simon?" she called out, frantic.

"Elysia," he said, and relief flooded into her. They might be prisoners, but at least they were together.

"Are you hurt?" She moved closer to the sound of his voice.

"I've seen far worse during training. Or even back in school when I challenged the teachers." She could feel his warmth, and carefully reached out her bound hands to touch him. She felt the sandpaper of his unshaven face, and his parched lips against her knuckles. "You?"

"It was only... like they were disciplining a naughty child. Nothing serious."

"Remeth? Yalath? Jukaro?" Simon called out. When there was no response, he repeated the call, louder in case they were in other rooms.

Silence.

"Where are they?" she asked. "This is some kind of makeshift cell."

"I'm more concerned about who our captors are. We're the only non-Maruthans here, so I'm wondering if that's why they separated us? Maybe someone doesn't want us in their tombs?"

"By kidnapping us? Armed soldiers?"

"But this is a Pazian province. The only soldiers are with the legions or garrisons. And I've never heard of even auxiliaries riding camels but..." He sounded worried.

"What is it, Simon?"

"They must be rebels. Unlike the other eastern provinces, which joined the Republic relatively peacefully, coming for protection against some greater evil, or for economic purposes... Marutha was won by war."

"But wouldn't the legions just crush them?"

"That's probably why they're hiding here, in the ruins. There's no legion presence here. But I wonder... how fast did news travel about what happened with the Scentari? The fact that the Scentari rose up in the first place might embolden others."

"Simon, I'm scared." He raised his bound wrists over her head, enveloping her in his arms to hold her tight.

"As long as we're together, we'll be safe."

"How can these people blame us for what they see as the sins of the Republic? It just doesn't make sense."

He sighed. "When I was young, I loved that idea of our fellow citizens leading us, not some man with a divine claim. But while it's easy to blame a figurehead for your problems, what happens when you don't have that? You make one. And we... might be an easy foreign target."

"Jukaro sure was quick to give us up."

"I'm worried that others might be in on this too. They must be turning a blind eye at the very least, if not collaborating."

Elysia gasped. "Surely not Yalath? He's obnoxious, but if Xelos trusted him I can't imagine…"

"No, nor Remeth. But maybe Eppeth? Or his men?"

"I thought they looked at us strangely. Jukaro too."

"It just seems like too much of a coincidence that they came looking for us right when we were heading to the other camp."

"Any ideas for getting out of here?"

"Not yet. But if we're going to be stuck here for a while…" He pressed closer to her. "Can't we enjoy the privacy a little?" His lips brushed against hers, but she pulled back. "What is it?"

"Sorry, I just…" After swirling the saliva in her mouth, she spat into the darkness off to the side. "Sorry, the sand. It gets everywhere!" He chuckled. "Now where were we?"

Despite all the fear, it felt so good. After being with Yalath for days now, they'd had only a few fleeting moments together. In a world of such uncertainty, he was her rock. She lost herself in his kiss.

Curled up together in the darkness, the hours melted away without any way to mark them. Elysia had drifted in and out of sleep, but rest was proving elusive now that her stomach was rumbling. *Surely, it must be night by now?*

Without use of her hands or eyes, all Elysia was left with were her mind and voice. Her thoughts returned again and again to the damaged frieze that seemed to be deliberately concealing what might be useful to them. If only she could see those fragments. If they even had them. What if they had been destroyed? Lost to time?

Or purposely ruined? That thought drove her further, to come up with a solution. If only she could remake it somehow.

What if I could?

"Simon?" she said into the darkness. From his even breathing, he was asleep again.

"What is it?" he asked, groggy.

"I think… I have an idea for rebuilding the frieze." Excitement banished any latent exhaustion from her body.

"How?"

107

"If I could get some soft rock... maybe even clay? I could... listen? I guess it is partly listening to what the stone has to say... partly seeing what could be there. If I do that... I'm thinking I could get the new stone or clay or whatever I can use... to talk to what's already there. And then it can tell me how to shape it."

"You think that would work?"

"I do."

He sat silently, thinking through the details and possibilities like he always did. That always made her nervous. What objection would he throw at her? He was good at objections.

"But..."

Here it comes. She reminded herself that he really did mean well. Still, she braced herself. "What if the writing is the key? The inscription."

In her mind she saw the frieze shattering into a thousand useless shards. "You're right... and that's not part of the sculpture. It would have been added after. As an engraving... text." Somehow she knew that part wouldn't come to her. She didn't even speak the language.

Suddenly he straightened, and she felt his face very close to hers.

"But what if we worked together?"

"What do you mean?"

"Maybe I can do the inscription... it's more like drawing or painting. Maybe my Talent can tap into it... especially with our close connection." He sounded so alive, and she hated to bear the bad news.

"That sounds like a great idea... but there's still one problem."

"Really?" He sounded crestfallen.

"We have to get out of here alive."

"I'm not sure that's even—"

Footsteps approached from the other side of the door, and she sat bolt upright. Keys scraped in the lock. The door creaked open and light spilled in around the silhouette of a robed figure, looking like death coming to take them.

Elysia huddled against Simon as they rose to their feet. Simon held his bound hands out in front of them as a feeble defense.

Is this the end? Please don't take him... or me!

A second robed figure entered, shorter, slower and carrying a lamp.

"How are you two?" said Remeth, the taller figure. He pulled back his hood and scarf and flashed his winning smile, setting their packs on the floor.

"But how?" Elysia asked as Yalath showed himself as well.

"I'll explain as we go. We have to hurry. Put these on." He produced two more robes from a fifth pack.

Simon held out his hands and Remeth looked sheepish. "Sorry, of course..."

"Jukaro?" Simon asked when his hands were free.

"They let him go, the weasel." Remeth started on Elysia's ropes.

"Did you escape?" she asked him.

"We were taken for questioning, about why we were bringing Pazian unbelievers into the sites."

Yalath smiled, uncharacteristically. "Remeth put on quite the show."

"What do you mean?" Elysia asked.

Simon raised an eyebrow. "Talent?"

Remeth grinned. "Let's just say I played the part of an academic sympathetic to their cause. That you two are visiting scholars we need to unlock what we're looking for."

Elysia rubbed her wrists together, smiling in thanks. The skin was raw but not bleeding. She busied herself putting on the robe. It was too big, so she'd have to walk carefully.

"What were they going to do with us?" Simon asked.

"Some still think you're Pazian spies, or worse... that Elysia is somehow trying to reawaken Zalikko and destroy us all. They were going to keep you here, until their leader arrived to make the decision."

"So how did you get all this?"

Yalath waggled a small flute in his fingers. "When they took us back to our packs, I played them a little song as thanks. They should sleep through the night and give us enough time to leave."

"But what will happen when they wake up?" Elysia asked.

Remeth peeked out the door. "If you don't hurry, we might be around to find out."

"How do I look?" Simon asked her. With the hood and the scarf and a curved sword in hand, she couldn't tell him apart from the others, or the men who had captured them earlier. Except for his much darker hand.

"Keep your skin covered, like one of these ruffians. And me?"

"Aren't you a little short to be a bandit?" She tried to stand on her toes, and he laughed.

Remeth's voice was urgent from the door. "Let's go! And don't say a word until we're well out of the camp. I'll do all the talking."

From the outside, their jail looked like just another ancient house.

None challenged them through several turns on empty streets until they climbed a set of wooden steps to where two sentries looked out into the night. They turned at the sound of the approach, and one held up a hand. Remeth opened his scarf and spoke to them. He sounded different again, like he was one of them. Gone was the genial artist, replaced by the grating tones that matched a hard life in the desert. Satisfied, the sentries pressed their palms against his in turn, and parted to let them pass. Fear clutched her throat when she thought they might offer Simon or herself the same ritual goodbye, but they turned back to their post without another word.

The bright starlight painted the desert sand an eerie silver. She found herself seeing clearer than she did by day, without the sun's glare on the sand. If anyone else was looking for them, they'd be spotted immediately.

It wasn't until they were halfway back to their original camp that anyone dared speak.

"Yalath," Simon asked, "who are those people?"

"Rebels. I'd heard word that they were more organized now, and working outside the major cities. But not this close to the capital. And not this many. Few of my people have ever been happy with the Pazian occupation."

"Occupation?" Simon asked, incredulous. "You've been part of the Republic for centuries!"

"Never willingly," Yalath said, his eyes hard.

"Now is not the time for politics," Remeth said with a voice so conciliatory that Elysia dropped all thought of it.

She asked a question instead. "But if they think we're spies, won't it be proof now that we've escaped?"

Yalath nodded. "Which is exactly why we're going to have to keep up this guise. Obviously Jukaro and Eppeth know of these people. Some of them must even be complicit. I can't say I totally blame them. Only Maruthans show proper respect to our relics. The Pazians would rather take them away to decorate their villas, or sell them to fund the army that keeps us down."

"That sounds awfully like treason," Simon said.

"Says the deserter."

Even covered like he was, Elysia caught Simon's wince. "We'd better hurry with our exploration," she said, doing her part to dispel the tension. "Simon and I have an idea."

Simon explained their collaboration plan to Remeth and Yalath.

"But how will we get back into the temple?" Yalath asked. "Without drawing further attention to ourselves? I don't think they'll let me out again if the rebels catch us."

"What if we draw attention to the rebels instead?" Remeth said, a smile in his voice. "I can play the part, and we can go down into the temple dressed like this. We can demand it, in the name of the revolution. Can you two work quickly?"

Elysia looked at Simon. They both nodded.

"Night is as good a time as any down here," Yalath said, "Let's go."

XIII

ᎶᏋᎶᏋᎶᏋᎶ

Restoration

The sentries at their original camp tried to block them from entering, so Yalath played a lullaby while Elysia covered her ears, like Remeth had advised her. Even if the guards were woken up by a shift change they wouldn't be able to determine where the rebels had gone.

Back in the temple of Zalikko, Remeth stood lookout at the stairs, and Elysia approached the frieze, to start her attempt at direct communication with the stonework. Simon set up several sources of light with his magic to keep the wall well-illuminated.

Yalath's mouth twisted like he was sucking a lemon.

"What?" Elysia asked.

"Are you sure this won't damage the stonework? This is my heritage."

"I'm sure The Devourer would be ever so careful with all these relics if she takes over the world!"

The old man wiped sweat from his brow and waved for her to begin. He looked so nervous that she almost felt sorry for him.

With her left hand on an undamaged part of the frieze and her right hovering over an adjacent missing portion, she closed her eyes. A hazy image of what was still there floated into her mind, with the gaps like swirling wisps of smoke. As she traced each curve and crevice of the sculpture, the image sharpened, becoming distinct and very real. It felt as if the stone yearned to tell her its story after so many centuries of silence. Images of more of Zalikko's female followers along with the male priests of Kashaka became so clear that it was as if she were watching the scene unfold before her. As her hand reached the first gap, where half a woman was missing, she stubbed her finger into what felt like a solid continuation of the figure. Luminous blue stone filled the gap

112

wherever her fingers touched, at least inside her mind, and the carving became not just complete, but glowed with a new life. Both hands danced along the panel, the strands of ether knitting together into glowing solid revelation. With the first panel complete, she pushed herself to the missing panels beside and below, and line by line she traced them into existence. She had to share what she was seeing.

"It's all here. The stone remembers, and is telling me. I see the men. They're coming to the temple hand in hand with the follow- ers of... of this temple. Like couples. They join hands together... it's like they're one big family. All bowing down to the central statue. Coming together... and so happy. It's like they're leading them into... some kind of paradise. That's the feeling I get. I wish I could read the inscription." She remembered Simon's idea. "Simon, come to me. Bring a brush. And blue paint. Take my hand. I think... I think I can show you."

Without opening her eyes, she reached out when she heard his footsteps approach. His hand felt so warm, so wonderful... the image in her mind wavered for a moment, competing with other pleasant visions. She focused, and it became sharp again.

"Simon, can you feel this?" She guided his hand along one of the missing portions, of the pairs of worshipers in a circle around the statue.

"I... I... I feel something, but it's impossible. It's not there. My hand pushes through it."

"Close your eyes." She pulled his hand away, and then brought it back to the surface. "Now can you feel it?"

His voice was full of awe. "It's as real as the other stone."

She smiled. "Now I'm going to guide your hand over the inscriptions. I'm hoping you can feel them enough so that you can paint them, and Yalath will be able to see it."

"But will I be painting on stone... or in the air?"

She squeezed his hand. "Just feel it. It will work." They started with the panel with the men approaching, starting first with the figures before continuing with the missing inscription. She guided his finger to trace the lines of the inscriptions, which were in a mix of pictographs and the wedge-like script. Then she imagined him dipping his brush into those spaces and making it visible.

"Is it working, Yalath? Can you see it?"

"It's incredible, seeing the full panels. The script is a bit messy, but yes... I can read it. I'll copy it out so I can decipher it later... in case it disappears."

They worked their way through the text on that panel and into the other missing ones. There was a special shared intimacy in working in this way, her hand and Talent both joined to Simon's. It was almost... she felt herself blush, happy that Yalath couldn't see her face. *Did Simon feel it too?*

The inscription at the end of the last panel looked different, like it came later, in another hand. She opened her eyes, delighting in the earnest concentration on Simon's face. He opened his eyes.

"Are we done?" he asked.

She nodded, grinning. "Wasn't that fun?" She blew him a kiss, safe in the knowledge that Yalath couldn't see. Simon smiled back.

"It was... amazing. It was almost like I could see it through my fingers. Is that how it happens when you see something trapped in the stone, for you to carve out?"

"Not exactly. This was new... it glowed. But imagine the possibilities! I want to explore ancient sites everywhere!"

"So how did it look to you?" he asked Yalath.

The old man looked at them with a strange expression. "Look for yourself."

Elysia clapped her hands and grabbed Simon's arm. In glowing blue, the completed figures and inscription hung suspended in the air. Parts touched the stone, but the rest just floated. In some ways it was the most magical manifestation of Talent she'd yet witnessed; so simple, yet so impossible.

Simon beamed, looking like a proud little boy. Yes, he was fully an adult and had seen so much in these past months, but it touched her to see him equally delighted.

Remeth walked in. "Were you calling for me? I heard noise—wow!" He gaped at their glowing handiwork.

"So what does it say?" Elysia asked.

Holding up a hand, Yalath scowled, furrowing his brow. "My translation is still very rough, I need more time... but..."

Elysia huffed, making the old man even more flustered.

"Yes... yes... a hurry. I know. But it can't be right... It would be considered almost blasphemy... from the dominant viewpoint. But it mentions the *cousins* again. I... I think we're on to something."

"Which is?" Simon asked, sharing her impatience.

114

"It seems like the followers of..." Yalath looked around, as if for evil spirits lurking, "*her* followers look forward to a time when their *cousins* will couple... no... merge with them, and they will unite in the new kingdom. But following *her* was outlawed. Why would Kashaka's followers have anything to do with them? Kashaka has been ascendant in all recorded Maruthan history, and... *she*... has never been anything more than an outsider. What do they mean, *cousins*?"

Simon shook his head, but Elysia knew they were missing something... in what Yalath had just said... something about...

"Wait! What is a cousin?"

Yalath's withering glare intended to show her what an idiot he believed her to be.

"I'm not stupid. I know the word. I just wanted you to say it out loud."

Simon stepped in. "A cousin is the child of your mother or father's sibling. I haven't seen any of mine since I was little. But what do you mean?"

"Yalath, what do you call the priesthood of Kashaka. In relation to the goddess?"

The condescension in his tone was almost too much to take. "Her sons?" He went white.

Simon's eyes opened wide. "But if they're her sons," he said, "and these women are Za—*her* daughters... then if the inscriptions refer to them as cousins..."

Elysia looked smug. "The one we're worried about is Kashaka's sister. Or at least that's what her followers considered her."

Yalath rolled his eyes. "There must be some mistake... that's ridiculous. Kashaka is our goddess, not some Damoz—"

Elysia cut him off. "If the women of this temple followed a goddess who was actually a Damoz, why not a whole nation?"

The idea seemed to shake him more than she expected. "But... my forefathers wouldn't have served such evil. And besides, this idea of Damoz having sisters? Ridiculous. And why would sisters be fighting?"

"You don't have any siblings, do you?" Elysia asked. "You should meet—" She went silent. While she never really liked Alexander, speaking ill of the dead was something she wouldn't do.

"So, if this is true..." Simon said, "then do you think the one I saw with Persei... do you think she's looking for her sister?"

One Damoz was almost unstoppable, but two?

"Was that all the inscription said?" Simon asked.

Yalath chewed his lip as he looked at the last part again, shaking his head. "I have no idea what this means. Are you sure it looked like this?"

Simon and Elysia nodded.

"It says: *When she falls, her blood will lead us back to her arms.* Blood of a goddess? Mythological rubbish."

"Wouldn't most say the same about the Damoz?" Simon asked. "Think, Yalath. Have you seen or read anything about the blood of Kashaka? I've seen the Blood of Tamar, but don't think that's relevant. What other references might make sense... maybe a heart?"

"The Heart of Kashaka?" Elysia repeated.

Yalath perked up. "What did you say? Heart of... of course!" He clapped his hands together, looking almost personable. "In the other dig site. The main temple of Kashaka. There's a vessel that seemed to translate as... the Heart of Kashaka. Could the blood be inside?"

"That's how hearts usually work," Elysia said in a mock scholarly tone. "But do you really think it would lead us to where Kashaka is now?"

"You're going to believe the scribblings of some outlawed ancient cult?" Yalath said.

"But what if it's true?" she asked. "What if this is the secret to finding another Damoz, and bringing her back into this world?"

"I've seen the destruction from one Damoz," Simon said. "I can't imagine two working together."

"Then we'd better stop *her* from finding her sister," Elysia said.

Yalath scoffed. "You think you can stop *her*? With your rudimentary skills? You need more training, more precision..."

"While you wait for her to take over the world? With her sister's help?"

Yalath's nostrils flared. "Woman, don't speak to me like—"

"Like what? Like someone who actually wants to stop these Damoz from getting what they want?"

"I think she's right," Simon said. "We have to stop them from getting together. Especially if *she* has some sway over Persei, and access to the might of the legions."

"Of course you'd defend her," Yalath said. "You're just as

reckless. And foolish. You're not powerful enough to stand a chance."

"We're more powerful than you!" Elysia shouted.

"She's right, you know," Simon said, looking thoughtful. "And you know why, don't you? Wasn't it your theory?"

"My what?" Simon's more measured tone seemed to be breaking through to Yalath.

"You and Master Xelos had postulated that proximity to the Damoz somehow brings out our power."

"Yes, yes. . that was my theory."

"Well, Elysia and I were closer to both *her* and Shadush when he was wielding his power. That's what let our Talent advance much more quickly than Xelos had ever seen."

"That's it?" Elysia said, tapping her hands against her face. "I know what we should do. We're certain these Damoz must be kept apart..."

"I still don't think they'll ever work together," Yalath said.

"But if they did, that would be the worst possible outcome," Simon said.

"So we need to prevent that worst case," Elysia said. "If we can locate Kashaka, wherever she is—"

"Our stories speak of her being taken away, imprisoned by the Izari," Remeth said.

"Then hopefully she's still in her prison," Simon said. "And we can keep her there."

"Let me finish, please. So we find her, then we stand guard, and make sure *she* doesn't break her sister out."

"Folly," Yalath said, sweat pouring down his face.

She glared at him "If *you're* right, then being close to Kashaka, even in her prison, should draw out more of our Talent. And if we get there soon enough, we can practice, set traps, and be ready for Za—for *her* when she comes."

Remeth nodded. "And with four of us all gaining power—"

"Four?" Yalath said, spluttering.

"Master, you've devoted your life to being ready for these Damoz when they reappeared. Now they have, and her idea sounds like our best chance."

"I agree," Simon said.

Yalath shook his head, wiping away the sweat. "I can't condone you throwing your lives away. However, I do think you're right that we need to locate this Kashaka. With enough preparation—"

"Then let's go take a look at her temple," Remeth said.

Yalath looked at the hanging inscription. "I've copied this down, but we can't leave this here. There will be enough questions already."

Simon laughed. "Good idea. I... I think water should do it? I've never tried this before." He took out a waterskin and poured water into his hand. He frowned. "This seems like such a shame."

Elysia thought so too. Destroying anything they created seemed like a sin against Talent, and its source. The gods, or... She shook off the dark thought.

"Just do it. We need to get out of here. Especially if we want to head over to the temple of Kashaka before daylight. They start early out there, and it's a busy site."

Simon rubbed his hands together, getting them wet, and proceeded to scoop the inscription out of the air, one section at a time. He made it almost like a game, catching and crushing the symbols into trailing wisps of pigment. He even flicked one at Elysia, spraying a line of paint across her nose. If they weren't rushing, she too would have made a game of it. They would have so much fun together, when this was all over.

When he was finished, he rinsed off his hands, now covered in paint. She leaned in and kissed him, making sure to share her mark with his nose.

"Let's go follow some blood," she said.

He looked troubled. "I'm just worried. If *she* is looking for Kashaka, then won't she be following the same path?"

"If they're coming here... the sooner we leave Gardisha, the better."

XIV
ᏅᏛᏅᏛᏅᏛᏅ
Heart

Remeth led them back out the way they came in, and the sleeping guards still lay undisturbed.

"This one certainly isn't a military camp," Simon whispered to Elysia, relieved they didn't have to fight their way out. He was barely a soldier himself, only assuming the role in comparison to his creative companions, and he fretted he would be unable to protect the others if it came to a pitched battle. The sooner they could get away from these unpredictable rebels, the better.

While they trudged again across the shifting sands, Simon pieced together the details required to make their ultimate escape: retrieve Zeno from the stables and the rest of their baggage from their room in the Zalikko camp, dodge the rebels, avoid any rebel sympathizers... or Jukaro, who likely feared the rebels enough to turn them in? Too many things to settle. And they hadn't even made it to the water temple yet.

Elysia walked with Yalath. The old man seemed to have given up on trying to teach her about a woman's appropriate place in Maruthan society. "Are you sure you know the way to the temple?" she asked.

"Remeth was with me once, and I've been there four other times. It shouldn't be a problem."

"We don't want any wrong turns," Simon said. "We have no idea who is with us, or against us."

"Which us?" Remeth asked, tugging on his cloak. "Don't forget, we're rebels."

"Is your flute ready?" Elysia asked Yalath. He patted the front of his robe. Their four disparate Talents were all proving useful in equal measure for the success of their mission.

After Remeth shushed them, they approached the lights of the larger dig site that housed the temple of Kashaka.

When they reached the threshold, the two guards looked alarmed, raising curved swords to challenge Remeth. He held up his empty hands and said something in confident Maruthan, sounding very much like one of their captors. The guards' eyes flicked from covered face to covered face. The taller guard on the left barked a command to Remeth, who shook his head.

The guard advanced toward them.

Simon stepped forward, making a show of touching the hilt of his own sword. A hiss from the shorter guard resulted in the taller one backing off, his lips a tight line.

From Simon's right, the trill of Yalath's flute billowed through his robe and into their ears... a haunting, sleepy melody. Before his eyes grew too heavy, Simon covered his ears. The shorter guard swooned and fell face first into the sand, while the taller staggered toward Yalath while trying to shut out the music. With hands on his ears, he barreled into Yalath, sending them both sprawling onto the sand. The flute clattered away, and Yalath's hood fell down. The big man's eyes flashed in recognition.

Instinct and training seized control. Simon closed the steps to the tall guard, the curved sword suddenly in his hand. It was long and the balance was wrong, totally different from the thrusting legionary short sword. *If he's any good, I couldn't beat him in a fight.* But instead, Simon stood menacing over the sentry, who pleaded in Maruthan.

Remeth was at his side, responding in a threatening tone. Simon cocked back his arm, and when he faked a slash the man's face crumpled.

Remeth covered Simon's ears with his soft hands. It made Simon uncomfortable, especially with the I-told-you-so look in Elysia's eyes, but he knew what would happen next. Yalath crawled across the ground to retrieve his flute and began to play again. Terror drained away in the man's eyes, replaced with a kind of hazy bliss, and he nodded off.

"He recognized you," Simon said to Yalath.

Remeth helped the old man up, who brushed the sand off his robe. "Yes, I've met him many times."

"Then this is your last time here, especially after what we're going to do next."

Yalath frowned, but nodded. "Follow me."

Elysia tugged at Remeth's arm. "But how come the music didn't—"

"Training," he said, with a mysterious twinkle in his eye.

The main camp was more permanent than the first one, and far more extensive. Many more streets and buildings had been cleared, and appeared to be in use. But it was still early morning and not a soul challenged them. How much longer would night last? The horizon already showed signs of light when they left the sentries.

Yalath led them through wide streets to the epicenter of the excavation efforts: a grand temple complex. They entered through large double doors, past an inner courtyard, and into another large building. Simon had to keep Elysia moving; she kept slowing down to admire the sculpture. He had to admit they were impressive, even though many were missing half or more of their limbs. These were confident expressions of devotion, not muted friezes hiding in secret temples.

Their path took them deeper, through several concentric rings of ruined halls and gardens, until finally they arrived at another door. "The central chamber," Yalath announced.

A giant fountain adorned with all manner of sea and river creatures dominated the center of the octagonal room. But what would have been stunningly beautiful was made grim and somber by the thick layers of dirt that coated the sculptures. A great eye in the ceiling that would have opened up to the sky, allowing light and rain into the central pool of the fountain, was blocked instead by a crumbling layer of sandy earth. When the alternating floods and drought had covered the city, the inside of this temple would have been filled. Simon marveled at the amount of work that had already been done just to excavate this much space. And would that earth on top hold? At least it made a protective dome to keep out the sand.

"I wish I could have seen it when the fountain was working," Elysia said, holding his hand. She could see past the grime and appreciate the underlying artistry.

Up close, the fountain was even larger than it looked from the doorway. Thirty or forty followers could stand comfortably inside the pool. And the central tower rose taller than Simon, covered with steps that looked like they could have housed plants as they channeled the water down into the pool. *There must be some kind of impressive mechanism inside to pump all that water...*

"So where is this heart?" Elysia asked Yalath.

"Where would you put a heart?" he responded, his voice as flippant as she had been before.

"Inside?" Simon said, stepping into the pool to examine the tower. No seams were visible. "Is there a door?"

With an air of self-importance, Yalath strode over to join Simon. He placed his hands on two sculptures of water birds and pulled on them together. A tray about the width of a thumb slid out, making an audible click. He walked around to the opposite side and pulled on a stone water lily. The face of the tower opened outward with a creak. Inside the crawlspace a ladder led down into darkness.

Simon was impressed. "How did you ever figure that one out?"

"My old books are good for something. The process was described in detail in an old scroll I found last year at one of our sites in Uraka. It's tight in here. Simon, why don't you come with me first? Remeth, you stand guard." Simon looked to Elysia, who nodded.

Simon shone the coin-light on Yalath as he cautiously climbed down. At that pace, it would be daybreak before they knew it. There was barely enough room for the old man, and Simon had to stoop when his turn came. The descent was constricted by metal pipes that shared the interior space with the ladder.

When he reached the bottom, it was like entering a secret world. Gone was the grime of the room up above. The walls appeared to be large metal tanks, with pipes connecting to them in multiple places, and all of them linking through a central pedestal of indeterminate function. With more time, Simon would have loved to examine the mechanisms involved. Perhaps some capability to collect water in rainy season for use in drier times, to give the illusion of ever-full water? That would certainly serve the interests of the priesthood.

"Who else knows about this place?"

"Just Eppeth and a couple of senior academics involved in the excavation. Well, and Xelos knew too." Yalath looked around. "We found the skeleton of the high priest in here when we first excavated. He was right here." He pointed to the front of the pedestal.

"Let me guess, the heart is there?" Simon pointed at the clay vessel on top, about the height of a child, but with a stylized woman's face. "So how do we use it?"

Yalath frowned. "I have no idea. We haven't tried to move it. The chief supervisor of the site is a... a very pious man with a special interest in Kashaka. He considers it one of the holiest relics. In fact, we're treading on sacred ground. Only the high priest was even permitted to know about this place."

"How do you feel about it?"

"Simon, this is one of the holiest relics of my people. We must preserve it... at all costs."

There had to be some way to use it. Simon ran his hand over the smooth surface, looking for any imperfections, markings or anything useful. Nothing. "Maybe Elysia can find something?"

Yalath's face twisted before he reluctantly nodded, and Simon climbed up to get her.

While he was clinical in his examination of the relic, she was reverent. Delicate fingers caressed the flawless surface, her eyes closing as she tapped into her Talent.

With a gasp, her hand recoiled.

"What is it?" Simon asked, rushing to her side. "Are you hurt?"

She shook her head vigorously. "It's... it feels like it's alive. It was pulsing.. like a heartbeat."

Yalath shook his head, bewildered.

Grimacing, Simon looked at the base. "If it's beating, it must be connected somehow. What if we..." He put his hands on either side to attempt to lift it.

"No!" Elysia and Yalath cried out in unison.

"You might damage it!" Yalath said.

"I... I felt it... it's afraid," Elysia said.

"Well, can either of you think of a better idea?" Simon asked. "How are we going to make the blood lead us to Kashaka? Do we have to make it bleed? If we just cut open..."

Elysia, whose hand was still touching the relic, swooned into Simon's arms. She looked like she was about to be sick.

"Are you all right?" he asked, frantic.

She clutched at his arm. "You can't hurt it. Not like that... I felt its pain, revulsion." She gagged. "There has to be another way."

"It's not like a human body, where we could just prick its finger, or draw blood from a vein..." The pipes drew his gaze and everything clicked into place. His head snapped up. "If this is the heart somehow, and it's connected to everything else, then maybe there's a place we can take a little of the blood. Just enough to somehow point the way?"

"Maybe... maybe I can... ask it?" Elysia said.

The look on Yalath's face was a strange combination of horror and fascination. He seemed to have a lot more faith in the gods than Xelos ever did. Very different from Simon's own propensity for questioning and challenging everything.

"It's worth a shot. If it has some kind of awareness... maybe you can threaten it?"

When Elysia turned a withering stare at him, he threw up his hands. "Hey, a little drop of blood is better than being sliced open, right? Just ask it."

Elysia placed her hands tenderly this time, like she didn't want to scare the relic. She closed her eyes. Were her hands pulsating with the beat she could feel? The movement was minute, but Simon thought he could see it. Her eyelids fluttered, and Simon was about to pull her away when they burst open.

"I... I told it we're looking to reunite it with Kashaka. It suddenly calmed down—felt at peace. It will let me lift it up, and a few drops of its... blood should collect at the bottom. We need some kind of a container. Yalath?"

He fumbled in his pack, before producing a small stoppered jar. "Ink," he said. Very reluctantly, like he was pouring out pure gold, Yalath carefully removed the wax plug and emptied the ink onto the floor. He looked like he might cry at the waste.

"We don't want to contaminate this... this blood," Simon said. He took out his waterskin. "Rinse it out first." After it was clean, Yalath gave the jar to Simon.

"So I'll lift the heart," Elysia said, "and you put the jar below to catch the blood."

"The opening isn't very big," Simon said, "but it will have to do." His arms were tense as he set up opposite Elysia. *What if it was poisonous? Damaging to the touch? Or real blood?*

"Ready?" He nodded. With the utmost care, she lifted the vessel. What looked like liquid silver puddled in an opening at the bottom, and a drip splashed into the base. "Quick!" she said, and he held the jar underneath. He caught the steady flow of drips, while praying that none of it would splash and hurt his hands... or be lost.

When the jar was half full, he nodded.

"Move your hands," she said. When he withdrew the jar, she

settled the vessel back into place. Her hair was drenched with sweat, and she was shaking.

Simon peered into the jar, and the strange liquid clung impossibly to one side, as if the side was the bottom and it had settled in place.

Elysia spoke again, her voice weary. "It said that... the blood will lead us to her. It cannot bear to be separated."

Sudden realization dawned on him. "It's not figurative at all. The liquid is actually trying to move in that direction." He showed the others the phenomenon inside the jar. "See how it's all on one side? It's pointing the way. If we could make a vessel in the right shape... then we could follow it like a road sign. Elysia, you did it!"

"It is not clear where it's pointing from down here," Yalath said. "I barely know which way is up. Let's return to the surface before anyone discovers us, and see where this leads." He held out his hand, and Simon gave him the jar, which Yalath painstakingly stoppered.

Elysia looked like she was going to faint again. "Are you strong enough to climb out?" Simon asked.

"I... I'm so tired, Simon. I feel like it drained all my energy, just doing that."

Yalath grinned. It was off-putting. "I have a remedy for that." Carefully packing the jar in his pack, Yalath again produced his flute. "Let me cheer you up a bit." His face lit up as he played a lively tune that perked up Simon's spirits. All his cares seemed to float away, and it was as if energy was flowing into his body, making him feel like dancing. His foot started to tap in time with the music.

Elysia was smiling too, and stood up straighter, all traces of weariness gone. She looked like she was about to twirl with glee when Yalath stopped playing.

"I feel better than I have in days!" Simon said. "Is it safe? We could do that all the time."

That brought out the usual scowl. "This is not some child's toy to abuse. This is serious magic. Only to be used in times of need. And this qualifies. Let's get Remeth, and get out of here."

They managed to leave the camp with the sentries still soundly asleep, though the sky in the east betrayed the imminent arrival of the sun. Yet another slog across the sand was the last thing Simon's tired body needed, but they didn't have much choice. It was surprisingly cool without the sun beating down on his skin.

He walked alongside Yalath. "So we go into the original camp, retrieve Zeno and the rest of our supplies, and then leave?"

"I think that would be prudent. But we should shed these disguises before we go in, unless we want to answer a lot more questions."

"But whoever in the camp is sympathizing with the rebels..."

"Then we must make haste." Yalath led the way in beginning to remove his robe. They were too big to stash in their packs, so they just buried them under the sand.

Being separated from Zeno for so long was making Elysia skittish, and Simon would rather be high in the air and on their way. The sky grew lighter even while they were changing. He could only imagine the spectacle they'd see from Zeno's back. *But there's no way four of us could ride Zeno together. Not for long.*

It was Yalath who talked his way through the suspicious sentries back at the original camp. If they had been ordered to watch for them, they didn't betray that fact, and let them pass. Elysia breathed a sigh of relief, and Simon shared the sentiment.

ᏮᏋᏮᏋᏮᏋᏮ

Glebric, Zustar and three of his best disciples attended yet another slave auction. *Every week!* Prices were depressed with the flood on the market from the survivors of the Scentari campaign. It was a great opportunity, but it still made him sad how frequently the sales came up. Slaves were the foundation of the Republic, even if nobody acknowledged it.

They were finishing their pre-auction inspection of the poor people when Glebric heard the shout. A young girl with fiery red hair, one of the last in line, had fainted, and her owner was bent over her with his whip ready. He shook the wicked barbs as he demanded that she stand up. She cowered, terror and... hopelessness in her eyes. It tugged at Glebric's soul. She couldn't be more than ten. *If I buy her—*

The first strike hit her arm, and the girl only whimpered. *She was probably starving.*

The second hit her shoulder, tearing a line in the cloth. She covered her face.

Driven mad by her seeming defiance, the angry slave dealer's screams reached a fever pitch. His arm cocked back further but a flash of darkness seized it. The slave dealer turned his fury to Azzam, the Alkazy who held the whip steady, the cords of his muscle bulging with the strain.

"Restrain this black dog!" the slave dealer screamed.

"No," said Azzam in his impossibly deep voice. "You will stop."

The slave dealer spat in his face. "I sold you, and I can break you."

"You have broken your last," the Alkazy said with finality. Before Glebric or anyone could stop him, his knife out of its sheath and buried in the side of the slave dealer's neck.

Stunned silence enveloped the crowd as time stood still.

A torrent of emotions rushed through Glebric as the sound returned: pride, righteous anger, disgust, and terror. The slave dealer's guards rushed the Alkazy, who adopted the stance Zustar had taught all of them. Azzam was his star pupil.

Zustar grabbed Glebric's arm. "This will turn ugly. Let's get out of here." The trainer was already holding his weapon, and the other two followed suit.

Something snapped in Glebric. "No, Azzam is right. This has gone too slow, too long."

Glebric stepped onto the podium where the sale would take place. Zustar and one guard flanked him, while the other went to Azzam's side, ready should the guards try to advance. The faces in the crowd varied from irritated to mocking to confused.

He breathed deep. This would take all the voice he could muster. "People of Attarsus. Slaves. Buyers and sellers." He pointed to the dead slave dealer. "This man has sinned against the gods."

A shout came up from one of the other dealers. "It's his right to beat a bad slave!"

"Silence!" Glebric shouted. "No man or woman should ever be slave to another."

"Who let this crazy kid in here?" the dealer shouted back. The laughs from others agreed with him. "Yanos was right, you need a better leash for your cog."

Azzam snarled at the outspoken dealer. "Yanos is dead."

Glebric looked at the terrified faces of the slaves. In the eyes of a few he saw something else—hope—and that pushed him forward. *I have to take control.*

"Slaving is still legal, but I mean to change that here. If I see anyone mistreating their slave… then you've seen what will happen. You!" he pointed to Yanos' guard. "Who speaks for your dead employer?"

Another man stepped forward from the end of the line. "He was my half-brother."

This one doesn't seem too upset. Likely just got the other half of the business.

"I am sorry for your loss. I will pay market rates for all your slaves. Double for the girl."

The other dealer sneered. "So the high and mighty young gentleman doesn't eat his own cooking? What a fraud. You've quickly become the biggest slave owner here in Attarsus."

Glebric nodded. "I would be, except I've set them all free." A gasp went up from the crowd, and the dealer's eyes bulged. "And I will do the same for the others. These," he said, pointing to the Alkazy and his other guards, "are freedmen in my employ. Remember that."

"Then the dog must answer for his crimes!" the frothing slave dealer said.

"Are you going to make him?" Glebric asked.

"Call the watch!" said another.

Zustar grabbed his arm again. "Now is not the time," he whispered. "You have to know when to retreat."

Glebric nodded, recognizing the wisdom in the advice. "Half-brother, deliver the purchases to my house and we'll have the gold for you. I'll be going now."

"No you won't," said the dealer. "You'll be waiting for the watch—" His anger turned to terror as he felt Azzam's blade touch the back of his neck.

Glebric stepped down from the podium, with Zustar and the other guard in tow. "If the watch needs to speak to me, they can come to my home. Good day, everyone."

Azzam released the man and the five of them left the slave market at a brisk pace. Glebric's pulse was still racing.

The first to break the silence was Azzam. "We should have released all the slaves."

"In good time, my friend. We were ill-prepared to start a riot."

Zustar stepped in. "And you're good, Azzam, but the others aren't ready. They need more training."

Azzam snarled. "Enough of us are ready now. How can you bear to watch as scum like that treats a young girl worse than an animal!"

Glebric held up a hand. "We have all seen this. Felt this way. We will make changes."

The Alkazy kept his head high. "We can take the city watch. We can make things right in all of Attarsus tomorrow. I would do it, if you would let me." The other two men grunted their approval of the plan.

Glebric considered it. The watch was weak. His trained men already outnumbered them. There was no Pazian garrison here in Attarsus. There was no need. The population was docile, more concerned with making money. And the navy served as all the walls the city needed to defend from without. He nodded. "You're right. It's the right thing to do. But be patient. Zustar, let's work on a plan. Let's get our new people integrated and then we will face the watch."

What had Ventus said to him this morning before he left?

Do you want more power, Glebric? Just take it.

It had felt good to assert control over the slave market. And right. And this was only the beginning.

XV
ᘓᘓᘓᘓᘓᘓᘓ
Escape

When they found Zeno, he whickered impatiently. "Don't worry," Elysia said. "We're safe, and leaving this nasty place."

Back at their quarters, they packed the rest of their supplies.

"We should check... the direction," Simon said. "Quickly, while we're alone."

Yalath produced the jar, and dug out the wax stopper. They all peered in at the unnatural liquid metal, which clung very clearly to one side.

"Can you tell which way that is?" Elysia asked.

"More toward Jeppo than Uraka," Simon said, and all eyes turned to him. He shrugged. "What? I keep a good mental map. It's what I do."

"It could really be anywhere," Yalath said. "In the desert, the sea, or even mainland Pazh. But not Uraka, because the river heads west. This is a crude instrument. We would be well served to devise something a little more refined."

"I was already thinking about that," Elysia said. "If I could get some clay, I could fashion a small bowl where we could pour the liquid into the middle, but have a lip catch it when it flows to the edge, and rotate it to pour out through a spout and back into our little jar to keep it safe."

Remeth's eyes glazed over. "I can't picture it."

"The important thing is that she can," Simon said, squeezing her hand.

"Well, you'll have to think on it," Yalath said, "because we don't have the materials or the time now. We'd better get back to the harbor."

"Do you think it's safe for us to leave by boat?" Simon asked. "If it's not even taking us in the right direction, and they move so

130

slow… won't they be able to catch—"

He was interrupted by a knock. Yalath stoppered the jar and stashed it in his pack, waving for Remeth to open the door when it was secure.

Eppeth, his men, and several guards stood outside. Eppeth nodded. "Good, you are back. We were beginning to worry about you when you did not return last night. Surely you didn't experience any trouble?"

Yalath stepped to the front. "We worked late at the other camp, and decided to spend the night."

One of the men raised an eyebrow. Eppeth peered in at them, seeing them readying their gear. "Leaving so soon? Aren't you going to show us your find?" He looked hard at Yalath. "And where is our friend Jukaro?"

Simon's heart sank. He'd completely forgotten their minder. Of course that would be unusual. He sized up the guards. Three of them, all armed with those curved Maruthan swords. The old man wouldn't be much of a challenge, but if they called for help…

Remeth spoke up. "Jukaro wished to file a report, so he didn't stay the night with us. Said something about preferring his own bed. We told him we would likely be leaving when we finished, so he could brief you about the results." *Was that subtle use of his Talent?* Simon found himself becoming convinced of the lie.

"And what results were those?"

"The statue in the temple of Zalikko appears to be genuine," Yalath said, "and we left it in the main hall. From our review of materials at the other camp, your men actually set off the last of the traps. It should be quite safe down there now."

"You have done us a great service, Yalath," Eppeth said, his eyes alight with curiosity. "But surely you can stay a little longer to walk us through this find? This is a historic day, and you of all people would relish the chance to be a part of it."

"I fear my Master's health is giving him trouble," Remeth said before Yalath could respond. "And you know him, he's so ornery about such things. But I've put my foot down. I'm taking him back to his physician in Jeppo."

Yalath sputtered with irritation, but it seemed to be having the desired impact. Concern filled Eppeth's eyes. "Yalath, you know we're not as young as we once were. You're lucky you have an… assistant…" he said, raising an eyebrow, "who takes such good care of you. So you're leaving today?"

"Yes, we were just packing up," Yalath said, putting a hand on Remeth's shoulder as if his feet were unsteady. Remeth adjusted himself to support the weight, looking very much the doting apprentice. *He's very good at this.*

"Then I'll leave you to your preparations. I'll send Jukaro in to check back with you when he comes. He'll want you to file a report, even if he didn't mention it last night. You can leave as soon as he's met with you."

"Of course," Yalath said, "thank you for all your help."

Eppeth made to leave, but one of his men whispered to him. "Oh yes, he just reminded me. Yalath, if you or your people plan to bring any... outsiders... here again, I suggest that you either rethink it, or make sure to contact us in advance. There are those who don't look kindly on such things."

"My apologies. I understand. Thank you for your assistance."

Remeth closed the door behind them when they left.

"Good work," Simon said to Remeth, shaking his head with a grin.

"I think we're still in trouble," Elysia said, "Even if he's not in on it, his men are. We should leave now, before it's too late."

"How do you know?" Yalath asked.

"Their faces betrayed them."

"Another part of her Talent," Simon said.

Yalath started wringing his hands. "We'll never make it back to the boats. And there might not even be one available right away. If they're sending more of those riders after us... I don't want to be taken by them again."

Elysia looked at Simon and Zeno, and Simon frowned in response. "But there isn't room."

"Room for what?" Yalath asked.

"We could fly out, on Zeno," Elysia said. "But he can manage three only for short distances. I don't think he can carry four at all, especially with all our supplies."

"Out of the question," Yalath said. "I'm not flying anywhere." Remeth looked disappointed. "Remeth was exaggerating the immediacy of my health issues, but there is a grain of truth to it. My heart can barely take this excitement on the ground. Flying could be the death of me. I'm at my best surrounded by my books, at home."

His library was impressive. Simon had marveled at it in the short time they'd spent at his house. The house around it might have been simple, but his collection was even more extensive than that of Xelos, which was good in its own right. The image of the library in his mind seemed so peaceful, yet so far away...

"That's it!" Simon said. "Or at least it could be. Well... I think it would be worth a try."

"What would?" Yalath asked.

"Your library. There wasn't much else you let us do back in Jeppo, so I got a very good look at it. There's something I've been meaning to attempt, and it might be the only way for you. If I paint a picture of your library, it might function as a kind of doorway, and if I do it just right... I think you could walk through."

Remeth's face lit up, but Yalath remained as skeptical as ever. "If you think I'll—"

"You'd rather try to be the fourth one on Zeno?" Remeth asked. "Simon is right. This would be a much better option for you."

The old man's lip was a tight line, but he appeared to be considering it. "But your panels and paper, they're much too small..."

"I was going to try painting it on the wall."

"But we can't just leave it there after—"

"Then we'll wash it away."

"You're not coming with me?" Yalath asked.

Simon had meant to ask first, but he knew Elysia would be fine seeing the last of Yalath. "No, I was thinking Elysia and I could ride Zeno and follow the blood to Kashaka. We could always use similar magic to contact you. But like you said, you're better off at home."

It was Remeth's turn to protest. "I hope you don't think you'll be shipping me off to Jeppo. I'm coming with you. I want to fly. See the world, wherever this blood takes us. And besides, three stand a better chance than two if we have to face Zaliakara."

Yalath looked crestfallen. *The old curmudgeon actually did care.* "I ... no... you're right, Remeth. You should go. You three make a good team. But we're getting ahead of ourselves. What if this doesn't work?"

"At least say you'll try?" Simon said. When Yalath nodded, Simon set to work.

Blocking in the lines went very quickly, as well as adding the tomes. Yalath gave specific advice about where the chair should be, particular words on the volumes, and other details to make it as realistic as possible. Simon was thankful for the lack of figures and decoration. The elements themselves were simple, though he worried about how exhausting it would be to send Yalath through. And he had yet to test it on a living creature...

When he had everything together, he closed his eyes and mentally reached out for his Talent. He was becoming more familiar with the feeling, and it was now as natural as mixing paint. Without opening his eyes, he made the final brushstrokes to complete the work. When he opened them again, Yalath beheld it with serene admiration.

"Touch it," Simon said.

"Are you sure it's safe?"

"It's your best chance," Remeth said.

Yalath reached out and the wall shimmered where his finger made contact, sending a ripple of light outward in concentric circles like he had dipped it into a perfectly still pond.

"Amazing," he said, reaching his entire hand through. "Remarkable, even the air feels different on the other side. None of this dry desert heat."

Simon gritted his teeth. Holding the door open was like lifting a boulder, and his arms felt weak.

"The jar?" Elysia asked.

Yalath withdrew his hand, startled. "Of course." He searched through his pack again, and handed the jar to Remeth. "Take good care of this. And each other. You are doing very important work. And keep me informed... maybe you can send a message like this. It truly is remarkable. Think of the possibilities? If you set these pictures up in the different houses I own, we could travel between them instantly... even back to Pazh! This bears further discussion, and study—"

"There is no time, Master," Remeth said, his voice gently urging. "Thank you for everything you've taught me. You've changed my life. Shown me so much." Remeth looked like he might cry, and Yalath was mortified. He started spluttering.

"Yes... well... take care of yourselves. You must stop Zaliakara. If she can unite with Kashaka... the world will be doomed." He turned and sized up the picture again. Nodding, he tried pushing the pack through first, and when Simon stopped painting, it appeared on the floor in the picture. He clapped like a little girl. "Incredible! I have to tell the others."

"Goodbye, Yalath," Elysia said.

Simon strained to focus on the reality of the image, of this door to another part of the world.

The old man put one foot through, and with a deep breath lowered his head and his entire body shimmered with dazzling colors. Simon felt drained, except for a throbbing in his hand, as if the image called out to it, and it buzzed to life, repainting the picture until it showed Yalath on the other side, waving.

Simon sat down on the floor.

"Are you all right?" Elysia asked.

He nodded, but felt weak. It took more out of him than he expected, especially with the lack of sleep or food. He pointed to the waterskin. Remeth wiped down the wall from the corner of the picture. The paint came off as if it were completely ordinary, first the shelves and walls and finally Yalath himself.

"So, I guess you can't do that again to get us out of here?" Remeth asked.

"No. We're going to have to go the... well, another unusual route. And I don't think we should wait for Jukaro, do you?"

"No," said Elysia. "Let's go."

A guard was posted outside the door, who looked shocked when he saw Remeth. He said something in Maruthan as he looked past Remeth to Simon and Elysia in the doorway. Charming as ever, Remeth's attempt to talk his way past only served to make the guard more uncertain. He drew his sword and pointed for them to go back inside. Remeth held up his hands and took a step toward the man, but was met by the lowering of the point to his chest. Frantic, the man shouted at them again, jerking his chin back the way they came.

"I think we should do it," Simon said in Pazian.

"Let me handle this," Remeth said.

"No, let's go back inside to *Yalath*," Simon said.

Elysia slipped back inside, followed by Simon, and finally Remeth, who kept talking to the guard until he closed the door.

"It's only one guard," Remeth said. "We can overpower him. He said his orders are to stay here until Jukaro comes to see us, and advised us to remain as well."

"But we risk sounding the alarm. Now he has only two options, leave us unguarded and go for help, or stay and do his duty. But I have another idea."

"Another doorway to a far off place?" Elysia asked. "But I thought you said you were too weak?"

"Too weak for something complicated. And that also means too weak for a fight. And I'm the only one of us with any experience with a sword, right? So we don't want to risk it. But what if we could sneak out the back?"

Remeth looked at the bare wall and wrinkled his brow.

"I think it would be a lot less... taxing to create a usable door. It just has to be big enough for Zeno to fit through."

He took quick measurements with his outstretched arms, marking the borders on a plain section of the back wall. Using the other door as a reference, he quickly painted in the frame, door, and handle. Then he channeled his Talent for the finishing touches, in theory to make this image of a door into one that functioned. The trick was projecting beyond the visible. He was right—compared to the portal for Yalath, it barely drew on his Talent at all.

"There, that should do it." He looked back to the others and smiled. He wondered if he'd ever get tired of showing off new things that his Talent could do. While focusing his Talent, he turned the handle easily, but the door stuck, as if the wood had swelled. Putting his shoulder into it as he pushed did the trick, and the door opened into an alley behind the house. After a quick peek to make sure it was empty, he waved the others through.

"Wait," Elysia said, "I have an idea." She took a blanket from the bed and tacked it up to the wall, covering their new door.

"But won't that look odd?" Remeth asked.

"Our disappearance will be the first distraction, and will likely result in some tough questions for our guard there. That might buy us a bit more time."

After they quietly closed the door, he and Elysia both got the same idea. Even on careful inspection, the outside wall still looked whole, with just the slightest line where the edges of the door would be. So the visual effect only worked on the painted side, even if functionally it went through. So many more boundaries to explore. But no time for that now.

Simon frowned. Avoiding the front door would take them off the route he'd memorized. He tapped Remeth on the shoulder and turned up his hands, but was met with a similarly blank look.

Navigating his mental map and looking at the branches in front of him, he tried to piece together the best possible path to get back on course, but it wasn't clear. He pointed in the direction that took them further away first.

The best they could manage was a quick walk; any louder and Zeno's hoof-beats would draw attention. It felt agonizingly slow given Simon's drive to get away as quickly as they could.

The surrounding neighborhood contained block after block of houses similar to the one they'd been assigned, likely for the other workers and specialists that supported them in the community. The next few alleys he'd hoped to explore were all filled with sandy soil, and even the first cross street. They obviously hadn't been worth clearing to this point. Simon swore under his breath. *We could try hiding in another building, but to what end?* When their disappearance was discovered, it would send the whole camp into an uproar.

They were just about to hit the second cross-street when they heard raised voices from back the way they'd come. A quick glance back didn't reveal the source of the sound, but he feared the worst. Peering around the next corner and seeing it empty, he waved frantically for them to follow.

He dared a whisper. "This should intersect with the way we came in, after a few blocks. We should go faster now, and break into a run the moment a guard spots us."

Rushing block by block, they passed several workers coming out of their doors. They were noticed, but not recognized or confronted.

Just one more street...

Louder shouts behind them, and the sound of running feet. Four guards.

"Go!" Simon said. He gave Elysia a boost so she could climb on Zeno's back, and he and Remeth broke into a full sprint toward the intersection. "Left!" he shouted, while peeking to the right. Two more guards spotted them and started shouting in Maruthan as they gave chase.

Simon dashed past the large tent where they'd first had their audience with Eppeth, which was thankfully unguarded, at least on the outside. Even with fear fueling him, Simon's legs were on the verge of failing, and Remeth was panting hard, unused to such exertion. Another turn right, past another street, up toward the...

Two guards stood at the exit looming fifty feet in front of them.

They drew their swords, and shouted something. Simon kept running, drawing his own short sword with a quivering hand. The others matched his pace. Did he even have the strength to face them? One on two... he hoped they weren't very professional. But if he could hold them off so at least Elysia, Zeno and Remeth could escape...

A bright streak whizzed over Simon's head. The guards waved their swords ineffectually at something flitting around their heads.

Simon forced out a scream as he rushed one. The guard looked from Simon to Remeth to Zeno barreling down on him, and might have turned and fled, if not for the guards now in view on their tail. Instead, he recovered his resolve and shouted to the guards behind while still waving at the flying creature. Simon used the extra momentum to ward off a clumsy slash from the first guard's curved sword and raised his free elbow to smash into the man's chin. His opponent crumpled to the ground and almost brought Simon with him, but he caught his balance at the last second. He hadn't seen what Remeth did, but the other guard was down. Zeno was already past the bodies, climbing up the stairs and out into the morning sun. Simon willed his tired legs to follow, the panic from a glimpse of the six guards behind them giving his muscles a burst of new life.

At the top, blinding sunlight dazzled him while biting sand blew into his face.

"Quick," Elysia said, holding out her hand. A white butterfly perched on her shoulder. "Climb up!"

Remeth swore loudly in Maruthan before switching to Pazian. "We have more company!"

Shielding his eyes, Simon saw the swirling sand surrounding camel riders racing toward them, the sun glinting off their raised swords. He took Elysia's hand, vaulted onto Zeno's back, and helped Remeth up. He gripped Simon's waist tight, with equal measures of excitement and fear in his expression.

"Away, Zeno!" Elysia shouted. The magnificent steed surged into motion, bolting away from the incoming riders. Simon's stomach sank as he felt Zeno's gait slip every few strides on the shifting sands.

Please, God of my mother, let him take flight!

Zeno's sliding gallop took them down the gentle slope toward the river.

Simon glanced back. The camels were closing on them, but there was no sign of the guards, who probably retreated at the first sign of a dozen rebel riders.

As they closed toward the river, the less sandy soil gave them an advantage and their lead opened up. Zeno opened his wings and began flapping furiously in the last fifty feet before taking off with one final leap. They were airborne, and Remeth did his best to squeeze the life out of Simon. Without his armor to protect him like when they'd flown with Kyso, it really hurt.

Zeno kept low over the water, clearing the other side before banking right and following the river downstream. If the riders couldn't see the wings, they would be left more confused than awed by the presence of magic. What explanation would they give for the horse to have crossed the river and eluded them?

"We did it!" Remeth said, when the riders were finally out of sight. Zeno soared higher into the air. Enough merchant ships plied this route that the less visible they could be, the better.

XVI

Direction

After an hour or more of flying above the trackless desert, Elysia suggested they touch down quickly to get their bearings, and Simon spotted an oasis that would make a good stop.

"Some are salty or foul," Remeth said as they approached it to drink. "A traveler parched to the edge of madness might drink themselves to death. But this one, quite perfect." Without Yalath looking over his shoulder, Remeth was much more forthcoming, even when he wasn't performing.

Elysia tended to Zeno, washing down the sweat that slicked his fine coat. He didn't complain, but she knew that it was a struggle to carry all three of them in this heat.

"Thank you for saving us yet again," she said as she massaged his wings.

She watched as Simon and Remeth huddled over the jar to get their rough bearings again. As Simon balanced to scoop out the wax that sealed the opening, the sand shifted beneath him and the jar tilted. A drop of the precious liquid fell to the sand and reflected the gold of the sun. Simon swore and tried to catch it, but in vain, and it skated over a dune and away to the northwest.

"Well, it's definitely not heading to Uraka," Simon said. "But it's so frustrating. If we had a good map, and a better pot to work with then we'd stand a chance of tracking this down. A few more accidents like this and we won't have any left."

"Maybe we should stop in Jeppo," Remeth suggested. "Yalath has lots of maps, and he can help Elysia get what she needs to make us a better house for this... blood."

"But what if that drop signals that we're coming?" Simon asked.

"To Kashaka?" Remeth asked.

"If she's loose already. Or somehow Zaliakara knows where she

140

is? We have no idea, but should go as fast as we can."

"I agree with Remeth," Elysia said, coming up beside them. "We have to know where we're going, or we won't know when we've arrived. And it shouldn't take more than a few hours in Jeppo."

"If our route brings us close to there, then we should certainly make the stop. We'll be able to tell once we reach the coast. But let's not waste any more time here. Zeno, are you ready?"

The horse nodded, and in just a few moments, they were airborne again, following after the memory of the metal streaking away.

ᏀᎵᏀᎵᏀᎵᏀ

By the time Simon and the others spotted the coast on the horizon, Remeth recognized familiar towns on the road to Jeppo, so they decided they were close enough to warrant the stop. Zeno banked slightly to the right and they made short work of identifying an inconspicuous landing spot beside a pond lined with sycamore trees, about an hour's ride from the city walls.

For the second time, Simon and Elysia made their way into the city of Jeppo with empty bellies and seeking Yalath. But this time they knew where to find him. They picked up some clay from the market along the way—Remeth knew a potter.

Yalath answered on the second knock, with a face more deeply creased than usual.

"She's here in Jeppo?" he asked.

"Nice to see you too, Master," said Remeth. "No, or at least not quite."

"Then why did you stop?" He started to shut the door.

"Our last bearings were pointing us more to the northwest, but we need supplies and maps."

Yalath grumbled and let them in. "At least you're in luck. I've been looking over some maps, wondering where you might be headed."

Simon hurried over to the table. "These are old, but very, very good."

"Of course," Yalath said. "Who do you think taught your people mapmaking?"

Elysia mumbled something about Izari maps beating them all,

141

but Simon shushed her, away from Yalath's glare.

"We were also hoping to fashion something better to hold… the blood," Simon said.

"What do you need?"

"We already have it," said Elysia, drawing out the clay.

"I'll head off to the market to get us some lunch," Remeth said. "I know you weren't expecting visitors. But I also know you're glad to see us."

Yalath rolled his eyes, and Remeth chuckled before he went out.

Elysia set to work fashioning the strange little pot she'd envisioned. First she formed the round plate as a base, sloping slightly upward at the edges, but not enough to make a bowl. Then she rolled up a tall lip around the edge, and at the top curled it back inward toward the center. They hoped this would be sufficient to catch the liquid and prevent it from leaking out. At one part of the lip, she added a small spout pointing straight up that they could use to pour the liquid back out again, if necessary. Finally she created a lid that would fit into the open top, to keep it covered while in flight, and a removable wax plug for the spout. The whole thing fit into one of her hands.

Yalath watched in silence, entranced by the display of craftsmanship.

Remeth was back by the time she looked up, satisfied.

"Should we try it?" Simon asked.

"Wait," Yalath said, and he rearranged the map. "Now it's oriented properly."

Simon removed the stopper from the precious vial of liquid from his pack. Elysia nodded him on. "Don't you need to… make it hard first?"

"We should test to make sure the form works, then Remeth can take it back to his friend for firing."

Simon was both excited and nervous. To spill another drop of the blood could be a disaster. They set down her creation with the spout on Jeppo, and Simon used the utmost care to pour the liquid into the base. It immediately lurched to one side, disappearing under the lip. Simon tried to peek in to see exactly where it had gone.

"It's a bit awkward," he said, looking through the top. "Could we even check it from the air?"

She pointed to the spout. "Here's the trick," she said. "You look in the spout, and see if the liquid has pooled there. If it has, then that marks the direction we go."

"But if it doesn't?" Yalath asked, looking skeptical.

She rotated it until the spout was pointing approximately west-northwest by the map and looked inside. Still not satisfied, she did three rounds of slight rotations, each time checking the spout. Finally she nodded. "There, take a look." Simon and the others each took a turn confirming with their own eyes that the liquid had pooled under the spout.

Simon took the straightedge and lined it up with the hole. It extended to the west and north into the Near Sea, across the island of Aktiri and several others just southwest of Attarsus in the Izar Archipelago, and onward into the north-central plains of mainland Pazh. And theoretically beyond that into the Far Sea and somewhere in Randesh. They had absolutely no idea how far Kaskaka was from them. And the device wouldn't help until they went past her.

Yalath actually looked like he was enjoying himself. "So then if we need to put it away—"

Elysia demonstrated. "You just take the jar, put it over the spout, and then tilt it so the spout is facing out in the direction it wants to flow." She completed the action and resealed the jar without losing a drop. Simon breathed out, realizing how tense he had been. Elysia handed it to Remeth.

"It's a marvelous idea, but still a shame you couldn't just see inside," Remeth said.

"Clear glass?" Yalath asked.

Simon shook his head. "But it would be too fragile, and besides, where are we going to get glass like that—oh!" He smiled. "When you get back, I could paint it to make it clear. Then we'll be able to check it from the air, without having to put it away. But we wouldn't want the potter to see that. And maybe you could get me more paints?"

Remeth nodded. "Help yourselves to the food. I'll take this to my friend and get an idea of when it will be ready."

୧୧୧୧୧୧୧

Persei reclined comfortably on a silk couch in the wing of the palace in Uraka that had become his quarters. *If there's one thing these Maruthan rulers knew, it was how to live in luxury.* The legion was stationed outside the city, since the Garrison quarters were already full and insufficient for a force of that size. Persei, however, had taken up residence in the former emperor's palace that now served as both the governor's mansion and housed much of the local bureaucracy. He was certain the slaves resented him, but he was the master, the embodiment of the force that kept this fractious province part of the Republic.

Mirasha walked in, so elegant in another one of the local Maruthan dresses. *How the locals must stare!* The very thought made him jealous of her walking through the streets unattended. He'd been stuck here for the last day, while Mirasha had been exploring some of the local sites that could prove useful. Ilson's contacts had been a big help, but if Persei hadn't threatened them, they might not have been so willing to let a woman see their work. Persei, meanwhile, spent the day reading through reams of reports of local disturbances, issues that might require a strong hand, and disturbing rumors of uprisings deeper in the south of the country. He had just decided that an investigation would be prudent, and couldn't wait to tell Mirasha.

He stood up to greet her with a kiss. "I just had something to tell you."

Bubbling over with excitement, she shared her news first. "We have to go to Gardisha," she said. "I found reference to the temple of Zalikko... Oh, I've been meaning to ask you, have you ever heard the name?"

He shook his head.

"It seems like another guise of the fire goddess, and may be connected to the one that..." She looked down, sorrow in her eyes, and he stepped in to put his arm around her. "That my father discovered. I think there might be some link to what we are looking for."

"Gardisha, hmm? That just might work."

"Why?"

"Rebels, or at least rumor of them. One of the governor's spies has reported that they are starting to hide out in the ruins, since we rooted them out of the major cities. He mentioned Gardisha as a source of particular concern, given its proximity to us here in Uraka."

"And that scholar that Ilson mentioned, Yalath. He was here but left for Gardisha a couple of days ago. But he wasn't alone. You know who was with him?"

That regained his full attention. *Surely not...*

"One local and two obvious foreigners; they stuck out quite clearly compared to these honey-colored locals. It's so different here, there's so few... outsiders. I've never felt so... like I stick out. Even Jeppo wasn't quite like this."

He knew what she meant; he felt it too. "Marutha is an old .. no, ancient place. People have lived here far longer than in Pelusia, Pazh or even Attarsus. There's just so many people, and they tend to keep to themselves, so unlike the other ports you've seen, where you get people coming from all over the Republic and beyond for trade or work. Here it's pretty much just locals. And they're none too happy that we're in charge. I guess in a way, it would be like a worker from Uraka spending time on the banks of the Sentusi, in the heart of Scentar."

"If they are so much trouble, why bother keeping the province? Why not let them be independent?"

He sighed. "They would arm themselves before we knew it, take back the neighboring provinces, and ultimately try to challenge us directly. Their empire stretched all the way to Egaras at its height. I'm sure many would love to get it all back, lining up to prove their claim to the throne so they could sit with scores of slaves bowing down to them. Did you know the old emperors believed themselves to be demigods?"

"I've read the stories. They're very helpful. The locals completely reject the Pazian gods, and cling to their own beliefs. So there are far more useful references to both Kashaka and the water, and even some underground references to this Zalikko. I would really love to see the dig sites in Gardisha. Can you take me there, with the legion?" She stroked her finger along his arm, and pleasure rippled outward from her touch.

"That would be perfect. I was hoping I wouldn't have to leave you here to continue your investigation." Something tickled the back of his mind, and he frowned.

"What is it?" she asked, with obvious concern.

"Those outsiders, the ones you said were with Yalath, did you get a description?"

"Sorry, I got sidetracked. Yes. A man with curiously dark

bronze skin, and a paler dark-haired woman, both obviously from far away from these Eastern provinces. It does sound like them, doesn't it?"

"Simon and Elysia, here?" he asked, incredulous. "Then everything is pointing us to Gardisha. I can do my duty and maybe earn more favor back home, while you search for power, and together we can get my revenge. This is going to be a good trip. Come, I must send word for the legion to prepare. We leave in the morning with half the men, and it's a couple of days march."

ᎶᏋᎶᏋᎶᏋᎶ

Insistent pounding on the door roused Glebric from his paperwork.

Zustar burst through, livid.

"Those idiots, they left!"

"Who, what?" Glebric stood up.

"Ten of our best. I told them to wait for you. But the Alkazy's eyes were like flames and he whipped them up into a frenzy. You know we're not ready yet. But he'd have none of it. They took their weapons and marched out for retribution. It's starting, Glebric."

"Retribution for what?" Glebric motioned for Zustar to follow him and they headed to the front gates.

"One of the young women from the kitchen was on her way back from the market, and she saw a group of rich boys pestering a slave girl. Our girl ran, screaming, and several boys chased her all the way here."

Glebric felt his own anger rising. *In broad daylight!* Just because they were rich, it didn't justify savagery. They thought they owned everything and everyone in this city. *No longer.*

"She came back and told one of the men, and the Alkazy overheard and you know how he gets. They grabbed their weapons and went hunting for the boys."

Any assault by freedmen on nobles would bring out the watch. Glebric had to stop a war from breaking out. Zustar was right, they really weren't ready yet. And many of their men were off on Corus, using Ventus' villa as a training ground. Zustar had only just returned to give him an update and was supposed to head back in the morning. Ventus was still there.

Be decisive. Swift action.

146

"Where did you say this happened?"

"Just west of here. They only just left. We might catch them if we leave now."

They collected weapons and more men in case Glebric needed muscle to make his case.

The light was starting to fade, so early in midwinter, as they rushed through the streets. Several turns brought them around the corner from the alley, and they heard shouts, and screams of agony. From men, not women. A sinking feeling accompanied Glebric as he dashed to see the scene.

A screaming youth writhed on the ground, clutching his groin with bloody hands. The Alkazy stood over him, his blade dripping red. A second youth squirmed in the grip of another trusted lieu-tenant. Six more Izari teen boys dressed in fine wool tunics were on their knees, faces in the dirt, each one held down by one of his men. A red-haired young woman, barely more than a girl, huddled in the corner, whimpering. She could be the older sister of the one he'd saved last time, and the similarity focused his anger. But first he had to get things under control, if he still could.

"Azzam!" Glebric called out. "What is the meaning of this?"

The booming voice of the Alkazy sounded like judgment. "The vermin treat this girl as a toy to sate their lust. They must pay the price."

"Azzam!" Glebric shouted again, advancing on him. "Don't do this!" Sure, they deserved retribution, but this was too barbaric.

Azzam shook his head, and before Glebric could breach the gap, reached down to slice off the manhood of the boy in front of him. The boy's wail was inhuman, sudden, and short-lived, before he fainted.

"Who is next?" Azzam asked, his voice other-worldly in its lack of emotion.

The boys wet themselves with terror and two fainted. But one looked on all of them with disdain. *Brave? Or stupid?*

Glebric rushed forward. "Azzam, this isn't how we wanted it. This is disgusting."

"It's better than they deserve. In my country they would already be dead."

"But this is not your country. We can't just do this. There are laws, processes."

The Alkazy looked him in the eye, and Glebric recoiled. "Laws that made you and I into property. Processes that would let these brutes walk free to do this again and again. Maybe in the privacy of their house, where none can hear the girls scream. Don't you believe this is wrong?" He turned to the other men, who nodded.

The brave youth flipped his head up high and addressed Azzam. "The abomination is when a foreign dog like you bites the hand of his master." High cheekbones and pale skin marked him as pure-blood Pazian, probably the son of some local official. "If your daughter was here I'd make her beg for more."

Glebric tried to hold Azzam's arm, but he was too quick. In a flash, his sword punched through the windpipe of the insolent youth. Azzam wiped off his blade on the soft, embroidered tunic.

"No man is above another," he said with finality.

"We are better than this, Azzam," Glebric said, pleading, trying to buy time. One dead noble. Two more emasculated. They'd die too, if he didn't do something about it. He narrowed his eyes, focusing on the bloody mess that was the groin of the second boy. Pinching his fingers together, he connected to his power and tried to use it for good, and stopped the bleeding. He quickly did the same for the other, without drawing any attention to it.

"Master Glebric, look," Zustar said from behind him. A crowd was forming at the junction, attracted by the screams. Fear and outrage rang out in equal measure. Some were running away, but more were joining the crowd.

"That's Lukas!" came a shout from the crowd. "Lukas Porunna is dead! Killed by the black slave!"

It will mean war. And it starts now. He had to take the lead.

"Azzam, leave the boys. We have to get back to the house. Word is getting out."

"Let it!" said another of his men, Taddash, the big Scentari. His beard was growing in again, but far from long enough for him to braid. He complained about the indignity of having been shaved when he was sold into slavery. "Time to change!"

"But we're not ready!" Glebric said.

"If you're not," Azzam said, "then it starts without you. Kill them."

Four of the men slit the throats of the boys they held, while two wavered, looking to Zustar. Not even to Glebric. Taddash held up a dying youth, blood dripping from his neck. Screams of horror erupted from the crowd. Most turned and fled, among shouts of "call the watch!", "run!", and "savages!"

No! No! This wasn't how it was supposed to be!

Zustar was at his side, catching Glebric as he wavered on his feet. His voice was a harsh whisper of command: "If you don't bind them to you, you'll lose them. And they'll take out their anger in even greater savagery. Do you really want to make a change, for the better?"

Glebric nodded.

"Then I'll get the girl, you honor the men. This is war. They'll follow a general."

Righteous anger surged through Glebric, dispelling the fear. Zustar was right. He would not allow a reign of terror. There would be laws, justice, equality. He coughed away the thick residue of fear and disgust, and addressed his men.

"You are right, Azzam. No man is above another. You were right to stop these savages. But we will not stoop to their level.

"Taddash is also right. The time for change is now. But change for the better. Not chaos where might makes right. You are the best of my men. You are all committed to this cause. To free all the slaves and create a new world where everyone has a chance, an opportunity. And we have to fight for that cause, because the slavers will not relinquish control without bloodshed." They all nodded. The speech was exactly what they wanted to hear. "But we must do this with order, not chaos. If you will join me, I will swear an oath to you, as my…" He spotted the puddle of red around the body of the noble Lukas. "As my blood-brothers." His mind searched for the right words to bind them to him. Like the chains of slaves, but broken. "Will you swear to me, as the brotherhood of the broken chain?"

He sent out a tendril of power, pointing at the pool of blood. A stream of red rose into the air and darted toward him. The men were startled, and several backed up. He only wanted to impress them, but the effect was much stronger with blood instead of water. He pulled up the sleeve of his tunic. "I will mark us all as brothers." The blood darted in to draw a design on his right shoulder, of three links of chain, the middle one broken. He bit his lip at the scalding pain as it seared the red mark onto his flesh.

"I swear I will fight for the right of all people to live free. To be fair and just, never considering myself above another. But also to treat everyone with dignity and respect for what is right. And to protect my brothers and sisters who desire the same. Who is with me?"

Zustar was the first to bare his arm, with Azzam and Taddash right behind him, and the rest falling into line. Glebric approached each man in turn, streaks of blood whirling around him like crimson butterflies.

Azzam kissed his forehead and called him the Alkazy word for brother after receiving his brand. He even smiled. Glebric got a glimpse of the power of the bond, which to some meant as much as family. When he was done, they clapped each other on the back and embraced, this diverse band of brothers. He had re-established control over their group, even if events were spinning away from him on the larger scale. That was next. He had to send for Ventus and the others.

"Back to the house. The watch will be coming, and we want to be ready for them, with numbers."

The crowd parted like Glebric had only seen for a visiting official. He felt disgusted at their willingness to submit to any master. It went against everything they were now fighting for.

He was even more disgusted that he liked it.

150

XVII
୧ୡ୧ୡ୧ୡ୧
Rebels

Persei rode with supreme confidence at the head of his column of three thousand battle-hardened veterans, marching along the road that snaked parallel to the riverbank. Mirasha matched their progress aboard one of the triangular-sailed local boats. While he hated to be apart from her, at least she would be cool, and if they found any relevant relics, they'd be easier to transport back by boat. Until he could be certain that the dig sites were safe from these rumored rebels, he wouldn't be allowing her off the boat in any event. And it was easier this way, not having to explain away her presence to the troops. Sure, he was the legate in charge of the legion and his word was law without a higher senatorial commander present, but it was bad for discipline if the commander was seen to be cavorting with women while the men marched through the scorching terrain, putting their lives at risk.

A drink from his waterskin cooled his parched lips. Despite the lush greenery of the farms that lined the river, it was still far too hot to be riding. As they approached Gardisha, the stretch of farmland was receding, pushed back by the encroaching desert. What once had reportedly been some of the most fertile land in the whole province was dry and cracking. No wonder the city had been abandoned for almost a millennium.

Persei had sent a scouting party of ten horsemen ahead to see if there was any sign of the rebels, and they'd come back safely with nothing to report. The city wasn't a city at all, just a series of camps reclaimed from the sandy waste. The blowing sand covered any tracks, but there was no sign of large-scale troop movement. Mirasha was interested in the two closer camps, while the latest information from his informants was that the last of the three was the main home of the rebels.

Out in the open, battle will be easy. But how to flush them out without antagonizing the locals? That's if the reports are true. He was still suspicious of the idea that any would be foolish enough to challenge the Legions of Pazh.

Callus, one of his best scouts, approached on horseback. Pale and blonde, he was good Pazian stock, but had grown up the son of a *mercati* in Kawan, spending his youth on a horse like all the boys there. Persei trusted him more than the Kawanians. With their eyes like slits, they always looked suspicious, or mistrustful of him.

"Legate, after crossing this crest we'll reach the bowl that Gardisha sits in. What are your orders?"

"Have the scouts taken another look?"

"No sign of movement. Just a handful of people coming and going from the river port. Most look like academics, not combatants."

"Excellent." He summoned Bellos, the handsome dark-haired *digniti* second son—one of his better tribunes, and effectively his second in command. He'd been Persei's drinking partner and shared his tastes for the finer things in life. "I want to split the force in three. I will take three cohorts and circle around to the east out of sight, coming back to the far camp. Bellos will take one to the middle camp, and you, Callus, will take the last cohort to the near camp. I want to surround them all. I'd have you build palisades to box them in, but on this sand I don't think they would stick. No wood, in any event. We'll split the scouts evenly, because at the first sign of resistance, or the all clear, I want word sent to the other groups. All three groups will move in together, so have the men ready when you see us enter the bowl from the far side. Javelins ready. If any of those rebels walk out the door, I want them skewered immediately."

"But how will we search inside the camps?" Bellos asked.

"Choose twenty of your best men, and lead them personally. Approach the entrances, and declare an inspection on the governor's orders. Keep an eye out for suspicious behavior. Ask to see the leaders of the camp, and if anyone tries to run off, bring them in for questioning. I don't expect they'll talk about the rebels— they're probably in bed with them. But if there are rebels here, they'll either show their hands or try to sneak out. "

"What if they don't?"

"If they try to fight us inside the camps? Then we'll kill them with superior training and organization. But at the first sign of opposition I want you to withdraw from inside the city and notify the others. We have no idea how many of these rebels are hiding in there. You have your orders."

The two men nodded and snapped salutes before riding off to organize the troops.

It was mid-afternoon by the time Persei's group crested the south side of the bowl, and they waved their 7th Legion standard in the air to give the signal. With barely a breeze, the air was clear of sand, and Persei was happy to see his other troops march over the ridge in response.

Would surprise have been better? No time for second-guessing now. Any sentries inside would be sounding the alarm, but they'd be surrounded soon enough.

He led the men at a light jog toward their destination: the black flags that seemed to mark the entrance of the third camp. Squinting, he thought he made out movement in the space below the flag.

A few short minutes later and his men were in position, in a ring around the camp several men deep. He had the rear line face outward in case of secret tunnels, but he doubted it was necessary. Leading his group of twenty toward the largest of three open doorways, he sat up a little higher in the saddle. *Maybe they'd surrender, but I'd almost prefer a fight. Although the slave sale…*

Two very nervous sentries stood at the entrance, in flowing robes almost indistinguishable from their skin or the sand around them. They each carried a sword, and their long robes could conceal other weapons. They evaluated Persei and his men and traded a glance, but stood their ground. Persei held up his hand in greeting.

"I am Persei Lokuta, Legate of the 7th Legion, and acting representative of the Senate of the Republic of Pazh." One seemed to understand, while the other betrayed fear. Persei pointed to him. This one was a little taller, with an ugly scar running across his cheek. Unwisely, his hand was on the hilt of the curved sword sheathed at his left hip. "You understand. We wish to see the leader of this camp."

The sentry said something in Maruthan to his counterpart. Persei scolded himself for not bringing more of the locals with him, and none in his party of twenty. *These must be rebels if they don't even learn the language. But it could prove limiting.* Not limiting enough that Persei would show weakness and withdraw.

"Hey!" Persei shouted at the man. "I didn't give you permission to speak. I said I want you to bring us to your commanding officer."

The man jumped. His Pazian was halting. "This... is... dig camp. Not war. Leader is bookman."

Persei rolled his eyes. "Just take us to him. Now."

"Must stay watch." The guard lifted a horn from a chain on his neck. "I call—"

"No!" Persei shouted again. "I will keep two of my men here in your place. *You* will lead us." Persei looked one of his men in the eye, and then jerked his chin toward the man's spot. "Take his place." The big legionary saluted and took a position next to the sentry.

The sentry's shoulders slumped, and he handed the horn to his counterpart with a defeated sigh. "Come," he said to Persei.

Persei dismounted and handed the reins of his horse to another of the men and leaned in to give his command. "At the first sign of trouble, kill the sentry and ride to the rest of the force. They should send in more troops to relieve us immediately." The man nodded.

The sentry walked down the stairs into the gloom like he was heading to his execution, his eyes darting around nervously, which put Persei on high alert. He turned back to his men, pointing two fingers to his eyes, and then around. He also made a show of putting his hand on the hilt of his short sword, which the men copied.

It was an impressive setup, with the tents covering the site of the excavation. Persei imagined the months of work this would have taken to reclaim it from the sand. These Maruthans might not enjoy Pazian rule, but they sure had an interest in the past.

Persei hoped all was well with Mirasha on the boat, and that she had the sense to stay away until he sent for her. That was the weak point of his plan—she was just headstrong and impatient enough that she might walk into the middle of a battle. The thought drove him onward to get the matter dealt with as quickly as possible.

Ilson's maps mainly covered the other two sites, so Persei had to trust this guard's route through the half-buried city. Most of the time they walked through streets that were open to the tented roof above, but a few times they went through actual tunnels. The men they passed looked like tradesmen doing various kinds of excavation-related activities: fixing posts, digging, carrying loads of sand and earth around. None of them took off to report their presence. *Could the reports have been wrong?*

After turning a corner, the guard led them toward a large building that looked like it might have once served as some sort of government office. "Bookman," he said. As they approached the entrance, two bored-looking guards snapped to attention and called out something in Maruthan to Persei's guide. One drew his sword, and the other opened one of the double doors and slipped in.

Persei swore at the guide. "What did he say?"

Golden eyes filled with the steel of resolve as the man reached for his own weapon, but instead found himself on the receiving end of a legionary short sword. Looking down at the point protruding from the front of his throat, the guard slumped forward, dead. Persei nodded thanks to his man as he drew his own sword. "We'll have to fight our way in."

"But sir, you said we were to withdraw—"

"We have to teach these bastards a lesson."

At the sight of nineteen fully armored legionaries charging his position, the second guard fled through the double doors, slamming them shut behind him.

Persei's first man tried the doors, but they were barred from the inside.

"You five, go around to the left to see if there are any other escape routes. You five do the same for the right. The rest of you, see if there's anything we can use to ram the doors."

A gong sounded inside the building, reverberating off the buildings on all sides.

"Sir, if that is their alarm, we don't know how many we are facing."

Damn the man for challenging his orders, but he was right. How many miles of streets and tunnels lay below the sand? How many of these rebel warriors? *But the chance at the leaders...*

"You two, go back to the entrance, do you remember the way?" They nodded. "Make sure that they take my horse and get reinforcements. If the alarm is heard that far, they'll have sent word already if the guard turns on them. But if not, give the order to break through all the entrances, capturing any they can, and killing any who resist. Leave only one cohort to surround the entrances."

The two snapped salutes and sprinted off.

"The rest of you will be heroes once again. I chose you because you fought in the first surge with me against the Scentari. Those dogs were far better warriors than this rabble. And far more prepared. Wet your blades with these sons of the sand, offering their blood to Salar, the Iron One!" Shouts went up from his men. They were his best, and they were worth many times their number in rebel scum.

"Find me something to knock down this door!" It didn't look to be reinforced, and anything would make a good ram.

His men reported smaller locked doors on two other sides of the building, and he was forced to divert them to hold those exits. The groups were to stay close to the walls so they couldn't be seen from inside, and capture or kill any non-legionaries who came through while sounding horn blasts with the numbers, one blast for every five opponents.

Two men came back with a wheelbarrow full of rocks, and a shovel. "Did the man give it over willingly?" Persei asked with a smirk.

"He left. We didn't see anyone else in the street. They must have fled with the alarm."

Persei scowled. Just as he feared. He nodded to the door. Four of his biggest men strained to pick up the wheelbarrow between them and walked back to the opposite side of the street. On the count of three they charged the doors, and the wheelbarrow punched through with a loud crash, sending splinters flying in all directions.

Two astonished guards scrambled along the floor toward a door on the opposite side of the room, but Persei's men cut them down before they could escape. Persei ignored closed doors to the left and right and signaled for his men to advance on the middle door as a wall of shields three abreast and two deep, Persei in the very middle. The last man took a lamp from a fallen Maruthan and brought up the rear, keeping a watch for attacks from behind. He swung the door open and let his fellows burst through crying: "For Pazh!"

Persei scanned the door for threats and means of escape. Tables were laid out in a square in the middle of the room, covered in papers and pieces of stone, set up for some kind of meeting or discussion. Five guards stood at the ready, swords drawn, at the left side of the room, while two older scholars huddled behind them. One made for the far door.

"Surrender," Persei called out, "and you will be spared. Your men have attacked the Legions of Pazh, an act of war."

The second scholar raised his hands and shouted "Spare me!" One of the guards smacked him across the back of the head and he went down in a heap. The other man had the door open.

"Charge!" Persei shouted, and his men ran forward in formation. Two guards were through before they could reach them, but the others were impaled quickly on superior Pazian steel, their curved swords unable to breach the shield wall.

"He's still alive, but unconscious," one of his men said, checking the fallen scholar.

"Stay here," Persei ordered, "and try to bring him round. He may know something, and seems to value his life more than the others. The rest of you, with me!" He charged through the open door.

At the end of a hallway, the old man was unlocking another door while the guards set up behind him. When it opened and the man burst through, Persei saw his other soldiers grab the scholar and easily dispatch the guards, who tried to fight.

Persei sent men to round up the soldiers from the other side while he interrogated the scholar. Completely bald and covered in wrinkles, he looked like a dried apricot. And while there was fear in his eyes, he was defiant. *Definitely sympathetic to the rebels, if not a leader.*

"Are you in charge of this camp?" Persei asked.

"Yes." His Pazian was much better than the guard's, with only a trace of the Maruthan accent. "Why are you killing my guards?"

"Why did they try to kill me, first? We're tracking down rebels known to be operating here. I'm guessing that's what these guards are?"

The man's eyes narrowed. "There are no rebels here, just loyal Maruthans."

"Loyal to the Republic?" Persei asked, eyebrow raised.

"Loyal to Kashaka," the man shouted. One of the guards restraining the man slapped him in the face.

"Your false gods won't save you now. You'll die a traitor to Pazh."

The distinctive ring of metal on metal could be heard from back the way they came, and the sounds of hobnailed sandals striking

157

the street in great number. Persei stood a little straighter, knowing he had the backing of numbers as well as skill.

"My legion will crush your rebels. You're surrounded. There is no escape."

"Then we will take out as many of you as we can, for the glory of Kashaka!" The scholar spat, but it fell short of Persei's sandal.

"Bind this one and turn this building into a prison. Maybe he'll talk later with a little more encouragement. See if that other one has anything more to share."

Several squads sprinted up to their position, led by the two men he'd sent. Persei smiled and returned their salute. "Follow me, men. Let's hunt us some rebels!"

ᏰᏋᏯᏋᏯᏋᏯᏰ

Numerius woke with a start at the sound of the door opening. *At least Ventus feeds me well. Or is it Glebric?* His stomach didn't particularly care.

Fiery red hair glinted in the light filtering through the half-open door. *Ah, the new one again.* He'd tried to be nice. He didn't have to try—he was generally nice. And no harm in trying to curry favor with the ones who took care of his well-being during this imprisonment.

Especially this one. Even with the beating she'd suffered, leaving her face swollen and now darkening to an ugly purple, she was still beautiful. And sweet.

He'd tried Izari when she'd brought him his food, and she'd recoiled from him, though progressively less each time. She was likely afraid of the shadow of those who had done this to her. He thought he'd give Pazian a shot.

"Thank you for bringing me the food," he said, keeping his voice gentle, and careful not to make a move to approach her.

She nodded, in the kind of instinctive deference a slave would show a kind master. *Another one of their recently freed slaves?*

"I'm so sorry for what you've gone through," he said.

Looking at him much closer, a tear welled up in her eye. "I... thank you."

"Don't worry, you're safe with me."

"Why are you being so kind? You're a prisoner here."

"I had come as a guest, and hoped to leave as one. But it was

158

not to be. The masters here are much kinder to the slaves than to those who try to protect this world from evil."

"But they also protect people!"

Numerius was taken aback. "The Master's men rescued you?"

"Yes, and I am very thankful!"

Defiantly so. There's something more here. "As you should be."

"They not only saved me from... from those monsters, but Glebric gave me my freedom!"

"Then what is on your mind, my child? Something is bothering you."

Her whole bearing changed, looking like a beggar caught with his hand in the temple donation box.

Oozing compassion, he put up his hands. "I'm only here to help. If something is troubling you... something about this house or the Master, your secret is safe with me."

"Why should I trust you?"

Did I strike true? I have to push through the opening. "Because the enemy of your enemy just might be your best friend. Maybe your only friend."

Her eyes betrayed a great weight. "I... it's just a dream. It's nothing."

"Dreams are important, miss... what is your name?"

"Kallara."

He nodded. "My name is Numerius. Pleased to meet you, Kallara. As I was saying, dreams are important. Sometimes they are a way for the mind to remind us of something that our waking eyes can't comprehend."

"Every night since I got here. I'm alone, in a room in this beautiful house. I'm singing." She paused, and Numerius wasn't sure if she would continue.

"Do you like to sing? Or only in your dreams?"

"When I was a girl... I used to sing to my mother. She said it made her happier than anything else in this world. That when I sang the old songs of the gods, of the heroes, that she could see them in her mind. But after she died, I couldn't sing anymore. Soon after, my uncle sold me as a slave. I was six. I haven't really sung for anyone in ten years."

Talent? In a slave? She must have kept it well buried not to have come to their attention sooner.

"I would love to hear you sing for me someday, Kallara. So now

159

you sing in your dreams?"

"Yes, and it is beautiful. I see the ghost of my mother, and I sing for her. I feel such joy, such passion. But then..." she looked around furtively. "Hold on." She peeked out the door and returned. Now her voice was barely a whisper: "The guards are there, but they're talking."

He nodded again for her to continue.

"Every time, in the dream, I feel this darkness nearby. In the house. It's... it's evil. Somehow I know it is. And it hears my song. Then my feet are suddenly wet. I look down and there's water covering the floor, and it's rising." Her eyes stared past him, haunted and afraid. "It rises like a washtub being filled with darkness, and I can't swim, and when I try to sing it away it enters my mouth and I'm coughing, choking... and then I wake up."

If he wasn't sure it would spook her, he would have hugged her. The poor girl was rattled. He would have dismissed it as crazy, too, if he hadn't already seen Glebric willing wine through the air with just the power of his mind. *A dream, about the magic here? The Keepers must learn about this.*

"Do you think I'm losing my mind?"

"No. Not at all."

Hope suddenly flushed her face, her eyes wide and pleading.

"Then you think..."

"Just as I said, I think you are attuned to a very real danger here, in this house."

"But the people are so kind, and they took care of me. Where can I go? If the families of those boys, the ones who..." Her words broke down in sobs.

Someone knocked on the door. "Is everything all right in there?"

"Yes, sorry, the prisoner was just making a long list of requests about the food."

The guard laughed. "Who does he think he is, a visiting prince?"

She laughed, putting a finger to her lips. "It seems so. But the Master does treat even his prisoners well."

Numerius nodded and waved for her to leave.

Her voice was barely audible: "I will return to speak with you more."

"Sing sweetly in your dreams," he said, just as quietly.

She closed the door and left him to eat his meal alone with his thoughts. And what thoughts.

Talent and dark magic both running wild, and I'm stuck in here unable to tell anyone or call for help. Numerius shook his head. *But this girl could be the key.*

XVIII

ᕮᕯᕮᕯᕮᕯᕮ
Aktiri

The lone island of Aktiri rose up like a solitary peak above the flat plain of the Near Sea. Simon did his best to imprint the natural beauty of the scene in his mind for a future painting, wishing once again there was some way to use his brushes while high in the air on Zeno's back.

Other than the wilds north and west of Pelusia, the independent island of Aktiri was the only shore of the Near Sea not a part of the Pazian Republic. Simon, always trying to make sense of every inch of the maps he pored over, had once asked his teacher about it. He'd been told not to worry, that the people of the dark island kept their strange beliefs to themselves. They didn't travel and they didn't trade. Neither Elysia nor Remeth knew even that much. Simon was content to keep it that way. As curious as he was to explore the mysterious island, he felt a much stronger pull to find Kashaka before she could be united with her sister.

Remeth had other ideas, and was making them known. "If there's any danger once we find Kashaka," he said, "we'll need to make sure we're as well rested as possible."

"Then we'll tie you to Zeno and you can nod off while we fly," Simon said.

"But we have no idea how far she might be."

"All the more reason to get there as fast as we can. If these two Damoz sisters start working together..."

"But aren't you in the slightest bit curious about this so called 'Dark Island'?"

"Yes, but—"

"Then why don't we set down near the city, and spend the night there?"

"Remeth, I know you're excited about your first trip outside of

Marutha, but there will be plenty of time—"

"Will there? We've barely had a chance to catch our breath since we reached Gardisha. Something tells me things will only get more hectic."

"I just don't think—"

Zeno shuddered, and Remeth's grip tightened around Simon's waist.

Elysia whispered into the ear of their mount, and now that Simon was focused on it, he recognized Zeno's wings were faltering.

"We'll have to get him down," Elysia said, "for a night, maybe longer. Between this wind and the extra weight, he can't go this far at one stretch."

Simon turned back to Remeth. With the incessant roaring of the headwind, Simon was barely able to speak to either of his companions, and they couldn't hear each other at all. "Looks like you'll get your wish," he said.

"For the night?" Remeth asked, grinning like a child receiving a surprise gift.

"Maybe longer." He turned back to Elysia. "Tell Zeno to pick the best spot for both landing and another takeoff." For the first time since they began flying with Zeno, Simon felt a level of panic seeping in. *What if Zeno tired somewhere over the sea? Could Zeno swim? Could the others?*

Simon's initial impression was more true than he'd realized. The island was one jagged mountain, with the whole southern face a sheer wall of rock, and no place to land. Laboring now despite Elysia's encouragement, Zeno made for the right around a cape that looked a little less steep. He flew low over the land, sheltered now from the worst of the wind, and Simon appreciated the sudden silence.

Zeno banked sharply upward, snapping Simon's head back to hit Remeth's, who swore in response. Looking down and ahead, Simon saw the reason for the change of altitude: a dark watchtower in the distance. As long as they flew high above, they might be mistaken for a small seabird. He would rather not explain themselves to these guardians of the strange island. Unfortunately, the watchtower dominated the only plateau they'd seen that would be suitable for a night's camp. Twice more their hopes at a resting place were dashed by similar fortifications.

As the afternoon wore on, the looming shadow of the mountain peak engulfed them as they continued along the coastline. The light made it seem like early evening, even if the sky behind them still shone bright.

Zeno groaned.

"What was that?" Remeth asked.

"Hold on!" Elysia shouted, and this time Remeth heard her too.

Zeno spread his sagging wings and soared downward, the mountainside closing on them far too fast.

Remeth squeezed Simon so tight he coughed. When he opened his eyes again, Zeno crested a hill and leveled off, bringing them in for a smooth landing on a sloping plain of soil rather than the barren rock of the rest of the island.

"Everyone off!" Elysia said, jumping down first.

Remeth let go, and Simon could breathe again, turning to glare at the sheepish face behind him.

"It was scary," Remeth said. Unsteady on his feet, he almost fell backward on the sloping ground.

"Walk slowly at first," Simon said. "The legs take a little while to recover, especially after crossing water. I don't know why."

Zeno slumped down onto his knees. Elysia stroked his mane as he rolled over on his side.

Simon put his arm around her. She was trembling. "Is he..."

She frowned. "Exhausted. It's too much strain on him, three of us for such a distance. I don't know if one night will even be enough."

Simon looked around. No watchtowers in sight, but at the bottom of the slope loomed the walls of the city. Maybe a couple of hours walk. He checked the blood of Kashaka and was not surprised to see it point straight toward the settlement.

"Then I guess we stay here for a while."

"You can, but I want to look at the city," Remeth said. He held up his hand when Simon started to protest. "You two have been all over the Republic, but I haven't. This is my chance. And we should make sure *she's* not in there." He pointed to the device Simon held. "What better place to imprison her than an island everyone avoids? This could be it!"

Simon frowned, but conceded that point with a nod. "It could be dangerous," Simon said, knowing he was speaking in vain.

"Everything has been varying degrees of dangerous since I met you two. So who is coming with me?"

Elysia's eyes lit up. She was equally curious about every new place. "But I should stay with Zeno. In case he needs something."

Simon felt pulled in both directions. He didn't want to leave Elysia alone, but Remeth had absolutely no experience of foreign lands. And the excitement of the new city…

"You go with him," Elysia said, as she laid a blanket over Zeno to cover his wings. "Bring back some new food to try. And fruit for Zeno." Her eyes said it would be all right, but Simon still felt like he was deserting her.

With their mount seemingly asleep, Simon snuck in a kiss with Elysia before turning down the slope with Remeth.

They had been walking slowly through treacherous rocky ground for what seemed like an hour before they found the faint sign of wagon tracks leading up from the city.

"Is that a wagon?" Remeth asked, pointing down the slope toward the city walls.

Simon nodded. "Coming this way. We should hide."

Remeth laughed. "If we were rats, there'd be lots of little cracks to hide in. But for us…"

Simon frowned. While the slope was full of sharp rocks that made walking difficult anywhere outside of the wagon track, there were no good hiding places. "Maybe I could use my Talent to paint us like rocks before the wagon gets here?"

"No," said Remeth. "I think we should talk to them. One wagon won't be a danger. And what's the worst that could happen? He's going away from the city. And even if he turned to head back downhill, he'd have to go slow to avoid overturning the cart. Let's see what I can find out from the driver."

Remeth laughed again, this time at Simon's expression. While Remeth had been happy to follow Yalath's lead, now that he was away from his mentor he was proving to be more independent and headstrong than Simon would have liked.

"Fine. You do the talking. I'll have my sword ready in case anything goes badly."

A sturdy mountain pony led the closed back wagon, with a single driver sitting up front.

"Probably resupplying the watchtowers," Simon said, more to

himself. "He might be a guard, and could be armed."

"Then if it comes to that, I'll leave it to you, soldier."

The driver reined his pony to a stop when he saw them. He called out a challenge, but not in any language Simon could understand. Maybe Kawanian?

"Wait here," Remeth said to Simon, and stepped toward the wagon with his hands raised, responding in a similar tongue.

The driver barked something back, but Simon gave up trying to understand. The man was a head or more shorter than Simon himself, but twice as wide. His skin was very dark brown, even darker than Simon's own, and he wore his black hair cropped close to his skull. His shirt and pants were dark gray wool, almost the color of the rocks around him. He didn't look happy, but at least he didn't raise a weapon against them.

Remeth got close, showing his empty hands with a grand flourish. *Always the showman.* Simon kept a close watch on the driver's expression as the two of them traded words, with Remeth's speech punctuated by theatrical gestures. At one point he was waving his hands violently down like they were crashing into the mountain, and finally the driver nodded and pointed back toward the city. He did shrug his shoulders and shake his head, as if in warning. Remeth finished the conversation with a bow and a wave.

The pony started up again, and Simon stepped out of the way. The man looked at him with piercing eyes of unnaturally light gray. The cart was odd. *Metal wheels. Metal frame. Not wood?*

"Could you actually understand him?"

"Not totally. I had to use a few different words. It's similar to Kawanian, which I don't speak that well. But there's a few words that sound more like old Maruthan. And then others unlike anything I've ever heard."

"What did you tell him?"

Remeth smiled. "That our ship crashed, and we escaped on a rowboat, but were dashed against the rocks. We made it through, but were heading to the city to get supplies and maybe find a boat out of here."

Simon nodded. "Not bad. I guess that's believable."

"Here's the bad part. Very few outsiders come here. Don't want them. Don't like them. So we're not likely to get a good reception." He broke out in a sly grin. "But I have an idea!"

"What?"

"How about you paint me up a bit, to make me look like him. Do you think that would work?"

Simon furrowed his brow. "Did you get a good look at him?'

"Why?"

"He was a lot shorter than us. If that's typical, then we'll still stand out. Might even be more strange. I could make you look a little different, and changing the skin color is easy. Even adding some hair. But I don't know how I could make you look shorter and wider."

Remeth slumped down, moping. "I guess it's on me to just talk us in?" Then he brightened again. "That's it! Paint me anyway. You just follow my lead. You're almost dark enough to pass for one of them in dim light. If you crouch."

"But if they're not friendly and we get caught…"

"Oh come on, it'll be fun. Even if we just get to try some new foods. What's the worst that could happen?"

Simon sighed. He'd seen far too many plans go horribly wrong of late. But Remeth was so excited. Simon rummaged around in his pack for his paints. "Just stay quiet while I paint, otherwise it will look ridiculous. And wipe that grin off your face."

"I'm used to stage makeup, for the shows without masks. I won't move a muscle."

It was a new experience, painting someone else's face. But at least Remeth was an obedient subject. Since Simon hadn't been able to understand the conversation he'd focused more than usual on the driver's face. He tapped into that mental image as he mixed the brown darker and darker until it looked like the expensive cuttlefish ink he'd seen in some official documents.

Focusing on that image in his mind he applied the paint in broad strokes, and Remeth didn't even flinch.

"I can feel it," Remeth said, "the power. It's a tingling sensation, like new skin after it heals."

"I can go faster if you're quiet."

The paint seemed to melt into his skin, and settled in at a color that seemed a perfect match to Simon's eye. The features would be more problematic.

"The driver's nose was wider than yours… I'm going to try something."

Simon imagined the other nose transposed over Remeth's, and painted from the edge of his face over the space where the extra flesh would sit. And it appeared, solidifying into an extension of his actual facial structure. Simon felt considerable pride at creating something out of nothing. The possibilities were dizzying.

After finishing off the nose and making the lips a bit thicker, he had Remeth stand up so he could get a good look at him. The long golden ponytail, which they'd tied back out of the way for the flight, hung down below his shoulders.

"What are we going to do with that? Chop it off?"

Remeth grabbed it protectively. "Over my dead body."

"Did you see the man's hair? He was practically shaved bald."

"Can you paint it away?"

"I... I haven't tried."

"Then get to it, if we want to get in there for dinner."

Simon pulled the hair back and tucked the ponytail into the back of Remeth's tunic. It bulged awkwardly, but would be hidden by his pack.

He dipped his brush back in the new skin color and painted over the hair that hung along the back of the neck, watching with delight as it seemed to meld into the skin, leaving only what appeared to be shorter hair above. Not quite the close-shaven look of the driver, but the best he could do. Finally, he painted the remaining hair black.

When he finished, he stood back to look at the whole again. "It's a good thing we convinced you to wear a tunic. It will fit in better here, and pretty much anywhere we go."

Remeth wrinkled his new nose. "I don't know how you can get used to wearing so much."

"Wait until you see what winter is like anywhere outside of Marutha. You'll be happy for it. Especially with your thin blood."

"It's a shame though, people covering up so much. Obscuring the beauty of the human form. As a painter, I thought you'd appreciate that."

"Not everyone is so worthy of being shown."

"But some are," Remeth said, his golden eyes smiling as they dipped down to Simon's chest.

Simon felt slightly uncomfortable, but it did remind him of something. "Right, your eyes. I'll have to dull them down a bit."

For the first time Remeth looked apprehensive, at the brush looming over his eyeball.

"I can't say it won't hurt, because I have no idea. But they need to be much lighter, even gray. And they'll be looking closely at your eyes if you're the one doing all the talking."

Remeth tensed up. "Do it."

It took only a lightest daub with the brush to change the color, but still Remeth's eyes were watering and bloodshot when he was done..

"Did it work?"

Simon nodded. "You look the part. But you're still too tall."

"Oh, leave that to me." Remeth hunched over, spreading his shoulders a little wider and puffing out his chest. The transformation was uncanny. He looked a good foot shorter, and wider too. To finish off the display he said something in that strange tongue.

Simon shook his head, incredulous. "You really do have a Talent for acting."

"That's what they tell me."

XIX

ଌଌଌଌଌଌ

Ignition

With useful information from the more forthcoming scholar, the hunt was less sport and more slaughter. Persei's troops combed through the streets, tunnels and buildings of the camp with brutal efficiency, slaughtering the woefully unprepared rebels. The idea of a direct assault by a Pazian legion must never have crossed their minds, with their defenses so lacking. This was a base built for secrecy, not defense.

Several pockets were harder to crack, and while Persei returned to the surface, some of his best men were still rooting them out. And the enemy wasn't completely inept, with several dozen wounded legionaries as evidence. But at a cost of many hundreds of dead rebels. Did they really think that a thousand of this rabble would do anything against the might of the legions? Or was this just the vanguard?

Marutha was a huge province, and much of it far away from the Near Sea and direct Pazian control. Sure, there were garrison forts along the frontier, especially in the east to keep an eye on the Marassani, and in the south to regulate trade across the desert with the Empire of Chaleth. But there were far more ruins, and they could all house multitudes of disgruntled young men, like this one. For the first time in his life, Persei was seeing the limits—even fragility—of Pazian might.

Callus and Bellos hadn't faced any direct opposition, and their questioning of the leadership had yielded a few details he wanted to share with Mirasha. Having left things in good hands as his force was setting up camp for the night, he was riding down to the river port with two trusted men and an extra horse. Mirasha's boat was one of only a handful at the pier, and he located it immediately. When he spotted her on his approach, his heart lit up and the day's slaughter was forgotten. She didn't see him right away, and the fiery orange of the setting sun reflected highlights in her hair, looking almost like a wreath of flames. He felt himself stir.

"Legate!" she called out when she saw him, in deference to his men. She was making an effort not to undermine his status.

"Mirasha, the sites are ready for you," he said with a smile. He kissed her hand, feeling so stilted in the formality. How he wished to whisk her away to private quarters and feel that hair in his hands, to feel the soft skin of—

"Was there serious opposition?" She examined the bandage on his left forearm. The wound throbbed in response.

"The third camp was their base. The others seem to be purely archaeological."

She waved to a slave and he went below, returning soon after with a chest of her belongings.

"The slave will have to walk. I only have one horse for you and your things. Should have brought a camel."

The slave strapped the chest to the back of the horse, and Persei helped Mirasha up into the saddle. It was awkward but would have to do. He'd far prefer to feel her in front of him on his horse, but that wouldn't play well with the men as they passed through the camp.

As they rode slowly over the dunes, that reflected red with the glow of evening, Persei told her what he'd learned.

"*They* were here."

"Yalath and…"

"And another Maruthan, as well as foreigners exactly matching Simon and Elysia. They were especially suspicious of Elysia, as a foreign woman trying to get into the fire temple. They associate Zalikko with women and evil foreign influences."

She put her hands on her hips and scowled at him. "Will they think the same of me?"

"Sometimes even I wonder about your foreign influence on me." She wrinkled her nose, and he knew she'd try to hit him playfully if they weren't on separate horses. And that would degenerate into…

"So it was only their presence that was considered strange?"

"They were able to recover a statue in the temple, which had previously burned the worker who tried to retrieve it."

"In the temple of Zalikko? I'd like to see that."

Persei nodded. He'd already had his men send word that he would be personally inspecting some of the sites, looking for anything about the rebels. "Apparently they also had a run in with the rebels and disappeared for a while. Later, at the other camp, where the main temple of Kashaka is situated, there was some kind of night raid. Yalath was part of a group that broke in, dressed like rebels. The head of the camp believes they might have taken something from the water temple. But they couldn't find anything missing, and the group escaped, pursued by rebels. That's all they know."

"They must have found what they were looking for. What we seek. We will go to both sites."

"I don't know if we can manage both tonight, so which one first?"

"Zalikko. Since they went there first, and I want to see that statue. It might..."

"It might what?" There was something in her look that drew him in.

With a glance at his men, she lowered her voice. "If my guess is right, it might be the key to unlocking power for you. For us."

Persei's heart beat faster at the prospect. Of uncovering this ancient power and seizing it for himself. With her. He told the slave to follow their tracks and kicked his horse into a light trot. He didn't want to wait any longer.

"This is Jukaro," Callus said, introducing an unremarkable little Maruthan with beady eyes. Persei was relieved Mirasha had the sense to wear a long veil, because he didn't want this one getting a close look at her. "He is the scholar from the office of the Prefect of Antiquities, the one who was responsible for showing Yalath and his company around. He'll take you down to the temple you've asked about."

"You knew Yalath well?" Persei asked.

"Uh... I had met him many times. He was frequently involved in the dig sites."

"Did you know his assistants?"

"Only Remeth. He had come before. It was my first time meeting Simon and Elysia."

Persei exchanged a glance with Mirasha.

"I have to say," Jukaro said, "it is highly unusual for a woman to be involved in one of our dig sites. And now a second woman in as many days…"

"She is a specialist in such things," Persei said.

"Ah yes, a specialist. As was this Elysia, apparently. What is your specialty Miss—"

"That is not your concern," Persei said, and Jukaro flinched. "Where is this temple?"

The man settled in a bit more once he was focused on the details of the dig. "Underneath one of the noble houses. In a hidden basement. They used to have…"

Persei's mind wandered as the man droned on about the history of the place. No overt signs of rebel activity, but he kept his eyes moving, watching the actions of every worker. Most wore sullen stares, but a few looked openly hostile. Word of the battle at the other camp was making the rounds, and the legionaries were even less popular than usual.

Jukaro's running commentary continued as they went into the ancient villa, down the stairs, and into the temple below. Old, dead stone to Persei. Nothing special or magical about it.

"You will see the fallen statue on the altar. The one that Yaath and his associates retrieved. With… all the excitement, we haven't begun our analysis of this rare and important relic."

Persei had his men do a quick sweep of the other rooms to confirm there were no rebels hiding anywhere, and had them stand guard at the top of the stairs. Mirasha wanted them to be alone, with this Jukaro. He would talk.

"Can you read the old Maruthan?" Mirasha asked Jukaro, the first words she'd said to him. She took off the veil, revealing her dark hair and those mysterious eyes. And with the slightest shift of balance her light dress pressed against her figure. Persei hated to share even the view of her with someone like this, but her eyes told him to back off.

The little Maruthan's eyes wandered all the way down to her legs. "Of course, it is one of my specialties, I'd be happy to translate anything for you…"

She smiled at him and he beamed, like a child hearing praise from their teacher.

"I would like that… very much." She gestured toward the statue.

Persei's eyes lingered on the statue's bronze curves. Taller than any man, with only a few wisps of flame slapped on in the name of modesty, her assets were in full view, and in Persei's mind, perfect. The beautiful face seemed almost familiar. Maybe one of the Pazian sculptors copied the piece? He'd seen so many statues in all the temples and especially Daymar's collection, and only the most beautiful goddesses ever made any kind of impression on him. It was good for Mirasha that this one wasn't alive and trying to bed him, because he might not be able to resist her advances.

"Oh, I haven't had a chance to decipher this one yet, but..." Jukaro leaned in toward the inscription on the back of the statue.

Mirasha moved over to Persei and whispered to him. "Father mentioned something like this. Like the statue. He had to put it back where it belonged, and then it was able to grant him power in response to his offering."

"So you think I could do the same?"

"I think you should try."

Jukaro looked up at them. "I... yes... I think I have it." He straightened slightly, like he was about to recite poetry. Persei fought hard not to roll his eyes. "*I accept your offering, my daughters, to the flame of purification.*"

"That's it?" Persei said.

Jukaro looked mortified. "These are ancient words on a delicate relic that was only recovered yesterday! We are the first to read them in a millennium."

Mirasha nudged Persei in the ribs. "Do you know why the statue came down?" she asked.

"It seems it was hidden away in a back room... and the room was trapped. To protect it?"

"Could we put it back where it belongs?" Persei asked.

The idea rattled Jukaro. "Well, it needs to be officially cataloged, and studied... it is ancient after all. We can't just go around—"

"I think we should try," Mirasha said. "Look at the frieze behind it. Look at the walls. All this will make more sense if it is set up as it was meant to be. Restored to its former glory."

"Where does it go?" Persei asked, looking around for some sign, Mirasha joining him in the inspection. It was difficult in the wavering light of the lamp, but he located rough portions of the floor that matched up with the broken bottom of the statue, roughly in the center of the raised altar area. "This looks like the spot."

Sweating profusely, Jukaro shook his head. "I can't sanction this... we could get in so much trouble."

Mirasha put her hand on his quivering arm and looked into his eyes. "But my dear Jukaro, if you were excited just to read the inscription, how much more exhilarating would it be to witness this statue returned to its rightful home? You would be living history, not just cataloging it! Just imagining it makes me..." She shivered as her voice trailed off.

Poor bastard. How can he resist?

Jukaro couldn't. His eyes darted around, from the statue to her face to her chest and back again in a fitful circuit. He could barely form words with her so close. "Well... I guess... it would be incredible. But how are we going to lift it up?"

Persei snorted, but got a good grip on the statue, making sure one was on a breast and the other started on a hip before sliding slightly behind. To make her jealous somehow? Even though he knew she was just using the pathetic scholar, it still hurt on some level to have to watch.

"Just make sure to guide the flames so they can connect," Jukaro said as Persei heaved it up, muscles flexing. If the bronze weren't hollow he would have needed to ask for help.

He lifted the statue onto its former home, facing the entrance, while the others helped nudge it into place. He felt a surge of heat on his sandaled feet, and suddenly the jagged edge was gone. The statue looked like it had been there forever.

Jukaro's eyes bugged out, and he tottered on the verge of fainting.

"So what do we do now?" Persei asked.

"Follow the inscription," Mirasha said.

"But the instructions were not very specific," Jukaro said. "We would need the right type of livestock... and besides, actually performing these kind of rites is strictly prohibited, both by Maruthan traditional religious law, not to mention by the Pazian edicts."

Mirasha's eyes flicked from Jukaro to the statue with a sly smile.

There was something intoxicating about the illicit nature of what she seemed to be suggesting. Persei gestured for Jukaro to join him in front of the statue. "Jukaro, come here for a moment. I think I understand."

The scholar walked over to stand next to him, Mirasha's eyes following him with what looked like... *hunger?* Anger and jealousy burned inside Persei, but he strained to keep his voice level. "They would kneel here, wouldn't you think? Let's try it." Jukaro reluctantly joined him on his knees before the beautiful statue.

In a flash, Persei grabbed Jukaro and pressed his face to the floor. The man yelped. "What... what are you doing?"

"Don't you think the old goddess should be respected? She was very powerful, you know." Persei turned the scholar's face so he could look in his beady eyes. "You know more than you're telling us. I suggest you spit it out. Unless you'd rather experience the delights of Zalikko's purifying flame."

He flinched at the name, but his fear was mixed with an equal measure of bewilderment. "I don't know what you're talking about!"

"You seemed awfully interested in what Yalath and the others were doing. How did you lose track of them?"

"The rebels... the rebels caught us, and I gave them up."

"Why did they leave this temple? Did they find what they seek?"

"They found some clue, but they needed to look at the fragments of the frieze that had been recovered... and cataloged. They're at the other dig site."

Mirasha walked over to the damaged frieze. "This one?" she asked.

Jukaro nodded his head. "They thought it was significant, somehow. But I don't know what they were looking for."

"Where did they go after they disappeared?" Persei asked.

"I don't know. They were missing for almost a day. And of course there's a rumor they were involved in the break-in at the other camp. But nothing seemed to be missing from the storehouse, and no signs of entry at the other sites. The next day they resurfaced here, and were being detained until I could see them to get their final report before they left."

"Detained?"

"They were going to leave without talking to me, but official policy dictates that they must check in and give their full report."

"But they never did?"

"No, they... they somehow broke out. It's a matter of some confusion. The front door was guarded, but somehow there was an unknown back door that they used to escape. And there was a chase… None of us know what happened to them. But only three of them ran from the rebels, along with their horse."

"Who was missing?"

"The old man, Yalath. He wasn't here, he was nowhere to be found. He must have slipped out by himself, or be hiding here somewhere. He couldn't have just vanished."

Persei and Mirasha traded a look.

"And the rebels lost them as well?" Persei asked.

"Apparently. Maybe you should ask them."

"Who do you really work for, Jukaro?" she asked, her tone becoming much more threatening.

"I work for the office of the Prefect of Antiquities, like I already told you. I'm just here to make sure everything is preserved."

"I know a liar. Though you conceal it well. Do you know who I am?"

Persei considered stopping her. It would complicate things if the knowledge got out that he was harboring the daughter of the greatest threat to Pazh in a generation.

Again the man shook his head.

"My father was Shadush, Grand Thane of the Scentari. He discovered an ancient holy place, much like this one. He made a sacrifice, and unlocked great power. The power of dark flames."

A deeper, more complete terror filled Jukaro's eyes. Terror born from understanding.

"What do you know of what happened with the Scentari?" Persei asked him.

"Just rumor that he was a warlock, used dark magic… killed so many."

Persei grabbed a fistful of hair and yanked the head back. "Liar! Only the military had the full information. Rumors would barely have reached here by now. No, you have sources… connections. Who are they?"

Jukaro stared up at him with open mouth but no voice escaping. Something was still holding him back.

"Do you want to live, Jukaro?" Persei asked. "Or would you rather be my sacrifice to The Devourer? That is your choice. Tell me who you are working for. Who else wants to know what Yalath and the others are doing?"

The quivering scholar's voice came out a whisper: "They only ask me to report what I see. They told me about Shadush. They were very concerned about any outsiders coming to visit the temples. They were Pazian."

"Who? I want names!" Persei put his hobnailed sandal on the man's back, but only with enough pressure to cause mild discomfort.

"I don't have names." Persei put half his weight on that foot. Jukaro gasped. "My rib! Keepers! They call themselves the Keepers. I don't know of what. But definitely Pazian. Please, just let me go. I won't tell a soul."

"What do you think, Mirasha?"

She shook her head at the pathetic figure lying before the statue. "I think he knows too much."

"But you said..." Jukaro began struggling, and Persei had to actually put some muscle into holding his arms down. His legs thrashed wildly. Persei yanked the man's arms back, using his boot as leverage, and twisted the hobnails into Jukaro's back. Screams of pain echoed off the walls.

Mirasha looked at Persei expectantly. "Say the prayer. Make your offering."

Persei tried to form the words from what he remembered Jukaro saying. No chance to ask him now. He'd have to improvise. "Oh Zalikko..." The words sounded flat, hollow.

"Do you mean it, or not?" Mirasha asked, recognizing his reluctance. "Do you truly want this?" Her challenge angered him. And more. If he didn't do this, he'd lose her respect... lose her. Burning anger, fear and all different colors of lust mixed together, warming his body all the way up to his tongue.

The words leaped out, fully formed. "Oh, Zalikko, I offer myself to you for your purification. Take this gift, this offering. Burn it! Consume it! Share with me a spark of your glory!"

What came next seemed like a dream.

The eyes of the statue blazed like hot coals, and waves of heat shimmered in the air around him, spreading to his hands. They became so hot it was almost unbearable, and Jukaro's screams turned to shrieks of agony as black flames erupted from Persei's fingers onto the spindly golden arms. That same dark fire that haunted Persei's dreams, calling to him, was now consuming another victim. Just like all his fellows and superiors on the banks of the Sentusi. Only this time he had called it into existence.

Jukaro flailed against his grip as the flames trickled down his arms to his back. But Persei was left untouched, unharmed. He locked eyes with Mirasha, who drank it all in with the same elation he felt. Exultant in the unlocking of this power. She wanted to share in this with him. She wanted to be with him in every way, at his side, as he channeled this power into the future he deserved. The feelings sweeping through him blocked out the pitiful wailing of Jukaro's final moments.

Visions flashed through Persei's head. Himself on a throne, a crown on his head. Mirasha at his side. Not just fire at his command, but water too. Daymar begging at his feet. Or dead, giving Persei his rightful place in the Senate. Multitudes bowing before him. It would all be his, but he needed to secure not just this power, but water as well. He saw himself in the bowels of the water temple, drawing on something that looked like liquid metal...

The visions cleared and he once again saw Mirasha standing next to the statue, two beauties in his life. His sandal sunk through the pile of ashes that was all that remained of Jukaro. Yet the skin on his hands was smooth and perfect, other than a coating of black ash.

"You did it!" Mirasha said, her voice filled with almost girlish excitement as she skipped to his side.

Persei nodded. She had never looked more beautiful. All that lust and desire was channeled into the one avenue right in front of him. He wanted her. Now.

"How did it feel?"

Was she also feeling it? The power? She looked hungry for him—to share it.

"Incredible. Like I was made for this."

"So can you control it now? Like my father could?"

He held out one hand and willed the flames to reappear. Down deep, somewhere, the power was there, but out of reach. The anger of futility coursed through his body. "It's there... but I can't. I can't tap into it."

Her disappointment was like a slap in the face. He couldn't bear to fall short in her eyes. But her voice was understanding. "Maybe it's because the goddess isn't really here? Maybe this is just some kind of echo, accepting the sacrifice? But doesn't have the power to grant you what you want."

"But I had visions. I saw myself wielding both fire and water. It seemed like a promise. But first I have to find the water."

"Did the vision show you where?"

"The water temple. Where the others went. Our trails continue to converge. We will find them, seize the power, and kill them. And in the vision, I saw what we need." He took her in his arms, and she didn't resist, despite the ash. Her closeness stirred him.

Her look changed. "I can feel what *you* need."

"Don't some of these pagan goddesses accept *other* kinds of offerings?" He did his best to wipe his hands on his tunic before pulling off her dress.

"It's worth a try," she breathed into his ear, lifting up his tunic.

XX

ᎶᏋᎶᏋᎶᏋᎶ

Leisure

Walls of the same dark stone as the cliff face loomed before Simon and Remeth, spreading out in both directions, from the mountain all the way to the water. Taller than those of the capital. The inhabitants certainly wanted to keep people out. *Or in?*

They had spent much of the walk discussing how strange it would be to live in such isolation, shut off from world trade and relying solely on local products and materials. The idea was completely foreign to Simon, having grown up among merchants and goods flowing into the capital from all over the Republic and beyond.

The wagon track led down to a small gate, a metal door barely larger than the wagon.

"I don't think they have much wood here," Simon said.

Remeth gave him a puzzled look.

"Never mind. So how do we get in? I don't see any sentries."

Remeth knocked.

Simon scanned the wall, catching a flash of movement in one of the arrow-slits above the gate.

"They know we're here."

Remeth shrugged again. He was too comfortable just talking his way through anything. Hopefully his Talent still worked despite a comprehension gap.

The door swung open, nearly knocking them over. Simon hunched over like he'd been practicing. He cursed Remeth inwardly, who looked far more comfortable in the pose.

Six short, dark and sturdy men strode out, encircling Simon. Clad in leather armor and round metal helmets, they brandished oversized hammers and looked surly enough to use them.

Simon and Remeth held up their hands at the same time.

One guard flashed bright white teeth in a snarl. His eyes were that same light gray as the wagon driver, almost white. The contrast from the skin was striking, and very unnatural. The little man held up his hammer to threaten Simon, and barked a command in Aktirian. While Simon didn't understand a word, he was starting to recognize the sound and rhythm.

You're up, Remeth.

Remeth made conciliatory gestures to the lead guard, speaking slowly and simply. *Was he playing a fool?* The lead guard looked from Remeth to Simon and back again before pointing the hammer at Simon with a grunted challenge.

With no possible explanation for why Remeth might be able to translate, he spoke for himself in Pazian. "My ship hit the rocks off the coast. I'm the only survivor."

The guards looked at him in uncomprehending wonder. He could only imagine how strange his words would sound to those who had never heard a foreign tongue.

He put his hands to his mouth to mime eating and drinking. "Food? Water?"

The lead guard peered up at him with those disconcerting eyes and breath that reeked of salted fish. He fingered Simon's tunic before flicking it away in dismissal. He questioned Remeth, who replied with a slow explanation, miming the shape of a box. The guard tapped his foot through it all, before jabbing a dark finger into Remeth's face, as if addressing a disobedient child. Remeth nodded in response to the stern warning, bowing almost to the ground. The guard huffed and signaled the others, who ushered Simon and Remeth through the doorway.

The corridor spanned ten feet and was well lit. *So much stone—*

The guards shoved them through a similar doorway at the opposite end, and into the city. Though it was late afternoon, the shadow of the mountain cast everything in the gray light of dusk.

The last guard shook his head before slamming the door shut behind them. Simon breathed a sigh of relief, but kept his voice low. "What did you say to them?"

Remeth's vacant expression and bemused smile perfectly fit his new role. "The simpleton was out walking and saw you crawling in from the shore. I helped you up and you were nice, so I was bringing you for dinner. They chastised me for going outside the walls alone, and never want to see me again." He laughed. "Oh, and to take good care of my new pet."

"Well at least they didn't take me away to prison, or kill me on sight. So maybe they're not totally against strangers?" He pulled the hood of his cloak over his face to divert at least some of the attention. "But how can we go out the gate again?"

Remeth stared blankly, playing his new role.

"Great, so now you do the talking, but you're an idiot?"

"Look at all the tall buildings," Remeth said, with a look of slack-jawed amazement.

Simon scowled, already tired of the act, but followed his gaze. All the buildings were that same dark gray stone, and three and four stories weren't unusual. They were more solid and practical than pretty, built to last. Peering over the tallest buildings was an imposing fortress. *Who is in charge of this place?* Simon checked the blood again, thankful that his little window made it easier. It pointed straight to the fortress, which Remeth noted with a nod.

Remeth shambled along, gawking at all the new sights, while Simon followed a half-step behind. The gravel street was nearly empty, and the dull iron doors of the buildings closed. In Pazh iron was not only expensive, but sacred to Salar, the Iron One. Outfitting the legions was the first priority, leaving cheaper metals for most regular uses. For it to be so plentiful here was intriguing.

They passed their first locals: a young couple in love who didn't give them even a glance. Both wore the same plain gray wool, him in shirt and pants, the woman in shirt and a long skirt. She was similar height to her man, and squat in her case translated into pleasantly curvy. *More to Persei's taste. Where is he? And more importantly, Zaliakara?* The thought refocused Simon on their goal, and highlighted the frivolity of their current sightseeing.

"This is a waste of time," Simon said after they were out of earshot. "We should do our best to rule out Kashaka being here, then get back to Elysia and Zeno."

"I'm enjoying it. Did you see that couple? So sweet."

Was he still acting as the simpleton? Though he seemed to be genuinely happy for them.

Another block, and Remeth was pointing again. This time to what looked like a tavern, with the front of the building open into the street. Half the iron tables were full of locals eating and drinking, mostly men, other than a server with a shorter skirt and her hair tied back.

Simon's stomach rumbled, so he followed the simpleton inside.

The woman cocked an eyebrow when she saw the two of them and started to turn away, but Remeth was insistent in holding up two fingers. Her accent sounded a bit less harsh in her reply, and she led them to a table behind four burly men. They were clean-shaven, again with the close-cropped hair, one balding. All wore matching iron gray robes that left their arms bare, and chains around their necks holding smooth iron disks. None paid him any heed, focusing instead on the rear end of the serving woman as she walked to the back of the shop.

She returned with a steaming platter of fish surrounded with piles of mushy yellow goo. It didn't look very appetizing, but Remeth smiled and pointed, clapping his hands. She smiled at Remeth like she would to a child, but frowned when Simon kept his hood low.

Remeth answered her question deliberately, pointing to what the other men were eating. When she tried to ask Simon, Remeth again answered for him, this time sticking out his tongue and miming cutting it off.

Now I'm a mute?

She flinched, wrinkling her nose, but to her credit tried to cover it with an apologetic tone and Remeth nodded, matching her frown. But when he pointed to the clay mugs of the men at the other table, the simple delight returned. He signaled first two, then with a sly grin pried open two more fingers to proudly hold up four. She nodded, patted his arm, and headed back to the kitchen. Simon had to admit, the robed men were on to something with the view. Which sent a pang of guilt through him as he imagined Elysia out in the cool evening with just the sleeping Zeno for company.

"Four drinks?" he whispered to Remeth when he made sure nobody was looking.

"Relax."

"But we still have to check—"

Remeth shushed him when the server returned to set four mugs on the table, two in front of each of them. She loomed over the table with an expectant look. Remeth made a great show of rifling through his pouch, before giving up, confused. He held out one finger to Simon. Simon reached into his pouch and withdrew a silver Pazian coin and held it out to her.

The woman's eyes lit up as she palmed the coin and Remeth

smiled his big dumb smile. One of the other patrons called out to her from inside the shop, and she bowed her head slightly and excused herself.

"You sure know how to charm them," Remeth said. "I told her to keep the change. I think we're going to get some excellent service." He held up a mug to Simon, who reluctantly took it.

The dark brown liquid gave off a pungent mix of smells: sour and yeasty, almost like bread, with an undercurrent of alcohol.

Remeth took a big sip while Simon was still inspecting his. "Try it," he said.

Simon was more tentative. It tasted sour and more than a little bitter, with a definite grainy flavor. "I prefer wine," he said quietly, his mouth blocked by the mug.

"Live a little. Enjoy something new, like the locals do!"

The second drink was somewhat better. "Maybe with food—"

He swallowed his words as the server returned with their platter and a couple of plates. It was half as large as what the other men had almost finished devouring. Steaming hot fish with the skin removed, the white flesh juicy and succulent, seasoned with… definitely pepper, and some other more acid smell. Vinegar? And other spices he couldn't recognize. His stomach rumbled its approval.

When she set it on the table, another smell assaulted them, sour and almost sweaty, wafting from the circle of mushy yellow balls that surrounded the fish. A closer inspection revealed a bumpy texture like lumps of yellow tongues, each about the size of a fig. Remeth clapped again, his eyes looking almost as large as the dish, while Simon had to steel himself to have a taste. It appeared she was going to stay for the show.

Remeth popped one into his mouth. After chewing it slowly and carefully, he beamed at her, sighing with delight as he turned to Simon. Was there a wicked gleam in his eye?

Simon's stomach tightened as he plucked a single squishy ball. *What in the world are these?* A slightly salty smell behind the sour hinted at a maritime origin. The bumps on the surface were soft and fleshy. Not enjoying the feel of it in his hand, he slurped it into his mouth.

And was surprisingly not disgusted by the taste: creamy, almost nutty, but with a heavy layer of salt. He felt the tension float away, and almost licked his lips, before remembering not to show the tongue that wasn't supposed to be there. The server chuckled and left them to their food.

Remeth scooped several more handfuls of the yellow mystery seafood. "Don't know, don't want to know. But good, huh?"

Simon allowed himself a nod and chased it down with another drink. The flavor was starting to grow on him.

"Admit it, you're having fun too!" Remeth reached over to tear open the fish and yelped when steam poured out. He licked his hand, and two men from the other table pointed at him and laughed. Simon shrunk a little lower in his seat, burying his face in his mug. The last thing he wanted was more attention.

Simon gingerly peeled away the sides of the fish, down to the bone, letting the steam escape without harming his fingers. He'd learned the trick in the wild. The first piece was warm and firm in his mouth, with a nice crust of pepper, and a fruity tang. Whoever these people were, they sure could cook.

"This is fantastic," Remeth said, his mouth half full.

"We should save some for Elysia."

"Will be a shame to miss out on the opportunity to have it warm, and accompanied by this sweet nectar." Remeth downed his second mug and waved to the server.

"Settle down," Simon said. "You're becoming a little verbose for a simpleton."

"Maybe I found my inspiration?" He licked his lips and held his mug upside down toward the server, with two fingers raised on the other hand. "I wonder what they call this delightful drink? Shame they don't export it. All of it. But if the food and drink is this good, no wonder they don't want to leave. And the locals have a certain... robust charm." His eyes danced from the server to linger on the men at the other table.

Remeth downed the next mug at one go, drawing a roll of the server's eyes, but applause from the other table. Simon groaned.

The bald man walked toward them, mug in hand, while hailing the server and pointing to Remeth. His features were strong and square, like they were carved out of the ubiquitous stone of this strange city. Simon reckoned the men to be about a head shorter than him if he weren't forced to slouch. His companions followed him, with the bald leader choosing the seat to Simon's right on the iron bench, with another man on his left and two more flanking Remeth, who grinned stupidly.

The server returned with a platter full of mugs, twelve in all. The bald man assigned them two each. But while similar, this drink looked a bit darker and smelled at least twice as strong. *This could get messy.*

Simon tried to wave it away, but the bald man laughed and put a strong arm around him. Remeth rubbed his hands together, patted his two new neighbors on their bare shoulders, and raised a mug as a toast. With a hearty cheer the others all downed their first.

Shaking his head, Simon took a large sip that burned in his throat. It earned him another clap on the back from the bald man, who was already on to his second. The man said something in an accusatory voice, which elicited more mime from Remeth about the missing tongue. The bald man was incredulous, and Simon cringed when he thought the man might want to see proof... but instead he seemed intent on encouraging Simon to finish the drink. Any late afternoon cold was gone as the dark liquid warmed him from the inside. Simon's head felt a little lighter, but he kept his tongue firmly hidden in his mouth.

Remeth led them in draining the next round, and his mug put a dent in the table when he slammed it down with a resounding clang. It earned a hearty chorus of laughter from men, but a stern rebuke from the server.

Remeth's babbling only increased as the server returned for round after round. Simon lagged well behind them and the bald man soon lost interest in his consumption.

When their cups were empty again, Remeth put a hand on the shoulders of his two neighbors, attempting to stand up to order another round. But instead of letting go, he gave them a squeeze and after an appraising look ran both hands down the right man's arm, caressing the well-defined muscles and making approving noises. While he looked to be enjoying himself immensely, the man grew increasingly tense. When Remeth's hand strayed under the man's shirt to his chest, the man slapped it away and jumped to his feet.

Simon reached under his cloak for the hilt of his sword.

The man raised his fist, but Remeth smiled and licked his lips, saying something far too sassy for the heated situation. The fist connected, sending Remeth sprawling face first into the remains of the fish.

The bald man seized Simon's sword arm with one meaty hand,

and with the other pulled back his hood. The other men gasped, but the bald man stuck out his tongue. Simon gagged on the strong smell of alcohol, but not seeing any other option, he opened his mouth to show his whole tongue.

"Remeth?" he asked.

The puncher held Remeth down on the table, while his neighbor pressed the remains of the fish in his hair.

The frantic server screamed at them, pointing out of the shop. The bald man reached into a pouch and tossed a few gray coins—*iron again?*—to the woman with a grunt, and with the assistance of his colleague pulled Simon roughly to his feet. Pinned, Simon was powerless to stop him from drawing the sword. With narrowed eyes he inspected Simon's features and yelled something to the others. They yanked the struggling Remeth away from the table. A yellow glob covered one eye, while shards of fish surrounded his inane grin.

The bald man shouted a question. It all seemed surreal, being tipsy and at the opposite end of his own sword, interrogated in an foreign tongue.

"Remeth? What is he saying?"

Remeth belched. "Why are you here?"

The bald man switched the point to Remeth's chest, and his next question was vicious. Simon was effectively inventing his own translations based on context and inflection.

"Yeah, Remeth, how can you understand the foreigner?"

"His big strong companions are quite handsome, in their rugged way. But I don't like this bald one very much."

"He has my sword, so I think it's time to use that charm."

Remeth winked with his uncovered eye, but one of his captors slapped away his attempt at a question. With a shove, they urged them to get moving. Remeth could barely keep his feet and put his arms around his grumbling new friends as they half-dragged him along.

Simon, despite the slight woolliness in his head, was able to keep walking unsupported. The sword point at the small of his back helped to focus his wits.

"Where are they taking us?" Simon asked.

"It sounded like 'Lord of the Coin', but that sounds a little silly." One of the men cuffed Remeth, and he shut up.

Despite the deepening shadows, Simon tried to keep a mental

map of their route. A left, then a right, onto a more major street toward the keep. *And Kashaka?*

Chubby little children huddled behind their parents, eyes wide. They were dressed in shirts and pants or skirts like the other commoners, marking their captors as different. And from the reactions of the bystanders, worthy of deference and respect. All eyes stared at him. These men were already taller than the local average, so Simon towered over the rest. For the first time in his life, it was his height that marked Simon as different—not the color of his skin. So he stood up proud.

But nobody would be helping him escape.

ଵେଵେଵେଵ

Elysia sat on the scraggly grass, curled up next to the snoring Zeno. The sky deepened in color to match the shadow of the mountain. She was taking a break from another attempt at carving that strange wooden snake. The form still eluded her, with everything but the head amorphous and unclear. Instead of revenge, frustration dominated her mind, as she imagined the exotic delicacies Simon and Remeth were sampling behind the walls of the city while she chewed on day-old flatbread. She wished she could be with them, experiencing the sights, smells and tastes of a new place, but she couldn't leave Zeno alone.

Not that it looked like anyone would be coming along to visit.

No sooner had the thought crossed her mind but the faint sound of hooves clapping on stone filtered over the hill. A rattling sound followed close behind—a wagon? With no cover, she was exposed, and hid her carving tool under her cloak, while clutching the bag of her other carvings.

There was nowhere to run or hide. And she couldn't leave Zeno. She'd just have to hope that whoever was coming would ignore them, or at least leave her be. She crouched next to Zeno, wary and watchful, ready to respond to any situation.

A shaggy pony crested the hill first, pulling a wagon with a driver. The man was big. Not tall, but very wide and dark—even darker than Simon. It was the pony that noticed them first, sniffing and turning to look straight at them.

Even from thirty feet away, and in the low light, the man's eyes shone pale and eerie. He reined his pony to a stop and called out to her, gesturing for her to approach.

She gripped the handle of her carving knife, willing him to go on his way.

He strained to look past her, at Zeno's covered form, and he pointed with another question. When again she didn't respond, he climbed down from his wagon and started toward her. He was short, squat, and very powerfully built.

She stood, panicked thoughts racing through limited options. She couldn't fight him off. She might be able to outrun him, but couldn't leave Zeno. But what if... She didn't even want to think of what this man would want. *Oh Simon, where are you?*

As he approached, his gaze lingered on her chest, and when he was close enough that she could make out his features, he stared at her skin with a leering curiosity that made her skin crawl. His next question was followed by a knowing smile, but not a kind one. Her heart sank.

Zeno stirred behind her, weakly turning his head to size up the approaching threat. His ears flattened and he snarled, but Elysia could tell that even the show of defiance was a strain. He couldn't protect her. It was all on her.

The man stopped, taking a closer look at Zeno. A different kind of desire took hold in his eyes, and he muttered to himself. Now less than ten feet away, he waved his meaty hand, again asking her to come to him.

She chided herself for not acting first. But how? She had no magic to wield against him; she hadn't brought anything close to life in weeks. Not with her thoughts so dark and muddled, thinking always of Persei and death.

He advanced again, walking faster now. He was too close.

She held out her carving knife, bringing him to a halt, and he raised his hands in surprise. But her cloak parted, drawing his gaze down to her chest, with a more brazen leer.

Her hand shook, but more with fear than anger.

He forced a laugh, but his body tensed up, as he bent his knees slightly as if he were about to...

He charged.

Waving the knife around kept the big hands from clutching her. When she nicked his arm, he bellowed and bared ugly teeth. Strong fingers struggled to grab her, but she twisted and slashed until he let go with a gasp that reeked of alcohol.

Panic blanked her mind and she bolted, stumbling over loose stones and bare rock but never losing her footing. She had to get away. Away from this brute of a man and his desires and...

She dared a backward glance to gauge his pursuit, but he wasn't following. He was eying her as he crouched next to Zeno, who was hissing and snarling, but unable to fend him off.

"No!"

He laughed again and pointed first to her then Zeno, before holding up both palms like a set of scales. Giving her the choice.

She froze, not wanting to forget her friend, her baby, her creation. But could she even buy his safety by giving herself up to this foul man?

He laughed again and yanked away the blanket, exposing all of Zeno. His light eyes flared wide and he jumped to his feet, warding himself. But when Zeno didn't make any move to harm him, he started flapping his arms like wings, mocking both of them as he danced around.

She was so alone, so helpless.

XXI
ᘒᘒᘒᘒᘒᘒᘒ
Prisoners

The keep stuck out from the face of the mountain like a massive square jaw. The bald man spoke with familiarity to the two armed guards flanking iron double-doors, and they waved them through.

The square room inside was dimly lit by torches along the walls. Simon and Remeth were prodded left and walked down a corridor to another iron door on the right, again manned by two guards. The door opened on a set of stairs leading down.

The whole group descended slowly, careful on their drink-addled feet. Simon only felt a little unsteady, but tried to mimic their shuffling gait. Near the bottom, one of Remeth's captors stumbled, sending the three of them sprawling down the remaining steps to land in a jumbled heap.

"At least wait until we're alone," Remeth said, earning himself another smack in the face. Simon couldn't imagine how he had survived Yalath's truculence. Or was this the release after bottling himself up too long?

Simon had to crouch so he wouldn't hit his head on the low ceiling, drawing a laugh from one of the men.

The bald man rapped on another door. When it opened, a stale mix of sweat and urine assaulted Simon's nose, and the man who peered out wore a twisted frown and a nose that turned sharply like it had been broken in two different places. He brightened at the sign of the two captives and ushered them inside.

Iron bars fenced off five separate pens in the large room, suitable for keeping animals. *Or people.* Several feet separated the pens, and faintly human shadows huddled in the far corners of two.

The ugly man directed their captors to take everything but their clothes, placing the packs, pouches, and Simon's sheath on a table in the middle of the room.

Simon cursed himself for not secreting some of his painting supplies in his clothes. They were all in his pack. Remeth and Simon were shoved into cells on opposite sides of the room, and the jailer locked them in. After a low conversation with the jailer, the bald man left with his men.

Simon's cell was completely empty. "What did they say?" Simon called out to Remeth, who had sprawled out like he was falling asleep.

No response from Remeth, but the jailer shouted at him. Simon held up his hands in apology and slunk deeper in his cell.

The shape in the cell next to Simon shuffled closer.

"Pazian?" the man asked, in a voice creaking from disuse, and intonation that sounded similar to the locals.

"Yes," Simon said, moving to that side of the cell. In the dim light the gray eyes looked eerily inhuman. His broad frame and dark skin resembled the locals, but his clothes were in tatters, his face emaciated, and his long scraggly hair and beard set him apart from the rest. He also stank. "How can you speak Pazian?"

"Live in Pazh. Many years before." His speech was slow and halting, like he was having trouble remembering the words.

"You left here? And then came back?"

The man nodded. "Mother sick. Medicine."

"Why are you a prisoner?"

"Outside people, outside ideas... not... not good here."

"So I see."

"Why you here?"

"My friend got into some trouble with the bald man."

"Yurek? Bad idea."

"Bad idea."

"Your friend, not from here. Look Aktirian. But no Aktirian start trouble with Coinbrother."

"No, he's... well... it's complicated. We just need to get out."

The man sighed. "Me too."

"Did you hear what... Yurek said to the jailer?"

"J... jailer? Kalnek?" The jailer, who had appeared to be dozing, opened his eyes and looked at them. He grunted and stretched out in his chair while watching them. "Yurek say Lord of Coin see him in morning."

"Who is the Lord of Coin?"

The man looked at Simon like he was the simpleton. "You

don't know Lord of Coin? You have problem with Coinbrother? How long in Aktiri?"

"We... got here this morning."

Curiosity simmered in those unsettling eyes. "By ship?"

Simon paused, considered his words carefully. "What's your name?" Simon asked.

"Tirin. You?"

"Simon Baroba. Pleased to meet you Tirin. How long have you been in here?"

"Too long. Many years."

"Did your Mother come back to see you after you were captured?"

His eyes blazed, like embers flickering with the memory of past rage.

"Dead. They let her die, with me here."

"Family?"

The hard face wilted. "Wife... gone, children... never saw my children."

Simon sobered up, imagining Elysia and his father living the rest of their lives never knowing how or why he disappeared.

"Tell me more about the Lord of the Coin."

"First, tell me how you get here. Not by ship? Then how?"

The enemy of my captor is my friend. "By horse."

Tirin swatted away his words like an annoying fly. "You crazy like your friend." He jerked his thumb at Remeth's snoring body.

"It's true. We flew here on a horse."

"What you say? Ride?" The curiosity was back.

"Fly, like a bird."

Tirin's eyes opened impossibly wide, and Simon could see the blood vessels streaking them like a labyrinth.

Simon nodded. "A flying horse. Magic."

Tirin shook his head. "Kid story."

"That's what I thought, until a few months ago."

"Your magic?"

"No."

"*His?*"

"No."

"Where is flying horse?"

"Outside the city, a few hours walk through... the southeast gate?"

"You leave magic horse, come to city, and get captured?" The words were flowing faster now, more naturally. The man pursed his lips. "Not sure you have good idea to get out."

Simon laughed at the absurdity of the situation, rousing the jailer. He shouted at Tirin, who bowed his head and apologized. The jailer grunted again and went back to his rest.

"He said not to wake him again."

"Sorry."

"Why in Aktiri?"

"Our horse was tired from carrying all of us."

"All? How many more?"

Damn, he was quick. Simon sighed, resigned to trusting this man as their best bet for local information. "My... wife to be. She is watching the horse."

"Wife? But Yurek said..."

"What did Yurek say?"

He flushed. "Don't turn back on them or might..." He paused, either unsure of what to say, or unwilling to say it.

"They took my sword. I'm no threat."

Tirin shook his head. "No, no... he mean..." Tirin thrust his hips forward.

Shocked, Simon held up his own hands. "No, no... not..." But then he looked over at Remeth and remembered his behavior.

"Man love man... against law here... against Book of Coin."

Remeth, you stupid ass... of all the things to joke about. Simon shook his head. "Well I can assure you I am not... I... a woman has my heart."

"And your friend?" Tirin looked at Remeth with more than a little unease, or even disgust.

"He was just playing around," Simon said, without being totally sure. "You keep mentioning the Coin. What is all of this about the Coin?"

"You know nothing of Aktiri?"

"I don't think anyone from Pazh does."

"All connected. Lord of Coin rule island, like father before him, and son after him. Except son dumber than your friend. Lord is like... your President, but for life, and High Priest. Coin is symbol of Shygakar, our creator. He made Aktiri out of his body, give himself for us, protect and give what we need. He leave son as Lord of the Coin. Chosen ones are Coinbrothers, like Yurek. Only strong, loyal men. People think they protect us from outside, who want to steal what we have."

"Like what?"

"Shygakar's Blood. Iron. From inside his body... the mountain."

"And the Coinbrothers control that?"

"Control everything." His tone turned bitter. "Use faith and fear for control my people. Not like your people, free. I see life outside, but they don't want people to know. Stupid one easy to control."

"So that's why they locked you up?"

Tirin nodded.

"But why would Pazh just leave Aktiri alone here? You're in the middle of the Near Sea, and they control everything around you."

"Treaty."

Simon raised an eyebrow. "But I thought you were shut off?"

"Treaty from early days of Pazh. Aktiri and Pazh leave other alone."

"From the early days? You mean after they conquered Marutha?"

"No. Back to beginning. Five hundred years? More?"

"That doesn't make sense." Simon sighed, letting it all sink in. Remeth had broken the law and violated the religion with his actions, and now had them locked up on the order of the theocratic absolute rulers. Without any way to get out, and no way to let Elysia know where they were or that they needed help.

Simon glanced at his pack on the table.

"Tirin, do you think you could convince K... the jailer to give me something from my pack?"

"Like what? You have magic key?"

"No, but... I'm a painter. I have paints and brushes there in my pack. If I'm going to be here a while, it would help me pass the time."

"He is greedy, bad man."

"So if there was something in it for him?"

"He not like me."

"Remeth," Simon whispered. The jailer didn't stir, but neither did Remeth.

"Your friend? Remeth?" Tirin said.

Simon nodded, and Tirin went to the far side of his cell and spoke to Remeth. He eventually stirred and looked up, groggy and dazed.

"Remeth, it's me, Simon."

"Nice place they put us up in."

"Thanks to you."

Remeth sat up. "I was just trying to be a good sport."

"You were fondling the priests."

"Fondling? No, just appreciating—" His eyes cleared a bit. "Priests?"

"The ones with the coin necklaces. They run the place."

Remeth cursed in Maruthan. "I wish the priests looked like that back where I come from."

"Enough of that. Our new friend Tirin here said that... loving men, or anything to do with it, is illegal here. Against their holy book."

"Barbarians," Remeth said, indignant.

"You can discuss the merits of tolerance another time. Right now I need you to use that famous charm on our overseer there." He indicated Kalnek with a jerk of his chin. "Encourage him to give me my paints, and I might be able to get us out of here."

Remeth sat up and brushed himself off, preening a little.

Simon held up a hand. "Charm, but for Salar's sake don't flirt with him."

Remeth wrinkled his nose. "I have standards..."

"Not good idea," said Tirin.

"You speak Pazian?"

"Remeth, Tirin. He's been to Pazh and back again. That's why he's a prisoner here. Contaminated with outside ideas."

"If this is purity, I'll take the cesspool. Pleased to meet you, Tirin."

Tirin looked warily at Remeth.

"He's greedy, this jailer," Simon said. "We could try offering some coin, or maybe I could paint him something."

Remeth nodded and got to his feet. He straightened his tunic and reached up to smooth his hair before remembering his disguise. "Tirin, Simon, pretend you're sleeping. I think this would be best one on one. Don't get me wrong, I love an audience, but conspiracy works best in the shadows. What's his name? Our sleeping overseer?"

"Kalnek," Tirin said.

The jailer twitched.

Tirin laid down in his cell and turned toward the wall, while Simon positioned himself to have a view of the jailer and Remeth's cell.

"Kalnek?" Remeth said, a little louder, toward the jailer.

The jailer blinked twice and asked Remeth a question. After a short mime-assisted exchange, punctuated by several glances at Simon, Kalnek walked back to the table where their packs lay. Remeth pointed to Simon's, and the jailer rifled through it. He held up a brush and one of the little wooden boards Simon carried with him.

"Simon," Remeth called out. Simon faked being groggy, shaking his head as he sat up.

"What? I was sleeping."

"Kalnek here," he said, pointing to the jailer, "heard you're a famous Pazian painter, and your work is quite rare and valuable."

"Oh?"

"And if you were to..." Remeth looked to Kalnek for approval, miming painting, "paint something for him, as a... gift... then he might be inclined to improve our stay here."

Simon nodded. "Tell him it would be an honor. Does he have a request?"

The jailer screwed up his face in response to Remeth's question. With a leer he mimed a large bust and hourglass figure.

Such strange patrons. My first commissions as an artist for a general and a jailer.

"He wants a picture of a well-endowed Pazian beauty." The jailer added something, patting his head. "With golden hair."

"Tell him that would normally take a few days, and cost as much as a small villa. But I'll see what I can do with these limited resources. Bring me my things."

Remeth relayed the message, and the jailer nodded eagerly, rushing over to Simon with his pack. Simon pointed out what he needed and the jailer handed the supplies over one by one.

"Can he set up a candle a little closer to my cell for me to see by? No need to worry, I'm not going to burn the place down."

Kalnek set up the light and stood expectantly at the edge of the cell.

Simon sniffed. "I don't like to be watched while I work. Spoils the inspiration."

With a mumbling apology, Kalnek returned to his seat and put up his feet, turning away from Simon.

"What did you tell him you get out of this?" Simon asked.

"As your agent, I get to share in the better treatment. So what do you plan to do?"

"At first I was thinking I could contact Elysia. But I don't want a picture of her falling into the hands of these types. Then I was thinking of painting a hole for us to escape. But we're already underground, and it might be a long way through the stone."

The jailer opened his eyes and glared at Remeth.

"I'll let you get to your work. Let me know if you need anything."

"I'll call when I need a distraction. For now I just need him to fall asleep."

Simon sat with the blank board before him, absently twirling the brush in his fingers.

Think, Simon!

A key? No, Elysia would do a better job of sculpting something like that.

Something for the mechanism?

What about the lock itself? An iron padlock about the size of his hand sealed him in, while the key ring sat safely on the jailer's belt. He'd used a different key on each lock. The lock looked new, well-oiled, with no signs of weakness or corrosion. Even with one of those hammers the guards carried it would take a long while and a lot of noise to open it. *If it were old and rusted maybe, but...*

Rust!

Simon went back to the corner of his cell and started mixing reds and browns. It just might work. He checked over his shoulder and the jailer was sprawled out, snoring. He waited longer, just to make sure, spending the time to get it clear in his head. Simon imagined rust encrusting the part of the lock where it inserted in the rectangular base that housed the spring. In his mind it was weak and thin and with just a hard tug would split apart and grant him freedom. His head felt warm, like it was glowing, and the feeling spread down into his right hand that held the brush.

Armed with the brownish-red paint, Simon reached through the wide bars and began to apply it to the lock. Channeling the idea through his hand, he added first speckles to the metal, then more, and as he worked he felt the texture change from smooth and perfect to rough and pitted.

The other prisoner, who to this point had huddled in the far side of his cell, stood up and stared at Simon, his light eyes like two burning beacons in the reflected candlelight. His beard was barely more than stubble, and his clothes less tattered than Tirin's. Simon put his finger to his lip and prayed the man wouldn't interfere. The man pointed to himself and the door. Simon nodded, and continued his delicate work.

The lock shifted, with the weight pulling down, stressing the now rusted metal. Flakes peeled off with each stroke, exposing undamaged iron below, and Simon repeated the process to work his way through. Sweat beaded on his brow with the exertion and awkward position, but the lock transformed before his eyes until finally it hung by a thin brown thread.

Simon put down his brush and paint to grip the lock with two hands. He pulled, and with a faint groan the metal gave way too quickly, dropping out of his hands when they hit the bars.

The lock hit the floor with a resounding clang.

ᎶᏋᏮᏋᏮᏋᏮ

Elysia watched the man grab Zeno's reins, but shake his head when he noticed there was no bit. He tried coaxing Zeno to stand, but Zeno just closed his eyes and laid down his head.

My poor Zeno.

After more tugging and prodding, and even a slap that was almost enough to send Elysia charging back, the man stopped, his face screwed up in frustration.

He started back toward his wagon, and Elysia retreated to the crest of the hill—as far as she could while still keeping sight of Zeno.

The man kept checking on her as he rifled through his cargo, coming up with a coiled rope that he slung over his shoulder, along with a hammer and an axe.

She felt herself slump at the lost opportunity. Now he was armed, and about to bind her friend. Her hand hurt from squeezing the hilt of the knife.

The man waved his hammer in the air, taunting her again before returning to Zeno. He bound Zeno's legs together, and her majestic steed was too tired to struggle. When the man secured his beautiful wings to his body she cried silent tears.

Simon! Remeth! Where are you?

With a grin in her direction, he picked up the axe. He approached one of the few trees in the area and pulled a branch toward him, hacking it free with a few mighty swings. After chopping it into several pieces, he used the stakes to stretch the ropes tight. Even at full strength, Zeno would be powerless to escape.

Again he called something out, a challenge or a request. Shrugging at her silence, he gathered up their saddlebags and her pack—she realized now she dropped it when she fled—braced them across his wide shoulders, and walked back to his wagon. He stowed them away in the back, under the cover.

When he was done, he urged her once more to come to him. It was darker now, and she couldn't make out his expression. The last light of the sky was fading, and soon it would be night. With the axe in his hand, he took one step toward her, and she flinched. Another, and she backed up. He broke into a run.

She turned and sprinted as fast as she could. She could hear him laughing behind her, but it was getting further away as she went down, down toward the city, away from the wagon and this man and Zeno. She slipped on loose gravel and her ankle twisted, sending her crashing down on jagged stones.

XXII
Guards

The jailer jumped out of his chair, searching for the source of the noise.

Remeth screamed.

When the jailer turned, Simon swung open his cell door and picked up the candle and lock.

Remeth kept shouting while the jailer sneered and brandished Simon's knife, his eyes darting between Simon and the captives.

Short, but sturdy.

Simon edged sideways in front of Tirin's cell, trying to keep his distance. Kalnek snarled a warning, but his eyes betrayed a measure of fear. He stepped clear of the table, but didn't advance any further.

"Not used to anyone being able to fight back?" Simon asked, trying to get closer to Remeth. "Get ready!" he shouted, making it sound like another threat. He waved the rusted lock at Kalnek. "Come on! Are you a coward?"

He must have chosen just the right inflection. The jailer charged knife-first. Simon tossed the candle at Kalnek's face and ducked to swing the lock. A pained shriek masked the crunch of iron on bone, and the man toppled head-first into the bars of Remeth's cell.

Kalnek struggled to his feet with murder in his eyes and wax oozing down his right cheek. Simon brandished the lock, but was out of ideas. His eyes moved to the knife, glinting in the lamplight.

The jailer squealed and went down in a heap, clutching at his crotch.

Remeth grinned as he pulled his leg back through the bars.

"You didn't leave me much room to work with."

"Thanks," Simon said, retrieving his knife and holding it to the jailer's throat. "Tell him if he makes another sound, his tongue will be coming out his neck." He tossed the keys to Remeth. "Let out the others."

"Tirin I understand, but are you sure about the other one?"

"Rapist and murderer," Tirin said, his eyes hard.

"Then leave him in there," Remeth said.

"No, he'll alert the others." Simon looked at the man, and nodded. "And I gave my word."

Remeth freed Tirin first, but took his time letting out the criminal, who immediately strode over to Simon, looked him in the eye, and without warning stomped his bare heel on Kalnek's head. The criminal spat in his now-glassy eye.

"Hey!" Simon said, far too late. "What's his name?" he asked Tirin, who only shook his head.

Remeth translated, but the criminal ignored him, bound and gagged the jailer with rope, and rolled him into the far corner of his former cell, facing the wall.

"Warl," the criminal said when he stepped out.

"Tell Warl that he'll do what we say, at least until we get out of this stronghold. We want to escape, not seek revenge."

"Not able to control him," Tirin said while Remeth relayed the message, "bad idea."

"I hope you're wrong, but there's no turning back now," Simon said.

"Tell that to girls and parents who will suffer."

Warl smirked at Tirin and began rifling through the items on the table. Remeth warded him away from their packs. Simon took his and recovered the materials from the cell.

"Tirin, is this guy the only jailer?"

"Another for night."

"Soon?"

Tirin shrugged his shoulders.

"Anyone else visit?"

"Not often."

"What's the best way out?"

"Front door, or mines."

"Mines? Into the mountain?" Simon shook his head. "But the front door is guarded. And we have only one knife." *Bastard Coinbrother took my sword.*

"Or magic?" Tirin pointed back at the lock.

"You could paint another door, like you did back in Gardisha," Remeth said.

"But where? We'll still need to be at ground level. I wish I had a floor plan."

"Maybe Warl knows something," Remeth said, and Warl gave a one word reply. He'd found another knife, a pouch, and was wearing a cloak that looked like it belonged to the jailer.

"See, not going to listen," Tirin said, "going to mines."

"Then we'll let him go. We need to get out of the city, not go deeper inside. And once the night jailer comes, we could have a full scale manhunt on our hands."

Remeth picked up a short staff and held it up toward Tirin, who flinched. He made a motion of smacking himself with it, and Remeth nodded, handing one to Tirin and keeping one for himself. "What's beside the keep, Tirin?"

"Nothing. Just wall. Blocks mine from city. Not sure why he goes to mine. Get to mine only through keep."

"Do the miners live in the mine?"

"No, in city."

"What do they wear?" Remeth asked.

"More importantly, how many are there?" Simon asked. "If the guards would recognize them, then a disguise won't work. And do they leave all at once at the end of a shift?"

Tirin shrugged again.

"We should get moving," Remeth said, looking at the jailer.

"I know," Simon said, "but I don't like to move without a plan."

Remeth grinned. "Then we'll just have to improvise."

"Your improvisation got us in here in the first place."

"Then I owe you to get us out." Remeth pointed to Warl, who was about to open the door. "If he's going, we should too."

Simon huffed, but nodded. "We'll have to think of something. Just stay quiet."

They followed Warl out into the empty hallway.

"What else is down here?" Simon asked Tirin, who shrugged yet again.

Simon's hand twitched on the hilt of his knife. Since Warl held the only other real weapon, Simon wanted to stay close to him. He wasn't sure Tirin or Remeth could do more than stun anyone with their makeshift arms.

Warl didn't make a sound in his bare feet, while Simon's hobnailed sandals scraped on the stone steps. At the top, Warl met Simon's eye. He held up two fingers and then drew one across his throat. *The guards!* Simon gulped and nodded. He pointed to Warl then to the right. Simon relaxed his hand to get a good grip on the knife, then opened the door, which swung inward.

Warl sprung like a cat with claws bared, slashing at his mark. Simon kicked himself into motion and stabbed the guard on the left in the throat before he had could turn, jerking the blade to tearing open an ugly gash. Blood gushed everywhere, and only fear kept Simon from gagging. He tried to think of Elysia, needing to get back to her and how it justified the action, but he still felt dirty.

Warl was already dragging the body onto the stairs. Remeth whimpered, but Warl silenced him with a hiss. Simon pulled the bloody mess of his own guard through the open door. The guard's hammer hung from his belt, and Tirin freed it, testing the weight. Warl reached for the other one, but Simon grabbed it first. He offered the knife to Remeth, who turned his face away. Simon looked down at the blood dripping from the blade, and wiped it on the guard's pants.

"Take it," he whispered, "it may be all that stands between you and dying here." Remeth accepted it like he wished it would crawl away.

"Won't it be suspicious if the guards are gone?" Remeth asked.

"The pool of blood will be more telling," Simon said, pointing to the ground. Remeth clutched at his mouth and turned away.

Warl was already on the move, his head darting back and forth like a lizard stalking its prey and he took off down the corridor to the right—away from the front doors. He seemed too comfortable with all of this, and with what Tirin had told them. Simon already regretted letting the man go free. But his gut said their chances were better following him, for now. Safety in numbers, such as they were.

Warl disappeared around a corner to the right, bypassing another iron door that faced them at an angle, set into a curved wall. *A tower? The outside?* He could use his Talent to open a doorway, but if there was anywhere they would come into contact with guards, it was likely a tower. *Too risky, with Warl almost out of sight.* He hurried to make up the ground.

Lucky for them, the long corridor was empty, with doors only on the right, none on what Simon guessed was the outer wall. They passed one hall, then a second as they followed Warl. "Do people sleep early here?" Simon asked Tirin, in a whisper.

Tirin nodded. "Sleep after nightfall, wake with first light."

"Then we might have a chance if we can find a good spot to get out."

"But where?" Remeth asked. "There are no rooms on this side. I say we make for the mines. At least there won't be as many guards there."

"But how will we get past the ones that will be there?"

"Leave it to me," Remeth said with a vacant grin.

Warl stopped at another corner up ahead, at what looked like the entrance to the other tower. They'd come the full length of the keep. He held his finger up to his mouth while pointing around the corner. Simon stood with him at the edge of the wall, but approaching footsteps stopped him from looking. He frowned at the other two, taking the hammer in two hands. It was heavy, but well balanced, and would do serious damage to any bones if a blow connected. Remeth held up the knife, and Tirin his hammer.

Simon crouched down to almost floor level to hazard a peek. Two big guards walked toward them at a regular pace, hammers strung from their belts, engaged in what sounded like idle conversation.

Regaining his feet, Simon held up two fingers. Warl gave an appraising nod.

Simon's heart beat in time with the last few footfalls of the approaching guards. One-two, one-two, one—and the head was in sight, one arm outstretched holding a key.

Warl blurred forward and Simon charged three steps while swinging his hammer overhead. With a crack it connected with the man's neck, and he collapsed to the ground, head lolling to the side.

A flash of metal disappeared into the other man's mouth as Warl withdrew his knife from under the jaw. The half-severed tongue bobbed around on a wave of blood. Choking and gagging, the man slumped to the floor.

Remeth turned away, falling to his knees and retching. Alcohol and bile added to the metallic smell of so much blood.

Warl hunched over the body, rifling through pouches. Tirin was on him in a flash, but Warl's parry was too late. Tirin's momentum drove his hammer through Warl's skull like it was a summer melon. The glimpse of the interior was more than Simon could stand. The strange food and drink roiled in his belly, the muscles clenching once, twice, before he was sick on the corpse in front of him. His head spun and he fell toward the mess but Tirin caught his arm.

"Why?" Simon asked.

Tirin's face was resolute. "For my daughter. He could not go free."

Simon nodded. The man likely deserved it, and it might serve to at least confuse the trail. It had been very quiet, for a battle. For a slaughter. Simon felt empty, but any lingering effects of the liquor were gone.

"Looks like they were going up to relieve the guards in the tower," Simon said, pointing to the key. "Which might mean only two in there? Do you think it's worth a shot?"

Tirin nodded. "At least two at mine gate."

"Still feel up to charming your way past more guards?" Simon asked.

Remeth shook his head, looking somehow pale despite his magically darkened skin. "I'll defer to your judgment here."

"Let's try the guard tower."

"Then I have an idea," Remeth said. He crossed over to Simon's fallen opponent, and untied the helmet's leather chin-strap. He tried it on and it rattled a bit. He wrinkled his nose. "Don't your people wash?"

Tirin scowled at him. "You, talking again?"

"I think it can get us the surprise we need. This time, follow my lead. I'd get you to put on the other helmet but..." He didn't even look at the mess of the other two mangled and bloodied bodies sprawled one on top of the other. He handed the knife back to Simon, and took a hammer for himself. He held it a little more comfortably than the knife. *So the blood, more than the violence.*

Simon unlocked the door. A staircase spiraled up to the right, lit by a single torch, leaving the left side in shadow. "Maybe you two can keep them busy, and I can start work on our way out of here?" He locked the door behind them.

Tirin leveled his hammer at Remeth. "Fight? Him?"

Remeth bristled and took a few practice swings with the hammer. "You look like you've barely eaten in years, and I keep myself in shape."

"Why you leave your dinner out there?"

Huffing, Remeth started up the stairs. "A drink says we don't even have to fight."

"You will lose." Tirin shook his head at Simon. "How long?"

Simon was happy to leave the potential fighting to the others. Only with his artist friends would he ever be considered the warrior of the group. In the legion he was far more comfortable with logistics.

"I'll go as fast as I can. Shout if you need me." Tirin disappeared up the stairs behind Remeth, leaving Simon to his work.

Simon faced the exterior wall, envisioning a waist-high tunnel they could crawl through, with the heavy stone sliding outward on runners with just one man pushing. With eyes now adjusting to the low light, he let his Talent flow through him into the outline on the stone.

The painted line opened into a gap, getting deeper and deeper until Simon felt the hint of a cool breeze on his arm. The stairs were quiet and he worked quickly, adding a handle in the middle. This took an even greater exercise of will, to paint lines like Elysia would cut away the stone until the rounded forms were comfortable to the hand. If only she were here to help, but he couldn't live with himself if he put her in such danger. Sweating with the intense exertion, he gripped the handle, bracing his foot against the bottom stair.

God of my mother, let this work.

He put all his remaining strength into the push and... it held fast. He swore under his breath. *Why isn't it... oh.* He'd tried brute force, not connecting to his Talent.

Crouching down again into position for another try, this time he used the tricks Xelos had taught him to channel his desire for freedom and to see Elysia safe.

One... two... three... The stone shuddered and creaked back an inch, then another, sliding more easily until it jumped out to crash onto the street. A gust of wind chilled the sweat dripping down Simon's face.

Echoes of clashing metal reverberated down the stairway.

ᎾᏋᏣᏋᏣᏋᏣ

The only sound Elysia could hear was her own rapid breaths as terror welled up inside her in the near-darkness. She turned back and saw... nothing. The man was gone.

She was totally alone.

The city loomed tall, forbidding and foreign. Filled with how many more men like the one she had just escaped? And only two friends.

She rubbed at her bleeding knees and wept.

ᏀᏋᏩᏋᏩᏋᏩᏀ

With hammer in hand, Simon dashed up three steps at a time. Two floors up and his legs were already complaining, but concern for his friend willed him three more.

Blinding light shone through the doorway at the top. With no chance to hide, Simon caught his breath and bounded up the final steps into the room.

Tirin and a guard danced, with hammers swinging at each other. When the guard's eyes darted over to Simon, Tirin attacked but the guard deflected the strike. While Tirin was tiring, the guard hadn't broken a sweat.

A huge second guard leaned over Remeth's prone body, one hand on his neck and the other competing to reach for a fallen hammer.

Simon charged the big guard, but Tirin's opponent shouted a warning. The brute released the spluttering Remeth and swooped the hammer to meet Simon's blow. The vibration jarred Simon's grip and his feet gave way, swept out from underneath him, and he slammed down hard on his left elbow.

The guard and Simon both gained their feet.

Simon faked a strike, but the guard didn't bite. They traded blows, iron meeting iron, each blow shooting pain through his forearm and driving him back a step. Simon danced away from a sidearm swing.

Remeth sat on the floor, still clutching his throat.

A wounded roar from the other pair drew the brute's attention for a moment, and Simon's wild swing glanced off the guard's retreating forearm. The guard bellowed, and Simon's follow-through caught the head of the counterattack. His arm went numb, but he jabbed his right knee into the gut of the guard and the man toppled toward him in a cloud of hot, foul breath. Simon rolled to the side to avoid being pinned under the brute's girth, but his hammer was stuck. Grabbing the guard's arm he brought his elbow down hard on the already injured spot. The guard screamed as bone gave way but still had the strength to swing wildly with the hammer, forcing Simon to roll further away.

"Remeth!" Simon shouted from the floor. His friend was on his feet, the other hammer in his hands. He gaped at the brute, who was using his good arm to push himself up.

Tirin screamed and fell to his knees, his hands gripping his chest. The sound snapped Remeth into motion and he charged to relieve him, swinging the hammer into the back of the helmeted head to fell the guard.

Simon scurried toward Remeth, and away from the rising brute. The big man's left arm dangled useless and twisted, but he brandished the hammer in his still functional right. After glancing at the doorway he lumbered forward, and his savage blow smashed Remeth's hammer out of his hands and forced Remeth to the ground.

Simon grabbed Tirin's hammer from the floor.

The guard reared back to finish Remeth, but Simon hurled his hammer at the guard's good shoulder, striking true. The brute snarled at Simon, who tried madly to pull the other guard's hammer from beneath his body. On the second lumbering step, the big guard pitched forward to crack his chin down on the back of his own hammer.

Remeth had his arms wrapped tight around brute's foot, twisting it so he couldn't get back on his feet until the brute kicked him off.

Giving up on the hammer, Simon took two steps and jumped on to the man's face. One sandal caught only helmet, but the hobnails of the other tore through soft cheek to mash the guard's face into a bloody mess. The guard's flailing hammer blow struck Simon on the shin, and his eyes went white with pain.

Remeth had almost reached the thrown hammer. Scuttling backward like a crab on two hands and one good leg, Simon backed out of reach.

"Come get me!" he shouted.

The brute's shredded and bleeding lips exposed red teeth, and the eyes betrayed furious agony. Impossibly, the brute got to one knee, the other, one foot, and crashed to the floor when Remeth's hammer connected with the back of his helmet. After smashing him once more in the face, Remeth looked around. His eyes bugged out and he gagged, dropping the bloody hammer to the ground. He fell to his knees, dry heaving.

Simon picked up the bloody hammer, removed the other guard's helmet, and turned away before smashing his skull.

He crouched in front of Tirin, his leg almost giving out with the pain. "How bad?"

Tirin tried to speak, but coughed instead, his face twisting in agony. A thin line of blood trailed down his cheek.

"Can you walk?" Simon asked. Tirin nodded. "Someone must have heard, or found the other bodies by now." His leg screamed when he tried to stand up, and Remeth guided Simon's arm around his shoulder to help him to his feet.

Simon flinched from that touch, some part of him suspicious of this man who might love men, but he fought it off. He was just trying to help a friend.

"Did you paint us an exit?" Remeth asked.

Simon nodded. "Was just about to give you the good news when I heard the battle break out." They slowly descended the stairs. "What happened to your charm?"

Remeth's cheek was pink and puffing up. "I went in first, Tirin hid. Said I was a new recruit, and my shift mate had the runs so I was going solo. I asked if they'd stay a bit before leaving me here alone. It was all going well until the small one asked me which trainer I liked. Shame, I had them buying everything to that point."

"So then you called Tirin?"

"Not exactly... I said, 'did you hear that?' and the shorter one ran to the door. Tirin tried to pop him when he opened it, but missed. I hit the big one from behind but... it didn't do much."

"Tough bastard, that one. He'd make one hell of a bodyguard... sorry." Simon stopped, as Remeth started to gag again.

When they reached the bottom, Simon put his things away. "Remeth, you go first. You're not hurt." Remeth made to protest but Tirin's pained wheeze shut him up. He crawled into the stone passage.

"Couldn't you have made it a little wider? It's a tight squeeze."

"You shouldn't have eaten so much."

Tirin looked at him with more than just skepticism.

"I know, you don't trust magic."

The sound of a key scraping in the lock jolted him to action, and Tirin practically dove through the gap. Simon pushed his pack in first, and crawled inside. The stink of sweat, blood and bile in the enclosed space was almost unbearable. When his head poked out in the cool of night, he breathed the sweet air.

"Give me a hand," he said. "Let's see if we can push this back in." Even with three men working together the stone was too heavy.

"They may not even notice it," Remeth said.

Simon shook his head. "Tirin, where to?"

His eyes were wet. "My family."

XXIII

ⓈⓈⓈ

Carving

How long had Elysia sat there, checking one way for the horrible man and the other for a sign of Simon's return from the city? It was fully dark, and a cold wind had picked up, carrying the chill of the sea right through to her bones.

But somehow the cold cut deep enough, to her very core, that it awoke something inside her.

A stubborn refusal to leave Zeno alone.

If the man had bound him, then he was leaving him, to return later. The least she could do was free him. But she'd have to do it herself.

It took some effort to regain her feet, but her ankle's protest was more whine than scream. With limping steps she walked back up the hill, finally reaching the point where she could peer over the top of the crest. The wagon was barely visible, heading toward the closest of the towers they'd spotted. How long until he reached there? An hour? Two? And then how many more would know about her, and Zeno? Would they come back in the night? Or did she have until morning? But there was no way to stop him before he reached the tower.

She hobbled back to Zeno, who looked so pitiful trussed up, but so tired that he slept anyway. Hopefully he was comfortable enough to recover his strength. She leaned down to stroke his mane, careful not to wake him. The carving knife was still fused in her aching hand, and she set to work sawing him free. The blade caught on a knotted part and she nicked her finger, crying out with yet more pain.

As she pressed at the wound, the swaying of the branches of the tree caught her eye. Like it was waving to her, but it was only the wind. One solitary and twisted tree, looking as lonely and forlorn as she felt. The branch the man had hacked apart pointed straight down, to the ground, broken and unnatural. And... something more. Something in the wood. Something only she could see. She had to get a closer look.

Curiosity muted the pain as she walked closer. The branch swayed and danced for her in the gray starlight. The jagged slash reminded her of her own wound, and the whole tree looked like it was mourning, in pain.

She reached out to grasp the branch, her touch gentle on the rough bark. She caressed it, inspecting it, anger welling up inside her. Anger at what the man had done so casually to another living thing. Did the branch tremble with the same fury? She turned it over and...

There were two forms trapped inside the wood.

The first was a long knife, curved and wicked. Like something used for a sacrifice. Definitely more of a weapon than the blade she held.

The second would have scared her away before, but now it seemed to match her mood perfectly. Even in the dim light she could see every exacting detail. The terrible little creature was the size of her hand, with wings not of feathers, but skin, like a fantastical dragon. Its head was more rodent, but with rows of razor sharp teeth. Hungry and vengeful, it wanted blood. It was perfect.

The branch came free in her hand, offering itself to her.

She sat down on the rocks and began to work, her blade peeling the bark like the skin of a ripe fruit; it came off so easily. The wood underneath was soft and dark, but still strong. Not rotten.

Inspired by the intensity of her isolation, fear, and righteous anger at the treatment of her dear friend Zeno, her hand moved faster than ever before as it removed everything that was not a part of her vengeance.

This little creature would stalk her prey, and keep them safe. Time had no meaning in her communion with the wood, and a faint glow guided her way, showing her each stroke and where to move next to unlock the life that was hidden inside.

When she finished, her hands shook and tears of pain and worry splashed the form in her hands.

"Help me, my little friend."

The wood turned warm and the smooth body of the little creature wriggled in her hands. The little face peered up at her, hissing between menacing rows of teeth, and… nodded? She held it up, pointing toward the wagon, barely a speck in the distance, on the road to the tower.

"Go. Stop him."

The little creature's tongue flicked out, long and thin, tickling her hand. When she smiled, it shook off its wings and a cloud of dust filled the air. She coughed and closed her eyes, but felt the weight go, and when she opened them again it was streaking in the direction she had pointed.

෧෧෧෧෧෧෧

Remeth looked at Simon with a raised eyebrow. "Are you sure that's wise?"

"The man just got out of captivity. Of course he wants to see his family. And maybe they can help us get out."

Remeth let out a sigh. "If we go with you to your family, will you help us get out of the city?"

"On my children life," Tirin said.

"Wouldn't that be the first place you'd look for an escaped prisoner?" Remeth asked.

"Then we'd better hurry," Simon said.

Tirin stayed in the shadow of the keep as he led them toward the wall that separated the mine from the city. They rushed along the sheer face, and even at that late hour, faint peals of metal striking stone rang out.

Imagining tunnels in the mines beyond the wall made Simon think of the excavation site and… "Kashaka!" Simon searched frantically for the special clay jar. Tirin looked skeptically at him as he watched the blood settle to one side.

"Looks like it's pointing through the mountain," Remeth said.

"She's not in the city." They both sighed with relief.

"Who?" Tirin asked.

"A goddess," Remeth said, "or a demon. Or both."

"Is there any water god here?" Simon asked.

Tirin frowned. "Spirit of sea is treacherous. Give us food, but steal our men and boats."

"Do you worship this sea spirit?" Remeth asked.

"No! Only Shygakar. All temples, gifts, even painting like yours… go to him. His son, Lord of Coin."

215

Simon and Remeth exchanged a look.

"Do you have painters?" Simon asked.

"Coinbrothers bring them to Keep. Serve Lord. Serve Shygakar."

Remeth put a hand on Simon's shoulder and gave him a hard look. "This is all fascinating, but all that matters is Kashaka isn't here. Let's see his wife and get out of here."

Tirin led them on a twisting route through shadowy alleys before stopping in front of a two story apartment block. Tirin looked at the door like he'd seen a ghost.

"Are you sure you want to do this?" Simon asked.

"I must."

"Can you invite us in?" Remeth asked, indicating a robed figure that had just turned onto the street.

They ducked inside to the bottom of a flight of stairs and Tirin shut the door, engulfing them in total darkness.

Simon rifled through his pack for the cloth-wrapped coin and opened it by feel. The cool magical light illuminated the stairs, and Remeth's smug smile. It had been his idea in the first place, but Simon had prepared another one back in Jeppo, just in case. *Thank Salar the guards didn't find it.*

Tirin edged up the stairs, keeping his distance from the light. "She might have moved," he said, hesitating in front of the third door on the left from the top of the stairs.

"Or she could be dead," Remeth said, "or with another man. Or woman?"

Simon elbowed him in the ribs. "Tirin, we don't have much time."

Tirin took a deep breath and tried the door. It was locked.

Remeth turned up his palms. "Great, then we'll have to go…"

Tirin knocked. A hesitant, uncertain knock.

Remeth rolled his eyes. "If she's asleep, you're not going to wake her like that." He rapped his knuckles much harder against the wood.

Simon and Remeth backed away from the door as soft foot-steps approached from inside. Simon rewrapped the coin, sending the hallway back into darkness.

A woman's voice called out a question, and Tirin's trembled as he responded.

She gasped. "Tirin? Tirin!" The door opened and a sliver of

light fell on Tirin's face.

"Lara?" His voice was thick with emotion.

The door opened wider, bathing Tirin in light. She gasped as she beheld his wild, dirty and emaciated form. He cringed.

"Tirin…" she said, her voice trailing off into sobs.

He reached out to her, tears streaming down his face. "Lara…" His smile showed several blackened and missing teeth, making him look even wilder.

Her voice turned suddenly harsh, accusatory. She slapped at his chest, and he winced, clutching his ribs.

Tirin reached out to her again, pleading.

She snapped back at him, and when Tirin tried to reach in she closed the door on his hand. He bit his lip against the pain, not making a sound. When he pulled the hand away, they were left in darkness.

"She said he's dead to the kids," Remeth whispered.

"Come on, Tirin," Simon said. "Let's go." He unwrapped the coin just a little, and his heart went out to the broken, dejected figure clutching injured hand to injured ribs.

"They call me traitor. Was executed. What can I live for?"

"Don't let them be right," Simon said. "But you look like death. Clean yourself up, and then find a way to come back to her. This was just too much of a shock all at once. Think of your kids. She has to protect them."

"Help us get away," Remeth said, "and we'll do whatever we can to help you."

"You care only for yourself," Tirin said.

Simon stood between them. "Tirin, I know you're in all kinds of pain. But you're endangering them by even being here."

Sudden realization hit Tirin's face. He knocked again. "Lara?"

Harsh words came from just inside the door. She hadn't left. His response was so heartfelt that Simon was moved to tears even without comprehending. Remeth surreptitiously wiped at his eye.

Tirin ushered them back down the stairs and out to the street, checking first to make sure the route was clear.

"The harbor," Simon said when Tirin pointed the direction he intended to go. Tirin nodded. "Maybe a fishing boat? Do any leave at night?"

"Many. My father was fisherman. One uncle too. Cousin still. Good friend. We go to him."

The sound of men shouting in the distance pushed them to pick up the pace, taking chances a few times by sprinting across open lanes.

The flash of torches coming around one corner drove them skittering into the alcove in front of a closed shop, trusting in shadows to hide them. Four guards ran by and Simon's heart pounded in time with their steps.

"Sealing the gates," Tirin said when the light had disappeared several streets past their location.

"Will they also seal the port?" Simon asked.

Tirin frowned. "Wall around, small gate for ships." He gulped. "Chain from tower to tower at gate."

Remeth swore. "How are we going to get a ship out through that?"

"Get us a boat and we'll think of something," Simon said.

"But guards in port and tower?"

"Can you swim, Remeth?"

"I grew up in the Vanusa Delta," Remeth said. "Of course I can swim. Why?"

"They'll be looking for three men. Tirin, wear my cloak and take our things so they don't get wet. Find us a boat. We'll try to follow along under the dock, so leave us a sign in the water."

"I'd rather just talk my way through," Remeth said, standing tall and attentive, no longer looking the bumbling simpleton that had been arrested. He wouldn't match the description...

"This way," Tirin said, hurrying them down another alley. No sooner had they returned to the safety of darkness, but two more guards went running down the way they came.

Simon exchanged a worried glance with Remeth, holding a finger to his lips. He handed his cloak and pack to Tirin and looked pointedly at Remeth. Sullen, he handed over his pack as well.

It might have just been hope, but Simon thought he could smell the sea as they came to the end of the alley. The wide street in front of them was brighter, illuminated by a half moon shining unobstructed on the stone. Which meant there were no shadows to work with.

"Water behind those buildings. I go first," Tirin said, holding out his hand. Simon reached to clasp his forearm in his traditional greeting, but Tirin's grabbed only the hand. He shook it, leaving Simon slightly unsettled by the difference. Tirin offered Remeth only a curt nod. After pulling the cloak over his face, he walked out into the street at a casual pace, heading to the left.

"What's wrong with you?" Simon asked Remeth.

"What?"

"Why are you being so obnoxious to him?"

"I... I'm just on edge. I have a pounding headache, I'm sore, I'm tired... and my throat feels like something died in it."

"That's why I don't usually drink. Your revels got us into this mess."

"I'll make it up to you later," Remeth said with a wink.

Simon threw up his hands in exasperation. "That again? How can you even joke about... that? Our lives are on the line. And I'm worried about Elysia."

Remeth's face fell. "You... you really care about her."

Simon nodded, missing her so much in that moment. *At least she's safe with Zeno.*

"You're lucky. To have found someone, someone who under-stands you. That you can talk to. As well as..." He looked at Simon with wistful longing. "When I first met you—"

Simon cut him off, turning away. "The water, we have to get to the boat."

He scanned the other side of the street, looking for access to the water around the building. The left side lane was twice as far as the right. "We should split up. I'll take the right, you take the left."

Remeth's face was composed again. "Why do you get the short run?"

"The docks are to the left. More likely to run into someone. At least you can talk your way out."

Remeth nodded. "So slip into the water unnoticed, then swim around looking for a sign from Tirin?"

"That's the plan."

"Not how I'd prefer to spend the night."

"A swim sounds refreshing."

Remeth shuddered. "You really think we can trust him?"

"We don't have much choice. And he's got nothing to lose now."

"I just hope they don't cut him a deal."

Simon hadn't considered the possibility. "But... surely they'd think he's the bigger risk than some foreigners?"

"Not if we're spies."

"Still, now we're all murderers. And I'm willing to put my faith in him."

"And I'll just have to trust you." Remeth sighed, and held out his arm. "See you in the water?"

Simon clasped it and nodded. "For Pazh," he said, automatically.

Remeth snorted and shook his head. "For the Talented. For us, Simon."

Remeth was right. There was deeper meaning even in a farewell. Whose side was he really on now?

Once Remeth reached the alley and disappeared from view, Simon checked that his way was clear and took off in a sprint to the narrow line of shadows next to the warehouse.

Breathing heavily, he shuffled along with his back to the stone wall and peeked around the corner. For the first time, he could match the smell of the sea with the sight. Fifty feet away was a large pier holding dozens of military galleys.

Simon swore under his breath.

It made sense. Without trade, the only boats they were likely to find here were for fishing or defense. And he'd unwittingly angled himself toward the military side of the harbor. Would they muster ships to make sure they didn't get out?

The smaller pier on the far side of the harbor was teeming with life, with fishing boats preparing for the day's work, and two already rowing out toward the harbor gate.

Two tall towers flanked the small opening, big enough for only a pair of war galleys to go through abreast. The outer wall of the city connected to the two towers, with no sign of stairs anywhere.

The city would be difficult to attack, if anyone ever tried, especially with this navy lying in wait to defend the small entrance and inhospitable terrain limiting the possibility of a land attack. Surely Kyso would love to develop a strategy to break it.

But right now, Simon's concern was getting out. And that meant the fishing boats. He could either dive off the military pier and swim across the harbor, or make his way around on land. Squinting, he could make out the forms of two groups of five or more guards going from boat to boat, searching among the fishermen. For them.

Two more guards were walking his way, along the shore between the two piers. Heading right toward them was... Remeth?

Simon swore again. *What is he doing?* One guard waved him over to speak with them.

It's as good a chance as any.

Simon walked out from the darkness with purpose, like he had a reason to be going to the military pier in the dead of night. His skin prickled in the brisk wind blowing in off the water, without a cloak to cover him. At least his skin color would look the same by moonlight.

Eyes forward, not looking toward Remeth and the guards, he made for the second galley on the right side. *So far, so good, not a soul to…*

A voice called out to him from the first boat, and he could see hands waving in the corner of his eye.

He kept moving.

The voice grew louder, more insistent.

Sighing, Simon turned to look at the man, who held his palm out. The only thing that made him any different from most of the men of Aktiri he'd met that day was that he was not obviously armed. He was also alone. Simon pointed at himself.

The man stepped onto the pier and walked toward Simon. With a glance, Simon confirmed they were still alone.

When the man was within a few paces and Simon could see his features, the gray eyes opened wide in shock.

Simon charged, closing the distance before the man cried out. Lowering his shoulder at the last second, he connected with the man's midsection and wrapped his arms around the bulk on the follow through. His momentum took them over the side.

Simon took a last gulp of air while the man's arms flailed around in the weightless moment before…

ତ୧ତ୧ତ୧ତ

Elysia looked down to the remainder of the wood at her feet, at the form of the blade. Exactly what she needed. She went to work on it, even faster now, her hand warmed up and one with her Talent. In what felt like moments, she was holding the simple carving tool in one hand, a wicked blade capable of dealing death in the other. It was also meant for *him*. She put down her carving knife and held the new blade in two hands, slashing at the air to vent her anger. The balance was perfect. And like the now living creature, it also sought blood. Revenge. Which she understood too well.

Elysia hobbled after the wagon.

ᏜᏋᏜᏋᏜᏋᏜ

The man's body hit the water with a dull slap, which Simon barely registered before they plunged into darkness. A stream of bubbles rippled across Simon's face, while the man writhed and struggled below him, hands tearing at Simon's but unable to break free.

Simon held on, focusing his attention on his grip, and on breathing out ever so slightly through his nose. The bubbles abruptly stopped escaping from the man, but the thrashing became more violent, panicked. After sinking on impact they had bobbed up slightly, but settled far enough below the water that air was not within reach.

The taste of salt on his lips and air going stale in his mouth sent waves of panic through his body. Still he held on to the man, whose jerking movements were becoming more erratic, less coordinated.

Simon pulled his knees up and in one motion released his grip while pushing off the man's chest, shooting himself up toward the surface.

A hand closed around his ankle, pulling him back.

Simon's lungs burned, screaming for him to breathe. Now he was the one kicking, jabbing wildly with his sandals, the nails of his sole tearing at the man. Another hand grabbed higher on his leg, desperately trying to climb up, but instead dragging Simon back down. One more wild kick connected with a squish, and the grip slackened just enough that Simon could wriggle free and surge upward.

His head broke the surface and he gasped for air. Treading water, he settled himself by counting each breath, scanning back and forth for any sign of the other man reaching the surface. By thirty he was calm and settled. By fifty, his gut wrenched with the realization that the man would never breathe again.

The chill of the cold seawater began to seep through his skin. He shivered and retreated into the darkness under the pier.

XXIV
ᏀᏋᏀᏋᏀᏋᏀ
Revenge

In the fading light, Elysia couldn't be sure, but the wagon seemed to have stopped. It gave her hope.

Gingerly at first, but with every step bringing her more urgency and confidence, she walked faster and faster until she broke out into a run, the wooden blade cutting through the air as she pumped her arms. There was no pain now. Just singular focus. On vengeance, for her and for her new friend and his home.

ᏀᏋᏀᏋᏀᏋᏀ

At least the blood will wash away. Simon shuddered. Where did such thoughts come from? Alone and far from help, a vicious murderer, and his first thought was getting cleaned up?

Simon kept his strokes under the water to blend in with the gentle lapping of waves against the hulls of the ships. Nobody seemed to have noticed the scuffle in the water or the sailor's disappearance.

He lost his sense of time as he passed galley after galley. He was using too much of his arms, with his legs already tired, and he clung to the last post to take stock of his surroundings.

More fishing boats were heading out toward the harbor gate, but the majority remained moored at the pier. The distance between the piers looked to be more than half again as far as he'd already swam. His limbs cried out at the breadth of the gulf.

With the search focused on the shore, the piers, the boats and even the water near the mouth of the harbor, he was going to be swimming in just about the last place they'd look, and his dark skin and hair wouldn't give much contrast in the moonlight. Even still, he kept his arms and legs fully submerged while he swam. At least the waves flowed across his path, not against it.

His mind wandered back to Tirin. Exploration and news of the wider world had branded him a pariah, while with Simon it was allowing himself to express his natural Talent. They both went against some societal construct, some rule that on first glance made no sense, but was the result of generations of acceptance of an idea.

But there was a big difference. Here the ruling class could justify their stance. An ignorant populace, kept fed and happy in their walled city surrounded by the sea, was not a threat to the Lord and his favorites.

Was the same true of Pazh? Did they fear Talent as something that could upset rule by the families of the *digniti* and *suprati* that made up the Senatorial classes?

But Lokas Lepilla was a Senator that didn't seem to fear him, and instead made him his ally—tried to protect him. Or was he just a pawn? Simon's mind chewed on the ideas as he made his slow progress.

And where is Remeth? Simon scanned the fishing pier, but from the distance and low angle he detected only movement, not details.

I'm in this mess because of him. Yet as angry as that made Simon, it piqued his curiosity. Who was Remeth, really? Xelos endorsed Yalath, and Remeth by association, but the actor couldn't be more different from the two old men. Tonight, he'd been like a legionary on leave from his post, trying to cram as much hedonistic pleasure as he could into one night off.

He'd been acting on the stage most of his life, but had he ever stopped acting offstage? Hiding his Talent, but also these... desires? The legionaries joked about men who preferred each other's company, but if it took place, it was far away from the watchful eyes of the others. Simon had been the butt of Persei's jokes placing him and Lokas in that camp, but while Remeth was handsome, no man had ever stirred any kind of desire in Simon. Thoughts of Elysia lying next to him brought some measure of warmth to a body growing increasingly numb in the cold water. She understood him better than anyone he'd ever met.

That's what Remeth wanted. It wasn't him. It was the idea of him. Of someone who could understand. Simon hoped he could at least be that friend.

But first, he had to get to the pier.

ᏬᏋᏬᏋᏬᏋᏬ

The wagon had stopped, and Elysia closed the distance quickly. Once she got close, she slowed down, approaching cautiously from behind. The man was out in front, by the pony, waving his axe around in the air, striking at some unseen opponent. No, not unseen, just dark and fast. Her little friend swooped and dove at the man and his pony, evading his counterstrikes.

She crouched low behind the wagon, shuffling sideways to get closer without being seen. The blade pulsed with life, desire... and thirst.

She rounded the side, and still the man continued his awkward dance, striking at the air where the creature no longer was, just out of reach. It whizzed by his head. The man cursed, wiping at the side of his face, and the hand came away bloody. His face and neck bore other signs of attack, as did the pony.

Although coiled and ready, her heart failed her. A man that strong, with an axe? She wasn't as quick as her little friend, and one blow could mean the end of her, without even the chance to say goodbye to Simon.

Without vengeance for the tree.

And for Father and Xelos.

Images of their faces burned in her mind, lending her strength.

The man twirled again but his mighty blow cut only air, useless.

Summoning all that righteous anger, she charged.

Her blow connected with his neck, slicing through flesh until it struck bone.

His arms flailed out, one knocking her back before the axe could connect. She fell, all the fear returning as the furious hulk of a man loomed over her, blood pouring out despite the hand that clutched at his wound. His impossibly light eyes burned with pain and rage inside his dark face and no longer did she have to fear his desire, only for her life.

Wings whirred and her creation alighted on his neck, sinking sharp teeth into the bloody mess and lapping up blood. The man screamed, trying in vain to swat it away, tearing at it with bloody fingers and the axe, striking both its body and himself. His movements slowed, becoming sluggish and ineffectual until he sank to his knees, his eyes glassy. The axe fell from his grip, but still his hands clutched at the little creature, slick fingers never getting a grip as it dug deeper into his throat.

Elysia felt no pity. She stood up, gripping her blade again with two hands.

"You attacked his home. You stole our things. You threatened me. And now, you die."

He cried out, begging. But she had no room for mercy.

She plunged the blade down through the space above his collarbone, into his chest. The body fell back to the ground. She released the knife, letting it drink. Her little friend remained next to it, chomping and slurping at the dead man's neck. They were satisfied, and so was she.

She readied the sorry-looking pony for the drive back to Zeno.

�6Ᏹ�6ᏱᏆᏱᏓ

Lost in his thoughts, Simon found himself only a few lengths away from the first moored fishing boat. The mountain partially obscured the moon, casting long shadows over the city, but not yet the harbor. He felt naked in the cold white light; now close enough to be seen.

He took a deep breath and submerged, swimming as far as he could underwater before gently resurfacing. He paused to catch his breath and look for any sign that he'd been noticed, and then repeated the process until he came up within reach of the boat. He gripped the side, shuddering relief coursing through his body at the chance to let something else bear his weight. Even the smell of dead fish was somehow welcome.

The relief was short-lived, with the sounds of too many people nearby; ropes and nets thrown around in boats, conversations on the dock, and oars splashing the water. He dipped under once more, resurfacing in a dark forest where the hulls of more than twenty fishing craft lined the space like huge trees, with the posts that supported the structure as small saplings. The pier sat almost on the surface of the water, only barely giving him room for his head.

Which boat? And did Tirin even make it?

He didn't notice anything distinctive about the boat next to him.

From the next boat over, Simon heard multiple voices raised in disagreement, but none of them familiar. Using the sounds as a cover, he swam in the opposite direction and searched boat by boat for any kind of sign, finding nothing. Each one made his arms and legs feel heavier. He couldn't keep this up much longer.

When the search party came back his way he sat low and still in the water, keeping only his eyes and nostrils above. More boats left, including the one where he'd heard the disagreement. The guards were likely inspecting each boat before they let them leave. Maybe if he waited until they'd checked all the boats? But then there would be little cover.

Another two yielded nothing, but what was that hanging down from the third? A net? His heart leaped at the sign. He swam faster, reaching out for this device that would bring fish to their deaths but might be a lifeline for him…

It pulled out of the water before he could reach it. Then ducked back in again, shook, and pulled out again.

Disappointment weighed so heavy it threatened to sink him. A loud voice called out from the boat and drew heavy footsteps as a group approached. Simon curled his arms and legs around a post and hung on. The boat dipped lower in the water once, twice, as people boarded. After a gruff conversation, the boat jerked again and rose back up to its original level. When the footsteps receded, Simon finally breathed again.

There were only two more boats nearby, before he'd have to return to the half dozen nearest to land.

Were his eyes playing tricks on him? Or was that a glint of metal on the waterline of the last boat? He mustered the last of his energy and swam twenty feet. It was a coin. A Pazian silver zal sparkled in a fine net intended for small fish. Braced as it was against the hull of the boat, it would be invisible from the pier, but a beacon to Simon in the water. Tears streamed down his face, so happy to see Salar's image on the coin.

Simon tried pulling on the net, with no response, nor any to his soft knock on the side. He tried a whisper, but only the weakest croak escaped from his salt-encrusted lips. Exhausted and alone… so close to help, but he didn't even have the strength to lift himself up to attract Tirin's attention.

He pulled on the net one more time…

A face looked over the side. It was clean shaven, with gray eyes… strange yet faintly familiar… Tirin?

The man curled his finger up ever so slightly to his lips before disappearing.

Simon cried more tears of joy.

A thin coil of rope dropped over the side, hitting Simon on the head. A hand reached over and made a circular motion. With feeble hands Simon threaded it around his chest below the armpits and into a messy but effective knot. He loosened his grip and sunk down several inches, but it bore his water-buoyed weight. For the first time since entering the city, he relaxed, letting his limbs go limp, slipping into the shadow of the boat to wait for some sign from Tirin.

Was it minutes or hours he huddled there just below the water-line? Everything felt numb, bloated, waterlogged. He had to set his jaw to keep his teeth from chattering, a noise that sounded to him as loud as horses galloping on a Pazian road.

Voices, somewhere in the haze high above him, almost on the edge of his consciousness. Strangely familiar voices, one… or was it two? But in an unfamiliar language. He felt an itch trying to bring him back, but he was too tired, too cold, too…

The boat shifted suddenly, smacking him on the back of the head so that he bit his lip. The salt and blood in his mouth pierced through the haze, tasting vividly of life and rousing him from his stupor. Input from his senses coalesced into coherent thought…

Someone was boarding the boat! *But who?*

Simon huddled down in the water, gripping the rope and straining to listen. Scratching, shifting, scuffling… the sounds of searching. More unintelligible conversation, and the click of boots on the deck. Questions, answers, then a voice… a distantly familiar voice… calling out louder, to the pier. A barked response, and movement again. Simon braced himself so he wouldn't be hit again by the hull, just in time to roll with the shift. Feet struck the pier again and started walking away.

The almost familiar voice again asked a question, closer now, almost at the edge on his side, and after a pause the other voice… *Tirin…* was evasive, hesitant in his response. There was a tug on the rope, and Simon took a breath and pulled his head under the water, hoping to make himself as invisible as possible. He held himself down under the side, his lungs screaming but his terrified mind maintaining control. Finally when he could hold no longer he slipped his head up and used every last ounce of control to release the breath slowly and silently.

A shadowed face looked straight at him.

XXV

Vessel

Persei's body burned with pleasant warmth in the cool of night, as he and Mirasha walked through the rows of legionary tents on their way to the other dig site. The heat of his shared passion with Mirasha in the temple of Zalikko was deliciously illicit, yet so appropriate as an offering to the goddess. Mirasha had found a small votive figurine and told him to keep it with him, as a reminder, and a focus for his new connection with this one who would give him power.

Eppeth, the overall supervisor of the site, had accepted their explanation of Jukaro's foolhardy plan to re-mount the statue, and how it burned him to ashes. He'd asked them to keep it quiet.

Persei had declared the camp free of rebel influence, figuring Eppeth would be happy to be rid of the legionary distraction. The old man was more of Ilson's ilk, focused on the discovery of ancient things, believing contemporary politics to be an annoyance, and beneath him.

The Temple of Kashaka was Persei's destination, where he hoped to match up reality with his vision. Despite his grumbling about the late hour, Eppeth accompanied them as the leading expert on the temple. Moving slowly with his cane, he led them through the quiet streets of the site, four of his own guards giving him numbers over Persei's two. But that didn't count Persei himself, and this new fire inside him.

Along the way, Eppeth pointed out aspects of the design and statuary that he deemed worthy of their attention. Persei didn't agree with his judgment, but Mirasha was riveted.

Though he hadn't seen anything yet from his vision, somehow Persei knew they were going in the right direction, deeper into the ancient structure. *To the central temple—to the heart.*

"Is this what you're looking for?" Eppeth asked as he led them through a final doorway into a central chamber. Above a large fountain in the middle, a hole in the ceiling was filled with earth.

Persei nodded, and pointed to the central tower. "We need to go in there." He circled around it, but saw neither door nor handle. "How do we get in?"

Mirasha shrugged with a curious look on her face. Eppeth narrowed his eyes. "Who told you about this?"

"I… read about it in a manuscript in Jeppo." He wasn't about to speak of his visions. "You know how to get in."

Eppeth turned his cane slowly in his hands. He looked so old, so frail. Persei could snap him in two if he didn't talk. The old man let out a deep sigh. "*She* cannot enter. It is our holiest of holy places."

Persei snorted, but a withering look from Mirasha stopped his tongue. He was about to mock the pagan gods, but he needed this man's cooperation. "I may need to call upon her expertise."

"Then you can describe it to her up here, and ask the questions. This is not negotiable."

Persei looked to Mirasha, who gave him an almost imperceptible nod. He didn't like leaving her here outnumbered, but if anything happened to them, his legionaries would slaughter all of Eppeth's men. He'd better keep his sacrilegious streak under control. If they were fanatics, they might choose a martyr's death.

"Agreed. And both our guards remain up here."

The old man nodded. "In fact, they can set up over there," he said, pointing to the entrance, "and turn their backs while I open the door."

"It's a deal. Let's get on with it. I know you'd rather be in bed."

"I don't see why this couldn't wait until a more civilized hour," Eppeth said to him quietly as they walked into the dry fountain together. "Look away."

Persei did as he was told, and heard a light click and a creak. *Mechanical… or magical?*

"It is ready." Inside the small door was a cramped space with a ladder stretching downward.

"We'll be back in a few minutes," Persei said to Mirasha and his men. "Do you need help climbing down?"

"I certainly do not." The voice softened a bit. "Though if you could go first, I'll pass you my cane. The last step is a bit awkward.

But I do well for eighty-three!"

Persei nodded, not just in agreement, but in legitimate admiration. Few apart from the wealthiest lived to see even fifty, and the man was as sharp as any.

Rung by rung, Persei made his way down into the gloom below. With a call down at the last possible second, Eppeth tossed the cane to him, nearly hitting him on the head. He more carefully handed Persei a lamp.

The flickering light revealed large metal tanks along the walls, pipes… and the clay vessel from his vision, mounted on a pedestal in the center of the room.

The old man proved to be stronger than he looked, climbing down with ease. He took the cane from Persei and used it to gently set his feet down onto the floor below.

"So," Eppeth said. "What is it you *really* want to see?"

Do I show you my cards, old man? First I test you.

Persei pointed to the vessel, seeing for the first time the woman's face at the top. "What is this?"

"An ancient relic. Sacred to my people."

"And what exactly is it? Or what does it do?"

"That is a mystery."

Persei's hand lowered to the hilt of his sword, and Eppeth's eyes followed the movement.

"You would threaten me here? Desecrating our most holy place? The heart of Kashaka?"

Persei withdrew his hand. "You mistake me. I mean you no harm." *But I need this… this heart. It would take some trade for him to give it to me. What can I even offer?*

"What would you give to be reunited with Kashaka?" Persei asked.

The old man laughed. "I suppose you know where she has been imprisoned? Don't mock me. My people have been looking for a thousand years."

"What if I could tell you how to find her? There is nothing you'd like more, is there?"

Eppeth looked on him first with disdain, then begrudging curiosity. "What do you know?"

"The secret is before you. But you wouldn't want that to get out, would you? I could share it with you."

"If you do possess such knowledge, which I already question, what do you have to gain?"

"I believe my people are short-sighted. And that the Izari that banished your goddess were misguided. All sources of power should be sought out, for the good of the people. I see how your rebels chafe against our rule. But this land has so much potential. Unite our might with the power of your goddess, reconnect her to your people, and it would be good for the entire Republic."

He'd struck a chord with the old man. "You're different, for a Pazian. But how do you know my people wouldn't rise up under Kashaka's wing and throw off the Pazian yoke?"

"That's why I'd like to be there when you find her. I need someone with foresight to work with, like yourself. I know you're not with the rebels."

Eppeth looked at him with what looked like a new appreciation. "How do you know?"

"I saw how the others reacted. You care only for the artifacts, for exploring the past. You yearn to be reconnected with the water mother. Don't you, Eppeth?"

"So if you know how to find her, why are you telling me all this?"

Because I can't risk killing you, not with the chance Mirasha could be hurt up there in an uneven fight. I should have brought more men. "Are you with me in this endeavor?"

Eppeth looked down to the sword again, but said nothing.

"You can die with your secret. But either way I'll need to touch this relic. Make it easier on yourself, and be a part of setting your goddess free."

Wrinkles creased Eppeth's forehead as he looked from the relic to Persei and back again, considering. He sighed. "One condition."

Persei cocked his head to the side, inviting him to go on.

Eppeth's voice turned solemn, reverent: "Offer yourself to her. Only the chosen men of Kashaka—the highest of the high priests and the emperors of the past dynasty—can even behold her heart."

A reasonable request, and a bridge I'll have to cross for her to grant me power. "What do I do?"

"Bow down before her heart. Gaze upon it. Touch your own. Repeat after me."

Persei followed each instruction to the letter, repeating the words as Eppeth bid him. "I swear, that with every drop of blood in my body, every life giving drop that comes from you, that I devote myself to you, Kashaka, water mother. I am your faithful servant. I go where you ask me to. Purify my blood. Make me one with you. Grant me the gift of your life-giving water. Let it flow through my veins, make me strong, so I can vanquish your enemies and lift you up into glory!"

The words felt strangely natural to Persei. But he'd grown up reciting prayers to Salar and all the other Pazian gods, both local and imported. The others had all been just that—words without meaning. But that had changed with his act on the altar of Zalikko. Here in this foreign ruin, for the first time in his life he meant the words he swore to the gods—to this foreign god. And for some reason he felt relieved that Mirasha wasn't here to witness this devotion to another woman.

With wrinkled lips, the old man kissed him on the forehead and laid hands on his shoulders. "Rise, brother of water, son of Kashaka."

"How do you know I speak true?"

Eppeth laughed. "Because if you're lying, then even touching her heart will consume you. Her blood will dissolve you like acid."

"You know about the blood?"

"Of course."

"Then you know it will lead us to her?"

A gasp. "What? But it would only come out to destroy a non-believer."

"Watch this." Persei lifted up the vessel and a metallic liquid dripped from a tiny hole in the bottom, one minute drop at a time. Persei tilted it to the side to slow the flow, and the small pool in the bottom of the rounded depression quivered slightly then rolled impossibly up the gentle slope in one definite direction. "Her blood seeks to be reunited with our lady. Where she is caged, victim of dark Izari sorcery."

Eppeth prostrated himself before the heart, his eyes wide as a true believer.

Persei set the heart carefully down in its base and retrieved the clay jar from his belt pouch, that he'd procured from the camp just for this purpose. He scooped out the wax stopper and handed it to Eppeth.

Eppeth looked on in a kind of captivated horror as Persei raised the heart again. "Now hold the jar steady and catch the flow." The first drop hit his hand and he flinched, but instead of burning him it rolled down his arm and impossibly sideways through the air before scuttling across the floor into the shadows.

"Your faith is true," Persei said.

After the initial shock, the old man's hand was surprisingly sure as he caught drop after drop until the jar was almost full and he withdrew it. Persei replaced the heart on the pedestal, giving it a delicate kiss for good measure.

Eppeth passed the jar reverently to Persei. "She is that way?" the old man asked, looking to the shadows.

"It appears so." Again with great care, Persei sealed the jar and stored it away in the pouch on his belt. He bowed low on the floor, joining Eppeth.

"Thank you, my lady Kashaka. We will be united soon."

He stood up and brushed himself off, though the floor was strangely spotless. Eppeth took his hand when he offered it, and he felt a new connection to the old man. *Good. I won't have to kill him after all. Not yet at least.*

Back in the main temple, Persei nodded to Mirasha and spoke to her in hushed tones. "I have what we need. Let's get back to the surface and see where it leads."

ᎾᏋᏂᏋᏂᏋᎾ

Simon's heart dropped, as if sinking to the bottom of the bay, lost forever like he would be.

But a dismissive remark from the strangely familiar voice made the head disappear. The rope slackened then caught Simon's weight. That voice shouted to the pier, and the boat rocked again as at least one man disembarked.

Simon's mind reeled with the impossibility of the situation.

"—down there?" came Tirin's voice, Simon's mind only latching onto the words mid-sentence.

His croaked response didn't even sound human. He tried tugging on the rope.

"Waiting for Remeth come back," Tirin said. "Wait bit longer."

Simon nodded.

"Hold on."

What else can I do? And come back? So he was here? Where is he now? At least it gave Simon something to think about while he waited in the darkness. It seemed like they'd passed the inspection, but what about the sea gate? If he were in charge, he'd check again, and they'd be found.

What if he painted himself to look like them? It might work, but how many manned a fishing boat? They didn't look very big. Four seemed excessive.

If they searched just as thoroughly then there was no way to hide out of sight. They'd look through the tackle and any blankets or storage or...

What if we could hide in sight? With a tarp or something to cover them, Simon could paint the surface to look like the empty floor of the boat. If Tirin had all his things, it just might work, but he'd have to work fast. It didn't look like a long row to the sea gate. *If only I could start now.*

More footsteps approached on the pier; one man, now that Simon was attuned to the differences. A barked order was answered by another voice, not Tirin this time. The boat shook one more time as someone came aboard.

After more scuffling above him, the boat pushed away from the dock. An oar splashed spray into Simon's face, waking him to full readiness. Simon gripped the rope harder and kicked his legs just to keep ahead of the oar.

"Simon?" came Remeth's voice over the side above the oar. "We'll pull you up once we're away from the pier."

With the possibility of escape so close, Simon felt one final surge of energy and kept pace, with his head just above the water.

After a few minutes of rowing they slowed and Tirin peered over the edge.

"We pull you up now."

Simon felt the sudden tension on the rope. Tirin reached out his hand and Simon grasped it with one, then both hands and between the rope and Tirin they pulled him on board.

Remeth wore a helmet and jerkin like the guards. "You look like death."

Simon stared at him, grasping at his throat. His mouth felt so dry...

A man held out a wineskin to him. It was Tirin, clean-shaven and scarred, but the same shrewd eyes stared out of the gaunt face. "Drink."

Simon did, the most soothing delicious water he had ever tasted. He took another long draft then coughed and choked.

"Don't kill yourself!" Remeth said, "Not after we just saved you."

Tirin sat at the oars with a third man, who looked entirely uncomfortable with everything. They resumed their rowing.

"I need to get started," Simon said. "Tirin, where is my pack?"

Remeth pouted. "Don't you want to know how we pulled this off?"

"First we have to be ready for the sea gate. In case they search us again. Tirin, how many fisherman normally go on one craft?"

Tirin asked his cousin and translated the response. "Two... three at the most."

"I'll bet they search every craft that goes through the gate. Look."

A boat passing through the gate pulled alongside one of the towers, while others waited in a queue behind it.

Simon found his paints. "Tirin, do you have a blanket, a tarp or something?"

Tirin frowned. "They will search again."

"They'll leave no stone unturned. But what if there are no stones. A tarp?"

Tirin nodded, reaching behind himself into the back of the boat. It looked big enough to cover the entire craft. One side was slicked with some kind of oil, but the other was unfinished.

"This will do."

Tirin translated his cousin's angry question. "What you do?"

"Remeth, I need you to lie down underneath. Sprawl out like there's two of you under there." The inside of the boat was plain wood with some staining. They could move the rest of the tackle a little further back to clear the space.

"Two of us? But they said three was acceptable. And besides, I'm a guard getting a lift to the sea gate."

"What if they ask you to stay at the tower? I don't want to leave anything to chance." He started mixing his paints. "How long to the sea gate?"

Tirin asked his cousin again. "Ten, fifteen minutes."

Simon sighed. "This won't be my best work."

Remeth grumbled, but laid down, holding the tarp stretched above him.

"I'm going to make it look like there's nothing there," Simon said to Tirin.

"How?"

"I'm going to paint it to look like what's underneath."

"Will it work?"

"In low light, it should. I think your cousin would throw us overboard if things take a bad turn."

Tirin sat on the front to give Simon a flat canvas. Even exhausted, desperation honed Simon's connection to his Talent, and he filled the space with the color of the wood. His brush moved fast but without any loss of control, and he added the joints, shadows, and weathered discolorations to give it depth.

By the time he finished, they reached the back of the queue of boats. Even to Simon's critical eye, it was hard to tell the difference.

"I'm going under," Simon said. "Knock three times when it's our turn, and again when we're done."

He slid first his supplies, then himself under the tarp to lie next to Remeth, their shoulders pressed together in the middle and bodies curved sideways with the shape of the boat.

Remeth recoiled from him. "You feel like a cold, dead fish!"

"Just be happy you didn't have to swim."

They each held a side and Tirin pulled it taut at his end.

"Will it work?" Remeth asked, whispering. Even with the stale smell of fish so strong, his breath still reeked of alcohol.

"It looks good," Simon said. "I think so. I know you're itching to tell me, so how did you get through the guards? I saw you go talk to those two."

"You did? From where?"

"The military pier. I..." The guilt at what he'd done hit him with a fresh wave of nausea. "So what did you say?"

"I told them I saw two people running. A big one and a smaller one. I sent one off the way we came, and stayed with the other to show him which apartment the big one slipped into. When he went through the door I grabbed his hammer and knocked him out."

"You?"

"What?" he said in a wounded voice. "I told you I keep in good shape. And I learn quickly. I've seen far too much damage done with those awful things."

"So you took his stuff?"

"It's my story! Yes, I borrowed his uniform and reported for duty to the docks, to help with the inspections. What a tedious job!

Once I found Tirin—can you believe how different he looks without the wild beard? It's obvious what his wife saw in him. A noble jawline ..."

Simon was suddenly too aware of having his flesh pressed against Remeth's.

"So you found him…"

"I barely recognized him. Took the lead on inspection of his boat once they said they were ready to shove off. Didn't find anything at first, so sent the others on while I finished off. Saw that strange rope hanging off the side so made a show of searching there too."

"So that was you?"

"Yes, and I nearly called out—you looked like you were dead!"

Simon winced. "Can you stop saying that?" It kept bringing his mind back to the corpse lying somewhere on the bottom of the bay, which could easily have been him.

"Sorry. So I went off to report my lack of findings, and help with one more inspection."

"But how could you come back on our boat?"

"I told them I needed to send word from the keep to the sea gate, so I'd catch a lift with one of the fishing boats. Keep an eye on things." Simon could hear the grin in his voice.

"Good work."

"Thank you. It was… exhilarating. Is that how you feel? Using your Talent with our lives on the line?"

"More nervous. But yes, it's a great feeling connecting to it. Even better afterward."

Tirin knocked three times.

Simon shut his mouth and slowed down his breathing, doing his best to keep it in time with Remeth's to limit the sound and movement, hoping they'd be disguised by the roll of the waves.

Tirin's cousin called out in a cheery voice, and another man responded from the distance.

The rowing sounds were only on the right side now, and Simon could feel the boat turning, angling toward the tower.

The left side thumped against stone, sending a shudder through the whole craft. The tarp rippled like it was trying to break free, and only quick reflexes allowed him to keep his hold. Remeth's side slipped from his hand, flapping slightly and letting in a bit of starlight before he caught it. Remeth's panicked heart beat like a drum next to him, and Simon wondered if his own would burst from his chest.

The voice called out again from the tower, this time questioning.

Their boat stopped.

Simon nudged his leg to the side, feeling for the hard sureness of one of the hammers they'd stashed out of sight beside him. In his mind he ran through the movements of an attack, hoping his body had something left if they were found out. Could he strike fast enough? How many would be in the tower? Or the other one? Reinforcements? A thousand worries vied for attention as he strained to listen for any signs of trouble.

Tirin was jovial in addressing the guard, who sounded friendly. He asked something else, and Tirin's response got them all laughing, even the nervous cousin.

Still Simon held his breath.

The voice spoke right above them, as if leaning over the boat for an inspection.

What if he steps into the empty space?

Simon felt ill, terrified that such a glaring hole might bring his plan crashing down.

Please just look, please!

Tirin's cousin laughed again and shared a few casual words with the guards before a short, clipped phrase—automatic, like a standard farewell.

The oars dipped into the water and they started moving again.

Simon exhaled very, very slowly, his body relaxing with every escaping puff of air. His eyes sagged, and Remeth's regular breathing faded into a light snore. The warmth, the rocking...

XXVI

Nature

Tirin's voice jolted Simon awake and his arm smacked Remeth.

"Coming ashore?"

"Watch it," Remeth said, his voice rough. "Can't a man get a good night's rest around here?"

Simon frowned. "Let's just hope Zeno slept better. The sooner we can get off this island, the better."

The tarp lifted, and Tirin peered in, dark against the lightening sky behind him. "My cousin… far as he will go."

Simon looked around, trying to get a sense of place. The coastline looked the same. They were a ways from the city, and he could see one of those towers…

"Did we come straight here?"

Tirin shook his head. "Too risky. First fishing, then circle back this way." His cousin sat behind him with his arms crossed. His eyes darted to the tower, back to the city, and everywhere else— expecting the worst.

"Thank your cousin. I know he did this for you, not for us. We appreciate it."

Tirin nodded. "This is way you came?"

"Yes. Our friend… our way out, should be up there." He pointed up to the plateau above them.

"How are we going to get up there?" Remeth asked, shaking his head. "We don't exactly have Zeno to help us."

"Do you think they'll send a search party out that way?" Simon asked Tirin.

Tirin's mouth twisted in thought. "You have problem at gate?"

Simon exchanged a glance with Remeth. "But that was hours before our escape."

"Way to Aktiri is by sea. But might follow strange happening.

241

You... we made big mess. Supplies to towers go often."

The wagon.

"We saw a wagon pass us on the way, so there won't be another for a few days?"

Tirin nodded.

"So what will you do, Tirin? Without the beard you look different for now, but won't others recognize the old you? You'll be in danger."

"Danger and free, not safe in prison."

"But you know what I mean... where will you go?"

"My people need truth. But..." He looked unsure. "Simon, could... I..." He took a deep breath. "What you do to tarp, and lock, and..." He pointed to Remeth's face. "Could you do for me?"

"Make you look different? It's the least I could do for all your help. Now, I have to warn you, I don't know how long it will last. It may wash away... or be permanent."

Remeth grabbed Simon's shoulder. "What do you mean, permanent? Simon, you—"

Simon raised a hand. "Later. Tirin?"

Tirin nodded.

When Simon took out his paints again, the cousin voiced a loud objection. Tirin shot him a pleading look, and the cousin huffed, grumbling, but appeared to concede.

"I'm going to scout for a path," Remeth said as he splashed into knee-deep water and waded to the shore. "Shout when you're done."

"I'll be quick," Simon said. He examined Tirin's face. "Anything in particular you want changed? What makes you most recognizable, to your people?"

"Make it last. My wife... she like shape of my face. This part." He pointed to his prominent cheekbones. "Change it."

"I don't know how this will feel. Try to relax." Despite his words, Tirin stiffened, almost recoiling from the first daub of paint.

Simon felt a surge of emotions: relief, gratitude, and concern for this noble man who put his life on the line for them. The brush swept along the cheekbones, flattening them out into a broader shape. He made the brows more prominent and added a slight turn to the nose and a scar at the corner of the mouth that pulled the left side of the lip down into a permanent frown. The chin he lengthened slightly, and stuck the detached earlobes to the side of the head with a daub of paint.

There was still some Tirin there if you searched hard, but the new features dominated the face, making him look more world-weary and sad. Unfortunately fitting.

"Ask your cousin what he thinks," Simon said.

The man's reaction gave Simon all the validation he needed— he nearly fell out of the boat. Appearing to ward himself against evil spirits, only Tirin's familiar voice calmed him down. Finally, he reached up and touched the new nose with eyes wide.

"My cousin not know me, so might be safe. Thank you."

The cousin scowled at Simon and pointed off the boat. Simon held up a hand while using the other to collect his paints back into his satchel.

"Sorry," Tirin said. "He—"

"No need to apologize. Thank him for me. He has done far more than I would have ever expected. I don't want to cause any more trouble."

"Will you return?"

"Here? No, we…" Simon thought for a moment. "I won't rule it out. I would say that you could seek us out again if you need a friend, but right now I have no idea where we'll even be." After closing his satchel, he held out his arm. Tirin clasped it in the classic Pazian farewell.

"Take care."

"For…" Simon had to stop himself. *No, not for Pazh. Not at all.* "We wish you all the best, in what you do for your people." Simon held his hand out to the cousin, but he looked away, toward the sea. "You'd better get going."

Simon stepped off the boat with a light splash, facing the forbidding central peak. He turned back. "Sorry Tirin, one more thing. What is the other side of the island like? Are there more settlements, towers, people?"

"Towers. Farms on good soil, no cities or towns."

"Thanks again." He waved at the already departing boat; the cousin put distance between them as quickly as possible.

Remeth was testing a rock wall for handholds, and Simon closed the gap before he made much headway. "Does this look like our best chance?" Simon asked.

Remeth pointed further down the narrow strip of sand.

"There's a rough path down there that winds up toward the city. But if we could climb up here, that flat part goes the other way. I don't know about you, but I'm staying away from the city walls."

"Agreed. I'm hoping Zeno has recovered enough that we can make a quick jump to the far side of the island, and rest further over there." Up close, he could see the handholds, but the better ones were just out of Remeth's reach.

"Maybe you can give me a boost?" Remeth said, readying himself. When Simon didn't immediately respond, he turned back with a pained, accusing expression. "What, you're afraid to touch me now? Afraid of what? That you might be too close to my ass?"

"I... I'm sorry. I didn't mean anything. I'm just tired." He interlaced his hands and held them out as a step. Remeth sighed, and the disappointment in his eyes made Simon feel horrible.

Simon's arms almost gave out when he boosted Remeth up; he was even heavier than he looked. But he caught the higher handholds and pulled himself up to a ledge, then turned around and offered Simon a hand. With shared strain they soon had him up on the narrow ledge as well.

"At least we can still make a team," Remeth said.

Simon's shoulders slumped. "I'm really sorry, Remeth. I haven't... I've never..."

"Met anyone like me? I could say the same. A dark-skinned Pazian with Talent, and as impressive as yours? It makes you different, just like me."

"I know. You're right. Please forgive me. We have to stick together. I just want to understand." He started walking up the narrow path.

"Understand why I'm like *this*? Why do you have Talent?"

"I don't know... I was born this way."

"Exactly."

"Did you always know?"

"That I like men? Did you always like women?"

"Well, no..."

"It's the same, Simon. My childhood was like any other, except I always loved telling stories, acting them out. But all kids do that, just like all kids try their hand at drawing, or sculpture if you have the materials. When I joined the troupe, met others with that love of acting... that's when I made my first good friends. People who understood me. Of course they were much older. I was twelve or thirteen when I first... first felt something for another man."

He sighed.

"Fallan. He was twice my age, one of the actors in our troupe. Had the face of a young god. I... I couldn't even speak to him, not that I had much of a chance. I was still getting the children's roles and he was a promising young lead. I wanted to touch that face, to feel those lips on mine... but a man with another man? In Martha they act like such feelings don't exist... could never exist. That's what women are for. To pleasure their men and bear them children. I hated myself... So I shut the thoughts away inside and tried to ignore them."

Their path switched back, leading them higher.

Simon wanted to understand. He was curious, and felt bad, but didn't know what to say, so continued in silence, waiting for Remeth to continue.

"But I was right about him! Just... not for me. When I was fifteen we were doing a show for the spring feast days, and at the end of the run there was a party for the whole troupe. It was the first time they let me have unwatered wine. I... I got a little drunk. I know, hard to believe? I saw Fallan head off into the garden, and the wine gave me courage to rush out and tell him how I felt. I lost my way in the trees, losing track of him, and even hit my head on a branch. But then I heard Fallan's voice, and another, and followed the sounds, but carefully. I didn't want to be seen."

He let out a sad and wistful sigh.

"I saw him. And another of the older players, Darish. He took Fallan by the wrists, and looked dangerous, even angry. I almost cried out, but then he leaned in and kissed him. My Fallan! And Fallan kissed him back. I was so jealous, I wanted to run and fight off this big brute that was doing what I wanted. But I also wanted to run away, in shame and horror. Instead, I watched. Off came their clothes, and for the first time I saw two men naked and in the throes of desire. And I burned to be a part of it. I wanted to feel his—"

Simon held up his hands. "I'm sorry Remeth, but..."

"Squeamish? Fine. But just remember that. Don't go telling me graphic tales of what you and Elysia do together."

"I would never! I'm not some philanderer like Persei. What I have with Elysia is special."

Remeth nodded, his eyes wet. "It is. And I'm happy for you. I really am. I wish I could have someone like that."

"So you never have?"

"Oh, I've had lovers. Other men from the troupe. It was surprisingly common, once I moved in those circles, but we were discreet. To hide from society we even hid from each other. But those relationships were nothing like what you have."

"Did you... keep seeing men like that when you were learning with Yalath?"

Remeth scoffed. "You think Yalath would allow it? No, he forbade it, the old prune. He doesn't like anything that gets in the way of connecting with your Talent. No relationships, no good wine... even keeps his food simple. I think he just likes denying himself."

"Did he ever have any women in his life?"

"Women? Yalath hates women. Well, people, really. If he ever had a lover, it wasn't something he talked about."

"So you were miserable with him?"

"Miserable? No... it's complicated. I learned so much. He's the only one who ever understood my Talent, and we connected in that way. But with all the other limitations, life was so different when I was living with him. So cold and austere. And the hiding! Our Talent was only to be used in extreme secrecy, or on one isolated subject at a time. Never in public. Not like what we've done here in Aktiri. He'd be apoplectic. Lecture us on how disrespectful we're being, and the danger we're bringing on ourselves by showing others our powers, and... well I guess he's right on that part.

"Simon, I'm... I'm sorry for what happened last night. I guess I needed the release. This was the longest I've ever been with Yalath without time with the troupe to break it up."

Simon nodded. "Just be careful. It's not just yourself that you might be endangering. And if anything happened to Elysia and we weren't able to help..."

The wagon sat right where they'd left Elysia.

No!

Ignoring the exhaustion, Simon broke into a run. The pony was covered in blood.

"Elysia!" he shouted, searching for her.

She stepped out from behind the wagon, her blood-streaked face lighting up when she saw him.

"What happened to you?" he shouted, frantic. "Are you hurt?"

She flew into his arms, holding him tight. "I'm safe. But what happened to you? You're wet, and cold!"

"But we saw a man?"

Her eyes flashed. "Dead." Her body went rigid. "Behind you! One of them! He's armed! Simon!" He spun around, raising his hammer to face the enemy.

It was Remeth, or rather the Aktirian version of him. Simon laughed.

Elysia drew a bloody blade that looked almost like... wood?

"Elysia, stop! It's Remeth!"

"It's one of those locals, coming to avenge the one I... I..."

His heart fell. She had been in danger, and he hadn't been able to protect her. But first... "Remeth! Say something. She doesn't know it's you!"

Remeth held up his hands. "Elysia! It's me, Remeth. Simon painted me so we could get in the city. This is no trick! But excellent work by our friend there."

She lowered the blade, now uncertain, and looked to Simon. "Is it true?"

He rushed to her side, and put his hand on her arm, gently encouraging it down. "Yes, after we met one of the locals with a wagon... what... what happened to him?"

"He came after me. I ran. He bound Zeno—I think he planned to come for him later. But I couldn't let that happen, so I made this." She lifted her sword. "And freed another little friend who had suffered at his hands. And we... we avenged him."

"Where is the body?"

"Up toward the tower. I left my friend there to... to clean up. Drove the wagon back here. He'd taken our things."

"I'm so sorry. I should have been here for you. How is Zeno?"

She led him around to where Zeno lay snoring.

"Did you rest?"

"No... I couldn't. So I carved." Her face lit up. "I finally figured it out. I was working on..." Her eyes searched for something and she grabbed it, trying to shield it from view.

"Can't you show me?"

Reluctantly she held it up for him to see. It was the dark piece he'd seen her working on for a while, but now it was clear and smooth, nearly finished. It wasn't a lizard at all; it was a serpent, except with vicious toothed heads at *both* ends of the sleek body.

Exquisite, yet grotesque...

"So what took you so long?" she asked, putting the piece away in her pack.

"We got caught up... in prison."

"Prison? Are you all right?" She looked him over for any signs of harm.

"Just exhausted. We had to escape, and then I had to swim across the harbor. And sneak out, with help—"

"Help? From these awful people?"

"I'll tell you everything while we get going. Do you think Zeno can fly now?"

"He's a bit better, but I don't think he could go far."

"The other side of the mountain is mostly unpopulated. But we can't stay here. They'll be looking for us, and when this delivery is missed they'll send someone to check on it. They might already be coming."

"Lots of food and supplies in here!" Remeth said from the side of the wagon. "Shame we don't have more bags."

"Let's fill what we have," Simon said.

"I'm happy you're safe," Elysia said. She leaned up to kiss him, but Simon jerked back, looking over at Remeth. There was a questioning hurt in her eyes.

"I'm sorry. Not now." He didn't want to rub it in Remeth's face. Not after all they'd shared. "We'll get the bags packed, you get Zeno ready." She didn't look happy, but went over to the sleeping mount.

Remeth had several piles ready in the cart. "Grain, dried meat, and a cask of that drink we had—"

"Absolutely not."

"I figured you were going to say that. And on second thought, I'd rather not drink and fly. How is Elysia? She looks pretty rough."

"She killed the wagon driver."

"Remind me not to make her mad."

Simon frowned.

Remeth looked at Elysia and back to Simon again. "I'll get the saddlebags."

The sun had just peeked over the horizon when they were ready to go, with all three of them up on Zeno's back. Simon was on edge. Elysia sat rigid in front of him, and try as he might to ignore it, he was painfully aware of Remeth's body behind him, not left with any space to hide on the small saddle.

"Are you sure Zeno is ready?" Remeth asked. "I don't fancy dropping on these rocks."

Elysia stroked his mane. "He's ready, aren't you my friend?"

Zeno snorted, sounding more like his usual self. He'd devoured several apples from the wagon. But what about the weight of the additional supplies?

Takeoff was sluggish, but Zeno used the downward slope to get momentum and they were airborne before they'd be visible from the city.

Zeno soared up around the mountain, giving them a good view of the entire island. Just as Tirin had explained, the western side was dotted with towers at regular intervals, with a few watching over small farms.

"What about there?" Elysia said, pointing to an isolated plateau.

Zeno brought them down without seeming too strained.

"Would one night's rest be enough?" Elysia asked him. The horse stamped once.

"Then let's get a camp together," Simon said. "I think we could all use the sleep. But first, Kashaka, just to be certain."

He took out the blood, hoping it would point away from this place. He'd had quite enough of Aktiri and its people. Remeth and Elysia crowded around him, waiting to see the direction, and they all breathed a sigh of relief when it pointed northwest, off into the depths of the sea.

"Then it's settled," said Remeth. "I'm going to bed."

Simon unfurled his map. "Izar?"

"Home?" Elysia said, hope in her eyes.

"At the very least, we'll need to stop there for Zeno's sake. Who knows how far this is leading us? But given that your Izari ancestors were her captors, it would make sense if they imprisoned her somewhere they could keep an eye on her."

She looked to the horizon. "Can we stop in Attarsus? I'd like the chance to really say goodbye. And maybe we could retrieve more of my things. Maybe even from Master Xelos' house?"

"Who knows, maybe he left something to you?"

"If those bastards didn't steal everything."

"I don't know... I did alert the watch. I doubt the killers stayed around long to take much. What would have happened with every-thing Master Xelos owned, since he didn't have an heir?"

"He never said anything to me about his plans." Her lips formed a tight line. "We should make sure that gets settled. To honor him. Both of them. My father's things are mine now."

"What if they're still searching for us?"

"In Attarsus? But why? You were seen in Tamar, and then they would have linked us to Bor…"

"We'll still need to be on guard. I wouldn't put it past Persei to have someone watching for us there."

"What if it's the one who did it?" Her eyes blazed.

"Please don't get your hopes up."

"I know, but still, it will be nice to be home. At least for a while."

"It will be different. And Kashaka might be far from there."

"I know, but you'll be with me."

He looked over to Remeth, already snoring with his head buried under a blanket to keep out the sunlight. Only then did he take her hand.

"I just wish we could have peace, alone together," she said, running her hand across his stubble. She'd need to give him another shave. She was getting good at it.

"We will, soon enough."

XXVII
༠༦༠༦༠༦
Performance

His people were calling it the celebration of freedom, which made Glebric even more nervous. He'd only intended for the meal to be a chance to bring together all his leaders, warriors and planners, so they could move forward as one.

The skirmish over the girl was the first of several in the past few days, and his men were increasingly brazen. They'd raided the slave market yesterday and killed the guards, bringing back another fifty souls to the house, which was too crowded already. There had been two separate battles with the city watch, and success had further emboldened the men. But things were moving too fast. Surely the governor would send for reinforcements from Pazh. Perhaps even a legion? They needed to get coordinated, and fast.

Fifty men and women were seated in chairs in the central courtyard of his house, with more than a hundred crammed into every space behind them. There was food for all, and well-watered wine. And to lighten the mood they'd asked several of their number to perform. Xelos might even have approved.

Glebric had been thinking about Xelos a lot lately. Had he really been so bad? Yes, he was rich, but had rejected the idea of slavery and always paid his people a fair wage, giving them an opportunity to improve themselves. How was that any different from what Glebric was doing now? But the doing was the difference. Action versus a life of leisure. Change was happening, because Glebric was willing it to happen.

Or allowing it. At this point he didn't think he could stop it if he tried.

His mother, Ventus, Zustar, and Azzam sat closest to him, all on the same kind of wooden chairs. He was one among the people, not better than them. Although his power set him apart.

That new girl, the redhead they'd saved—Kallara—was ready to sing for them, with accompaniment from another girl on flute, a young man on lyre, and one of the elders behind them with a drum. *Hopefully this puts them at ease. I have to rein them in so we can drive forward together.*

The flute led with a happy melody that tugged at Glebric's heart. So sweet and charming, like the flutist herself. He smiled at his mother, who was obviously enjoying it. The drum and lyre joined in, adding something masculine and grounded to the song. Glebric sipped his wine, feeling at peace and looking to the girl, Kallara. The bruises had mostly faded, but she looked nervous. Probably not used to such a large crowd. Their eyes caught for a moment, and he smiled to urge her on. Reflected back, he saw fear, and felt a slight pull inside him. A tug on his power, like a mother on the ear of a misbehaving child.

Her song poured out, ethereal in its beauty. That he didn't understand the language was irrelevant. It was original, nothing like the formulaic music of Izar. Waves of sound surrounded him, caressing his ears, filtering into his mind, carrying him away as if he were drifting off to sleep. He felt peace, wonder and…

A jab in the ribs brought the world sharply back into focus. Ventus glared at him with narrowed eyes.

"Later," Ventus said, his voice barely audible. "Guard your mind."

Glebric looked around at the still enraptured crowd. When he focused on the girl, he felt as if he could see things clearly, like his eyesight had become more attuned. The sound made ripples in the air. But instead of penetrating into him, affecting him, now they bounced off a hard outer shell.

Magic. And she was using it on them. *Knowingly? Or unwittingly? A plot? What about the other musicians? Enemies in my own house?* But like Ventus said, it would have to wait. He had a speech to give.

When the song finished, many rose to their feet and cheered. Glebric joined them to blend in. But when Kallara's eyes met his again, her joy in the adulation cracked, and the raw, naked fear returned. *Fear of me.* Her eyes slipped to Ventus before resuming their scan of the happy crowd. *She knows something. She's dangerous.*

Glebric raised his hands to speak. A hush fell over the crowd.

"What a wonderful way to celebrate our time together. One more round of applause for our own musicians." The four filed toward the back amid handshakes, smiles and loud cheers.

Glebric waited until the crowd settled.

"This is a celebration. Of freedom. Of life. Of being united in one goal."

Cheers punctuated every pause.

"Freedom for every living man and woman in this city. And beyond!"

"We'll kill every last one of those slaving bastards!" a warrior shouted, and far too many voiced their agreement.

Glebric held up a hand. "But that is not our intention. We do not kill for revenge. We only fight because we have to. Not because we want to. We are not savages. We do not aim to oppress, not after what we have all suffered." Another chorus of agreement, but the more belligerent faces looked chastised. He'd have to be very careful with them.

"Now is the time for action. Coordinated action. Our men," he said, indicating some of the warriors, "have already had success against the city watch. We can take them. Neutralize them. Offer them a chance to join us in the new order."

"But they oppress us in the name of Pazh!" chimed in another warrior. "I won't serve with the likes of them!"

Glebric shook his head. "They are just men, like us, doing a job for their employer. We need the numbers, and we need a united front. For as soon as we claim the city, it will set grander wheels in motion. The navy will be on us immediately, and make no mistake: the legions will come."

An equal number of gasps and defiant shouts rang out.

"Yes, the legions. The Republic does not brook opposition. Rebellion. They will aim to crush us. Only if we secure the city and show a united front can we negotiate with the Senate. If the people here declare for our new government, then we stand a chance. So we must keep the people on our side, while taking control.

"First, our men will take the watch. Tomorrow.

"Next, we will secure the other nobles. They can join us and free their own slaves, but many will fight and have their own guards. The wealth of those who fall will help to fund our cause

"Treat everyone with respect as you go out in the name of freedom. We will take our islands here in Izar one by one, freeing the slaves and workers and building support. We will be ready for the Pazians to recognize us when they come."

He read universal agreement in their faces. The ones who wanted a fight would get one, but properly constrained. No blood-bath. He would use his power to prevent it, if he had to. And to face the Pazians if they wouldn't meet them at the bargaining table. Ventus estimated they'd have weeks to secure the islands first, a month at most.

"So are we all in agreement?" he asked. The shouts were universal. "Then enjoy this banquet, for tomorrow we retake this city, and then the world!"

With everyone preoccupied with devouring the food, Ventus leaned in close to Glebric. He kept his voice low. "You saw it, didn't you?"

"With the musicians? Yes. What was that?"

"Magic. Power. Power that would challenge you."

"Really? They seem harmless," Glebric said, but in his heart he knew it wasn't true. Something opposed the power that flowed through him.

Ventus paused to take a bite of succulent steaming fish. "If you don't see it, then you deserve to fail. To give someone else the chance. Azzam wouldn't allow such a challenge."

"Azzam is ready to kill even the Pazians among us, for the dishonor they've caused him. Even you."

"Which is why you're a fool if you think that those with power won't use it against you. The girl might be grateful for her rescue, but did you see how she fears you?"

"She... she knows something."

"She sees both of us as something other than Glebric and Ventus."

"So she sees the truth."

"Yes, but that's not something we share lightly. Tell me, Glebric, how much power do you need, to make things right in this world? To do what your heart yearns to do?" The deep eyes bored into him; ancient and powerful and promising the world.

Glebric gulped, shrinking from the question. "We are doing everything we can."

"So you have enough power?" Ventus raised an eyebrow. "Do you really think the Pazians will offer you a treaty and let us sit here astride their shipping lanes? Choking their lifeblood? Collecting our own taxes?"

Of course not. I'm a fool.

"I could use my power."

Ventus laughed. "Those are parlor tricks compared to what is possible. What we can do together. But such power needs fuel."

Glebric dreaded even whispering the words. "What... fuel?"

Ventus smiled a cold, calculating smile. He glanced at the musicians.

"Do we make them play for us?" Glebric asked. But he knew it was much more.

"They won't be willing to do what you need. Choose one. You'll get a taste for what is possible. Four might even be enough."

"Enough for what?"

"To give you the power to move the sea against the navy, or against the legions when they come. You can force them to treat with you." Ventus stood up and wiped his mouth with a cloth. "Make your choice, and see me tonight."

The food lost all taste as Glebric mulled dark possibilities through the rest of the meal, with his eyes flicking to the musicians every few minutes.

The dream was worth any price.

He walked through the crowds, saying his pleasantries until he reached the musicians. They stood to meet him.

"Thank you for your wonderful performances, all of you."

"It was our pleasure," said Kallara, the redhead.

Glebric reached out his hand to the flute player, a sweet girl with bobbed hair. She was probably close to his seventeen years, slightly older than Kallara, but her innocence made her seem younger. She offered her hand very tentatively in return, sweetly shy. Glebric smiled to encourage her and kissed her hand. "You played so wonderfully... I don't know your name."

"Orna," she said. Her voice was surprisingly harsh. Glebric tried not to let his disappointment show.

"We are honored to have you among our number. I was hoping you might play for me and a friend, privately?"

Her nod was automatic, like a slave deferring to her master, and anger flared in Glebric. "It is only a request, we are all free here. Would you like to join us? Just music, nothing more."

She relaxed, but Glebric felt concern emanating from Kallara. *That one bears watching.* She was somehow more... aware. Not oblivious like this Orna.

"Would you come to my study now?" Glebric asked. "I have paperwork to attend to. Our plans to improve this world require such an investment of time and money."

"It is very good," she said, "what you are doing. I am honored to play my part."

We'll see if you change your tune.

Ventus was already in the study when Glebric arrived with Orna.

"This is Ventus," Glebric said. "He works very closely with me in planning our efforts, especially on the financial side. Ventus, Orna is here to play for us while we do our work."

"Welcome Orna, it will be a great help. Working with numbers all day is so... tiresome. Your talent should be the tonic we need to pick things up." He gave Glebric a knowing look, which made his stomach drop.

Are we really going to do this? Here?

"Won't I be interrupting... or hearing something that I shouldn't?"

Ventus waved his hand in dismissal. "Certainly not. You won't be a bother at all. Can I see your flute?"

Reluctantly, she offered it to him. "It's only simple wood. I'm saving for something better. But I only just started making money these last few weeks, thanks to your business."

She shone with a curious mix of heartfelt appreciation and shame at the simplicity of her possession. No longer was she denied that right of ownership. Here was a girl who was living the life he wished for everyone, proof that he was on the right track. And now he was going to take that away from her? He felt like a monster.

Ventus cradled the flute in long fingers, stroking the smooth wood. "It may be inexpensive, but you made it sing so beautifully. It's in the pastoral Borathi style, isn't it?"

She nodded.

"Have you always played?"

"As much as I could. My father was a shepherd and I grew up hearing him play. My village was taken by the Marassani and he died, so I was... sold. But I was one of the lucky ones. They didn't harm me. And I've worked with good families, helping the women. My mistress even let me play for her on special occasions. It's what kept me going all these years. And it helps me remember Papa."

Glebric caught Ventus' eye and shook his head slightly, but was met by a dark twinkle.

Ventus held up the flute in front of him, waving it at her with his next words. "Did you know, young Orna, that there is power in music? In all the arts?"

Her delicate brow furrowed. "I'm not sure what you mean."

"Power. Magic. Do they speak of that in the tales where you come from? Maybe from the old crones?"

"Like the one with the shepherd leading his sheep with just a flute? Or the ones about the wicked man charming young girls against their will? But that's just silly. They're only stories."

"What if I told you it's all true?"

Glebric felt sick. There was no turning back.

Her eyes widened in wonder, and she looked even younger. Was he wrong? Was she only fourteen or fifteen? Barely past childhood? Then they narrowed again.

"Master Ventus, are you making fun of me? I know I am but a simple country girl…"

"No, I speak true. What if I said that *you* have the power to do all those things, and so much more? That I saw it in you when you were playing? You're special, Orna."

Her face lit up. It almost brought a tear to Glebric's eye. This girl had probably never been told she was special.

"Can you… will you show me?"

Ventus held out the flute to her, and when she reached up to grasp it, he waved it away. "I'm sorry, I can't. I just want your Talent."

"I… I don't understand." She looked to Glebric, and he wanted to vomit.

"It has been a long night, Ventus," Glebric said. "Maybe we should let Orna go."

Ventus laughed, genial but with a velvet twist of cruelty. "Oh, I don't think so. It is much too late for that."

For the first time, fear began to creep into her eyes. Those innocent eyes If there was any plot to use magic against them, she was an unwitting accomplice. She had no idea that she even had an aptitude. *This is wrong.*

"Glebric here," Ventus said to her, his tone matter-of-fact, "wants to free the slaves. Every last one of them. Such a noble goal. Admirable. Worthy. What a delightful young man Master Glebric is, don't you think, young Orna?"

She looked at Glebric again, imploring, begging for help. She didn't understand what was going on, but she did think highly of him, and knew something terrible was about to happen. "Master Glebric, can I leave now?"

"The problem, young Orna," Ventus continued, "is that this Republic is built on slavery. Without the cheap labor the Senators would have to cook their own food, dump out their own excrement, mine their own iron. Can you even imagine it? Of course they'll fight for the right to keep slaves. Just like Glebric said in his speech. Wasn't it a wonderful speech?"

She nodded through silent tears.

"Have you seen Glebric's power? He's special too. Not like you, different. Glebric, show her a little something of your power. Is that a tear?" He pointed to the glistening drop running down her cheek. "Glebric has a special way of drying your eyes. Do it." His face turned deadly serious.

Glebric complied. Pointing a finger at her eye, he called upon the power to pull the liquid into a round ball, away from her face and into the air. One, two, three little globes glistened as they danced in a circle around the lamp. The wonder returned to her face, along with something that hurt Glebric even more: hope. Misplaced hope.

"So you see," Ventus said, "he can command water like this. But only in small amounts. Not enough to stop the Pazian fleet. And he might be able to use it to defeat one or two or a handful of legionaries sent to kill him. But not thousands of highly trained warriors bent on destruction and reclaiming slaves for their masters." He paused and looked at Glebric.

"Do you think Glebric is a good man, and would do what is needed to make things right?"

She looked in his eyes, and began to nod slowly.

"No matter the cost?"

"Yes," she said.

He turned on her. "What about you? Would you do everything you can to serve the cause?"

"But what can I do? Play the flute? Or would this... this Talent you described. Could I use it to help?"

Ventus gave a slow nod. "Oh yes. With your Talent inside him, it would magnify his power two or three times."

"What do you mean inside him?"

"Ah... there's the rub." With mock sadness, Ventus shook his head. "He has to take it from you."

She took a step back, hands up. "But how? It's a part of me."

Glebric had seen enough. "Stop it, Ventus, you're scaring her.'

"Can I have my flute back? I'd like to go."

"Glebric, it is time. Her Talent, it's in her blood. Take it, now."

"My blood?" She clutched one hand over her throat, the other over her heart.

"Ventus! I will not."

Now Ventus was the one to look shocked. "Until tonight, you didn't even know this girl's name. And now you will spare her and bring all this crashing down? She knows too much. Let her walk out the door and your dream dies."

"Please, Glebric!"

"She is innocent. She doesn't deserve this."

"Don't let this shell deceive you. You saw that Talent inside her. It senses you, like the other girl did. It is afraid of you. It hates you. It wants to destroy you for your power. In her eyes, *you* are the abomination."

"It's not me they hate. It's you, Ventus, or whatever you are!"

"You were nothing without me. I gave you everything you wanted."

"Just let me go!" Orna shuffled toward the door.

"Feel inside her, Glebric. All those with Talent seek to destroy ones like you. To imprison you. Or make you their slave!"

Something snapped. Glebric turned to her. "Is this true?"

"I don't know anything! Please, let me go."

"To the others," Ventus said, "where she will turn them against you. You can resist one, especially one so young. But four? They would imprison you. Glebric the slave for all eternity!"

"No!" Glebric's vision blurred. The helpless, hopeless feelings of his youth returned, but he rejected them. "No!" He was free, and he would never let someone take that away from him again.

His power flowed into her, grasping her blood.

Orna had reached the door, and opened her mouth to scream, but he pulled the moisture from her tongue and it came out a rasping wheeze.

Clenching his fist in the air, he drove deeper, feeling the blood warm around his hand. It resisted, with writhing antipathy. Hatred.

"How do I harvest the Talent?" His anger pulsed in time with the beat he felt through her blood.

Ventus smiled. "Pull it out, into you."

Horror was frozen on her face as he walked toward her.

"I can't let anyone stop this march to freedom. There will be sacrifices along the way. Thank you for your service, Orna."

He touched her chest over her heart and began to pull on her Talent-laden blood. First a trickle, then a steady flow out through his hands and into him. Her face contorted in silent agony as her very essence drained away. Her skin sagged and withered before him, her eyes shriveling into desiccated raisins. Every drop of life that left her surged into Glebric, making him stronger and so very alive.

"Take it all."

The flow slowed to a drip when the skin began to crack, and the hair fell out of her head. The lips sank away, exposing the grin of death. The dried up husk rattled to the floor in a heap of bones.

Ventus smiled, holding out the flute. "Would you like to keep this as a memento of your first? This is only the beginning."

XXVIII

༶༶༶༶༶༶

Home

A knock stirred Numerius from his thoughts. He'd been unable to sleep with all the noise of what sounded like a party.

"Yes?" he called out.

The door cracked open, splashing light on his face.

"Numerius?" Kallara, and she sounded worried.

"Come in, dear."

She carried a candle and looked over her shoulder before closing the door behind her.

"Glebric knows," she whispered.

"Knows what?"

"That there's more to my music... I... I shouldn't even be talking about this."

"You can trust me, my dear. Why do you think this?"

"He... there's something different about him, about the way he looks at me."

Numerius laughed. "You're a pretty young woman, and he's a young man. It's natural."

She pursed her lips. "Once I might have thought that's all it was. But when I was playing, he looked at me, and it was like he saw inside me. Saw my... saw that I'm special. And not just me."

"Oh? There was another?"

"Orna. She's one of the other players. We were performing for everyone. We were all so excited about this chance to show some of the new pieces we'd been working on. The crowd was mesmerized, enjoying it so much."

I'm sure they were. More than one with Talent?

"But when I saw Glebric, I felt the darkness... like from my dream. And not just from him, but the other man who is always with him."

"Ventus?"

"I don't know his name. He's Pazian."

Numerius nodded. "What about him?"

"I... I'm so scared of him. Is it wrong to think he's... evil?"

"Unfortunately there is a lot more evil in this world than any of us would like."

"I know that." She unconsciously touched the bruises on her face.

Poor girl. Worse is yet to come.

"But this is different. I think somehow Glebric and... Ventus? I think they're connected to the darkness from my dreams. And I think they have Orna."

"What do you mean?" *Everything is moving too fast.*

"Glebric asked her to come and play for him in private. I tried to get her to come with me, but I had to be careful. He is the master after all."

"But Kallara, you're free now. No longer a slave."

"I know, but this is his house. I... Numerius I'm scared. I think he'll come for me next. I don't know what to do."

"It is as I feared."

Her eyes went wide. "You knew about this?"

He nodded. "They are channeling dark magic."

She gasped. "But..."

"It's as real as your Talent. And you're right. They will be coming for you next. You have to get out of here."

"But where can I go? I can't go out in the city by myself." She shuddered, again touching the bruise.

If only I had more time. She might have been useful to get me out of here.

"I can help."

Hope dawned in her eyes. "You would do that for me? But you're a prisoner here."

"And I wish you could help me get out. But I have powerful friends. Friends that need to know what is happening here. They can take care of you. Can you write Pazian?"

Her face fell. "I... I can't. I'm sorry."

"Could you get me something to write with?"

"I... I don't know. What if they come for me tonight? I might not get back."

He took a deep breath.

"But I'm sure you have a good memory? For lyrics and songs?"

An excited nod confirmed his guess.

"Then I need you to go to Korg. He runs a warehouse by the harbor. Ask anyone down there and they'll send you to him."

Terror returned to her eyes. "The harbor at night? But I've heard…"

He nodded. "You're right, of course. Have you been to the temples on the acropolis? There's a shrine to Aliata. The priestesses there should give you a place for the night. There's one named Nyera. Tell her I sent you."

"Oh, thank you!"

"So Nyera at the shrine of Aliata. Then Korg in the morning, by the harbor. Do you have that?"

"Yes."

"Are you ready for the message?" She nodded. "Tell Korg that I'm held prisoner at the house of Xelos, now Glebric. They're raising an army here. The whole city is in danger. I need him to send an urgent letter to my home in Pazh. To my steward. He's to write a letter for Tullus. Tell him there are works of art here that are in danger. We must take care of them, or they'll turn dark, damaged by the elements. Extremely urgent. Did you get all that?"

"Can you say it again?" He let out an exasperated sigh, which crushed her. "No, I… I mostly got it. But I just wanted to make sure."

After a second time, she repeated the message verbatim. *This may yet work.*

"Do they allow you to come and go as you please? Or will getting out tonight be a problem?"

"I… I have an idea. I've made some friends among the guards."

"Be careful."

"Thank you, Numerius. I don't know what I would have done without you."

"It is I who must thank you. You've given me reason to hope again. Now get going. You don't want to be seen here."

She nodded with a smile. "Goodbye. I hope we will meet again."

"You and me both, my dear."

She closed the door, leaving him in darkness again.

A Talented girl is my only hope? She'd better hope my people find her first.

ᏩᎬᏩᎬᏩᎬᏩ

On Zeno's back, Elysia rode through the solid familiarity of the gates of Attarsus. The memory of departing that same way so many weeks ago seemed more dream than reality—hazy and indistinct.

Simon led the way, with Remeth trailing behind them. This time the guards did look at them funny. She could pass for a local, but few foreigners ever ventured outside the city itself.

Zeno had landed early in the morning at the same valley they'd used for his first flight. He was even more tired than when they'd reached Aktiri, and Elysia had decreed a minimum of two full days of rest for him, with three being preferable.

Before heading to the city, they'd taken a walk down to the coast to bathe—Simon's swimming escape was the only time any of them had a chance to get clean since they left Jeppo. Remeth had been relieved that he was able to wash away his Aktirian visage and return to his golden Maruthan self. Simon had somehow convinced him that it was permanent.

Simon had been somewhat distant since coming back from their little sojourn in Aktiri. Had he seen something that disturbed him? Had something happened between him and Remeth? She couldn't figure it out.

The guard at the gate smiled at her. "Coming to see the shows?" She was surprised how comforting it was to hear her native tongue for the first time in... months?

"Shows?"

"At the theater. There's a new troupe performing some of the classics. Two more nights, unless the people don't let them leave. I've heard they're incredible. I was hoping to go tomorrow when I'm off." He looked at the two men. "Maybe you could—"

"Thank you, but my husband would prefer if I went with him."

The guard looked from Remeth to Simon and back again, making a face. Less embarrassment than disappointment. And a hint of disdain. But he nodded respectfully as she passed by.

When they were out of earshot, Remeth came alongside her, grinning. "Did he say theater?"

"Yes. Some new group of players. I... I've never actually been."

"Well, maybe while you're taking care of your business, I can look into that. I love my Maruthan theater, but there are those that claim the superiority of your Izari style. You two said you want to look into Xelos' house, your father's house, and your workshop? Which first?"

264

She frowned, the horrible image of her brother's death blazing in her mind. "Simon, I don't want to go into the bakery. It would be too hard. I'll drop off Zeno at the workshop first, but then I want to see Xelos' house."

"Remeth and I will clean up," Simon said. "But I'd rather you stay in the workshop. You can get me the rest of the paints we left there."

"Simon, you're still jumping at shadows. Sure, I'd have cause to worry after dark, but in daylight? This is my home. I used to go everywhere by myself. Xelos' neighborhood is as safe as it comes. And I'll wear my cloak. It's cool enough that I'd want to anyway."

"I'd feel more comfortable if we stayed together."

She shook her head. "Your concern has been noted, but I fit in here. You two... you stick out. And you know yourself; few of my people are as open-minded as Master Xelos was."

"So we're settled then?" Remeth said. "Which way? And what's that? Is it on fire?" He pointed to the acropolis, where the morning light reflected off the gold decoration, shimmering like flames.

Elysia smiled. "It's the pride of Attarsus—the acropolis. All our great temples. Definitely worth your time."

Remeth shrugged. "I'll leave the visual stuff to you two. I'm much more excited to see the theater. Where is it?"

"On the other side of the hill," Elysia said. "Maybe Simon can point you the way later? Do you remember where it is?"

Simon nodded, still frowning. But she wasn't going to let him lock her away. It was too exciting to be home. And besides, she'd proven she could take of herself.

They walked the long way around to her workshop, so that she didn't have to pass the front door. The door was still locked, so she wasn't surprised to find things untouched inside. The rest of her sculptures were there, and Simon restocked his paints. "Come on, you'll have a good and uneventful rest down here. We'll bring you some food."

Simon's eyes darted around, looking back toward the entrance to the bakery. She squeezed his hand reassuringly.

"It will just be a short walk. I want to check with a few friends of the family at the agora. It will be so busy that nothing bad could ever happen to me. And then a quick walk by Master Xelos' house. I'll be back before you know it."

"Why don't I come with you?"

"If you can get the house cleaned up, we can sleep there instead of the hard floor of the workshop. I'm looking forward to a few nights in my own bed. With you."

"While you're off running errands?"

"These errands can get us supplies, and maybe money too. You said yourself that we're going to have to find a place to live, or source of income at some point. This should help with both." Her words set off that practical side of him, and she could tell he was processing the details.

"I could always join these players," Remeth said.

"Just be back as quickly as you can," Simon said.

Elysia kissed him, and led Zeno down into the basement.

୧୨୨୨୨୨୨

"She'll be fine," Remeth said, as he and Simon walked around the corner to the front door of the bakery.

"You don't understand. Last time we were here, she found her brother dead, and then I failed to rescue her father *and* Xelos. There are too many bad memories here. And they might still be looking for us."

"You're paranoid."

"Better safe than careless."

"So this is the place? Do you have the key?"

Simon nodded. He turned it in the lock and held his breath. Remeth copied him. He opened the door and looked where the sunlight illuminated the dusty floor.

And saw an arm.

Remeth made a strangled noise from behind him, gagging. "Gods, the stench!"

Simon closed the door again, and when he breathed in, the odor of mold and decay was still strong.

"I guess that answers one question," Simon said. "No one has been inside."

"The bodies have been here for how long? Weeks? Over a month?"

"Almost two months, by my count."

Remeth grimaced. "And now we're supposed to clean this place up?"

"It gives us a free place to live. Elysia's father owned the bakery and the apartment behind it."

Remeth pursed his lips. "I'd rather find an inn."

"But we should be more careful with our money. Would you prefer another night on the rocks? And it also gives us a bakery. Free food?"

"Now you're speaking my language. But dead bodies… how many?"

"She said three."

"What are we going to do with them? We can't exactly carry them out for burial. And where would we even do that in the city? It's a shame we don't have a hole to just dump them in."

"Hey, one of them was her brother."

"Family or not, they're still a bother. Maybe you could just make them disappear or something?"

"Magic of creation, remember? I can't just destroy something." But that did give Simon an idea. "But maybe you're onto something. I could paint us another hole, kind of like I did at the keep in Aktiri."

"What, and bury them inside the bakery?"

"Do you have a better idea? Although I don't know if it will help the smell."

"Once we clean up, I know ways to make the place smell better. Flowers, some spices. But mainly airing it out."

"But we can't air it out while the bodies are in there. Someone might get curious. We shouldn't even be standing around out here. Elysia was right, we stick out already."

"How long would it take you to paint the hole?"

"I'll try to do it as fast as I can."

"Can I wait out here?"

Simon scowled. "If I have to bear it, you can too."

"Can we at least get something nice-smelling to distract us?"

"Come on, let's just get on with it."

"I don't like you very much."

"I'll buy you a theater ticket."

"Deal." Remeth rummaged through his pack and pulled a bulb of garlic. He broke off a clove and handed it to Simon. "Chew on this. Yalath said it was good for you, but the smell is so strong it might help." He popped one into his own mouth. Simon took it and did the same. The taste was overpowering. He liked garlic, but not magnified a hundred times. But it filled his mouth and nose and he couldn't imagine another smell challenging it.

"Ready?" he said. Remeth nodded. Simon prepared to breathe through his garlic-filled mouth, and opened the door again. The musty, rotting smell mixed with the garlic, but the result didn't knock him down, and he was able to get a better look at the room. The floor was dusty, with the first body near the door, a second by the oven at the side of the room, and the third by a set of racks hanging off the wall.

Simon pointed to a broom and the space in the middle of the floor. While Remeth swept the dust, Simon got out his painting materials, and at the same time channeled his nervousness about being discovered, and his honor for the three dead men. He worked quickly in black, making a rectangle wide enough to fit a body, longer than himself, and added two sets of handles, one at each end, to be used to lift up the slab. At first he imagined the tomb underneath to be deep enough to fit all three men, but then he refined the idea, envisioning instead a moderately thick stone slab of the floor with another rock layer underneath. He waved Remeth over, and together they struggled to lift up the first layer.

"What?" Remeth said, and gagged at the extra inhalation. Just as Simon pictured it, there was solid rock underneath. Remeth threw up his hands, but Simon shook his head, pointing at his own eyes. He went back into his almost-trancelike state, outlining another similar door, but this one with hinges. Under this one would be the ultimate resting place for the three men. Remeth helped to pry it open, and this time they looked into a gaping hole, deep enough for the bodies.

Simon pointed to the feet of the guard by the door, and tried to mime Remeth dragging him by the sandals. He felt squeamish, and Remeth squeezed his eyes shut for a moment, choking back his gorge, but then settled down and approached the body. Very gingerly he tried grabbing a hold of just the sandals, twice recoiling when his hand brushed the dead flesh. Finally he got a good enough grip to pull the body along to the edge of the hole, and used his foot to push on the clothed part to roll him in.

Simon tried not to look at Alexander's face as he pulled him into the void. *I'm so sorry.* Pushing those thoughts from his mind, he rolled the other guard in, closing the first layer with Remeth.

"We should put something in between, to seal up the smell," Remeth said.

"Let's just close it for now. We might be able to get the bodies out of there at night. We should mop up. Maybe then Elysia can help us get rid of the spoiled food."

"I feel like I'm taking orders from Yalath again."

"The theater beckons, once we're done."

Remeth's grin returned.

XXIX
Master

Elysia stroked Zeno's head as he settled into a comfortable in her workshop. "You'll be all right here. You need the rest. I'll see if I can get you some fresh fruit." He nuzzled her and gave a little nod. "I won't be long."

She'd spent a few minutes going over her other sculptures, deciding which she might bring if they journeyed onward.

After failing to find a way to conceal the long wooden knife in her pack, she laid it on her worktable, patting it gently. She kept a few of her tools, in case she found something useful at Xelos' house, but took out the serpent, intending to leave it as well.

She stroked its long body with a mix of admiration and unease. It was some of her finest work, but disturbed her deeply. Beautiful, yet terrible. When she'd brought the wagon back to Zeno on Aktiri, she'd found the carving where the driver must have discarded it. And instead of cloudy and indistinct, for the first time the form had been clear. Not arms and legs like she'd been searching for, but two heads. One for the man who ordered her father dead, and another for the hand that carried it out. Did the body pulse under her touch? Feeding off her anger? She shook off the feeling, but stashed it in her pack.

She brushed the dust from a simple dress she'd left there months ago. After changing into it, she felt like herself again. Pulling the hood of her cloak over her face, she locked the door behind her.

She turned right, banishing thoughts of the bakery from her mind. *First, the agora, and maybe some answers.*

It was as busy as ever, with every kind of food and drink for sale. *I should have brought money, and I could have served up a feast.* Sausages from Akanos the butcher, the best swordfish from Thonis, and Gorgo's finest raisins; her mouth watered as she put together a menu of her favorites. After journeying to four other provinces and a mysterious island, everything familiar became new and exciting again.

Her heart fell when she saw the empty spot where Alexander used to pitch their stall. She approached the nearby stall of Zona, the buxom seller of fragrant oils who was always making eyes at her brother, or any prospective customers who happened to be male. Normally Elysia avoided her gossip, but today she was the best option. Zona's face lit up when she recognized her.

"Elysia? You're back! Where have you been? Everyone has been talking. Your whole family has been gone for… it must be two months now! Did you move away? I even walked by the shop, and thought you must have left some food out—the smell was rank."

Elysia finally got a word in, and her tears were genuine. "Father, you know he was ill. We took him away, to see if he'd improve. But he…"

Zona put a comforting hand on Elysia's shoulder. "Say no more. Then is your brother back?" There was more than a passing interest in her expression.

"No, he… he was struck down as well. I'm alone now."

Zona clutched her chest, looking like she might faint. "Not Alexander too! When?"

"I only completed my mourning and was able to return to the city."

"What will you do? You can't run the bakery by yourself. You need a man in your life."

"I haven't decided yet. But thank you for your concern."

"Anything you need, Elysia. I'm here for you."

"Thank you."

So the bodies were never discovered. Not even Father? Didn't the guards search Xelos' house?

She left the agora, intending to find out more.

Xelos' street was busier than she'd ever seen it, and not the usual wealthy people and their slaves or servants. Four women carried large sacks in front of her, trailing behind a heavily-loaded wagon. Commercial traffic was unusual in the exclusive neighborhood. A group of five tough men waved to the women, and one smiled at Elysia. She pulled the hood lower, and the men laughed. She watched in disbelief as the wagon approached Xelos' door, and the women lined up behind it. Men came out to unload sacks of grain and carry them into the house.

Elysia walked up to the women. Two looked like lighter northern barbarians, while the others were dark-skinned, likely from Egaras or beyond. All were dressed simply. *Certainly not like those Lokutan women.* They had put down their sacks full of fresh vegetables. "Is the Master in?" she asked them.

"In, but probably still asleep," the taller light one said. The others laughed.

"You should have seen the party," said a dark woman with long braids. "The music was so beautiful."

"I think Master Glebric liked the players even more," said a short-haired dark woman.

Glebric? Elysia's mouth hung open.

"What? You have designs on the young Master? Get in line. He had his pick of the players last night."

The tall woman lowered her voice. "He asked Orna to play for him, *in private.* I didn't see her yet this morning, did you?" The women tittered.

"I... I didn't know Glebric was the Master here?"

"Have you been living under a rock?" asked the woman with braids.

"I was away. But I knew Glebric."

"He's so lucky," said the short-haired woman. "My old master beat me. He didn't leave anything to me when he died."

"At least he died," said the braided woman. "And at a good time too, so the Master could buy you and set you free."

Too many questions vied for Elysia's attention. "What did Glebric inherit?"

The tall woman rolled her eyes. "Everything. Not just the house, but many businesses."

"I heard he has a whole island as a vacation home," said the youngest of the four, who hadn't spoken yet.

Xelos made Glebric his heir, when he was just a servant? It didn't make sense. *But maybe he can help?*

"I would like to see your Master."

The women exchanged knowing glances. "We'd all like a little time with him," said the curly-haired woman.

"Not me," said the tall one. "He's not my type."

"Should we remind you that when he comes calling?" asked the curly-haired one. The others laughed again.

The men had finished unloading the sacks, and the wagon moved out of their way.

"Why does he need so much food?" Elysia asked.

"For all of us!" the young woman said. "We all live here."

The guard at the door waved the women through, his eyes following them as they passed. He held up a hand to Elysia. He crooked his neck to try to see her face under the hood, but she pulled it tighter. "What is your business here?"

"I would like to see... Master Glebric."

He raised an eyebrow. "Do you have an appointment?"

"No."

"Then you'll need to speak to the steward to make one."

"Could I see the steward then?"

"He's busy."

This might be my only chance. She pulled open the hood, and the man's eyes changed from suspicious to curious, flicking further down the rest of her cloak. "I'm an old friend of Glebric's. I'm only in town for a short time and was hoping to see him. I'm sure he'd be happy if you could make that happen." She forced a smile, which he quickly matched.

"I'll see what I can do. What name can I give him?"

"Do you promise only to say it directly to him?" He nodded. "Elysia."

"I can't say whether he will see you soon. Do you want to wait out here? Or would you prefer to come inside?"

She smiled one more time before replacing her hood. "Inside, thank you."

Stepping out of her way, he let her pass, and she imagined his eyes searching her body and tried not to shudder. Another guard took his post.

The state of the receiving hall made her frown. It was nearly full, with a half dozen chairs at one side, five full. Seven more guards stood at various points around the room, dressed in the same sort of uniform as this one; leather armor, helmet, and short sword in a scabbard. *What are they defending against?* More attacks like the one that had killed her father? A group of unhealthy looking people—*slaves?*—sat huddled around a simple meal in one corner of the room. A woman in rags was washing a small boy in the now dirty fountain. It looked like a refugee camp.

"Who are all these people?" she asked the guard, doing her best to mask her horror.

"The new ones just arrived today, waiting for the Master or his steward to assign them a home and a job. You can sit over there." He pointed to the empty chair, between two middle-aged Izari men, dressed in fine tunics—likely merchants. "I'll see if I can find the Master for you. No guarantees, remember?" He walked off toward the study.

Why does Glebric need so many slaves? It made her think of the poor people she'd seen as they left Tamar. Some even looked Scentari, but were so dirty that it was hard to tell.

The merchant on her left kept mopping his brow with a cloth, and his sweat smelled foul. The one to her right had his arms crossed and wouldn't stop tapping his foot. She tried to ignore them and kept her face down.

Had other rooms had been similarly re-purposed? Retrieving any more of her work seemed a distant prospect at best. *And what of the talking statues?* If there was one thing she should do, it would be to protect Yalath and the others.

The guard returned, and gestured for her to follow. When she did, the merchant on her right stood up, exasperated.

"I've been waiting all morning!"

The guard laughed. "And you'll keep waiting until the Master is ready to see you. Making a scene won't get you in any faster. Come, milady." When she caught up to him, he leaned in to whisper: "It's your lucky day. That other man spoke true. He's been waiting for four hours, and was here yesterday."

"I will make sure to thank the Master."

He knocked on the study door.

"You may enter," came Glebric's voice from the other side. At least it sounded like him, but so much more assured. The guard opened the door and bid Elysia to go in.

Glebric looked up from the big desk—Xelos' desk, piled high with scrolls and sheaves of parchment. He had changed so much: more mature, with deep creases around his eyes, and wore a fine tunic of deep blue silk with a gold pattern. More extravagant than anything Xelos ever owned. He waved to the guard. "You can leave us alone, thank you."

The guard saluted and closed the door behind him.

Glebric looked at her questioningly. "Elysia? You don't need to hide yourself."

She felt a slight tug of worry, but despite it, removed her hood. Glebric's eyes drank her in, and he smiled, with genuine relief "It is so good to see you! I feared the worst, after the attack."

"How did you get away?" she asked, wondering for the first time. She'd thought everyone in the house would have perished.

He walked around the desk and pulled out a chair. "Please, have a seat."

"Thank you."

He returned to his chair. "Wine?" He poured two glasses. She hesitated. "Please, it's not often old friends are reunited. Let me be a worthy host." He passed her the glass, and she took a small sip. It was lightly sweet, and warmed her on the way down.

"So you were saying, how you got away?"

"Ah yes. Master Xelos, bless his soul, I have him to thank. For my life... for everything. He sent me off to the agora that morning, with Sofia, do you remember her? She's now in charge of my kitchen. She thought we were being followed, but I told her she was seeing things. But then at the agora even I could see the men on our tail. Eventually one of them bumped into me, knocking over the grapes I was buying. Even helped me pick them up, and then they left.

"The Master had given me the day off, so I was heading over to stay with my friend Hector. Did you meet him on the way in? He's become an excellent steward. My first hire. It's such a pleasure to be able to help my friends now. So I stayed with Hector, because I hadn't had a day off since Simon arrived." He watched her eyes, like he was looking for a reaction. "Where is our friend Simon?"

"He..." Something told her she should be cautious. "He went back to Pelusia, just before Tamar was attacked. Did you hear? The Scentari took the city in the battle, before the legions arrived to drive them off. I... there's been no word from him since. I think he must have fallen in the battle."

Glebric reached his hand tentatively across the table, just touching hers. "I'm so sorry. I know he was a dear friend."

"Yes, thank you So you never went back that night? When they..."

"No, I was completely oblivious. When I came back the next morning, the city watch were examining the house. There was this smell of death, and... oh Elysia, it was horrible. Bodies everywhere, of all the servants. Even poor Ycastros. And..." he gulped. "And the Master."

"Did you see it?"

"Thankfully, no. They wouldn't let me in there. But when they learned that I was one of the servants, they questioned me, trying to figure out whether I was a part of the attack."

"Were there... any other bodies?" *She had to know.*

"You mean of the attackers? No. If any had fallen, they must have taken them away. Or burned them."

"Burned them?"

"Yes, there was a fire in the courtyard, and apparently several human bones were found. Believed to be men. Mostly young and strong, but one older.

She couldn't hold back the tears. "I... I think my father was one of them."

"Oh Elysia, I'm so sorry. But why?"

"It was Simon they were after. They were trying to use my father to get to him."

"Why Simon?"

"Apparently he had angered some noble from Pazh who wanted revenge."

"So it was Simon's fault? He brought this doom on everyone we knew?"

She fought back the urge to argue. "Sorry, "But I don't under-stand, how did you come to inherit all this?"

Glebric's expression softened into a smile. "It was the most amazing thing. I had served the Master as best I could, and we were quite close. I never had a father growing up—he died in a fishing accident. That's why I've been serving since such a young age—to help support my mother. I used to help the Master file some of his documents sometimes, so when they asked me if he had a will, I was able to find it for them. Never could I have imagined he would leave everything to me."

"Everything?"

His eyes narrowed defensively. *I'm not greedy, just surprised.*

"Actually, he did instruct me to take care of his other servants, but I would have kept Sofia regardless." He paused, considering something. "His will *did* mention you. You are to have free access to your *remaining* works, and any tools. Is that why you're here?" Could she see a trace of embarrassment?

So Master Xelos didn't forget me.

"I... I would like to see my pieces. I just wanted to find out what happened."

"Where have you been?"

"I had to leave. Simon tried to stop the attack. He got away, but found out my father and the Master had died. He fled the city, and I hid on Nasos."

"Why come back now?"

"I heard... that you had survived. I wanted to come see you. And the house of course."

The hope she kindled in his eyes made her own heart sink.

"You came for me?" he asked, his voice quavering.

"And for the tools, of course. I wanted to get a few pieces too. I'm so... so thankful that Master Xelos thought of me."

"The tools, you can have them. But the artwork, much of Xelos', and your pieces as well... I... I sold them."

"Oh? All of them? Who bought them?"

"A visiting senator, if you'd believe it. A general no less?"

She clenched her teeth. *Lokuta? He sold Xelos' work to his murderer?*

"I'm sorry I didn't know you'd be back. I'll make it up to you. I'll give you your share." His imploring look blunted her anger.

"Oh, no... sorry, just a bad memory. I'm so happy for you. Was it a lot?"

"Enough to fund my dreams. That's why I had to do it."

"Your dreams? What do you mean to do with all this? And why all these people?"

"I'm setting them free." His voice burned with a drive she'd never heard before.

"Setting who free?"

"The slaves. It's deplorable. No man or woman should be the property of another. But these Pazians, and many among our own people... that's how they get rich. How they keep us down."

"That's... that's so noble. So ambitious. I've never really known many slaves. My family never had any, nor Xelos. I agree that it's a horrible practice. But won't the Pazians try to stop you?"

This smile didn't look so nice. "That's why I need my own army."

"You're going to fight for their freedom?"

"When I have to. First I used much of Xelos'... my inheritance to buy all the slaves I could. I set them to work in my businesses. Which are doing quite well, I might add. I've got some great people to run them, and the newly freed, they work five times as hard for their own coin and self-respect. I'm giving them not just freedom, but dignity and hope."

Every word he said resonated and she found herself getting swept up in his passion. She thought of the poor people outside Tamar, the losers in the war with Pazh, that were destined for just such an animal existence.

"But that was just the beginning. The other slave-owners aren't happy, obviously. Not only have I changed the market for slaves, but I've given new ideas to the ones they own. When they run away, we take them in and set them free."

"The owners must hate you."

"Indeed. There has been fighting in the streets. Did you come alone? I wouldn't want anything to happen to you out there."

"I did. I…"

"You're staying back at your house? I could send someone to escort you back when you leave… but why not stay here? You could have your old room." He reached his hand across the table, seeking hers. She flinched, and there was a bit of hurt in his face.

"Sorry, you scared me with talk of danger in the streets. I was just hoping to get some of my tools, and take them back to the bakery."

"But I could make space for you here. The workshop is being used for other purposes, but I could clear you a space. Your tools are locked in one of the cabinets. I'd just have to speak with—" His eyes narrowed.

"What is it?"

He shook his head. "It's nothing. I have something I must attend to. You know the way to the workshop. I'll send one of my staff to help you get what you need."

XXX
ᘓᘓᘓᘓᘓᘓ
Assistance

Remeth stood impatiently in front of Simon. "Now can we go?" he asked.

Simon had to admit that the bakery looked almost ready for business. "Which way to the theater?"

Directions!

"I can't believe we didn't check for Kashaka," Simon said. "Hold on, let's do that first."

"Can I point out that you promised we could go to the theater when we were done?"

When the liquid settled, it pointed northwest.

Remeth looked at him expectantly. "I... have no idea what direction that is, from in here."

"Northwest."

"Same as before then?"

"Not exactly. It's shifted slightly. I think we're closer."

"Which way to the theater?"

Simon thought for a moment. "Northwest."

"Maybe we'll see her at the show. Let's go!"

Simon nodded. At least it would give him something to do, though he was more enthusiastic about finding food in the agora than experiencing Izari theater. At least if Elysia had been with him, she could explain the stories and references.

It was early afternoon, and the streets were clear. He tried knocking on Elysia's door, with their agreed-upon code, but she didn't answer. "I don't like it," Simon said.

"She's probably off on her little walk. It's a beautiful day, not a cloud in the sky. And she knows this place far better than either of us. She'll be fine."

"I hope you're right."

Remeth put his arm around Simon. "You, my friend, worry too much. Maybe I should get you a drink. What do they like around here?"

"No more drinking in strange cities."

Remeth made a face.

The walk to the agora was uneventful, other than Remeth commenting on the Izari taste in clothes and beards. He wasn't a fan of the latter.

"Then I guess you're not going to meet the man of your dreams here," Simon said.

He actually looked disappointed. "Between the arts, and their reputation... do you know if it's true?"

"I always thought it was just a legion insult—sorry. I wasn't thinking. To be fair, Persei used to accuse..."

Remeth put his hand on Simon's shoulder. "I know *you* don't mean it. Thanks for trying. And I'm not ruling anything out."

The agora was packed and so different from the deserted space that he'd run through to flee Persei's assassins. Even by day, guards flanked the stairway up to the acropolis.

"What are you so happy about?" Remeth asked.

"This is where I met Elysia."

"How sweet. I'm hungry. Anything you recommend?"

"Fish, flatbread, and the olives are great."

Remeth wrinkled his nose. "Never liked them. Too salty."

"That's because you've never tried them fresh. Come on." He found a vendor selling different varieties of olives, a middle-aged Izari man with a long brown beard. "Do you speak Pazian?"

The man narrowed his eyes at Remeth, before turning back to his olives.

"Excuse me," said Remeth. "I believe my friend was speaking to you."

Still the man ignored them.

"Friendly," Remeth said.

"He probably doesn't speak Pazian."

They tried another stall, this one selling grilled fish. The smell made Simon's mouth water. He approached the young Izari woman at the grill.

"Do you speak Pazian?"

She glanced furtively behind her, where an older man, her

father by the resemblance, was cleaning fish. "What would you like?"

"Why are you so nervous?" Remeth asked. "Another man wouldn't even talk to us."

"Are you new freedmen?" she asked in a low voice.

Remeth snorted. "Of course not! I am no slave, never have been. And my friend served in the legions!"

Simon shushed him. "Why do you ask? Has there been trouble with freedmen lately?"

"You're not from here, are you?"

"No, just visiting. We just got in. Can we get two of those?" He pointed to a tray of large sardines. She nodded and stuck half a dozen on each skewer, drizzled them with oil, and laid them across the top of the hot coals. His stomach rumbled.

"You both smell like garlic, by the way."

Simon blushed, but Remeth laughed and answered. "Sorry. We were working with some foul-smelling cargo. I'd rather work with the odor of garlic, wouldn't you?"

She nodded.

"So you were saying, about the freedmen?" Simon asked.

Her father looked at them sideways and berated her in Izari.

Simon held up his hands and shook his head, and the woman seemed to be defending them. The father cooled down, but kept glancing at them suspiciously while he worked with his fish.

Their order sizzled and popped, the skin turning deliciously crispy. Remeth paid the price she indicated.

"Father doesn't want us to serve them. Says there will be trouble."

"I didn't realize there were that many freedmen here."

"There's some young noble, just came into great wealth. He's been going around buying all the slaves and setting them free."

"Sounds like a nice guy," Remeth said.

"The other nobles don't like it. Or the Pazians. They're worried the other slaves will revolt."

"Does your family have slaves?" Simon asked.

"Do we look like we have the money? That's why I work with my father. Your fish is done." She used cloths in each hand to grab the skewers and skillfully slide the cooked fish into two rough clay bowls. She handed one to each of them.

"You just eat it like this?" Remeth asked. At Simon's nod, he reached in. "Damn, that's hot!" He licked his finger.

Simon blew on his before picking one up, and again before taking his first bite. It was warm and crunchy, and his hunger salted it perfectly. "Thank you, it's excellent."

Remeth copied him. "So who is this young noble? Do you know his name?"

She shook her head. "Gre... Gle... something like that."

"Thanks for the fish, and the news," Simon said, finishing his lunch.

"Have you been to the theater?" Remeth asked. "I've heard there's a new troupe."

She smiled shyly and shook her head. "I wish I could."

"I was an actor, back home in Marutha."

Does he even realize she thinks he's asking her? "We should get going if you want to get your ticket. Finish up."

"My friend is right. Thank you again, and I'll think of you when we watch the show."

The young woman cast her eyes down, smiling, as they left.

"What are you doing?" Simon asked when they were out of ear-shot. "Flirting with a woman? Getting her hopes up?"

Remeth looked hurt. "She seemed nice! I didn't think..."

"You're a handsome young man, and far too charming. Don't go breaking any hearts."

Remeth beamed.

"And no, I'm not flirting with you either. Though you would make a fine model for a painting sometime."

"I would be honored. And you haven't even seen the best of me."

"Clothed, thank you. And I could use it to contact you if we're apart."

"Really?"

"And possibly more. We've been meaning to try some experiments... exploring the boundaries of our Talent. But we just haven't had the time. Did you do that sort of thing?"

"With Yalath? Barely. I'm so used to *not* using my Talent, but you know what? I should do some experiments here too. Might help us get better tickets. We should have asked her where to go."

"Was that enough to eat?"

Remeth patted his belly. "It will do. Tickets are priority number one."

"It's on the other side of the acropolis."

"Do we have to go up there?" Remeth said, looking at the stairs with disdain.

"No, we have to go around. Though I'd love to spend some time in the temples. You should see the artwork. Every piece is by an ancient master. Back when Talent must have been commonplace."

They walked to the base of the stairs, and even though he looked completely different, Simon was happy not to recognize the guards. He was about to turn away when a short, cloaked figure rushed by the guards, heading toward them. *Thin, a girl?* Her eyes caught his for a split second, and he saw a flash of fear. And something more.

"Remeth," he said. "Look."

"A girl, so what? Running from something. You're not distracting me from the tickets."

"No, look. Do you see anything different?" It was definitely there. Like light bent slightly around her, shimmering. "I think she's one of us. Come on. Besides, she's going the right way."

They matched her pace, following her to the left of the acropolis, out of the agora and down a busy street. She was going in the general direction of the harbor, and after the second turn, Remeth spoke up.

"Are you sure this is the same way?"

"Not exactly now. But this could be important. If something has scared her, we need to know about it. And if it were you, wouldn't you want us to help?" Remeth nodded.

At one intersection, the girl turned back and stared right at Simon. She froze.

He smiled and waved.

She bolted.

"Really?" Remeth said. "I don't want to run, not so soon after lunch."

Simon took off after her, not checking to see if Remeth was following.

Before the next intersection, he got close enough "Stop," he said. "I can help." But still she kept running. A few locals shouted at him as he ran, but he couldn't understand a word.

She ducked down a side street but it came to a dead end. She wheeled on him, and her hood fell, revealing a wild shock of red hair. She couldn't be more than sixteen. Strange bruises mottled her face.

Simon held his hands up. "I'm trying to help. I don't want to hurt you. I'm sorry that I scared you." He was pretty sure she understood. "You do speak Pazian, right?"

Her eyes darted around. "Why should I trust you?"

"You're an artist of some kind?" Her eyes narrowed and she backed up a step. "I don't know what kind. But I am too. And someone is after you. Someone wants to capture your power." Buried in the fear was a glimmer of hope. But then she looked away, behind him, coiled and ready to flee. She pulled up her hood.

"You're too fast," Remeth said, panting loudly.

The girl tried to run past him, but Simon and Remeth each caught an arm.

"Feisty one," Remeth said. She twisted back and forth.

"Ow!" Remeth yelled, letting go. "She bit me!"

"Wait!" Simon said, also releasing her. "I really mean it. My friend here, Remeth, he's an actor. I'm Simon. I draw and paint."

"Prove it," she said, with surprising challenge in her voice.

Simon rifled through his pack, and took out one of his brushes. "See?" The tiniest spark of curiosity gave him hope. "I only recently found out about my Talent. What do you do? Do you have a teacher?"

"I sing," she said. "No teacher. I only just met others like me. We played music together. But then..." Terror flooded into her face.

"Then what?" Simon asked, keeping his voice gentle. "Someone found you?"

"I... I think so. Or, I think he knows what we are... could see it in us."

Remeth and Simon exchanged a glance. Remeth spoke up. "It could mean that he has Talent too."

"No! There's something dark there. Something... evil."

Persei? It has to be. Simon's blood burned.

"What is his name?"

"Glebric."

Simon did a double-take. "Did you say Glebric?"

"Do you know him?" Remeth asked.

"Young Izari man, dark hair, thin, about this tall?" Simon held his hand up to eye level.

"Yes, that's the one." There was fear in her eyes. "He seemed so nice when he saved me."

"Saved you from who?"

She shivered. "Noble boys. Pazians. They... they..." Simon could tell he was losing her.

"Sorry for the reminder. I know Glebric. He was a servant of my former mentor. But my mentor is dead. Who does he now serve?"

"What do you mean?" she asked.

"He must serve a new master. Who is it?"

"Everyone calls him Master Glebric. He lives in a big house. He's very rich."

"Glebric?" Simon shook his head. "That's impossible! A big house? Don't tell me it's the one with the nice carvings, and a door knocker like a hammer and chisel?"

She nodded. "That's the one!"

"That's Xelos' house! How did Glebric take over? He couldn't have been the heir. Unless everyone else was dead? Xelos did send him out on the day of the attack."

Remeth shook his head. "Wasn't Elysia going to Xelos' house?"

Simon's heart dropped. "By Salar! We have to stop her!" Remeth held his shoulder before he could run off.

"Who?" the girl asked, looking from face to face.

"Elysia," Simon said. "She's another one, Talented like us."

"And she was going to that house? You must stop her. He'll get her, just like Orna."

"What do you mean, like Orna?" Remeth asked.

"After our performance last night, he took Orna back for a private concert. She didn't come back. I think he did something terrible to her. That's why I ran, Numerius told me to run."

"Who?" Remeth asked.

"Numerius. He's a fat old Pazian man, a prisoner. Glebric has him locked away. He seemed to know something about Talent, and he has friends that can help."

Remeth narrowed his eyes. "Numerius, you say? Simon, did Xelos mention anyone by that name?"

"No. And I'm guessing Yalath didn't either?"

"Then who is he? And what does he know?"

Simon turned back to the girl. "Uh... what is your name? Sorry, I don't want to call you girl."

"Kallara."

"Kallara, so how did this Numerius help you escape?"

"He couldn't. He's still a prisoner. Because he knows about Glebric and that... that there's something evil there. I saw it in my dreams."

Simon felt his stomach lurch. "Did you ever hear anyone speak of Persei Lokuta?" No spark of recognition. "Then what power does Glebric have? Could he also be following *her*?"

"Who?" Kallara asked.

"Z..." Simon looked to Remeth, and then sighed. "Zaliakara, the Damoz of Flame."

"Flames? I didn't see any flames. But in my dreams, there was too much water. And I know the water is evil."

Everything snapped into place.

Remeth paled, and had to grab Simon to restrain him from bolting again. "I think we've found Kashaka."

"Let me go! We have to get Elysia! If she's gone in there she's in horrible danger!"

"But the two of you won't be able to go alone," Kallara said.

"Why not?" Simon asked. "I know the place—I used to live there."

"Glebric is training an army."

"Wait, what?" Remeth asked. "An army? Why?"

"To free the slaves."

"Sounds like Kashaka has more noble aims than her sister," Remeth said.

"Who? You're very confusing." Kallara crossed her arms.

"Sorry," Simon said. "Kashaka is the Damoz of Water... and the sister of Zaliakara. They're ancient evil beings that grant power to those who submit to them... make sacrifices in the name of power. At least, that's what we think. Glebric must have given himself to Kashaka. We were actually tracking her here."

"It sounds so crazy." She searched their faces. "But I believe you. So what about the sister, Zaliakara?"

"I've fought her servants before. And now I think she's looking for her sister too. That's why we need to find her first. And..."

"And then what, Simon?" Remeth asked. "We thought we were going to keep her hidden, then fight off Zaliakara. Not try to put Kashaka back in her cage. We have no idea how to do that. We should ask Yalath for help."

"But Elysia!"

"Glebric knows you, right? And others might too. But only Elysia knows me. How about I go infiltrate the house and get her out. Or at least figure out what's going on. I can use my Talent." His eyes twinkled for Kallara, and she smiled. "You go back to the bakery and contact Yalath for advice."

"Bakery?" Kallara asked.

"Elysia's father was a baker. That's where we're staying, here in Attarsus."

"Can... can I stay with you? Learn more about my Talent?"

"I'm not sure how good of a teacher—"

Remeth cut him off. "Of course, young lady. Simon would be happy to take you with him. Where were you going when we accidentally started chasing you?"

"To deliver Numerius' message. To his friend. I stayed in the temple of Aliata for the night, so nobody would find me. I should deliver the message first. Simon, would you come with me?"

"What was the message?" Simon asked.

She closed her eyes and the message came out like lyrics to a song. "It's for a man named Korg. Numerius is a prisoner of Glebric, at the house of Xelos. They have an army. The city is in danger. Send word to his steward in Pazh, to write to Tullus. Tell him there's artwork in danger, that we must rescue or they'll turn dark, damaged by the elements. Urgent."

Rescue?

"Could it be?" Simon asked.

"More... like us?" Remeth answered with a question of his own. "What do you think?"

"I think we should ask Yalath first. Will that do, Kallara?"

"Where is this Yalath?"

"I can contact him from the bakery."

"Contact him? How? Using magic?" Her eyes lit up with anticipation.

"Yes."

"Then I can wait."

"So... how do I get to Xelos' house?" Remeth asked. "And why do I get the feeling I won't be going to the theater today?"

Kallara squinted at Remeth. "You don't look much like a merchant. Or a slave. You should be one or the other if you're going in there."

"She has a point," Simon said.

"If I'm a merchant, I should be more free to move around?"

She shook her head. "The merchants wait for meetings with Glebric, his steward, or the scary one... Ventus... his main advisor. But the slaves, once they decide where you'll be living and working, you can pretty much come and go as you please."

"Slave then." Remeth's brow creased in thought. "I have it! I'm Killeth, a Maruthan slave who heard Glebric is offering asylum to those who escape. I came straight away, offering my services. Will that do?"

"Do you have any special skills?"

"Take off your shirt," Simon said.

"But it's cool out!"

"Yes, and you're a slave. That's too fine a shirt for you. I'll keep it back at the bakery." He held his hand out. Pouting, Remeth first handed over his cloak, then lifted the Aktirian shirt above his head. Kallara's eyes went wide as his golden muscular chest was bared to the cool breeze and the afternoon sun. She blushed when Remeth winked at her.

"So which way to this house of Glebric?"

Simon winced to hear it called that.

"We'll walk you to the street—" Simon stopped when Kallara shook her head violently.

"I'm not going near there."

Simon groaned. "Remeth, are you good with directions?"

"Well..."

"What if I drew you a map?"

Remeth laughed. "I'm an escaping slave, not a tourist."

Simon looked around to get his bearings. "Do you remember how to get back to the agora?" Remeth nodded. Simon gave him the course from there.

"Don't worry, if I get lost, I'll just get someone to point my way. My Talent helps in that regard." He smiled again for Kallara and walked off toward the agora.

"He'd better get Elysia out," Simon said, "because otherwise I have no idea how he's going to find his way back to the bakery."

XXXI
ᏰᏋᏰᏋᏰᏋᏰ
Requiem

Persei, Mirasha and twenty hand-picked men rode into Jeppo in the afternoon. He hoped it would be enough. Kashaka's blood had pointed vaguely toward Jeppo from Gardisha, and into the Near Sea once they'd sailed downriver to Uraka. Now they headed into Jeppo with for two purposes: to catch Simon and Elysia, and hire a ship for the next leg of their journey.

Persei left Bellos in charge of mop-up in Gardisha, claiming his interrogation had unearthed urgent new leads he wanted to follow back in the cities. Bellos was to return to the barracks in Uraka when he was done, to await further orders.

How long would he be gone? How far would this trail take him? His position as legate required that he stay with the legion barring some new directive from the Senate in Pazh, and he was already in breach of protocol for leaving his men. Even for a matter theoretically of national security.

And it wasn't just Mirasha's urging for haste that had him charging forward on this quest for power. He also felt it. If he waited, he could lose this chance. Once he brought these elemental forces under his command, he'd smooth over any problems caused by his absence.

They stopped first at the garrison, in case there was any word from Pazh. And there were two letters, one with the seal of the President, and the other from Daymar.

The official letter ordered him back to Pazh by the end of the year. He was to leave the 7th in the charge of his second in command, and a new legate was on the way.

Daymar explained that he'd asked the President to recall him, and had a new charge for him once he took power in the new year. Signed, Daymar Lokuta, President-elect of Pazh.

Seeing the title would once have stirred fires of jealousy in Persei. But not now. He had discovered his own path to power. One that wouldn't make him wait, or shut him out. Power that would let him scale his brother's shoulders to reach heights never seen in the history of the Republic.

Persei laughed. For once Daymar was providing him with an opening, instead of slamming the door in his face.

So it was with a new bounce to his step that Persei took his men next to visit Ilson, for directions to Yalath's house. Ilson confirmed that Yalath had returned from Gardisha—he was hoping to meet with him soon to discuss his findings.

His instructions led them through the market and into a densely populated neighborhood of mud-brick apartments. The locals parted before their troop, looking sullen and mistrustful, but avoiding outward signs of disrespect.

Mirasha spoke to him through her veil. "How many men do you want to bring in with us to speak with Yalath?"

"All of them?"

"In an apartment? We may be discussing things you wouldn't want your men to hear. And what if you need to use your... powers."

She had a point. And he was itching to try calling on the fire. Part of him hoped he could roast Simon alive inside the house. He deserved it. "We'll bring in a pair, just to make sure things are safe, but have others waiting for our call if there's a problem."

She nodded.

The house sat at the end of a block, and in the noonday sun, no one seemed to be coming or going. He ordered most of the men to cordon off the area, four to stay ready at the doors, while two that he'd recruited to the legion himself would accompany them inside.

"These fugitives may say or do strange things. What happens inside does not leave these doors. Do I make myself perfectly clear?"

The two soldiers saluted. He could trust them.

He tried the wooden door, and found it locked. He had already dismissed the possibility of diplomacy. No, if this one was working with Simon, brute force would be necessary. He looked at the hinges. Bronze, and nothing special. *But what if?* He channeled his hatred of Simon into his hands until they radiated waves of heat. He leaned down to touch the hinge, willing the heat out into the metal. It began to glow.

"Break it down," he ordered two of his sentries. "When the door is down, the four of us go in to find him. Or them."

The two burly soldiers hit the door with a crash and the hinges tore apart. Persei, Mirasha and the other two soldiers dashed through, the three men with swords drawn. The corridor was dark, but some natural light filtered in from the room up ahead. When Persei and Mirasha entered the sitting room, strains of music—*some kind of flute?*—wafted into the room, tickling his ears like a feather. Enchanting music that welled up inside, drawing him forward...

Small, soft hands clapped over Persei's ears, almost muting the sound. He grabbed them, trying to wrench them away so he could hear more, but Mirasha's face was beside his, and she shook her head.

The soldiers brushed past them and into the room, following the source of the sound through another doorway. They paused at the entrance and turned back to Persei, their expressions distant, almost like they were lost. But recognition flared in their eyes and they raised their short swords, leveling them at Persei and Mirasha. One pointed at Persei's sword, and then to the ground.

"You dare challenge your legate?" Persei shouted, the angry words storming out of his mouth. The legionaries raised their swords in defiance, taking up fighting stances.

Livid, Persei broke free of Mirasha's grasp and charged at the nearer of the two legionaries. The drumbeat of his blood pulsing in his veins drowned out the music, and he attacked with a flurry of jabs and slashes that were met sword on sword. The soldier's blows were heavy and lethargic, and Persei pressed the advantage, catching the other man on the sword arm. The slash made him drop his weapon, and Persei's pommel smashed him on the chin, between the cheek guards of his helmet.

Persei turned and saw the other had grabbed Mirasha and was holding a sword to her throat.

"Submit, and she doesn't get hurt," the soldier said.

Blazing fury surged from his heart, and he stretched out a hand toward the mutinous soldier. Liquid black fire shot out in a stream, striking the man in the face. Dropping his sword and releasing Mirasha, he clutched at his eyes, screaming.

"Legate?" came a shout from down the hall.

"Stay back!" Persei shouted. He didn't need more men getting in the way. *And who else might be with the traitors?*

Persei charged the burning soldier, but Mirasha ran the man through with his fallen sword before Persei reached him.

The music changed to a soothing, haunting melody that curled into his ears and settled his mind, urging him to lie down, to sleep. Persei felt his lids sagging and…

�6Ꮻ�6Ꮻ�6Ꮻ�

"It smells funny in here," Kallara said when Simon brought her into the bakery. Simon winced, not wanting to explain. "How long was it closed for?"

"Almost two months."

So much had changed since Elysia found Alexander dead there. He'd traveled across all the eastern provinces of Pazh, defeated one grave threat to the Republic, and learned so much more about his magic. Yet here he was again, wondering how to get someone out of danger at Xelos' house. But this time he could turn to a mentor for advice. Even if Yalath was obnoxious. Simon wondered how much he might *not* have learned, had Yalath been his mentor instead of Xelos. And how much more could Remeth grow now that he was freed from the stifling teaching philosophy?

"Can I at least air it out a little?" Kallara asked. Simon nodded absently, looking around for the best place to do his work.

He walked through the smashed door to the back and found their family table. He imagined a young Elysia sitting and carving, or eating with her parents and brother. Her father's dead face loomed large in his mind, but he forced it out, thinking instead of Yalath's prominent hooked nose. He took out parchment and paints and started mixing. "I'll be working back here," he called out to Kallara.

She walked through the doorway. "What happened here? It's such a mess."

"Bad people attacked. Looking for Elysia, but really for me."

"I guess they didn't find you?"

"No. We were lucky to escape. I'm going to need to focus on this painting."

"Can I watch? I won't get in the way. I can sit behind you."

"Suit yourself. But I need to focus." She sat down on a chair out of his field of vision.

"How does it work? Where is he?"

"Jeppo, in Marutha. Do you know where that is?"

She shook her head. "Is it far?"

"A week by ship."

"But you can talk to him from here?"

"I... I think so. I haven't really tried. But if I can picture him, I can at least get him a message, and try to communicate. I've done that before."

"Sorry, I'll stop bothering you so you can work. This is very exciting. It's all so new to me."

Simon closed his eyes and centered himself, imagining Yalath speaking to them in his home back in Jeppo. The bald head, piercing eyes, and perpetual variations of frown and sneer. The glares at Elysia. Remembering that gave him a rope of emotion to grasp, and he followed it down into the well of his inspiration, becoming one with his Talent. His hand leaped into motion. First the distinctive nose, then the mouth and chin, the eyes, the head, all appearing in rapid succession on the page. *I need to speak with you, Yalath. I need your wisdom.* The urgency filtered into every stroke, and he felt that connection suddenly, to the man far away across the sea.

Yalath's cheeks were full, his flute at his lips.

"He's playing," Kallara said, with interest. "How will you get his attention?"

Something was wrong. Yalath's eyes were wide, and sweat beaded on his brow. He was scared of... someone?

"He's in trouble!"

ᎶᏋᏮᏋᏮᏋᎶ

A slap in the face brought Persei back to awareness. "Cover your ears!" Mirasha said. He did so, looking around with half-closed eyes for the musician. He located his sword on the floor, but couldn't retrieve it without opening himself up to the strange and powerful music.

Mirasha motioned for him to follow her, sword in her hand. He pushed his own blade forward with his sandal, trying not to cut himself. There was a safety, a solidity to having his blade within reach. From the middle of the room he could see through another doorway, into a bedroom where an older Maruthan man sat on the bed, cheeks working hard as he played a very ordinary looking reed flue. *That's it? Not some magical relic?*

He nudged the sword in front of him, on a direct line to the man. He was about ten feet away. A clear shot. Persei held his breath, trying to squeeze the pressure into his ears to somehow block the sound for the moment he needed.

In one fluid motion, he leaned down, took his hand off his right ear, grabbed the hilt of the sword, and in a sweeping circle launched it at the musician. It struck the flute, sending it and the sword flying past him to clatter on the floor.

No longer fearing the music, Persei sprinted into the room and clapped his hand over the old man's mouth, choking any possible song that might escape.

Mirasha held the sword to the musician's side. "Interrogate him."

Persei shook a finger in front of the man's nose, curved like the beak of a hawk. "If you try so much as another note, old man, you'll lose your tongue." He withdrew his hand from the mouth. "You're Yalath?"

"You take orders from a woman?" The man spat in his face.

Persei jabbed his elbow into the man's gut.

"I'll take that as a yes. Where are Simon and Elysia?"

A hint of recognition in the golden eyes, quickly covered with cold iron.

"I take it they're following the trail of Kashaka's blood?" Persei asked.

A sharp intake of breath and slight narrowing of the eyes, but silence.

"Then you'd be happy to know that we have our own vessel of her blood that will lead us there too."

"And then what?" Yalath's voice was resolute, defiant.

"I should ask you the same. What do your friends hope to achieve by finding Kashaka?"

"They can keep such evil power out of the hands of foolish men who would destroy us all."

Persei scoffed. "They'll try to seize it for themselves. And I will stop them. For Pazh."

"For Lokuta? Or is it just for Persei Lokuta? Ignorant fool of an inbred—"

Persei's fist hit him square in the jaw, drawing blood.

"Don't test me old man. I was going to let you live."

"That would be a mistake," Mirasha said.

Yalath's eyes were full of scorn. "Your commander says jump "

Mirasha seized his chin, her nails digging into his skin and forcing a grimace of pain. "This one has Talent. He used it to turn your men. With his music."

Persei stared at her. "Such a thing is possible? I thought it was the magic of the flute."

"No, this one has Talent with music. The flute just helps him focus, to twist the emotions and feelings and bodies of those who aren't protected against his attacks."

"And why was this wench safe?" Yalath asked Persei, his eyes shining in bizarre triumph.

The insult set off his fury, and Persei punched Yalath again in the cheek, harder this time. He heard a crack.

Yalath shook his head and spat a bloody tooth in Persei's face. "She's controlling you, you're the pawn of—"

Another blow from Persei and Yalath's eyes glazed over.

"We're not going to get anything else useful from the mouth of this one," Mirasha said.

"Then what do we do with him?"

Mirasha took out the votive figure of Zalikko and set it on the bed next to Yalath. "A man as a sacrifice is a meal, but one Talented man is like a feast. She will grant you great power if you dedicate this one to her."

Persei looked around the room. He found spare sheets, and used them to bind Yalath's hands behind his back, and his feet together. As he did so, he felt something strange, like a web of power around the man, just above his skin. The fire inside him stretched out to lick at it, hungry to devour this essence.

Yalath's head bobbed, the eyes straining to focus.

"Do it," Mirasha said. "Unleash your power. It needs to feed." She backed out to the doorway.

Yalath tried again to speak: "Persei. Don't trust her. She is—"

Dark flames leaped from Persei's fingertips to the man's tongue, devouring it first. His eyes widened with the excruciating pain, but no sound could escape. Just the hissing, crackling flames dancing along his form as they consumed every inch of his body and spread to the bed.

Persei felt threads of energy—of life force—shimmer in the air, swirl around the little votive figurine, and flow into his hands. It was ecstasy; the warmth that spread through him that was better than the finest wine.

Mirasha watched, her eyes never leaving the burning body, with the slightest hint of a smile on her face. She was his partner in this, in everything. And together they would master not just this power, but Kashaka's as well. He would be a god, and Mirasha his queen.

ᏩᏬᏩᏬᏩᏬᏩ

The flute was gone, replaced by terror on Yalath's face.

Kallara screamed.

Dark flames shot into his mouth, setting his tongue ablaze. The piercing eyes burned before Simon, becoming black and empty pits. With every stroke the flames danced across Yalath's flesh, in moments reducing him to a pile of charred bone and ash.

It happened so fast.

"No!" Simon slammed his hand on the desk, his brush stroking an angry black scar across the page. But anger was replaced by terror, and he tore the page to shreds, breaking any contact with the enemy.

How would Remeth react? Wanting revenge, just like Elysia? Simon wouldn't be able to stand in the way of both of them.

"Who did that?" asked Kallara, very pale and shaking.

"Zaliakara again. The Damoz of Flame. And Persei must be wielding her power now. If they found him..." Simon gulped. "They know about us. And Kashaka? I fear they'll be coming for us, and her."

"Then we must stop them."

Simon felt so old, so jaded. "But we understand so little."

"Then we'll have to think of something."

He admired her courage, but didn't share her optimism.

"We don't even know what to do with Numerius' message."

"I owe it to him to deliver it. He helped me."

What would Xelos do?

"But we don't know if he's truly a friend to people like us. I don't know how they treated you back where you grew up, but they tried to stomp the creativity out of me. To protect me."

"Why?"

"Because there are people out there that hunt for us. People inside the Republic."

296

"But if Glebric and his people are also hunting us, and Numerius is against him, then maybe they are our friends?"

"We just don't know."

"If I waited until I was sure, then Glebric would have me too."

She's right.

"Well, what we do know for sure is that Yalath is dead, Elysia is in danger, and now Remeth is putting himself in harm's way to get her out. And neither of us should go there. Not looking like ourselves."

"What do you mean? Like ourselves?"

He wished he hadn't said that.

"I... I've painted disguises before. It can work very well."

"But what if we're caught there?"

"Exactly. I don't want to risk it."

"But it would still be useful even if we're just out in the city, right?"

His mouth was a tight line, but he nodded. "Especially with that hair of yours."

She laughed. "You're one to talk." She touched his skin. "Where are you from?"

"Pazh." Her raised eyebrow challenged him. "But my mother was Benjish." She shrugged her shoulders. "From far west of Pazh, a country called Benjea. Well, it used to be a country, before it was conquered."

"By Pazh?"

"No, Benjea is part of the Kingdom of Randesh." She still looked blank. "Never mind. My father was Pazian. So my mother was even darker."

Kallara nodded. "One of Glebric's warriors has the darkest skin I've ever seen. It's like midnight with a new moon. He's... he's scary, even though he helped me get away from those brutes."

"How many warriors does he have?"

"At the house? Dozens." Simon's heart fell again. "And that's not all of them. I've heard them speak about training at more locations, here and on other islands too."

"Do you know what they're planning?"

"They're going to rise up and free the slaves."

"They want a war?"

"There's already been some... battles? But by accident. Like when they rescued me." She chewed at her lip. "That's what I just don't understand. Glebric is good, or... he's mostly good? Everything he does, or wants to do. But then Orna... and I felt this... not hate, but similar... against me. Does that make any sense?"

Simon thought back to his paintings of the dark flames. "Too much sense. That's what I felt when I went up against the one who controlled the dark fire. Their power, it hates us... but now I think it wants us too. If it..." He looked into her eyes and saw the fear there, the despair, and he couldn't continue. She was younger than any of them. She shouldn't have to see this, or even know about it.

"It what? Tell me. I'm a part of this now. Even more than you. Glebric will be looking for me, not you."

And she was right, again. *Her spirit matches her hair. I wonder how she pours that into her songs, and what she can do with it?* He sighed.

"If they consume us with their power... sacrifice us, any of us who are Talented, then I think that gives them even more power than the... consumption of a normal human. Once they know about us, I think they'll hunt us."

She crossed her arms. "We're not food. We have to rescue your friends, and mine."

Why was she so much more confident than he was?

"And how are we going to do that?"

"Magic."

Just like that. "Magic? What do you know about this magic? You don't have any training at all! I worked for weeks, non-stop, under Master Xelos. I learned from Elysia. I even learned from Yalath, poor Yalath." Another Talented mentor dead because he'd come into their life. He looked at Kallara, so young, and with so much ahead of her if he could just get her away from here... away from these ravenous beasts. He couldn't let someone else fall on his watch. "And now you think you're going to go in and do this? What, with me?" He blinked away tears of futility.

She turned away, sobbing. And he hated himself. He kneaded his face with his hands.

"I'm sorry Kallara, I shouldn't have said that. I..."

She wheeled on him, her eyes fierce. "Remeth said you'd help me. I know *he* would. Or are you too weak? Too scared?" The last word lilted with the first note of a song, and her voice rose, turning to a language he didn't understand. The swirling music leaped into his ears, invading his mind; waves of terrifying notes that beat him down, cowering against the table, his hands trying in vain to shield his ears from her attack.

Sudden silence, and the terror melted away. Her hands covered her mouth, her eyes even wider than his own.

"Did you practice that?" he asked. "Have you ever done it before?"

She shook her head, mute. He nodded, impressed.

"Maybe we have a chance to do something, if we work together. Forget everything I said before. Let this be your first lesson: your power is only limited by your imagination. If you can channel your emotion through your Talent, then I have no idea what you're capable of. I've barely tested the limits myself."

"I... I could feel it. Feel the emotions swirling out through my voice. Like the air coming out was heavy with... with power?"

"I could certainly feel it. So you were talking about me being scared, and in your anger, on some level you were trying to frighten me. And it worked. Have you done anything else?"

"It was the first time at Glebric's house, in front of the group. I sang, and I could feel the power going out through the room, touching them all."

"What feeling? What emotion?"

"It was an old Valtari song, about the beauty and wonder of the snow. I felt such peace. Everyone got so quiet, and listened—to me! And they were smiling and peaceful..." Her smile shone through her eyes. "But then after, they... I forgot! The watch! Today! They're going to attack the watch! That's what Glebric said in his speech."

"Maybe they changed their minds? We didn't see any sign of it." *Great, we get here just in time for fighting in the streets.* He had to get Elysia back. "But if I were going to start a revolt, I'd start at night."

"Let's get that message to Korg then, before things go crazy."

"We have to disguise ourselves first."

"Really? How does it work?" Her excitement lifted his heart just enough.

"I can paint on you, and it changes how you look."

"Forever?"

"I... I'm not actually sure. The first time it washed off when I went swimming. The second time we had to really scrub it off. I did it one more time with the intention of making it permanent, but then we left and I haven't seen the guy since. So what would you like?"

"So you can change the colors?"

"Definitely, as long as I can mix them. But I've also added hair, taken it away, changed the shape of a face."

"Wow! Let me think." She curled her red hair around her finger, eyes looking up in thought. "Could you..." She looked down at her chest, drawing his gaze down to the slight swell. She was still young, still... developing. He blushed.

"I... I don't think it wise. Try inconspicuous. Better if we can move around unnoticed."

She pursed her lips, and pulled the lock of red hair out in front of her eye. "Then this definitely has to go." She frowned. "I just started to like it too. I used to hate my hair. It was uncommon in my village, but very rare out here. The other girls always made fun of me."

"They were probably jealous. It's a beautiful color."

"Really? I never thought of it like that. It does stand out. But for blending in... I guess dark brown is good then? Most women around here have hair like that." She felt around her eye, at the remnants of the purplish bruise. "You'd better get rid of this too."

Anger churned in his stomach. *How could those boys do such a thing to a girl?* A thought occurred to him.

"Now that you know about your Talent, have you ever thought about..."

"About what?"

He sighed. "About going after the boys who did this to you?"

"Glebric's men already took care of that." She shuddered, frowning at the memory. "One died. Two others were... what's that word... Eww... eww?"

"Eunuch?" Simon squirmed at the mental image.

"That's the one. It wasn't even Glebric who did it. It was the really dark one. He's always angry. He believes what he's doing is right, but he's so savage. I wouldn't want your friends to get on the wrong side of him."

"Let's make sure Glebric and the others won't recognize either of us."

XXXII

ᏯᏌᏯᏌᏯᏌᏯᏌ

Commission

Too many memories swirled through Elysia's mind as she opened the door to the workshop. Some part of her held futile hope that Master Xelos would be inside, somehow safely hidden away.

Instead, she scarcely recognized the space, cluttered with more people than had ever been in Xelos' house at any one time. Half the room was filled with craftspeople: women sewing, men working leather into armor and polishing metal weapons. *Preparing for war. In my home city.* Elysia shuddered.

The other side had been converted into a dining hall for the mass of people. Women carried trays of food to waiting groups of men. The majority were brutish and loud, bearing scars on their arms and even faces.

I'll just get my things and get out of here.

An eager young man approached her. "Miss," he said in Izari, "the Master asked me to help you get your things?"

It made her suddenly self-conscious. If he could recognize her, how many others might? "Thank you, yes."

He led her to the cabinets next to... only a few shards clung stubbornly to the wall. Xelos' row of talking statues lay in ruin. She fought back a tear at the destruction of his finest achievement. *But by whose hand?* No matter. who did it, it kept Yalath and the others safe.

"Is everything all right?" the man asked.

"Yes, sorry. Just remembering something."

He nodded and unlocked the cabinet. "We keep these things out of the way." He lowered his voice. "The warriors tend to break things. Especially if they've been drinking. The Master likes things tidy." Inside were all of Xelos' tools, the ones she'd come to love over the years of practice together. "He said you could take whatever you like, as a gift. And I have a bag for you." He held out a sturdy canvas sack.

"Thank you." She looked over the chisels, drills, picks and files, first filling in gaps in the tools she'd brought with her, then adding a few of his favorites.

"Did you work with the late Master?"

She frowned, wishing he would just ignore her, but nodded.

"I'm sorry. It must have come as a shock to hear about the attack, and how he died. Did you know it was right here, in front of these ruined statues? What were they? That he would die to protect them?"

"He destroyed them?"

The man nodded. "There was apparently a hammer in his hand. What did they look like?"

"I... No. He kept them hidden. I don't know what they were."

He didn't seem to fully believe her, but thankfully didn't push further. Something about his probing made her uncomfortable.

"You knew Master Glebric then? He's so lucky, to have been so close to the late Master. What a generous gift, to leave all this to him." Was there a hint of ambition? This one was shrewd, and looking out for himself.

Glebric, be careful who you trust.

"Yes, I knew him. And yes, I'm very happy for him."

"He mentioned you might stay the night? That I should find you a room?" He looked around with some measure of disdain. "It's getting too full. But I'd expect that to change soon."

"Why?"

"Let's just say that I'd stay off the streets tonight."

"That's good advice on any night. Why tonight?"

His eyes darted over to the men eating and back to the weapons. "Our plan will see its first major test. Tonight."

I have to get back to the bakery.

"Then I'd better get going. Thank you for your help."

"Anything for a friend of the Master. Especially one as beautiful as yourself." He dipped his head with a charming smile. *Not charming enough.* He locked the cabinet and walked her out. "So, if you're leaving, the Master would want you sent with some protection. But he's busy. Ventus will arrange it."

"Oh that won't be necessary," she said. *Ventus?*

"Nonsense. He won't let you out without an escort. He was adamant, with what is to come. Please, this way." He led her past the crowd in the front room to what used to be Xelos' private receiving room. After knocking on the door, a voice bid him enter.

"Sorry to disturb you, Ventus, but here is the Master's friend, who you said would need an escort home?"

"Come in," Ventus said, in Izari but with a hint of a Pazian accent.

A middle-aged man with an aristocratic nose sat behind another of Xelos' desks, surrounded by papers. *Definitely Pazian.* He looked at her with a knowing smile, and cold eyes so deep she felt herself getting lost in them. A chill washed over her, raising goosebumps on her arm. *What is it about those eyes?*

"Elysia? Glebric has told me so much about you. What a pleasure to finally meet you. Please, come in."

ᎶᏋᎶᏋᎶᏋᎶ

Remeth had to stop for directions three times before finding the right street. It was busier than the other fine neighborhoods, with groups of people coming and going from one particularly large house. Despite the cool air, he found himself sweating after the running and walking. *And to think, I'm missing the theater for this?* He was in a foul mood as he approached the door, but filed in behind several men pushing covered wheelbarrows, trying to look like he was meant to be there.

Even he was impressed by the sculptures around the great doors, especially the handsome depictions of the Izari gods, so realistic compared to the classical Maruthan style he was used to. One especially caught his eye—a bare-chested hero battling a lion with his bare hands. *I'd worship him.*

A gaggle of giggling young women passed by after coming out the door, with two giving him a particularly long glance, and he answered with his most charming smile. They turned demurely away, tittering all the while. *Maybe I'll have better luck getting past women today.*

A bearded guard at the gates barred his way with an arm while the wheelbarrows passed through. *Might be handsome with a shave.* He said something in Izari, but Remeth just looked at him blankly. "New here?" the guard asked again in Pazian.

"Yes," Remeth said, making his words sound rough and awkward. "I escaped. I heard this master wants us all free."

The guard called out something in Izari through the door, summoning another, this one with a blond beard. "Telys here will take you for processing."

"Follow me," Telys said. He led Remeth through the grand gates into a large room with a central fountain. Between the doors in each of the four walls he counted a total of twelve guards. And with good reason. The room was packed. On the left side sat a group of well-dressed men.

A cloaked woman walked beside a young man. *Was that Elysia?* She passed through the door on the left. "This way," Telys said, giving him a slight shove in the opposite direction, toward a huddled group of women and children who ranged from disheveled to filthy. A middle-aged man with a neatly trimmed beard and a wax tablet made notes as he inspected each person. "Hector, I have a new man for you."

Hector looked up from his wax tablet, appraising Remeth. "Maruthan? Do you at least speak Pazian?" Remeth nodded. "Name?"

"Killeth."

Hector chuckled. "If you can hold a weapon, then that might be a good name for you yet." He recorded something on his tablet. "Can you? You look strong enough."

"I would fight for freedom."

"Definitely Maruthan. Telys, take him over to training. We can always use another, and not a moment too soon."

"This way," Telys said, and led him through the double doors opposite the front gates, into what would have been a beautifully quiet garden, if it weren't for the dozen pairs of sparring partners and the violent clatter of wood on wood.

Telys delivered him to a man whose shoulders looked like they were trying to swallow his bald head. His skin had a dark cast to it, which made the scars slightly less noticeable, except for the jagged one across his forehead.

To have survived such a blow, this one must be tough.

"Zustar, I have a late entrant for you. Killeth, Zustar will make sure you're outfitted. Might teach you a thing or two. Take heed, it could save your life tonight."

Tonight?

Zustar harrumphed. "Killeth is it? Maruthan? Then you'll be happy to join the fight. The master says we attack tonight, so tonight it is. Have you ever been in a fight?"

Remeth's mind flashed to the battle in the tower, and he gulped. *What have I got myself into?*

⚮⚮⚮⚮

"I can't believe it!" Kallara said. "I don't even recognize myself. It even feels real!" She touched her nose, where instead of the slightly upturned tip it pointed straight forward, with the taller bridge distinctive among the Izari. She ran her hand along the dark brown locks that framed her face. "All those times I wished I could be someone else… now I can. And you!" She tugged on Simon's short beard.

"Hey! That hurts." He batted her hand away.

"How does it feel to cover your skin like that?" She touched the creamy whiteness of his hand.

"It doesn't feel any different." Although she hit on something. It felt like a betrayal of his heritage, of his mother's people. He told himself the disguise was necessary, but this time it gnawed at him. "We should get moving."

"To deliver the message."

"I'm still not sure about that."

"But you said yourself; they might be the only friends we have left. And I owe it to Numerius."

He sighed, but nodded.

He retraced the route back to the port, the one he knew better than any other in this city of mixed memories. At least in the sun it seemed friendly. He'd changed into a tunic of Alexander's, while she wore one of Elysia's, and they walked down the street like any local brother and sister on a winter day. What struck him was that nobody paid them any heed. He fit in, but only in disguise.

They had no trouble finding Korg's warehouse by the harbor. He looked to be involved in importing wines and other goods from Pazh. Korg was tall and eminently respectable.

"I have a message from your friend Numerius," Kallara said.

"Who are you?"

"Kallara," she said before Simon could stop her. "He's in trouble."

305

Korg laughed. "Short of wine? Or food?"

"He's a prisoner at the house of Xelos—now Glebric. They have an army, and threaten the whole city."

Korg looked to Simon, who just nodded.

"He wants you to send an urgent letter to his steward in Pazh, to write a letter to..." She paused, thinking. "To Tullus. There are works of art here that are in danger, and need to be cared for, or they'll turn black. Damaged by the elements."

"Artwork? He's always going on about it. Never understood why. Not much money in that kind of thing."

"Can you send the message, right away?"

"Consider it done."

"Can you help him get out?"

Korg laughed again. "Can't spare the men. I'll be setting up extra guards here at the warehouse in case there's trouble. I'm not the only businessman doing the same. It's no secret things have been escalating. Those thugs think they run this place already."

"Why don't you send the watch after them?" Simon asked.

"The watch? They'll track down a cut-purse or swindler, but they don't want a fight."

"Thank you, Korg, for your help," Simon said.

"Who are you?"

"He's Simon," Kallara said before he could stop her.

"Zymon, really. But my sister here thinks I should use the Pazian version."

"Your Pazian is quite good," Korg said, before adding something in Izari.

"Have to go," Simon said, ushering Kallara out.

"I thought he was nice," she said when they were out in the late afternoon sun.

"Don't go telling people our names!"

She recoiled from the force of his words. "I'm sorry, but Numerius said—"

"I know you're just trying to help. But there are people looking for me, with my name. We look different, but if someone connects our real names with our new look..."

"Oh," she said, her face falling. "I understand now."

"Just keep quiet if we meet anyone else."

"Can I pick a new name?"

"Sure. Whatever you like."

"I'd like to be Ambrosia. And you can be… Antonos."

"Ambrosia? Don't you think that stands out a bit too much?"

"I like it."

"Antonos is serviceable enough."

"And you're my big brother."

"Sure."

"And our father is…"

"You can make up whatever you like, but just remember to keep quiet when we get to Xelos' house."

"You mean Glebric's."

"Are you trying to be an annoying younger sister?"

She grinned at him. "So the disguise is working?"

⟨⟨⟨⟨⟨⟨⟨

Thoughts swirled through Elysia's head, not making any sense.

"Glebric?" she asked.

"Yes," Ventus said. "He told me all about you, and the late master. About your beautiful work. He must be so happy to know you escaped from that dreadful attack. You absolutely must join us for dinner." His smile made her uncomfortable. *And those eyes.* She felt naked before them. Almost like he could see inside her.

"I… I would love to, but I was just about to leave. I found everything I was looking for. Perhaps tomorrow?"

"I'm afraid things are about to get a little… complicated out in the streets. Glebric would not want anything to happen to you. No, why don't you stay here. Which was your old room? You could rest until dinner. You seem tired."

She was, and didn't relish the thought of being out in the streets during a fight. But there was something about his look, how his words and eyes seemed disconnected in some way. "You work with him?"

"Yes, there is so much to organize for Glebric's grand vision. I take care of a lot of the logistics, calling on my mercantile background. Sorry, where are my manners. I'm Ventus."

"Nice to meet you. Glebric was always good to me."

"And he let you get all your tools? That's just wonderful." He tapped his chin. "You know, I've been looking for someone to work on a commission. Have you ever worked with the green marble from Jeppo?"

307

Her eyes lit up. "I've always wanted to!"

"A large piece arrived right after Glebric came into his inheritance. Master Xelos must have ordered it before his untimely demise."

For me? It was always my dream...

"It would be a shame if you left without taking a look. Or are you in a hurry to meet someone?"

"No, I... where is it?"

"In storage, but I could have it brought to you." He smiled. "Let me make you an offer. Take a look at the marble, and see if it has any potential. Perhaps some inspiration will come to you? Stay for dinner, and off the streets. I'll give you until dinner to decide on some ideas, and then if I like them we can talk of a price."

Simon said we do need the money. And the chance to carve that famous green stone? She nodded.

"Splendid. I'll have my man show you to your room, and others bring you the stone. You must be hungry?"

"Yes, but I wouldn't want to trouble you. Can I get started right away?"

"I thought you might say that. I'll have them bring the food to your room.

"Thank you, Ventus. I hope you'll like my ideas."

"I'm certain I will."

Elysia floated out of the room on a wave of excitement, thankful for this one last gift from Master Xelos.

ᎶᏋᏓᏋᏓᏋᎶ

A knock at his door interrupted Glebric while he pored over his maps of the city. "Yes?"

Ventus opened the door. "Are you almost ready?"

Glebric had reviewed the plans a hundred times, but still questioned everything. "Are you sure we can do this tonight? Maybe I should delay—"

"Nonsense. And look weak? You've delayed long enough as it is. Show me where you mean to strike first."

Glebric pointed to the port, agora, temple complex, barracks, and the city gates.

"Good, good. You know the port is the key."

"Yes, for the future. And I think we can fight the watch. But what if the nobles turn on us? With things getting a little rougher lately, they've been hiring more bodyguards. They could challenge us, and even turn the tide if they were to join the fight at the wrong time. I want to send men against some of the richer ones tonight, but do we have enough? If we could release their slaves... I pray fortune smiles on us."

Ventus nodded. "I would not trust in fate to secure our victory."

"No, so that's why I think we should wait. More men and we could guarantee—"

"I wasn't talking about more men."

"What?"

Ventus' cold smile tugged at something deep inside Glebric.

"You mean... my power?"

"You control the pieces in this game, but with your power you also load the dice."

Glebric stood up and paced the room. "I don't know, I don't think... I haven't really tested it. What could I even do?"

"You could take out the garrison by yourself. You just need more fuel to do it."

Fuel? No... Orna's terror was etched in his brain. *No, I can't do that again.* "I'd rather not..."

Ventus grimaced. "Then you'd rather not win. Glebric, you are so close to controlling this whole city. Making it a base for changing the world. You say you want to free every last slave in this decadent Republic, and beyond. We can do this together. But it will require more power. The pain of a few serves the good of the many."

"But it's murder."

"They would do the same to you! Don't forget that. They hate you. They're plotting to stop you right now. You already let the girl through your fingers. She could be rallying more of them against you!"

Glebric clenched his fists. "They wouldn't! The girl, Kallara, she just doesn't want to be a slave. She wouldn't—"

"Hatred is a powerful force. They will kill you so they can enslave others. What of that? Would you stop those that would make your mother their whore!"

"Stop it!" Glebric's blood boiled. "Why? Why would they do such a thing?"

"To punish you. You felt it, how they oppose you. How they hate you and everything you stand for."

Glebric clenched his teeth. He had felt it. "Bring them to me!"

"Already on their way. Feed your power, and you will bring us victory tonight."

XXXIII
ᎦᏎᎦᏎᎦᏎᎦ
Intersection

Remeth wanted to wilt under Zustar's penetrating glare. "Is that a no?" the trainer asked.

Remeth marshaled his Talent to cover his misgivings with bravado. "I had to fight my way out of my master's house. His guards will feel it for a week!"

"Well, it's no ordinary bodyguards we face tonight. The city watch, and a handful of legionaries."

"For freedom!" Remeth said, and pounded his bare chest. He had to admit, he liked the sound of it.

"I like this one, Telys. We might make a warrior of him yet." The guard nodded and walked off. Zustar searched the stand of wooden weapons and picked up a long knife. He tossed it to Remeth, who fumbled the catch, earning a scowl. "You'd best get a hold on it if you want to survive the night. This is no game."

"The Pazians will pay for holding us down."

"Aye, they will. But they'll take a few of our men with them, and you if you're sloppy. Look at them." They were a tough bunch, of every size, shape and color. But no Pazians, and only one Izari. No other Maruthans either, which suited him just fine. It might be harder to keep his cover. Zustar drew a short sword. "Show me what you've got."

I don't know how to fight with a knife. A wiry blonde man—*Gatraki maybe?*—danced with the knife held blade down. His sweeping slashes connected on the body of his Borathi opponent, but he whirled back out of reach of every counterstrike. *Dancing I can do.* Focusing the flow of his Talent, Remeth prepared himself to copy the motions. *But this Zustar looks like a tough judge.*

Zustar assumed a fighting stance, holding the blade parallel to the ground and pointed directly at Remeth, who answered by crouching low himself, holding the blade down like he'd seen. "Lefty," Zustar said with an approving nod. "That earns you a few points. I wish I had more time with you, but the basics will have to do." Without any further warning, Zustar's sword flashed, Remeth's hand stung, and the knife skittered away across the stones. Zustar shook his head. "Pick it up. You need a stronger grip. But not too tight."

Remeth grimaced at the sickening thought of drawing blood. He'd seen enough already. *How do I get myself into these things? All I want is to go to the theater.*

"Killeth? You'd be holding your own entrails if this were a real fight. Pick up the knife."

Nodding, Remeth retrieved it and resumed his stance.

Zustar clucked his tongue. "You're too tense." He rapped Remeth's shoulder with a meaty hand. "Here. Relax. If you're tight, you can't respond quick enough. And if you're using a knife and he's got a sword, reaction is all you have. Ready?"

Remeth waited, watching for any sign of attack. He kept his feet light, just like dancing. He'd been in a few choreographed fights on stage, and the footwork had come easily to him, while the slashing and parrying were a struggle. Zustar flicked out his sword and Remeth dodged to the right, earning an appreciative grunt from the master, who stepped back and tapped his chest.

"That's better, but you should have buried that knife in my heart. I left it exposed."

In his mind, Remeth saw the blood spurting out around a knife, and choked back a gag. Zustar pursed his lips. "Again."

Zustar's next attack jabbed his ribs, sending sparks of pain shooting through his whole body. When he clutched at his side, Zustar leveled the sword at his neck. "You think that's pain? Your dodge took away half the power, and I held back."

"I... I don't know if the knife is best for me."

"Your footwork is good, but your reactions are slow. But you're strong. Hmm." Zustar went back to the weapon rack and came back with a club. He tossed it to Remeth. "How about this?" At Remeth's quizzical look, he laughed. "You just bash them as hard as you can. Can you do that?"

Remeth nodded. At least there wouldn't be blood.

"Not much I can teach you on that. Get yourself to the armorer for some leather to protect your precious golden hide."

Remeth winced as he rubbed the scratch on his ribs. He wouldn't disagree.

"Aktar!" Zastar called out to an athletic Pazian man, who from his own set of scars appeared to be one of the more experienced warriors in the group. "Take Killeth to get some leather fitted. I might even send him with you tonight."

Aktar looked Remeth over and nodded, clasping Remeth's arm with a sturdy grip. *Keen eyes, and a whiff of danger to this one.* "Welcome to the team, Killeth."

ᏮᏋᏮᏌᏋᏮᏋᏮ

Kallara's warning about Glebric's force striking soon had Simon on edge. He couldn't remember the last time he walked through a city without looking over his shoulder; this time for thugs in general, rather than agents specifically seeking him. It didn't change his anxiety level. The few wealthy people they passed were accompanied by multiple guards, some as many as six, and they were tense, ready for a fight.

When they turned on the street that led to the house, the feeling changed. No commercial traffic, not even the usual messengers and residents on their way. The street was empty, except for rough-looking men walking in groups—organized squads, they walked in formation. Simon considered turning back, afraid for Kallara's safety even more than his own, but he had to get to Elysia.

The front doors were guarded by two big men on the outside, which evoked the memory of Simon's ill-fated previous visit. He froze for a moment, paralyzed by the shame and failure washing over him.

"Is there something wrong?" Kallara asked.

"No, sorry. Just a memory."

She lowered her voice to a whisper. "I'm scared. What if they catch us?"

"We have to risk it. I can't abandon Elysia."

"But what about Remeth? Couldn't we go back to the bakery and contact him? Like you tried to do with…"

"It would take too long, we're already here."

"I don't want to go back in there."

"Neither do I." He wasn't sure he could face the death. But he already felt anger welling up at the idea of a dark power inhabiting

313

Xelos' house. It was an affront to the master's legacy. "But let's try."

He put his hand on her shoulder and urged her to come with him to the door.

The guard was a big man, taller than Simon by several inches, and twice as wide. He held up a hand and challenged them in Izari.

"Pazian?" Simon asked.

The guard narrowed his eyes. "You two look as Izari as they come."

"It's a long story."

"What is your business here?"

"My sister and I escaped our master, and heard we can find solace here."

The guard's eyes flicked down Kallara's nondescript tunic and back to Simon. "Come back tomorrow. We're closed. The master is busy, and not taking in anyone new tonight."

"But we have nowhere to go…"

"That's not my problem. It's not too cold, find somewhere outside."

Kallara started sobbing, and the guard screwed up his face, looking around before leaning in to whisper. "If you want to stay safe, keep away from the agora tonight. And the gates. And maybe the port. I'm sorry, but I have my orders."

Simon nodded in resignation. "Come, Ambrosia," he said, putting his arm around Kallara. "There's nothing we can do."

"Just stay safe," the guard added helpfully as they turned away.

"Now what do we do?" she asked when they were out of earshot. "We have to get in there."

"This confirms it. The attack must be happening tonight. If we keep an eye on things, and figure out when the bulk of their men have left, we might be able to get in another way. I have an idea."

ᏮᏋᏮᏋᏮᏋᏮ

"How long have you been working with Glebric?" Remeth asked Aktar as they walked.

"A month now? Maybe longer? I saw the way this city is going. His vision is beautiful. No more slaves? Throw off the Pazian yoke?"

"But aren't you Pazian?"

314

"Sure, but *mundati* like me, what chance do we have but to serve the senators in their palatial homes?"

"Like this one?"

"Glebric is different. He's one of us."

It did appeal to his Maruthan independent streak.

"So where will you be attacking tonight?"

"You mean we? Glebric will be laying all that out, and soon. You'll just do as you're ordered."

"Just wondering where he means to strike."

"The port, the gates, anywhere there are guards. Any locations of strategic importance."

"But what about the nobles and their bodyguards? Aren't they the real power? They'll resist him."

"Of course. But they'll be huddled in their homes, enjoying the pleasures of wealth and power."

That reminded him. "What about the theater?"

Aktar raised an eyebrow.

"The theater! It's all they talked about at my master's house. Everyone is fawning over this new troupe. Won't most of the nobles be there tonight?"

Aktar nodded with new respect in his eyes. "You're right."

"Is that one of the targets?"

"It should be. I'll raise that to the others. I could lead that attack myself. The muster should be in another hour or so, just before dusk. And I'll recommend you get posted with me. Your club will be more use getting council members in line than against the few actual legionaries. You might earn yourself a little distinction on your first day. But wouldn't your old master recognize you there?"

"He was ill. That's how I was able to escape. He's not going anywhere tonight, or anytime soon." Remeth covered the grin that wanted to form. "I never did get to see the theater, I've heard—" He bumped into a man rounding the corner.

"Watch where you're going, you oaf!" the young man said.

Remeth bowed his head in apology. And saw her—Elysia, standing shocked next to the young man. "I'm sorry to have disturbed you, milady."

Elysia nodded, mute.

"We're all free men here, Killeth," Aktar said. "He meant no offense, this place is busier than it's meant to be." Aktar smiled at Elysia. "We didn't mean to scare you. You must be new."

"Have we met?" she asked, looking closer at Aktar's features, and avoiding Remeth's eyes. *Good. She's too straightforward and might give us away.*

"I'm sure I'd remember," Aktar said and smiled again. "Maybe just passed each other somewhere, sometime? In the agora? At the temple?" He shrugged his shoulders, not expecting a response. "Though I would certainly remember such a beauty."

The young man huffed. "I'm sorry," he said to Elysia, "but I still have much to do. Can I show you to your room?"

"You're staying?" Aktar asked. "I hope we will meet again."

Her smile was awkward, and her eyes flicked to Remeth for a moment. He stood a little straighter, tensing his muscles to try to look his best. Her eyes slipped to his chest and a hint of color brushed her cheeks before she rushed away.

"Looks like you might have made an impression on her," Aktar said.

"I... I am not used to the freedom to smile at beautiful women."

"No, I guess not. Well I am, and I saw the way she looked at you. Almost as if she recognized you?"

Remeth's heart skipped a beat. Aktar laughed and squeezed Remeth's bicep.

"I don't have the balls to walk around half-naked like men from your province, but I can see why the ladies might like it. She certainly did. You're a handsome man, Killeth. Now that you're free, that counts for something. Or did any of your former master's girls take a shine to you?"

"That wasn't permitted."

"Pity. Some actually breed their next generation of slaves. Nice strong bull like you would be in demand. Though that independent streak might worry them. Wouldn't have surprised me if the lady of the house herself brought you to her bed."

Remeth crafted the slightest smirk and Aktar clapped him on the back.

"Ho! Not so innocent are we? We're going to get along well, Killeth. Now let's get that chest of yours covered in leather before the armor is all gone."

⚏⚏⚏⚏⚏

"Thank you for coming," Glebric said to the two musicians standing in front of him in his study; the young man with the lyre, and the older who never went anywhere without his drum. Glebric didn't remember their names, but they were definitely Myraki, with black hair and that dark cast to their skin. And very suspicious.

Ventus stood behind them, a wolfish gleam in his eyes.

Glebric thought of Elysia sitting across from him in the same room, sounding so inspired by his ideas of freedom. He hoped she got back to the bakery safely. He would look for her tomorrow, after all this was over. That pang in his heart, was it guilt? *Elysia would never do anything like this.*

Ventus nodded impatiently.

"You probably wondered what happened to Orna and Kallara..." Glebric's voice faltered. These men didn't deserve to die. Neither did Orna. And where was Kallara? Ventus was convinced she was rallying forces against him, but she was just a girl! *Though some would say I am little more than a boy, and look at the power I now wield.*

The two men exchanged a worried glance. Glebric had rehearsed the lie, to get them comfortable. But why? *They were just going to die.* "Orna tried to kill me—"

"No!" said the young one, his eyes blazing. "She'd never hurt anyone."

Glebric held up a hand. "I couldn't believe it either. I invited her to play for me. I loved what she could do with her flute, the art... the magic." A flicker of worry creased the brow of the old man. "I was lucky to escape. She tried to use some kind of dark magic on me, to enslave me. I broke free just in time, and threw her off, and... I'm sorry to say she hurt her head when she fell."

The young man lunged over the desk at Glebric, too quick for the old man to stop him. "You monster!" he screamed, grabbing for Glebric's throat. He wasn't big, but he was fully grown while Glebric was still growing into his man's body. Panic attuned Glebric to the anger pulsing through the veins of his assailant, so full of life and power. Glebric's mouth watered, hungering for a taste, and he could control his emotions no longer. He opened up, and summoned that power into himself. The man's hands clenched tighter on his windpipe for a moment, but slackened when his body jerked back and forth. The blood vessels on his arms and face writhed like worms under his skin until they finally burst, spraying out blood in a cloud of droplets that froze in the air. With a final flash of horror, the light in his eyes died out.

Regaining his composure, Glebric willed the droplets to swirl around, forming into larger and larger globules until there was a single ball of power-laced blood hovering over his outstretched palm.

"So, he showed his true colors. He was a part of the plot to attack me too. Old man, tell me, were you the mastermind behind it all?"

The drummer fell to his knees, his beard touching the floor. "I knew nothing."

"Liar. But if you tell me where Kallara is, I may let you live."

Ventus raised an eyebrow, but Glebric shook his head.

The old man looked up. "She lives?" There was a frail hope in his eyes.

"Then you're useless to me."

The man raised his drum and tried to beat it, but Glebric yanked the man's blood out of his mouth in one rushing torrent. The withered old husk floated to the ground, lifeless and pathetic. Glebric's hands quivered as he stroked the rippling globes of blood. It suffused his skin, filling him with warmth and light. And Talent; fuel for the power he needed.

Ventus nodded his approval. "You have done well. And it feels even better than the last time, does it not?"

A new urgency flowed through Glebric. "Marshal the men. This power should not be wasted."

XXXIV
ᏬᏋᏬᏋᏬᏋᏬ
Mobilization

Persei stood with Mirasha on the foredeck of the *Stormrunner*, the fastest ship they could hire in Jeppo. The reds of the sunset set off her hair.

He'd brought ten men with him as his guard, as was his right as a traveling legate, though he felt now like they were more a hindrance than anything, with the new power inside him. Not that there would be any opposition between Jeppo and Pazh. But he felt more comfortable with the extra iron under his command. Who knew what waited for them at their stop, wherever that might be. The blood of Kashaka in its clay jar had pointed past the independent island of Aktiri, a strange place that Persei knew nothing about. He'd told the captain to keep a course for Attarsus, and they'd see if they needed to redirect him from there. It would cost the family a lot, but Persei would spare no expense in his pursuit of power.

"Do you think we'll find Kashaka in Attarsus?" he asked Mirasha.

"In the city? Would you imprison such a power in the middle of a settled area?"

She had a point. "No, that would be folly. If she's in Izar, she must be on one of the uninhabited islands. If she's even there." He was getting impatient with this sea travel. Even with a good wind, and this fast ship, it would still be several more days before they reached the archipelago. Of course the chance to be alone any time he wanted with Mirasha was a welcome diversion this time, with no trace of her former seasickness. Their lovemaking was reaching new heights of passion with all this extra fire inside him. It wasn't only affecting his desire; she couldn't keep her hands off him.

"I tire of this sunset," he said, taking her hand in his.

"Shall we go below?"

With the heat radiating from her body, he knew it would be another good night.

ᏮᏋᏮᏋᏮᏋᏮ

Returning to her old room was eerie, and especially uncomfortable when the young man had to evict the four girls who'd been sharing the room. Elysia tried to protest, but again, Glebric's instructions prevailed. If she were to do any real carving, she'd want privacy anyway.

Master Xelos had died protecting the identities of Yalath and the other masters—protecting her. So had her father. And now Xelos' heir was giving her the chance to work in her dream material. *I will do you proud.*

The knock brought her back to the present. She opened the door and four strong men struggled to push a wooden sledge bearing a shrouded block the height of a man.

"Just leave it on there, so we can get it out again," said one of the men, as he shook out his muscles.

"Thank you," she said, and they left her alone.

Her heart fluttered as she lifted a corner of the shroud, but she paused, imagining it first in her mind. What would she see inside? A great hero? An animal? An array of smaller pieces? She closed her eyes, savoring the moment, before opening them and drawing back the shroud.

She gasped at the beauty of the light green stone, with iridescent flecks that flashed silver in the flickering lamplight. Shadowy bands of darker green gave it depth and character. Her eyes searched deeper for hidden forms, for potential...

She recoiled, clutching her mouth. *No! It can't be.* Within the stone crouched a hideous beast, savage and angry at its captivity. Its narrow head resembled a fish, but with row after row of wickedly pointed teeth. But it stood on two feet, with arms and legs like a man. The feet were webbed, almost like fins, and each finger and toe ended in a sharp claw that looked capable of tearing through flesh like butter. Worst of all were the eyes. There was nothing human in those orbs of pure malevolence. Nothing but hate and destruction.

Sitting down on one of the beds, she buried her face in her

320

quivering hands, trying to banish the apparition from her mind. *No, I can't let such a thing loose in this world.*

But deep inside, she felt part of herself laugh. *No? You weren't shy about wanting revenge on the Lokuta and their agents. Or about unleashing your birds on the Scentari? And what about fashioning a blade and a killer on Aktiri? You're not so blameless.*

Horrified, she looked at her hands.

What have I done? What have I become? I'm so sorry, Simon. I don't deserve you.

But that reminded her of something he said, about his own art. He could envision something and then create it, not just unlock what was already there.

Maybe I can do the same?

She allowed her mind to wander to the realm of possibilities. There was definitely something about the color that made her think of water, and creatures that would plumb the depths of the sea. In her mind, it was a beautiful horse, like a graceful sister to Zeno. Except with fins and a fish's tail—a sea-horse to carry her over the green waves. The vision brought a smile to her face, and she opened her eyes to project it on the raw stone.

For a moment she could see the faint outline of the noble face, the sleek neck, and the scaled body. But it melted away, almost like it was consumed by the more powerful creature that lived within. It would not be denied. The horrible fish-man mocked her, defiant

"I will not free you from your prison," she vowed.

But she couldn't take her eyes from it. It was horrible, but there was a wild beauty to the lines. The marble called to her, and she ran her hand down the rough surface where the block had been wrested from some quarry across the sea. And brought it to her, here and now.

She steeled herself against the vision, and searched through her things to find the right tool. "My hand holds the chisel, and my Talent reveals it. I'm in control."

The toothy grin just smiled at her.

I hope.

With a light tap she broke into the soft marble, and felt her power connect to the stone.

ᏮᏋᏮᏋᏮᏋᏮ

The courtyard was full of Glebric's men—ten lieutenants of his army, along with the six squads that were stationed in his house. Seventy men in all, but just a fraction of his overall force. He'd spent dinner poring over the map and the battle plans with Zustar, Azzam and Ventus, and they'd come to the final dispositions. Now it was on him to show leadership, or so Ventus had urged him.

His body was the first battleground; with angry power urging him onward, while old thoughts and worries gnawed at his confidence. *Who am I to lead them in battle? I've never been in a fight! These men would sooner laugh at me than follow my charge.*

But the power fought back, filling him with a new strength and conviction. *I could end their lives in an instant, and it would only increase my power. Any who dare oppose me will just feed my strength.*

But there will be no opposition here. They share my vision.

"Are you ready?" he called out to the men and they snapped to attention. "You have tasted freedom, each and every one of you." He saw the nods and the yearning in their eyes. "As have I. I know what it is to be a slave, and I cannot bear for any other man, woman or child to be denied the right to freedom."

"But the Pazians would keep them in chains!" shouted Azzam, on cue. Angry shouts joined him.

"No more! Tonight, we share this gift, offering it to all of Attarsus. Are you with me?"

"Freedom!" shouted Zustar and Azzam in unison, and the men joined in behind them in a deep chorus of determination.

"Follow the captains of freedom, and you will be a part of history." He pointed to Zustar. "Our loyal trainer Zustar, who has made slaves and gladiators into a fighting force, you will command these three squads, and take the barracks. Azzam, you will take two squads to the port. Aktar, I have a list of noble houses—"

"What about the theater?" shouted one man, tall and blonde with golden skin. He looked like a god in leathers, and his eyes blazed with passion—passion for freedom. Many shot him angry stares, but at his side, Aktar raised a hand. Ventus had his misgivings about that one, and his closeness to that Pazian general who had bought the artwork, but he was skilled and the men respected his worldly experience. Glebric was happy to have him on his side, and who knew the depravity of the *digniti* better than someone who had worked so closely with them for so long?

"Aktar, why the theater?"

"Our new Maruthan friend has a point. Many of the wealthy will be at the theater tonight, watching the new players. They may be hiding behind their guards by day, but this rare pleasure will help them relax."

If we could round up the richest merchants and strong voices on the council, not to mention the wealthier Pazians... Zustar looked to be considering the possibilities too, while Azzam glared impatiently.

"What do you call yourself, Maruthan?" Glebric asked.

The man stepped forward. He looked strong, and carried a large club, but bowed his head with the deference of a slave. "Killeth."

"Killeth, do not bow your head to me. I am a free man like you, and your idea is worthy of praise."

Glebric raised his voice a level. "Aktar, take Killeth and two squads of strong men like him. If we want to control the city and release the remaining slaves, the theater is a prime target. I will accompany you myself. I will call on the slaves in the crowd to rise against their masters.

"Hector, send someone to procure the tickets, now. We don't want to show up uninvited. Spare no expense.

"Captains, speak to Zustar and he'll direct you to your targets for the night. Go swiftly to your men, for we strike one hour after darkness falls. If we all work together, the city will be ours by sunrise."

"Freedom!" the men shouted together.

He spoke faster now, with a new depth of conviction. "But freedom does not mean chaos. None of our number shall harm any women or children. There will be no looting. And if any watchman, bodyguard or soldier submits, bind him and bring him back. They will expect to be slaves, but we will show them our new order, ruled by equality and kindness."

"Freedom!" the men shouted again.

"Freedom!" Glebric shouted back. "To your squads!"

ᎶᏋᏮᏋᏮᏋᏋᎶ

Simon had taken Kallara back to the agora to get a simple dinner of fish and flatbread to pass the time until dusk. He'd learned from experience not to face the Attarsus night on an empty stomach. No telling what might happen. They'd taken the food back to the bakery, where he gathered his paints and laid out his idea.

Kallara was incredulous. "You can paint your way through a solid wall?"

Simon smiled. "I've done it in ruins, and a stout keep. And once through the lock in a prison."

Her eyes narrowed. "Why were you in prison?"

"A misunderstanding. And really, it was Remeth's fault."

"So where do you mean to enter the house? It's packed with people."

"Well, if most of the fighting men are out taking over the city, then I'm not so worried about the women and children."

"But every room is in use, except on the upper floor. And we can't climb up there... can we?"

"I hadn't thought of that, but it might actually work."

"I don't like climbing."

"It would be even more conspicuous. That's what I'm more worried about—someone on the street stopping us. If they're patrolling the perimeter, we'll be in big trouble." He drew her a quick map. "Our only chance is here." He pointed to the alley on the west side of the house. "The other wall is right up against the next house, but this side is open. If I can get my bearings right, we can go into this storeroom. Do you know what they're using it for?"

She shrugged her shoulders. "I've never been in there. I spent most of my time on the other side of the house. Where do you think Elysia might be?"

"I was hoping you'd have an idea."

She thought for a few moments. "The women without children are mostly in the east wing, either in the rooms on the way to the dining hall—"

"But the dining room is at the north end, coming out of the atrium."

"Not that one, that's where Glebric entertains his guests. The other dining room for the rest of us, it's in the east wing. Really good light and a lot of tables."

Simon grimaced. "The workshop? They must have converted it." It seemed the ultimate disrespect of Xelos and his art. *Our art.*

"Whatever you call it. So either those rooms, or the ones leading to the stairs." She looked down at her feet. "Though some of the women have been known to go upstairs with some of Glebric's warriors. But I never spoke with them of it."

Simon waved his hand to dispel the very idea. "I don't think she'll be up there." *Aüata, Salar, Choron? Whichever god will hear me, please keep her from such a fate.* "I have everything I need. Are you sure you want to come?" He really wished she wouldn't. He feared for his own safety, and she'd be in danger just walking in the street with so many brutes about spoiling for a fight, or worse. *Even if Glebric means well, how will he control every last freedman?*

She shuddered. "I'm not staying here by myself. There's something creepy about this place." He tried not to glance at the rug.

"Then let's go."

ᏩᏋᏩᏋᏩᏋᏩ

Remeth was to be the third from his squad to leave, which gave him a few precious moments to look for Elysia before he was out the door. To preserve the element of surprise they were leaving separately, other than the guards assigned directly to Glebric. Hidden under his cloak were the studded leather armor and the club tucked in his belt. In his hand he clutched the ticket to the night's theater show, which started in thirty minutes. He was impressed that the steward had been able to manage it, and wondered how much of a premium he paid for the tickets. He was to take his seat and listen for the signal from Glebric's men, then start taking out guards or other threats. Remeth would be seated next to Aktar, which made him feel a little more comfortable. He didn't think he'd actually draw a weapon against a noble's bodyguards if he were on his own.

Where is Elysia? He'd been sure she would be in the workshop getting her things, or maybe even carving something. But it was mostly empty; save for an old Izari who Aktar said was a former master doctor in the legions, and his two assistants. *They're expecting casualties tonight. I don't intend to be one of them. But I can't just stay here, or be branded a deserter.*

"Looking for something?" Aktar asked when he saw him.

"Still trying to get my bearings. The house is far bigger than my former master's. I still can't believe I'm staying here."

"It's nothing compared to the best of Pazh."

"Who were they? Your masters."

"*Digniti*, if you can believe it."

"Senators?" Remeth forced his eyes wide with feigned awe.

325

Aktar chuckled. "The President-elect himself!"

Now he didn't have to fake looking impressed. "Then why would you leave? Or did they treat their slaves badly?"

Aktar's smile turned sly. "Oh they love their slave girls, in bed. It was too painful, surrounded by such beauty but never able to touch them. And they didn't treat the men nearly as well. I'd love to set those ladies free."

"I'd be right there with you."

"Not going to happen, my friend. I don't want your golden skin to outshine me. I saw that earlier. Was *that* who you were looking for?" His eyes narrowed.

Damn this one. "In my country, you ask a woman's blessing before going into battle."

"Well I haven't seen her, so I guess you'll have to do without. Don't worry, you'll have me by your side. But not if you don't get going. One last trip to relieve myself and then I'll be on my way. Always better to be empty in a battle."

Remeth cringed. "See you at the theater."

"Indeed."

Remeth saw no further sign of Elysia on the way past the remaining guards manning the front gates. *I hope you got out, Elysia, or I have failed you.*

Out in the deepening darkness, with a cool wind raising goose-bumps, Remeth debated heading back to the bakery instead of continuing on to the theater. *If I go back, I'll be late for the opening act.* He so desperately wanted to see at least part of the show before the fighting broke out. And once things went crazy, there wasn't likely to be another show for a while yet. *But if they're back and safe, then I don't need to risk myself. I could run?*

He tried to straddle both options, walking quickly back toward the agora before making a decision. But how different the streets looked at night. He took two wrong turns and had to retrace his steps, costing himself what little buffer he had left. By the time he reached the agora, he realized he had no idea how to get back to the bakery in the dark. Or at all. And he couldn't exactly ask directions. He was alone. Unless he went to the theater.

Just make it back to Glebric's house tonight in one piece, and figure things out in the morning.

The amphitheater was a marvel, cut into the far side of the hill that housed the acropolis. Remeth found his way rather easily, with the few people out walking all headed that way. Merging into the line passing through the entrance arch, he handed his ticket to the usher and got directions up to his seat—dead center, only eight rows back from the stage. What a waste. He began to hope that the plans would fall through and he could just enjoy the show.

Rows of torches wreathed the stage in flames, which assisted the rising moon in spectacularly illuminating every detail. Remeth felt like a child waiting for a gift as he picked his way through the throng of people until he found his row.

He shuffled his way past a merchant, his wife, and their teenage sons, and settled into his seat. Anticipation and the brisk walk up the steps warmed him, even seated on the cold stone. He hadn't thought to bring a mat like the family beside him. And where would he get one? *There should be vendors selling them.* The boys whispered something to each other, looking in his direction, then tried to hide their laughter. He gave them a smile and a nod, and they shut up. *We'll see who's laughing when the fighting breaks out.*

Now where is Aktar?

⊙⊙⊙⊙⊙⊙⊙

On their short walk, Simon only had to stare off a couple of young men who loitered at a dark street corner. He thanked the gods that he was tall and they didn't seem up to the challenge, though they stared brazenly at Kallara until they were out of sight.

Xelos' street—he still couldn't call it anything else—was dead silent. If there were guards, they were on the inside. *Just like last time.* The night breeze cut a little closer to the bone as he remembered Elysia's father splayed out inside those doors. He was thankful he wasn't trying to sleep, fearing what visions of Remeth or Elysia meeting a similar fate might visit him in the dark of night.

They crossed over to hug the wall of the neighboring mansion, scanned the street one last time for any last minute observers and confirmed it was empty. They ducked around the corner between the high walls of the buildings. Simon had wondered what practical use the lane served, other than to give two wealthy individuals a little more privacy, but he hadn't gone ten feet before the smell supplied the missing information. Kallara gagged, and he clapped his cloak across his nose to keep out the dual stench of human filth and rotting food. The smell was surprising, with the lane appearing to be as clean as the street outside.

"Will you be able to paint here?" Kallara asked, holding her nose.

Simon nodded, not wanting to draw more breath than he had to. The smell worsened further down the lane, especially where it narrowed down to five feet across. Simon puzzled at the source until he saw the doors on the other side, where the stink reached its zenith.

"They must dump out the refuse here to be collected," he said and immediately regretted it as he took another whiff and felt his meal do a flip in his belly. He sprinted around the corner before hazarding another breath. It was better, but still smelled strongly. "It's a shame, that would be the best point to go in, but I wouldn't be able to stand it." Kallara wrinkled her nose and glanced nervously down the second lane that ran parallel to the main street, behind the houses.

"I wouldn't want to be the one who has to cart that filth away."

Simon grimaced. "I hadn't thought of that. They'll probably come during the night to take it. I'll try to work as quickly as I can. I never knew what was behind here. It sure makes it easier being at a corner—we won't end up in the wrong house by accident. Can you keep watch?"

"How long will it take?" Her eyes watered.

"I'll do the best I can. Want to see some magic?" He grinned and took out the glowing coin. It was still shining brightly and her delighted gasp gave him some hope. He propped it between a brush and a jar of paint, to illuminate a portion of the wall, and started summoning his Talent.

XXXV
Theater

Remeth's enjoyment of the show overshadowed any trepidation about the coming battle and how he might fit into it. In between scenes he'd located Glebric and his host of guards in seats in the second row, and a few other pairs of men from Glebric's army scattered around the front portion of the crowd. He felt for the club under his cloak, wishing it away as some bad dream. Aktar's nonappearance nagged at him. Had there already been a setback?

The hush of the crowd drew him back to the spectacle. Onto the stage strutted the lead actor, a gorgeous Izari man with a close-cropped beard, looking every bit the son of a god he was cast to play. He brought passion and flair to the role, convincing in his desire for revenge for the god's mistreatment of his mother.

Caught up in the emotion of the story, any thoughts of fighting someone else's battle drifted away.

These Izari sure know how to put on a show!

"Ambrosia?" Simon asked, his tone playful. "It's ready." She clasped her hands together and skipped over to him.

"No sign of the waste collectors," she said, almost proudly. She raised an eyebrow when she looked closer at his work. "What is it?"

He'd wanted to try something a little different, after the heavy stone back in Aktiri had almost been their undoing. He pointed to the top of the little door. "I put a hinge here so it will be easier to get back out this way, assuming we need to make a quick escape.

"Is it big enough for you? You're a lot taller than me."

"Don't worry, I can fit."

329

"Are you going first? I..."

"Of course. I need to make sure it's safe."

She pulled her cloak a little tighter and looked down both sides of the lane again. "Just don't leave me alone out here."

"I'll reach out my hand when you should follow."

"And it goes all the way through?"

"You're not going to get stuck inside the rock, if that's what you're thinking."

"All right."

"No more talking until I tell you to, got it?" She nodded. "And keep close while we're going through. It might be heavy."

He put away his paints and shouldered his pack. Kallara inhaled sharply when he drew his knife in his right hand. "Just in case," he whispered, but her lips still quavered. He wasn't feeling confident either. *Gods, let Elysia be safe.*

Focusing that concern, he knelt down, dug his hands into the handle he'd painted, and pulled it up. Kallara's little gasp chimed in time with his own sense of wonder. With every time becoming easier, would this ever seem commonplace, painting reality to suit his needs?

The tunnel yawned before him, barely wider than his shoulders, and only a few feet deep. He smiled reassuringly at Kallara, whose wide eyes shone with the reflected light from the coin. He ducked inside, supporting the hatch with his shoulders and back while nudging the glowing coin forward with his hand. He wriggled forward into the small space until the door sat heavy on his rump, with his sandals still out in the cool of the street.

Just before he opened the inner door, he covered the coin with his chest in case darkness was his friend. He strained to pull the hatch up until it was flush with the ceiling and peeked into the room beyond. The room was stuffy, but with a mix of welcome scents: pungent spices, ripe fruit, and fresh greens. After the brightness of the coin, his eyes couldn't make out any shapes in the darkness, but it seemed quiet enough.

He reached back and waved for Kallara to follow, and she responded with a light tap on his ankle. Her breaths were rapid and shallow, hot on the backs of his legs, as they wormed forward together. It was only then that modesty encroached on his mind. She'd have a clear view of the back of his loincloth. He palmed the coin to make sure it was fully covered, keeping the darkness total.

A more insistent tap on his ankle got him moving again.

When he was halfway through the second hatch, he rotated onto his back and she smacked into his knee. She stifled a giggle. He propped open the hatch and guided her through.

This time his eyes were more adjusted to the darkness, but he could only make out the faintest outline of large shapes—shelves and boxes? Not wanting to risk stumbling over random objects in the dark, he cracked his fingers apart, bathing the room in the coin's glow.

He'd been lucky enough to come out between two sets of shelves, both full of pots, jars and small boxes. They blocked his view of the rest of the room, so he stood and helped Kallara up.

A woman screamed.

$$\text{Ꮿ}\text{Ꮛ}\text{Ꮿ}\text{Ꮛ}\text{Ꮿ}\text{Ꮛ}\text{Ꮿ}$$

Elysia heard a sound, away in the distance. But she ignored it, so engrossed in clearing away handfuls of the green stone, getting closer and closer to the treasure hidden inside.

The sound was louder now, finally breaking her concentration. Knocking at the door. "What is it?" she asked, not even trying to hide the irritation in her voice.

"Can I enter?" A man's voice, and one she'd heard recently, but she couldn't place it. Not the one who showed her the room.

"I'm busy."

"You're in danger."

How long have I been here? Has Glebric's battle begun? Memories of Alexander and the guards lying dead in the bakery flashed through her mind, and her throat constricted.

"Is the house under attack?"

"Not yet, but soon."

She brushed marble dust from her hands and walked to the door. It was locked. Panic set in and she banged on it. "Is there a lock on your side?"

"I don't have a key." She heard jingling, rattling and clicking. "It may take a few minutes. Are you ready to leave?"

She turned back to the marble with a frown, not wanting to back away from the challenge. The creature inside sneered, like she was conceding defeat. Or… like it knew she would come back. She felt her skin crawl, and replaced the shroud to get it out of sight.

The door opened behind her just as she finished packing away her tools. It was the Pazian man who had been with Remeth. Her heart leaped. *Why wouldn't Remeth come himself?* She struggled to think of how to ask without giving anything away.

"Who are you? Why are you helping me?"

"I've been sent by a friend." He looked out in the corridor. "But it's not safe to speak of such things here. That one who locked you in is still about."

"Glebric?" She couldn't believe he'd hold her against her will. Or was he trying to shield her from danger?

He shook his head. "Ventus. But that's not who sent me.

"The streets will be perilous tonight, but the garrison caught word of the attack and we're no longer safe. Are you ready? We have no time to lose." He stood straight and confident, but the muscles in his neck were taut like rope. She nodded, and pulled her cloak back over her head.

"It would be best if you didn't speak until we're outside," he said. "Follow my lead." He put on a wide-brimmed Izari hat that left his face in shadow.

"Where—"

He put his finger to his lips as they rounded the corner to the front room. With only half a dozen guards and no trace of the newly freed slaves, it seemed sparse, almost empty. One of the guards nodded to her companion as they approached the front doors. "Aren't you cutting it a bit close? You're the last one out, Aktar."

Was there a slight flinch? Aktar. Unusual name, but not one she recognized.

"Special mission for the master," Aktar said with the same confidence. The guard raised an eyebrow, but when Aktar smiled, the man returned it. Aktar leaned in close to the man and spoke softly, but Elysia could still hear him. "Don't speak of it to anyone." The guard tapped his lips in response, and they clasped arms in farewell. The guard opened the door and they darted out.

The night air cut through her cloak. Or was it the memory of the last time she walked out through these doors, leaving Xelos for the last time? And it was on a night like this when her father fell on these very steps. She slowed for a moment, lost in thought, but Aktar grabbed her hand and pulled her forward.

ᏂᎬᏈᏂᎬᏈᏂᎬᏈ

Captivated by the lead actor's stirring speech to the people of ancient Attarsus, Remeth almost missed a flash of gold, off to the left in the crowd. Some sort of sign? He rued again Aktar's failure to present himself. *I don't even know what the signal for the attack will be!*

But with his attention focused, the shifting, tensing movements of his fellow conspirators stuck out in the crowd. His heart sank a little, knowing this wondrous interlude was about to come to an end. He savored the last few moments of the performance as best he could while keeping an eye on Glebric and the others.

The golden flash appeared again, from one of Glebric's men raising a polished cup. In front of him, an incensed middle-aged Izari in a fine tunic stood up and shouted, shaking an angry fist at Glebric. Two guards stood up beside the Izari. A murmur rippled through the crowd, and a few hecklers called for them to stop disrupting the show. The actors tried to ignore the distraction and carry on, but Remeth could see it was affecting their performance.

Glebric stood up and responded.

Remeth gulped. *Two squads, less Aktar, plus Glebric and his six?* He'd counted at least twice that many guards just among the wealthier theatergoers. *And how many of ours have only cursory training like me?* He chided himself for even thinking of Glebric's army as his own, but the speech had been compelling, and the personal recognition quite flattering. Not the joy of adulation he received on the stage, but a far cry from Yalath's tough love.

Half the crowd was watching Glebric's argument now, and catcalls rained out. Remeth felt sorry for the players and this capricious turn of fate that stole their audience from them.

The Izari man staggered back, clutching his throat, and tripped onto the stage, drawing a collective gasp. Remeth felt a clenching in his gut, like a hand squeezing his entrails.

Women screamed. The lead actor stared, slack-jawed, while others started rushing about.

Glebric stepped over the body and mounted the stage, nodding first to the shocked actors, then turning back to face the crowd. With the strange sensation gone, Remeth had to admit respect for Glebric's poise on such a large stage for what had to be the first time. Though he savored the thrill of so many eyes on him, Remeth still felt a fluttering lightness every time he took the stage.

Nerves. Did Glebric feel them now? Or did his dark power shield him from such emotions?

Glebric raised his hands against the cacophony of hundreds of voices wondering why he was interrupting the show, railing against his temerity, or curious about the fate of the fallen official.

"I apologize," he said in a voice pitched to carry to the back of the theater, "for interrupting your show." He turned to the actors and put his hand over his heart with an apologetic expression. The din died down, with most people straining to hear what he would say next.

Remeth gripped the club under his cloak. The mood in the place was bordering on ugly, and there were enough strong men in the crowd aside from the guards of the nobles to tip the scales. *Can you convince the slaves to join us against their masters?*

"But tonight is the beginning of a new era here in Attarsus. A time of freedom and equality for all."

"Says the young knave who stole an old man's fortune!" came a shout from the front, off to the side. A few other shouts agreed with the accusation. Glebric's face twitched toward a scowl, but he composed himself as he noted that particular face.

Undaunted, he raised his hand for silence again. "Attarsus has long been a bastion of equality and democratic participation, respected throughout the Near Sea. Until the council was cowed by Pazian might and forced to give up our traditions."

His words unsettled the crowd, evidenced by the equal mix of worried, angry, and supportive expressions. The family next to Remeth seemed concerned, while two young men on the other side echoed Glebric's defiance. And the slave of the family in front of him sat up straighter, raptly listening for more.

"Treason!" a richly attired Pazian in a toga shouted back as he stood up. "Call the watch to have this man arrested as a traitor to the Republic!"

Glebric pointed to the Pazian man, who appeared to be some sort of official. "This is the sort who lords over us, considering themselves above us. *Suprati?* Superior? *Digniti?* Dignified? As if the rest of us are lower and base?" The line earned him more supportive shouts.

"So you and a few men are going to lead a revolt?" the official asked, jeering. Two large Gathaki guards stood up to flank him.

"It is not my revolt. It is the will of the people. All the people."

Glebric pointed to a slave next to the Pazian man, holding a cup of wine. "You there. Are you a man, or a beast?"

The official's stern look cowed the slave to sullen silence.

Glebric shook his head sadly. "He treats a man like a beaten dog. Like *property*. The Senate treats our islands as their property as well, for them to use and abuse as they see fit. But no longer." He looked around, meeting the eyes of not just his men, but every slave or young man who reflected his anger. The cup-bearer looked up in response, earning him a slap from his master. Angry shouts broke out, with more slaves standing up. The naked fear in their masters almost made Remeth laugh.

Glebric raised a fist. "Rise up! In our new Attarsus, every slave will be free. Every man will have a vote! Join me, brothers and sisters, and take back rule by our people! For freedom!"

Glebric's men, interspersed throughout the crowd, were the first to stand and echo his call for freedom, but were soon joined by more and more of the slaves, as well as the common folk in the seats at the back. Even the cup-bearer stood up, but with so many more rising in their seats, Remeth didn't see what came of him. The father and mother beside him remained sitting, huddling their sons against them. They were right to be afraid.

A cry from the direction of the Pazian official drew more shouts, and most strained to see what had happened. When the actors rushed off the stage for the exits, the floodgates opened and suddenly everyone was scrambling for the stairways. Remeth, trapped in the center of the chaos, stood watching the scene unfold, paralyzed by indecision. And fear.

ᏮᏋᏮᏋᏮᏋᏮ

The woman cowered behind a thin sheet, sitting on a makeshift pallet. All Simon could see was the shock of black hair and terrified eyes flitting from knife to glowing coin and back again.

"What is wrong with you?" said another voice. A matronly woman peered around the shelf, rubbing sleep from her eyes until she started at the sight of him and Kallara. "How did you?" She backed off with arms held up to ward them away. "Guards! Guards! Thieves in the house!" The screams of two more women disappeared out the door.

So much for entering unnoticed.

"We mean you no harm!" Kallara said to the woman in the sheet as she scuttled away from them, but the screams drowned out any chance at communication.

Simon stood frozen with the coin in his hand.

Kallara tugged at his arm. "Put that away. I don't want to get caught here."

Elysia! His legs surged to life.

The matron and the screaming woman bolted out the door when Simon came out from behind the shelves, and by the time he reached the door they were disappearing down the hall toward the front entrance. "This way," he said to Kallara, and made for the atrium. He concealed the coin in one hand, and the knife in the sleeve of his cloak.

He swore under his breath. The atrium garden was another makeshift campground, with all the campers roused from their sleep. *But maybe with the added newcomers we won't be recognized—*

"What is it?" a worried old man asked them. "Has there been an attack on the house?"

Please let me channel a little Remeth. "Yes," Simon said, "and they're coming this way!"

Shouts rang out in at least five different languages as panic spread through the group. A baby wailed, while the women, children and elders scrambled to grab their belongings. They surged in a wave toward the double doors to the right and the perceived safety of the guards. Simon pulled Kallara by the hand across the atrium toward the doorway to the east wing.

"Can you help me?" asked an old woman, tugging at Kallara's arm. "My husband is ill, sleeping in one of those rooms."

Kallara nodded. "You go to the front, I'll make sure he gets out."

"Oh, thank you child!" The woman grabbed Kallara's hands and only let go when Simon wrenched them free.

"What do you think you're doing?"

Kallara shot him an angry glance. "We need an excuse to check the rooms."

Or not. All the doors in the east wing were open, and confused women and children were rushing to and fro, chattering excitedly.

Simon stood tall. "Get to the front doors! There are thieves in the house!" One woman fainted, and two others had to drag her away.

No sign of Elysia, in the hall or any of the rooms. Dread weighed heavy on him. *Upstairs?* Kallara grabbed his arm as he made to turn the corner.

"Where are you going?" She looked as distraught as the other residents.

"What if they have her up there?"

"But that's where Glebric stays, and that horrible Ventus. And his best warriors."

"Who are all likely out, terrorizing the city. Come on."

Kallara took a deep breath. "But what if they can see through our disguise? I... I'm scared Simon. You didn't see the way they looked at me."

"No, but I've looked into the eyes of a similar warlock, and defeated him." *With the help of another trained soldier, not a scared girl.*

Her pleading eyes attempted to dissuade him, but he walked up the stairs. When she didn't follow, he didn't blame her. She should prefer the safety of the group, and he had enough to worry about.

He gripped his knife tighter.

ᘯᘰᘯᘰᘯᘰᘯ

Elysia's heart pounded in her chest after the deception at the front doors. "Where do we go now?"

Aktar shushed her, and took them further into the neighborhood, away from the agora. She walked in silence for a few minutes, until they rounded a corner on a street that led back down into the lower part of the city.

"Now can you tell me?" she asked.

"I have a friend, with a house down by the harbor. But we must hurry. The streets will be full of blood before the night is through. Unless you want to add yours to the flood?"

"No, I... but won't they try to seize the harbor as well? I could seek refuge in a temple."

"Absolutely not. The acropolis is another target, and there will be nowhere to hide."

She frowned. For all Glebric's passion about freeing the slaves, his revolution would devastate the city. She had to warn her friends. "Then I would prefer to go my own way."

A brief flash of irritation was coated quickly with concern. "That's not wise." He pointed to a pair of ruffians eying them from

337

a dark corner. "It won't just be Glebric's men. Once things turn, all the scum of the city will run rampant. I couldn't in good conscience leave you alone on a night like tonight. I insist you come with me to my friend's house—"

"But I don't even know you. Who is this friend who sent you?"

"I'd rather show you." He took out a small stone disk, carved with the symbol of Xelos. The sight of it brought her comfort.

"You knew him? The late master…"

"Only in passing. But he had many friends, and wanted to keep an eye out for you. When I saw you in the house, I asked what I should do, and only just received word to break you out. I only worked with Glebric to serve their aims."

She closed her hand on the token, straining to feel a connection with the man who it represented. *Thank you for watching over me, even in death.* "Which way?"

XXXVI

ᏩᎬᏯᎬᏯᎬᎬ

Ventus

Light footsteps pattered up the stairs to join Simon, punctuated
with a sigh.

"Have you ever been up here?" Kallara asked.

Master Xelos gave them free run of the lower level, but only he
and a few of his servants ever spent time upstairs. And Simon had
no reason to challenge the unwritten rule. If anything he tried to
sneak private moments with Elysia, out of Xelos' sight. He shook
his head.

"Then you could use another set of eyes."

The top of the stairs turned to the left and opened in a corridor.
But what looked at first glance to be a wall was actually a sliding
screen, and behind it a balcony overlooking the atrium. Simon had
never realized that they could be watched from above, and thought
of one time he'd tried to kiss Elysia when they were alone by the
pool. With the angle of the wall it would be hard to see the opening
from below, but from above it gave a useful vantage point.

A door at each end of the corridor-balcony gave them their
options.

"Which way?" Kallara asked in a whisper.

The clamor from the atrium drowned out any sound that might
give a clue to Elysia's location. *If she's even here.* Simon looked at the
right side door, but Kallara yanked him to face the other way.

"Who are you?" asked a middle-aged Pazian man in a sleeping
tunic as he peered out the other door. He stared intently at first
Simon, then Kallara. With a flash of something that looked like
recognition, he straightened and darted back into the room behind
him, slamming the door.

Kallara's hands shook, and her voice wavered. "Ventus. And he
knew me."

339

"But if he knew you, there must be some dark power at play."

"Let's get out of here."

"He might have Elysia."

The other door was locked, but Simon wasn't about to let that stop him. "Hold this." He gave her the knife. He took out his paints and repeated the sequence he'd used to rust away the lock in the Aktiri prison, only faster this time. It dropped off in his hand, and he placed it quietly on the floor. The demonstration settled Kallara, at least slightly. He took back the knife, palmed the glowing coin in his off hand and pushed open the door.

It was dark. Deciding to push their edge of surprise, Simon opened his hand to shine the coin-light around the room, squinting to cope with the sudden brightness.

No signs of movement, or life. A huge bed dominated the room, surrounded by chests and a large desk. Simon looked for closets or other exits, finding none. "This must be Glebric's room, and I guess he's out?"

"What about Ventus?"

"He might be holding her. We have to check."

"Please S—"

"What, *Ambrosia?*"

"I... I just think we should leave."

"Your young friend is wiser than you," Ventus said from their doorway. "If less Talented."

ରେ୧ରେ୧ରେ

Remeth still hadn't drawn his club.

One richly dressed man and his three guards rushed onstage, but before they reached Glebric they were battered from behind by men with clubs. Glebric ran to them, and when he laid his hands on the fallen their bodies would quiver before falling limp.

Another wave of nausea hit Remeth, and he knew for certain it was Glebric using his dark power. It was an abomination—an affront to everything good in the world. It offended every fiber of Remeth's being.

The wife of the man next to him was sobbing. "You are not slaves or nobles," Remeth said to the husband. "You should be safe if you move to the back of the theater."

"But how will we get out?"

"Wait until everything settles." With his Talent backing his words, his smile must have been reassuring, even if inside he was screaming at himself to flee.

The man nodded. Remeth urged others around him to follow the family, both to remove them from danger and open up a gap leading downward. He made slow progress, row by row.

With a better view he identified several fronts in the battle, with groups of Glebric's men or slaves trying to overcome the wealthier Pazians or Izari and their guards.

Half-way down, Remeth was bumped off-balance by a large man and he fell to his knees. His club skittered away between the feet of two fleeing women. One yelped and pushed away from him into the crowd. Cursing, he scrambled to retrieve it and immediately saw the fear in the faces around him.

"No! I'm here to help!" Remeth shouted, but to no avail. These people could not hear him, nor would the words soothe them if they could. They were the terrified mob fleeing from the aggressors, and he was one of the armed. To Remeth, the performer, it was worse than scorn.

A rough hand grabbed his shoulder and pulled him around. His hand clenched the club, ready to swing, but the eyes were familiar—the burly Kawanian that had been sparring in the courtyard at Glebric's.

"Come," he said.

His club was slick with blood and Remeth's stomach roiled, but more desperate for a connection, he still followed him. The Kawanian shoved a path through the crowd, not caring if he knocked over women or children. They came out behind two guards facing off against more of Glebric's men. One mighty swing from the club and a guard was down, and Glebric's men bludgeoned the other into submission.

"There," said one of the men, pointing to another skirmish at the edge of the stage. The crowd was thinning out, with most of the non-combatants having either left or retreated to the highest ground. Bodies littered the ground, many injured and moaning, and not just men but women and children too. Remeth wanted to reach down and help them, but feared the more capable killers turning on him.

But he did pause to locate Glebric again, and his muscles froze. Glebric knelt over a dying man, his mouth drinking in the life force like glowing blood. Sacrificing another man for his power. Remeth couldn't just stand idle in the face of such depravity, and though his legs were jelly, he forced his first steps toward the stage.

"Where are you going?" the other man asked.

"Glebric," Remeth said.

"He's fine, help us with the others."

"I have to go to Glebric."

The man scowled, but didn't stop him.

Remeth reached Glebric just as he was standing up, unsteady on his feet, like he was drunk after his... feeding. His other men dragged bodies over to him, bringing more for the sacrifice. *Subdued, but still alive!*

Glebric straightened and when his eyes focused, they were on Remeth, who he waved to approach. "Killeth, was it? The theater—what a brilliant idea! More slaves came over than I would have dreamed! We have cut deep into the entrenched power of this city, and are taking what is theirs, to add to our might. We took down the governor, and the head of the assembly! On this night, the city will be ours. Your part will be remembered. Shame we had to miss the show."

The weight of responsibility crushed the fight from Remeth. He looked around at the withered husks lying before him; the fresh, plump bodies being brought to Glebric for him to feast; and the remains of the terrified masses scrambling over each other to scale the back wall to safety. There would have been death this night, but Remeth was the one who directed it here. His selfish desire to see the show had brought destruction on them all, and he would have to carry that burden on his heart.

Glebric must have seen something of the emotion in his face. "I don't revel in death. But to start a revolution, those who stand in our way will have to fall."

His men brought another two bodies, and now outnumbered, Remeth mourned the lost chance to stop the madness.

"I'm almost done here. Killeth, round up the rest of the men and tell them we're going to join the others at the harbor."

Remeth followed the order, praying for another chance to make things right. Or at least to stop further wrong.

Simon held out his knife, and Kallara slipped behind him.

"See?" Ventus said. "She is wise to fear me." He stepped into the room, brandishing a sword in his right hand. He looked pointedly at Simon's knife. "How about you put that down? And stay here as my guests." He tossed the rusted lock onto the floor between them and looked at the coin with a smirk. "And don't go trying anything that might give me reason to just kill you."

Simon's eyes darted around, looking for any possible escape route. The windows? They were only on the second floor. The fall wouldn't kill them. But in the time it took him to open the latch...

"You're not getting away," Ventus said. "I've already called for the guards, and some will be waiting in the alley."

He tapped Kallara's arm. "Sing?" he whispered.

She shook her head.

"Use your fear."

Ventus frowned. "I would prefer if you included me in your conversation. Maybe the young lady will entertain us while we are at this impasse? How about a song?"

"Simon?" she asked, uncertain.

Ventus smiled, but it was an awful, evil smile. "Simon! Of course! Come to save your dear Elysia! I'm afraid you're too late." He tapped his hand absently on the blade of the sword, looking wistful. "Such Talent. And a striking, unusual beauty. Glebric was quite happy to welcome her back into his life. And that bed."

"She would never—"

"Perhaps she prefers wealth and power over your sort of dabbling. Glebric has made himself into quite the impressive figure. And he was always quite fond of her. She's not the first to think the same of him. Is he... Kallara?"

She gasped, and those eyes froze Simon's heart. There was an ancient depth and menace, so very like the sea in a storm.

"Your friend, Orna was it? She wanted him so badly that it... consumed her."

Kallara stepped out from behind him, shaking, and opened her mouth. The song escaped first as a delicate thread, a thin and tremulous sound. Her fear joined with Simon's for a moment, locking every muscle in place, and he felt trapped. But she found her voice, and the vibrations entwined into thicker strands of power and emotion, giving him strength and inspiration. He could face this foe. And was he seeing things? Glowing strands, row thick as ropes, stretched out toward Ventus, reaching forward to entangle him in a musical prison. If Simon stood still now, it was only because of awe at this completely different display of power.

Ventus lifted his sword in mild surprise, watching as the golden ropes entwined his arm. "Impressive! Such confidence and control." He turned to her. "Who is your teacher? This one?" The ropes tugged at his arm, but couldn't move it. Kallara's voice faltered for a moment, and Ventus slashed the golden energy into oblivion. The rest of the ropes disappeared with Kallara's gasp, and Simon felt his grip waver on his knife.

Ventus cocked his head to the side. "Surely you didn't think you could defeat me with something so simple?"

"I brought down Shadush, the Scentari warlock, with a simple blade," Simon said.

"Pah. A mere slave. Now you face the master."

"What are you?" Kallara asked.

Ventus pointed the sword at her while nodding his head. "Again, this one has a good head on her shoulders. For now." Those ancient eyes in the middle-aged face looked into Simon's. "You know, don't you."

"I won't say your name, but I know who you are. But aren't you supposed to be a woman?"

Ventus' hearty laugh only inflamed Simon's defiance further. "I wish I were. Maybe we can make a deal? Offer me the girl, and I'll let you go." The eyes flicked up and down. "She's a more suitable host. Yes, I'd prefer that."

"What does he mean, Simon?" Kallara asked, with even more terror in her voice.

"That evil being I told you about. It's inside this man somehow. Living in there. If living is the right word."

Ventus nodded. "Better than being trapped in that dank prison, to be sure. But while your music might be able to control the mind of this body without my intervention, I won't let you do that. I can shield his mind. And this particular host has proved useful. Along with my servant, Glebric."

"But you serve Glebric," Kallara said.

"Only in his mind, child. In reality, all his power comes from me. I choose to grant it to him, because it serves my purpose."

"Why do you want to free the slaves?" Simon asked.

"I care not who serves me. Just that I have a nation of

worshipers. But I will take particular pleasure when these particular islands bow down to me. And I do so love to be by the sea."

Simon tried to process his words while figuring out how to escape. *Can this host be harmed?* "So this isn't about revenge? For the Izari people who locked you away?"

That laugh again. "Revenge? You sound like my sister. She always used to burn with that human idea. Or maybe she inspired it in the humans in the first place. No, all I want is dominion over the lands that are mine by rights."

"What lands?"

"Those that border every sea, river or lake. Anything that feeds on my life-giving waters is mine. But these few rocks will do, as a start."

"What happened to Elysia?"

"You care more for her than you do about this Republic you serve. How noble. More of my sister's kind of passion. Offer me the girl, and I'll tell you."

Kallara retreated a step, pulling even with Simon. She searched his eyes for any sign of betrayal, any hint that he would do what Ventus asked. He shook his head. But a part of him questioned that. He had only just met this girl, while Elysia was everything to him. His mind filled with anger, futility, and shame at failing Elysia again, driving out any of the remaining fear. He turned back to Ventus, pointing the knife at his enemy's chest.

"This body you inhabit. He looks to be a merchant, while I am a soldier of Fazh." He adopted a fighting stance. "The body will still bleed."

For the briefest instant, the fear of a middle-aged man flashed through those eyes, before the ancient depth returned, reasserting control over the flesh. "That may be true. But I have lived many lifetimes and have skill beyond your wildest imaginings. Do you dare to test that?" Ventus held the sword in two hands, setting his jaw in challenge. "And how do you know this Ventus didn't serve in the legions as a youth?"

Kallara's hand found his shoulder. "Simon, don't risk it. If he defeats you, he will feed on both of us."

"Wise words Simon. You should heed them. Though the question is not if, but when I will taste your Talents. Unless you accept my offer. Give her to me, and I will let you go free. Or I could grant you even greater power."

ᎶᏋᏨᏋᏨᏋᏨᏨ

Between Xelos' house and the harbor, the streets had been eerily quiet. Aktar led Elysia to a run-down neighborhood, and a similarly shabby apartment. Her misgivings grew at every turn.

"Your friend certainly doesn't live in a very nice area."

"We all must make do with what we have. We're not as lucky as Glebric." She bristled at the intimation that it was below her, and followed him in.

The dark stairwell felt like it was closing in, and a squeal from the corner made her miss a step and bang her knee.

"Careful, milady," Aktar said, giving her a hand.

On the second floor, he led her to the third door on the right, and produced a key.

"Your friend must trust you," she said.

He looked at her strangely for a moment before responding. "Yes, in case I need to come by while he's away." He opened the door, and the stale stench of sweat and spilled wine assaulted her from the gap.

She gagged. "He'd better be away." *How can someone stand this?* Alexander may have been messy, but even he couldn't live in filth. Xelos and Yalath kept their houses spotless.

Aktar lit a lamp. The room looked almost as bad as it smelled. Half-eaten food and overturned cups littered the table on one side, along with a jug of what she assumed must be wine. Clothes on the floor were covered with a layer of dust, and the sheets on the bed in the corner lay crumpled in a pile.

"Come in, you'll be safe here," Aktar said.

From outsiders, but how about the rats?

"Can I help you with your bag?"

Not wanting to appear ungrateful, she allowed him to put the heavy pack on the bed. He offered her a chair, and she took a seat. *How long must I stay here?*

"It's not much, but it will do for the night. Make yourself comfortable. I'll get us some food from around the corner, so we won't have to go out until morning."

She heard the click in the lock as he left, and wondered if she'd traded a nicer prison for a shabby one. *Simon, I hope you're safely inside tonight.*

XXXVII

⟨e⟨e⟨e⟨e

Duet

Simon stared at Ventus, trying to make sense of his words. *Why is he bargaining?*

"You control the mind of this host, but that's it," he said. "You don't have any power." He spoke more confidently as the ideas fit together, even if they were still no more than guesses. "You need the host just to move around. And you need the servant, someone who has given themselves over to you... you need them to be a vessel for your power. You can't do it alone. You need Glebric."

Ventus' smile had disappeared, replaced with a tight line.

"You can't feast on our Talent without someone to sacrifice us in your name."

I hope I'm right.

"So what happens if we kill this vessel?" Simon asked, taunting now. He took a step forward. "What happens to you? And Glebric's power?"

"Your power is nothing compared to what he wields," Ventus hissed. "But imagine, Simon, what you could do if you marry your power to his? I can give, but I can also take away. Offer me the girl, and you will see."

The idea was tempting. Not for power's sake—at least Simon wanted to believe that was the case. But if he could take away Glebric's power, then he would save the others. Or would this Ventus, this Kashaka, give them both the power and let them destroy each other? The Damoz could not be trusted with anything but their own aims.

"My answer is still no," Simon said, keeping his voice and the knife level.

Ventus sneered. "So we're back to you trying to overpower me with a knife."

"And you with just a sword. And I'm not alone," Simon said, almost absent-mindedly. "I'm not alone," he said again, this time for Kallara. He offered her the glowing coin. Though puzzled, she held it out just as Simon had. With his now empty hand, he reached into his satchel to feel for his brush and paints.

Ventus jabbed the sword in his direction. "What are you doing? Keep your hand where I can see it."

"You asked Kallara for a demonstration. So, I thought I'd join her." He nodded in response to Kallara's questioning look. She wet her lips and sang once more. Ventus shifted uncomfortably as her song started low and somber, like she was mourning the friend who had been sacrificed to this dark power.

Simon managed to work off the stopper of one of his jars of paint—he couldn't be sure which one—and tried his best to keep it upright to prevent a spill.

"Stop!" Ventus shouted, but creases on his forehead belied at least a crack in his resolve.

Or his body's.

Kallara's song lilted up from the ashes of despair, raising Simon's spirit and steadying his hand as he dipped his brush into the paint, swirling it around to get enough for his desperate attempt. Her voice rose higher and higher, and the air around them buzzed with life, with power, and she stood steady and confident, still pointing the coin at Ventus, who now looked frail by comparison. The energy crackling around her coalesced into physical form, more powerful than before—thick golden vines. Ventus slashed wildly at the approaching tentacles, and each one he touched disappeared with a sizzling hiss. Unbowed, Kallara's song reached a triumphant crescendo, sending more of the glowing tendrils to assail the Damoz. But with each defensive slash Ventus grew in confidence and composure, as if his muscles remembered old training. He was fighting Kallara's magical attack to a standstill.

In one motion, Simon switched hands for his knife and brush, now dripping with black paint. He sprinted toward Ventus, channeling all his anger and fear, and closed the gap with dagger ready to parry, and brush raised to attack.

A magical vine pinned Ventus' arm, forcing him to chop it off with a powerful stroke. He was sweaty and panting, but in fine form. His next slash went for Simon, who deflected it with his waiting knife, but had to abandon his intended counter-thrust with the brush. Without blinking, Ventus warded off two more vines, his stance now light on his feet, like a seasoned warrior.

Simon's shoulders sagged momentarily, before a heroic strain of Kallara's song lifted him on a golden wave of confidence. He felt the rhythm, how the vines would attack on certain notes, and he used his knife to beat out a counterpoint, following her thrusts. Ventus deflected her first strike, and Simon's knife blow, but Kallara's next beat struck him on the side, sending him back a few steps before he could turn it away. Simon was on him with another thrust, then Kallara again, one-two-one-two until they backed Ventus against the wall.

Simon seized his chance, following his knife thrust with a head-level stroke of his brush from right to left. It connected, smearing paint across Ventus' eyes with a surge of Talent. Ventus shrieked, stabbing blindly at the air in front of him, but Simon dodged easily. Kallara's golden tentacles avoided his wild blows, wrapping up first his legs, then his off-arm. Simon painted over Ventus' mouth and ears, covering his entire head in the sticky blackness he'd envisioned, brought to life by his Talent. Ventus abandoned the panicked slashes and tried instead to shave the black goo from his face, but it coated the blade and held it fast. Two more tendrils pinned his arms to his body, but Simon wasn't finished. Dipping his brush back in the spill inside his pack, Simon painted the wrists and ankles together to bind Ventus, who toppled over with a squelching splat, face down on the floor.

ᎶᏋᏳᏋᏳᏋᏳᎶ

Glebric swelled with pride, and more... with untapped power, as his band closed the short distance to the harbor. Shouts, screams, and other signs of battle came loudest from the direction of the water. His plan was working. Attarsus would be theirs, as long as they sealed control of the docks as the gateway to city's riches.

"Ready for a real battle?" he said to Killeth. He liked the Maruthan, even if he'd just met him. There was something about his manner, and his idea about the theater was a master-stroke. While his golden arms were well-muscled and the club like a deadly weapon just waiting to be unleashed, the man didn't seem too enthusiastic about joining the fray. He'd been tentative at the theater as well.

"I'm... I'm not used to this sort of thing." Killeth said.

Glebric put a reassuring hand on his shoulder. "None of us are. But we fight for freedom. For people like you and me, and for the generations to come. No more slaves will be born on these islands. And when I unleash my power and crush the Pazian fleets, we will take our cause across the Near Sea." Waves of that power rippled through him, the longing to use it so intense he almost swooned. Killeth reached out to steady him, concern in his eyes. Glebric nodded his thanks. "I'm not used to the exertion either."

Chaos reigned in the open space of the harbor. One ship was burning, with the fiery blaze illuminating the rest of the scene and a number of small battles. Glebric's men faced off against groups of city watch on the shore, and skirmished with crews on the docks and aboard a few ships.

A whirling streak of black charged down the pier toward one of the larger galleys. *Azzam*. He and his men were meeting with fierce resistance from the crew.

Glebric knew that ship—a large Pazian slaver. Was it the one that brought Azzam to captivity? Even from across the harbor, Azzam's lust for vengeance was contagious. "To Azzam!" He drew his sword and charged across the open space.

Azzam single-handedly drove back the slavers, but before he could board, the oars were in the water and the ship pushed away from the dock. The affront sent Glebric into a rage—*how dare they run from him!* Whether it was all the power churning inside him, or the proximity to so much water, he felt empowered to act. To unleash his fury and stop them from escaping.

He jutted both hands out and down toward the dark water on either side. Though his hands swirled through the night air, he felt the wetness of the inky depths below him, as he churned the water around and around into whirlpools. Bringing his hands together, he merged the two smaller eddies into a raging vortex that grew in size as it engulfed more water. No longer aware of the people around him, Glebric felt one with the sea.

The swaying of the dock barely registered on Glebric as his creation reached the hull of the slave ship. The galley rocked and heaved, the near side's oars first rising useless into the air like the legs of an overturned centipede, then shattering on impact with the waves on the way back down.

Other ships slammed together and against the docks with great groaning and crashing, and the screams of sailors and Glebric's men alike cut through the night.

But Glebric wasn't finished. The slave galley sat directly on top of the watery vortex. With a flick of his hand, Glebric battered the hull with wave after wave, and the most vicious washed across the deck to sweep away the crew. The ship spun faster, its oars wrecked and useless, looking like a child's toy in a tub.

"Enough!" came a shout from beside him, just insistent enough to grab his focus. He turned his anger on the source, Killeth. "You've stopped that one from escaping, but look." The golden hand pointed to the other ships. "You're damaging the rest of the fleet. Our fleet. Look at the flags!"

Where Pazian standards had flown atop the masts, now the crews were pulling them down, in surrender, or pledging their allegiance. To him. Glebric felt the pull of the words, the sense in them, and swelling pride...

But he shook it off. He would make one final offering to the sea that was his greatest ally. The ship rose on a swirling pillar of water, up, up, up...

ᎶᏋᏮᏋᏮᏋᏮᏮ

Kallara's song leaped with joy and ended. The air around Simon became still once more, the tendrils winking out of existence. Ventus writhed against his gooey bonds, but they adhered even to the floor.

"You were amazing!" Simon said.

She beamed back at him, her face glowing from the exertion. "So were you! How did you do that?"

"It just came to me. The body is still human. Still afraid. So even with his strong mind, he had to focus to fight off your Talent. I figured if I could break that focus, and stop the body from being able to see its environment—"

"So what do we do with him now?"

"Drive the Damoz out of him."

She recoiled, horrified. "Kill him? But he's defenseless."

"That might work... but I'd rather not be a murderer." He shivered at the thought. "No, I was thinking we could work our Talents together to force the spirit out of the body. To set him free. If the ancient Talented people were able to imprison this...

this thing, then why not us?"

"Because we have no idea what we're doing? How many of them were there? Did they have instructions? I just started using my power yesterday. Simon, I think we should just leave. He said he called the guards to surround us!"

"He was bluffing." Simon hoped he sounded confident in his guess. "They would have been up here by now. But Glebric is out there somewhere, attacking the city. If we can push out the source of his power, then the city could be saved."

Where Simon expected to see disagreement in Kallara's eyes, there was only pain and bitterness. "Saved from what? Glebric only wants to free the slaves. He was better to me than any master has ever been. This is not our fight. But if it were, I think Glebric is the one we should support."

"But what happens if he comes back here and frees this one? He's seen us. Knows about our power. And will come after us. We're too significant a threat."

Worry replaced her certainty, and Simon pressed on. "We know about them, and will try to stop them again. We're also a source of fuel for this dark power. Do you really think they'll let us live?"

"Are you sure you're not just seeking revenge for what he might have done to Elysia?"

Simon clenched his fists. *Why does she keep challenging me? Or is she right?* "We still don't know what happened to her. And no. I'm just thinking about the greater good."

"Of Pazh?"

"No, of... of humanity. These Damoz threaten everyone, but those of us with Talent most of all. Remember your friend... Orna was it?"

She shot him an angry look, but then turned it on the black cocoon on the floor. "If we did try to push the Damoz out, how would we even start?"

"I think I might have the key." He reached into his pack, and swore when black paint coated his hand. He withdrew the jar of Kashaka's blood.

"What is it?"

"Her blood."

"So it's really a her, that... that thing inside him?"

"I guess so? At least that's what the ancient Maruthans believed."

"So what are you going to do with it?"

"I think—"

"You think? Simon, is this just a guess?"

He felt sheepish. "An educated one. Just hear me out. This contains some of her blood, and it tries to get back to her. It led us here. But I'm guessing that there's a lot more of this blood inside Ventus right now. If we can draw it out, then maybe we can contain it somehow?"

"Is that an ordinary clay jar?"

"Yes. Other than this bit of magic, so we could see inside. I could use any kind of water-tight container to hold it, once we get the blood out of him. That's where I think you can help."

"Me?" She backed off, waving her hands in front of her. "I'm not touching any blood."

"But what if you could sing to him—the real him, the flesh that is Ventus—and have him work with you to expel the blood. Then I can see how much is there, and paint something to contain it."

"Where do you think it was before it went into Ventus?"

"Probably some kind of prison that the ancient Talented ones built just for that purpose."

"What if we could send it back there?"

"But we don't even know where that is."

"No, but Ventus must. Maybe Glebric too."

Simon scowled. "I'm not working with Glebric."

"See, you do want revenge. Do you really think so little of Elysia?"

"She would never share his bed!"

"Then why are you so against him?"

"I'm only against him because he's given himself over to Kashaka. And you should be too." But Ventus' words were like a tiny splinter in his mind, distracting him from something important... something Kallara had said.

"Kallara, you're right. Ventus must know, and maybe he could lead us to where the blood was imprisoned. What if there's some power in the prison that could help us?"

"But what if the real Ventus won't co-operate? What if he wanted this to happen?"

"More likely Glebric wanted this to happen, so he could gain power. Wait... that's it! They must have both been there. Glebric to gain power, and Ventus to be offered up to Kashaka. I think I know how to find the place."

Simon looked around for something to paint on, spotting a scroll rolled up on a side desk. He unfurled it and brought it back to the floor near the coin.

"What are you going to do? And how long do you think your ooze can hold him?"

Simon frowned. He had no idea. "I might be able to show us the prison. But I need you to be quiet. And watch the door. Take this."

Simon sat on the floor with the scroll unfurled face down in front of him, using his paint jars to hold the corners open. He placed the clay vessel of blood at another corner and took one last look at Ventus' body, which had stopped writhing, but still appeared alive with the chest rising and falling regularly.

Closing his eyes, Simon forced several images into his mind. First, the face of Ventus, stern and composed. Next he imagined the silvery sheen of the blood of Kashaka, and finally Glebric. *Show me where this happened.* Tapping into his well of emotion, he dipped his brush into the paint and without opening his eyes, let his Talent loose on the page. The two figures appeared first, Ventus' head pushed down, and the silver blood flowing in through his nose and mouth. Exultation on Glebric's face fueled Simon's anger, and the rest of the scene appeared on the page; damp floor and walls encrusted with slimy vegetation that wept seawater, and an altar made of some kind of irregular stone that looked almost alive. But it wasn't just an altar. Ventus' head was drowning in a basin full of the blood. A receptacle. The home of the blood for a thousand years.

"Kallara, I have it. Come look."

She bit her lip. "I don't want to go there. And how would we even bring this…" Ventus was struggling against his bonds again.

"We might be able to do it from here." Her eyes lit up. "Remember how I saw Yalath? How my picture was a window?"

She looked in wonder from the picture to him and back again. "You think we can just push the body through there?"

"That might be even easier than what I was thinking."

"What was your idea?"

"That you use your music to coax out the blood, and we send it through the picture. But moving the body might be wiser." Curiosity burned bright for a moment, before doubt and trepidation pulled him down from the moment of inspiration.

"What if we can't move it? Or we get stuck?"

"Would you rather try singing it out?"

She took one more look at the body, wrinkled her nose, and nodded.

"Let me try something first," he said. "We don't understand how that altar-prison works." He painted away the figures of Glebric and Ventus, leaving the shrine empty, and added the window frame around the picture.

Holding his breath, he slowly pushed the jar of Kashaka's blood down to the picture, concentrating his hope into opening a physical window. He braced himself for disappointment, but the resistance didn't feel like paper against the hard ground; it was flexible, almost gelatinous. Pushing further, he felt a rupture around his hand, and a clammy dampness in the air as the connection opened to this other place.

Kallara clapped her hand over her mouth, and Simon could barely control the shaking of his hand. He could travel anywhere his art could take him. He had only intended to deposit the jar, but the attraction was too strong. He dipped his head and fought through what his eyes told him was impossible, while his hand felt a rippling sensation like pushing through the surface of a pool, except finding air on the other side. He stumbled and fell the rest of the way, disoriented by the sudden change of perspective from looking down to sideways. Kallara's scream cut short.

When he looked back all he could see was a shimmering square of light hanging in the air behind him. Panic rushed through his mind. *Can I get back? And where am I?*

The room was like a cave, with the central altar-prison lit from within by a faint and unearthly glow. But before trying to get back, he wanted to settle something else. He tipped the clay jar so that a single drop of Kashaka's blood would escape. It dropped to the floor and first rolled back toward the portal he'd just come through, but slowed down, struggling against some force pulling it in the opposite direction, until it came to a shuddering stop. It fought the losing battle for a few moments before lurching backward toward the altar, one inch at a time until it rolled impossibly up the side and disappeared into the basin. Simon looked inside, and saw no sign of it.

The old magic still works. We might have a chance.

"Kallara?" Simon called out. He didn't hear any response, but through the glowing portal he could see a rippling shadow that vaguely resembled her. *This had better work both ways.* Steeling himself against the unnatural sensation, Simon reached his hand into the amorphous glow, feeling again the difference in the air and sudden contact as a soft hand closed over his and started pulling. Simon bit his lip and dipped his head through. His stomach lurched as his senses struggled to reconcile two different versions of up. When his eyes could focus, Kallara held his hand in hers, her eyes wide with wonder.

⊙૨⊙૨⊙૨⊙

Elysia hadn't moved from her seat while Aktar was gone to get the food. She certainly wasn't neat, but her eyes picked out every stain and crumb leaving nowhere safe to take a step. Finally she'd closed her eyes and nodded off, only to wake to the sound of his key in the lock again.

Aktar looked at the messy table with pursed lips.

What, you expect me to clean for your friend? Because I'm a woman?

He quickly marshaled his expression and carried his bundle to the table. When he moved the old plates it gave rise to a new stink—of mold—and Elysia wondered if she would even have an appetite.

"What did you get?"

He smiled self-consciously as he wiped the table with a rag. "Some bread and fish. Olives." When he unwrapped the food, the smell of grilled fish cut through the stale air and her mouth watered. She even allowed herself a smile, which he matched. "Wine?" he asked, raising a jug. "Sorry, my friend seems to be out of water."

"Only a little then," she said, wanting to keep her wits about her. She very rarely drank wine.

The food was excellent, and he seemed to be as hungry as she was. And thirstier; he drank three cups to her half cup, and seemed more relaxed with each gulp.

"So what will you do?" she asked. "Since you deserted your post with Glebric?"

"Things will take a while to settle down. But I'll help you get out of the city if you want."

"But I…"

He leaned forward. "It's not safe. And I wouldn't be comfortable sending you alone on a ship back to my friend. Not by yourself. I will accompany you." His eyes flicked down to her cloak. He poured himself another cup of wine, and refilled hers, despite her waving him away.

"But where?" *Just play along.*

"The capital would be safest."

"But I don't know anyone in Pazh."

"And there wouldn't be anyone looking for you. My friends could keep you safe."

"These friends you keep mentioning. Who are they? Can you tell me now? Now that we're alone?" At the last word, his eyes hinted a different sort of smile.

She was alone with this strange man, and her friends didn't know where she was. Her gaze wandered the room, flicking away when she caught herself looking at the bed. But he'd intercepted the look, and his smile broadened.

"I'm the only friend you need, Elysia."

XXXVIII
𝒢𝑒𝒢𝑒𝒢𝑒𝒢
Emancipation

Kallara stared at Simon. "That was incredible. So you *can* go through!"

With only one arm and his head back in the room, Simon felt exposed and vulnerable, but he had to hurry. Ventus' legs had broken free and flailed wildly. "Kallara, you need to do your part now. If you can draw her blood out and push it through the portal, the altar will do the rest. The blood tried to fight it, but the old magic is more powerful. It must have taken some special force to get it out and into this man."

"Like a sacrifice."

Simon nodded, having come to the same conclusion. Sacrifice seemed to be central to the transfer not only of power from the Damoz to their servants, but also of the Damoz themselves to their hosts. *Would it work in reverse?*

"Are you ready to drive this darkness out with your song?"

She released his hand and closed her eyes, standing so still that Simon wondered if she was still breathing. Without the conversation to focus on, the wrenching feeling returned; of being in-between, half here and half there. *What if something goes wrong with the picture? What if I'm trapped here? What if it cuts me in half?* Sweat trickled down his neck, through the picture, and dripped down to the temple floor.

Kallara poured out a long, low note that set the whole room resonating with its power. It rolled up and down, the words of her mother tongue pulling at him as they flowed past, beckoning to him. He strained to meet the call, yearning to unite with the music. His mouth hung open, helpless. Would she steal something from him as well?

The air around Kallara thickened and coiled, swirling in a

golden vortex, pulling on the fallen man's energy, his life force. The black ooze on Ventus' face began to bubble and froth, peeling away until a mouth-shaped void was exposed. The head jerked and spasmed, fighting against this strange song, and the mouth snapped shut for a moment before stretching impossibly wide. Waves shimmered in the air between them.

Simon gasped when the first glimpse of silver darted out between the lips, like a metallic tongue. It shifted and strained, warping from long and thin to wide and flat and back again as it struggled against the inexorable song. The silver stream arced and danced through the air toward Kallara.

It's working!

When the shining silver liquid was within arm's length it suddenly shifted, changing tack from struggling resistance to leap toward her open mouth.

"No!" Simon shouted.

Kallara's eyes hardened and a wave of violent song rushed from her lips, repelling the last gasp attack and diverting the silver stream down into the picture.

Simon stumbled to dodge the liquid as it passed him, his head pulling through to follow its course. Its momentum carried it halfway to the altar, which lit up with the glow of a cold full moon. The rush of liquid slipped toward it faster than the single crop before, and with a muted wail it fluttered through the air and down into the basin with a slurping sound. More and more of the stuff came through the picture and drained inside, until the altar blazed so brightly that he had to shield his eyes.

With a loud hiss it stopped, and the room went dark. When Simon opened his eyes, all he could see was the dim light of the portal, which seemed to be unraveling before his eyes. He dove for the light.

༄ළ6ළ6ළ6

"Glebric!" Killeth shouted.

The connection to the water evaporated. The pillar lost its form and the ship came crashing down, sending spray over all the docks. The waves continued to rock, but aimless and chaotic. Something had broken his control.

Was it the distraction?

Glebric stabbed his hands toward the water again, desperately trying to reclaim his grip on the depths, but nothing. Just an absence where his power had been. He felt empty, small... forsaken. Anguish filled the void.

His other men surrounded him as he clenched his fists. Had they set up a perimeter to protect him while he worked his magic? One kept flinching every time he moved, and the rest showed varying degrees of awe and terror.

But Glebric's own fear was far greater.

"The battle is won," Killeth said. His look contained a cautious curiosity, even concern.

"Where is Azzam?" Glebric asked, still shaking, and one of the men pointed to another ship, where he was the only one still fighting. "With me."

Azzam wasn't just fighting the men on that ship, he was slaughtering them. Glebric leaped aboard. "Azzam, we have won." Somehow his voice cut through to the dark Alkazy, who stopped, looked around at the few cowering and many more dead before him, and finally acknowledged Glebric with a nod.

"You have your city," Azzam said in that impossibly deep voice.

"We have freed it. Thanks to your help." He offered his arm.

Azzam pointed down to the deck they stood on. "I claim this ship, to return home."

Was everything slipping away at the height of his victory? *Without my power, or Azzam...* He felt like a child, begging. "Azzam, I..." He leaned in close and lowered his voice. "I need you. There is more work to be done."

The black hand gripped his arm so tight it hurt. "You have given me what I seek, and I have set you on your way. Your people need you. But I must return to mine. This is not my home, and never will be." His dark eyes flicked to the men around them. "See how the others view me, with fear and distrust in their eyes? I won't become the animal they believe me to be. I fight only for my freedom. And now I am free to go."

This noble warrior, a prince among his people, Glebric couldn't keep him caged here like an attack dog. As much as it pained him, he clasped the arm back, choking back the mix of fear and loss.

"Go, Azzam. You will always be a brother to me." He traced the sign of the broken chain on his friend's arm.

"And you to me. And Glebric—lead them. You have it in you."

He jabbed a finger into Glebric's chest. "Inside you. Not from that… power. Lead as a man, not as a sorcerer."

The confidence buoyed his spirits. With the money, and the support of others like Zustar, maybe, just maybe they could still be successful? He scanned the docks, taking in the fires, the damaged ships, and the debris strewn everywhere.

"Can you at least help me secure the ships first?"

The white teeth shone in the night. "Of course. I'm yours until dawn."

"Good. I'll need every hand. This place is a mess. We'll need to clear the harbor before you can even get this ship out of here."

ᏮᏆᏮᏆᏮᏆᏮ

Simon's nails scratched at the floor, desperately trying to keep his body from falling back through the picture. Kallara grabbed his hands to help him up.

"Did it work?" she asked.

Simon nodded weakly. The effort of multiple crossings had drained him, especially on the heels of so much worry and fighting. Kallara peered through the picture at the altar. "Will that keep her… contained?"

"I don't know. And I wouldn't want someone else to get in there. Like him." Ventus lay peacefully now, with the ooze peeled away to expose most of his face. "Is he dead?"

"I don't want to touch him," Kallara said.

Simon's leg buckled when he tried to walk. After righting himself, he crossed over to the prone body. The breathing was faint, but regular. "Out cold."

"Then let's get out of here."

"We shouldn't leave signs of our magic. The fewer that know about it, the better."

"But how are you going to get that stuff off?"

"It should wash." He retrieved a basin of water and some cloths.

"What if it wakes him up?"

Simon handed her the knife again. "If he looks like a threat, stab him in the throat." Though she recoiled from the suggestion, she looked ready to do it.

Dipping a cloth into the water, Simon tried releasing his Talent

361

and any sway it held over the sleeping man. The blackness washed away like ordinary paint, no longer tacky.

"Can you hurry it up?"

Simon glared at her. "You could help. It's just paint now. Nothing to worry about." He held up the other cloth and she reluctantly knelt and started washing off his arms and legs.

"Your song was so beautiful, so powerful. Was it one you already knew? Or do you make it up as you go along?"

"I… it's a combination. It started with a song the women in my village used to sing, but then I changed the words, calling for Ventus to expel the evil inside him, to reclaim his life. And I felt him respond."

"It certainly worked. Though for a moment there I thought it was going to take you over."

"I don't know how, but I knew it was coming for me. I had to open myself up like that to draw it closer to the picture. What do we do with the picture?"

"Take it with us. I'll roll it up like a scroll. I don't want anyone finding it, and I want to return to the temple to more permanently secure it."

"Why would the ones who imprisoned her leave it open like that?"

"I don't know. I'm wondering if they had it sealed but something changed to unleash her again. Like what happened with the Scentari and Zaliakara."

Kallara shuddered. "I don't want to meet her."

"Neither do I. And we can't let them unite. One is a tough match for all of us working together. Two would mean our doom."

"You said they're sisters. Do you think Zal—"

"Zaliakara will come looking for Kashaka?" Simon pursed his lips. "I'd bet on it. We'll have to do something about this soon. But first I want to find Elysia and Remeth."

Working quickly together, they finished washing off Ventus.

"Do you think he'll remember any of this?" Kallara asked. "He knows who we are."

"Our names anyway, not our faces."

"But he's seen my face, before. And apparently Elysia too."

Simon fought the concern welling up inside him. Now that the imminent threat was gone, he wanted desperately to find out what happened to her. And whether there was even a hint of truth to

Ventus' words. "We can't worry about that now—"

"We could. We could kill him." Kallara inched the knife toward the exposed throat, a strange fury in her eyes.

"But we won't, because that would be cold-blooded murder. It was that silver thing that pushed for Orna to be killed. Not this man. He was more of a slave than you ever were." He coaxed her hand down, but left the knife in her grip. "Can I trust you with that?" She nodded sullenly. Simon picked up the short sword and tested the weight. A fine blade, better even than the legion standard issue. He rolled up the scroll and the parchment cracked when bent against its former curvature. He furled the rest of it more carefully, tied it with a cord and stashed it in his pack. "Let's go look for some sign of Elysia and Remeth."

"What about Numerius?" Kallara said as Simon peeked through the screens to the courtyard below. It was empty now.

"Who? Oh, the man that gave you the message to deliver?"

"Yes, he's still here. We should free him. Who knows what might happen later. His room is on the way."

Before Simon could respond, she was halfway down the stairs. They turned right down a narrow corridor Simon had never had the occasion to explore. On the right side was a door, which Kallara found to be locked. "Can you open it?" she asked.

Simon huffed, but nodded. If he wanted her cooperation, there would have to be some give and take. He took out his paints and rusted off the lock again. Marveling at the efficiency that came with a little practice, he pined for some quiet time to just experiment and explore. Like he and Elysia had talked about. He couldn't bear the thought of never getting that chance.

"If he slows us down, he'll have to fend for himself."

Kallara scowled and opened the door. "Numerius?" she called out into the darkness.

"My dear," said an unctuous voice. "I told you to escape. What is happening? There was so much noise."

"We've come to let you out."

With the way he blinked his widely set eyes at the sudden light, coupled with the wiry patches of hair and fleshy pouch on his chin, he reminded Simon of a potato. His tunic was dirty, and he stank.

"Numerius Ontillus at your service," he said, his voice much smoother than he looked. "And my dear, who is my savior here?" His look was thankful, yet calculating.

"A friend," Kallara said.

He clucked his tongue, inspecting her face thoroughly. "What have you done with your beautiful hair?"

Damn, this one is too observant.

"I couldn't come back in looking like myself."

"If I did not know your voice, I'd scarcely believe it was you. Where are we going?"

"You're free to go your own way," Simon said.

"I was a prisoner here. I thank you for letting me out of my cell, but I can't just walk out the front gate."

"He's right," Kallara said. "We have to get him out."

"Will the guards recognize you?" Simon asked.

"I'm afraid so. They've all had a turn guarding my cell."

And I'm not showing this one my power with a disguise, or by sneaking him out the way we came in.

"Wait here," Simon said. He rushed back up the stairs to Ventus' room and found a simple cloak. Too tall, but might get him out unnoticed. When he brought it back, Numerius and Kallara were chatting away.

"Thank you for your help, Antonos," he said. "And for helping Kallara deliver my message."

Simon nodded and handed over the cloak.

"I am again in your thanks. Get me to a boat, and I'd be happy to grace you with some gold for your trouble."

Simon waved him off. "Just doing a favor for my friend."

"You're local then? Where did you learn to speak Pazian? Your accent is impeccable."

"My... good tutor."

"What line of work are you in, that you're here with Glebric?"

"I'm only here to help my friend. I don't work for this master."

"A wise choice. Shall we depart?"

"I... I want to make sure there aren't any other prisoners like yourself," Simon said.

"Oh? Did Glebric imprison another friend of yours?"

Kallara deflected the question. "His men have been causing trouble around the city. They're apparently taking it over tonight."

Simon wouldn't have thought the man could get any paler, but somehow Numerius managed. "Then we'd better go quickly. One thousand gold paz if you get me out now."

That would certainly help... but Elysia could still be here!

They hurried through the front entry room, now packed with all the cowering women, children and elders.

"Fire!" Kallara shouted. "Upstairs!"

The panic spread across the room like a spark on dry kindling. The crowd surged toward the doors and the guards had no choice but to let them out, or be crushed. Three guards sped past Simon to check on the fire.

"There's your opening," Simon said, giving Numerius a push on the arm. "Where can I collect?"

"Come back to the warehouse of Korg. I'll leave the payment for you. Kallara, aren't you coming?"

"Not yet." She kissed him on the cheek and he shambled after the crowd. Simon and Kallara turned down the corridor to their left, to search the final wing.

XXXIX
ᎦᏋᏋᏋᏋᏋᏋ
Searching

With no sign of Elysia as they searched the remaining rooms, warning those they encountered about the imaginary fire, Simon still wasn't ready to give up. Being in the workshop, even with the mess left by weeks of misuse, reminded him too much of her.

"She has to be here somewhere!" He even tried opening the locked closets, calling her name softly in case she was imprisoned.

"Maybe he was lying, and she left? We should too!" Kallara dragged him by the arm. "And what will we do when those guards find Ventus and no fire?" Her logic prevailed, and they rushed back to the front room. "We warned everyone down that way," she said to a guard, and he nodded thanks, stepping out of their way.

They pressed through the huddled crowd outside, where whispered rumors circulated. They were almost to the far edge of the crowd when he heard a familiar woman's scream.

"It's the thief!" she shouted.

Not again.

He brushed Kallara's arm. "Bakery," he whispered, and took off at a run.

This time at least he had a good lead on the guards. *Why are they always chasing me out this door?* He even followed the same route. *If anything I look less distinctive this time. I just hope Kallara can get away too.*

The other streets in that neighborhood were quiet, but the agora was full of people milling about, completely different from his last nighttime dash through the space. He slowed down, approaching a group of men to find out what was happening, except they were speaking Izari. He swore under his breath, but asked his question in Pazian.

"Why is the agora so full?"

He was met by shocked eyes. "You haven't heard?" said one

dark-haired and bearded man, not unlike Simon's current look. "There was an attack at the theater! That upstart Glebric and his men."

"Killed the governor!" said another man.

"Spoiled the show!" said third, earning glares from the rest.

"We were lucky to get out with our lives."

"But you heard him, he doesn't want to harm us ordinary folk, he wants to free the slaves."

"Pah! And make them his own army, I'd say. Then we'll see what he thinks of us."

One of the guards from the front of the house ran into the agora, but stopped, bewildered once he saw how many people were there, and Simon kept him in his sights while blending into the conversation.

"Any fighting in the streets?" Simon asked.

The first man nodded. "Something is happening by the port."

"Where is the watch? I reckon they've been attacked as well."

"There'll be looting!" said an older man with a cane.

"Then I should be getting home," Simon said. "Thank you."

"We should all get off the streets," said the first man, who was met with grunts of assent. "But stick together." The men broke up into groups of two or three after saying their goodbyes, and Simon fell into step with one pair that looked to be heading in his direction. Simon pulled up his hood and managed to get out of the agora and around a corner without further incident.

"My wife told me not to go to the theater," said the shorter of the two men. "Said the priest warned her no good comes of it. I'm never going to hear the end of this."

His friend clapped him on the back. "That's your worry? At least you don't have any slaves. I've got two at home and now I'm worried they'll be expecting their freedom. How about you? What takes you out at this time of night?"

"I was visiting a friend's house," Simon said. "How was the show? I hear those players are quite good."

"That's the shame of it all," the short man said, "they were excellent. I won't be voting for that Glebric, just on that basis alone."

"You think he'll be running for council?" the second man asked. "The watch should lock up him and his goons."

"They don't stand a chance. More likely he'll shut down the

council and make himself a tyrant."

The thought of Glebric being in charge of anything was completely alien to Simon. It was easier to imagine Persei as President of Pazh, a thought which made him shudder.

"This is my street," Simon said, somewhat unhappy to be leaving the company, but thankful he wouldn't have to explain anything about the bakery.

"Keep safe," the short man said. "It will be a new day tomorrow."

Simon waved his goodbye and walked the last two streets to the bakery, checking twice to make sure he wasn't being followed. The alley was dark, and he didn't see any signs of movement. He knocked his special knock on the workshop door and waited, hoping against hope that Elysia was somehow inside.

With the patter of approaching footsteps, anxiety surged into him. Brandishing his knife, he spun to face the shadow, which shrieked, holding up hands in surrender.

"Simon, it's me," Kallara said. "What took you so long?"

"How did you get here so quickly?"

"I ran the other way as soon as the guard passed me. Everyone looked confused, not expecting a girl to be going off on her own, and nobody followed. I ran the whole way here."

"I had to throw off the guard, so we're safe now. But where is Elysia? And Remeth?" While the hope of her being there, safe in her workshop had been enough while he ran, his worry turned to panic.

"Did you check the bakery?"

He shook his head and they walked to the front of the building. He unlocked the door, but the bakery was empty.

"If Remeth found her, he would have brought her back here. Unless…"

"Don't even think of bad things, Simon," Kallara said, putting a hand on his arm. "We'll find her."

"But how? Where?" He looked around her former home in vain, and when he saw the rug he imagined her dead brother's body below it, and pictured hers lying beside it. "I should never have let her go out by herself."

"Let her? What is she, your property?"

"No, but it's not safe…"

"To walk the streets by day, when nobody is looking for you?

You left me to run by myself at night. That's far worse."

It stung because she was right, but he still wouldn't forgive himself. It was his fault Elysia was out there, alone. Somewhere. *If only I could...*

"Picture her!" he shouted, and scrambled to retrieve more of his paints, his worry and love swirling around inside just waiting to be let out onto the page to show him the way.

Kallara's face lit up. "What can I do to help?"

He showed her how to mix some of the paints and he set to work, pouring his intense emotions into finding Elysia.

ᏩᏋᏩᏋᏩᏋᏩ

Elysia looked down at the deep red wine in her cup, trying to avoid Aktar's eyes and cover her discomfort.

Aktar shuffled his chair around the table beside her, and reached for her cloak. Drawing back, she put the wine cup down.

"Aktar, please. I only just met you. I... I'm very thankful you got me out of danger. And for the food. But I'm feeling tired. I can sleep in the chair." She stood up, with the wine rushing to her head and making her feel light.

"Nonsense," he said, and was beside her, gently holding her arm. "I insist that you take my bed."

"Your friend's bed," she said, correcting him before the realization pierced through the slight haze in her mind. "Aktar? Are you sure we haven't met before?"

"I believe I would remember speaking with someone as lovely as you."

"But you look so familiar."

"I feel like I've known you a long time." He took her hand in his, gently but firmly. She could read the lust in his face, the longing. But behind it, something more. He looked down through the top of her cloak toward her chest. "Stay with me, Elysia."

Hearing him say her name was jarring. "I... I don't feel comfortable with this. I'd like to leave."

She wasn't prepared for the flash of anger. "I'm not good enough for you? With everything I've risked... all the trouble you've caused me, I think I deserve some... compensation." His leer turned her stomach, and before she could move away he reached around her shoulders and tore open her cloak. She

369

screamed, and threw her cup at his face.

"Bitch!" he shouted, rubbing wine from his forehead. "You'll be in my bed tonight. I'd hoped you would come willingly, but I'll have my reward either way."

She backed off, taking slow steps toward the door. When she reached for the handle, he walked back to the table and picked up a key, dangling it mockingly toward her. "You'll be needing this, then?" He tapped it on his chin. "How about a deal? Spend the night in my bed, and I'll give you the key." No longer trying to hide his feelings, he stared brazenly at her chest.

She pulled the torn cloak across the bare patch of skin, as if it could give her time. Time to think. To find a way out. To find her friends.

"Well?" he asked, waving the key again.

"And if I refuse?"

The gleam didn't leave his eye. "Oh, I'll have what I want, Elysia. But you'll enjoy it much more if you're willing. So what is your choice?" He took a step toward her. The door behind her was wood, but felt like the stone wall of a prison.

Her mind reached for anything to stall him, but without making him angry. "Why me?"

"What?" He stopped, appearing genuinely confused.

"Why did you risk so much to save me? You're one of Glebric's lieutenants. You could be on the winning side."

His mocking laugh was at odds with the pain in his expression. "Maybe for today, but do you really think he can resist the might of Pazh?" He shook his head. "The overlord might be looking the other way for now, but the legions will be back, and Glebric and his men will all die for what they've done. They don't look kindly on slave revolts."

"So that's why you turned on him? To back the ultimate winner?"

"Bright and talented. You are a most impressive young lady, Elysia. You deserve a strong man at your side. One who can be your equal."

"Someone like you?"

The words sounded bitter to her, but he reached out, pleading and open, almost vulnerable.

"Yes, someone like me. I can keep you safe in these uncertain times. And with the backing of my friends—"

"You keep telling me of these friends. If I'm to listen to your entreaty, then I need to know more about you. I don't know what kind of women you're used to, but I would like to actually know the man I'm…" His eyes followed hers to the bed, where she saw her bag. He smiled.

"Wealthy Pazians. With lots of friends. I have a house in a quiet neighborhood. They've been very good to me."

"What do you do for them, that they reward you so handsomely?"

He pulled out two chairs and motioned her over to sit next to him. She tried to keep her eyes on his so that he wouldn't notice how much her legs shook.

"They have interests in many cities across the Republic and sometimes need someone to attend to business in person, on their behalf." He switched over to Izari. "They say my Izari is very good, so I'm a natural choice for this part of the world."

She nodded, impressed. "So why were you here in Attarsus?" she said, switching over to her native tongue. Somehow it gave her a greater feeling of control.

"I was sent to keep an eye on you. To keep you safe?"

"When?"

"Months ago. You're lucky they have the money to keep me posted here, otherwise I would have been long gone."

"But who sent that message?"

His eyes narrowed for the briefest moment, and he broke out in a smile. "Why Master Xelos of course! Who else would have your well-being at heart? If I could catch those bastards who killed him, why…"

She reached out to touch his arm, before she even realized what he was doing. But to hear another sharing her thoughts, her desire for revenge. She felt a closeness, shared understanding.

"And then when the bakery was attacked," he continued, "I feared the worst. That you were dead, like your family."

His gentle finger wiped a tear from her eye. The pain came flooding back, and she was thankful for the strong arm reaching around her shoulder to comfort her. Alexander's lifeless eyes stared into hers once more, and a chill went down her back. She flinched, staring at him in shock.

The bakery had been left untouched. How did he know…

His grip tightened on her shoulder.

XL

𝕰𝕰𝕰𝕰𝕰𝕰𝕰

Retribution

Any weariness was dispelled as Simon's passion surged onto the page into the form of Elysia. First came the outline of her face and hair, but lines of worry and discomfort lined her face, and there was fear in her eyes.

She's alive! She needs me!

It was too much emotion and he had to settle himself to avoid losing the connection. It was dread he channeled as he moved out from her body to get the context.

Where are you? He let that thought fly free in his mind, married to his frantic worry.

A table sat in front of her, simple wood, with food. It was nothing like Xelos'—Glebric's—house. His brush flicked to her shoulder, and she shied away from something—*a hand! A man's hand!*

Kallara gasped.

Elysia's cloak was torn, and the hand reached under the parted cloth to touch her exposed skin. Uniting the sudden wave of fury to his Talent, Simon's hand moved faster than he had ever imagined, filling in the cloak and body of a man...

It can't be Glebric!

The man faced Elysia, his back to the picture, and he pulled the cloak away...

Kallara's sobs turned frantic, an echo of past horror showing through her eyes. "Simon, you have to save her!"

His brush flicked to the edges of her form. Elysia struggled, but the man was pushing her toward a bed. Simon rushed to paint the frame, his hand shaking so violently that the lines swerved and dipped and crossed themselves. The furious mess seared deep into the page. He enclosed the scene.

"But where is it?" Kallara asked, her voice shrill. "How can we get there in—"

Simon drew his sword, closed his eyes, and dove into the page. Reality rippled around him, wrenching, twisting and... lancing pain in his elbows as he hit something hard.

He opened his eyes.

The man whirled to face Simon, his hands gripping Elysia's wrists as she thrashed against him.

"How?" he shouted, his scarred face angry. He shoved Elysia roughly onto the bed.

The mix of confusion and hope in her eyes startled Simon.

"How did you get in here?" the man said, his eyes flicking first to the door, then to the floor in front of Simon. Simon's sword. He must have dropped it when he crashed through.

Simon winced against the pain as he lunged for the hilt before the man could react. While he gained his feet, the man circled behind the table and drew a sword of his own. His hard eyes looked more perplexed than worried.

"Who are you?" the man said, moving around the table. "I expected someone to come for you," he said. "But is your Simon dead? I would have thought he'd be the one riding in to save you. Not some Izari. A cousin maybe?"

"Elysia, I've come for you," Simon said.

She stopped rubbing her wrists and stared, mouthing his name.

The man lunged forward two steps, drawing Simon to stab wildly at the air. Elysia made to stand up, but he waved her down, earning a scowl. She started rifling through her pack.

"So, you do know this one," the man said to her. "Tell him to leave us alone."

The look the man gave her rekindled Simon's fury, and he charged the man, but with a clang of steel his blow was deflected, and the force pushed him back.

The man fought professionally, like he had killed before. No nerves, not even a sweat.

"He'll fight you, Aktar," Elysia said.

"Then he'll die," Aktar said, rotating the blade to limber up as he assumed a fighting stance.

Aktar tried several times to bait him with feints, before withdrawing. Simon backed off, earning a sneer. "Not so brave now, are you?"

"Let us go, Aktar," Elysia said.

"I'll give him one more chance to leave, but you have to stay. You'll only be safe with me. And before he so rudely interrupted, I was going to show you what a real Pazian man is like. I think you'll enjoy—"

Simon slashed at his shoulder, but Aktar's sword deflected the blow and reversed with a flurry of slashes. Simon danced just out of reach of the first few blows, until the force of the last against his parry sent the blade skittering away.

Desperate, he kicked at Aktar's legs, toppling both of them to the floor.

Simon grabbed for the sword arm, locking it and the blade flat against Aktar's body, the tip just an inch from his face. A crushing blow to the side of his head and Simon lost his grip. The blade nicked his cheek before it hit the floor. Another blow to his head and his vision swam.

The wavering blade pulled back again and...

Aktar grunted in surprise and stood up, shouting and waving at something.

Simon blinked twice and his eyes cleared.

A creature coiled around Aktar's neck, hissing and biting.

Simon tried to stand, but his head swirled and he fell to his knees, on the verge of retching.

Aktar sliced the creature away from his neck, splitting it in two. He tossed one half to the ground in front of Simon, and held the other toward Elysia.

Her snake?

Aktar snarled like a cornered beast. "Witch! What is this sorcery?" He threw the limp remains at Elysia, whose eyes filled up not just with fear, but fury. He glanced back at Simon, sneered, and walked toward the bed.

Again Simon tried to gain his feet, and this time listed badly to the right, falling on his side, his ears ringing.

He felt so helpless as Elysia kicked at the advancing Aktar, lashing out with a small knife, but not strong enough to drive him back.

"Elysia! No!" he shouted, but his voice sounded weak.

Song broke through the ringing in Simon's ears; a clear, beautiful girl's voice. Familiar and soothing, a hauntingly mellow tune...

Aktar relaxed his grip on Elysia, who stopped kicking at him.

Wisps of golden light floated through the air.

Simon's eyes moistened, overcome with a melancholy calm. It was like a hazy, sad dream, as Kallara walked across the room. Aktar sat on the bed, tears streaming down his face. Elysia was weeping.

Kallara retrieved Aktar's sword, which lay discarded beside him, and cut strips of bedding to bind his hands and feet. She pulled over a chair, walked back to Simon and pressed the sword into his hand.

Her touch on his shoulder was comforting but insistent, yet he was powerless to move, to get up. The sorrow, the regret, the inconsolable desire to make things right with Kallara...

She clapped her hands over his ears and the world snapped back into focus.

Disoriented and weak, she helped him up, and walked with him to the bed. He checked the restraints before struggling to heave Aktar into the chair, and tied him into place. When Simon nodded that he was done, Kallara stopped singing.

Aktar shook his head, as if waking from a dream. He beheld Kallara with surprise, then Simon's sword, and struggled against the bonds. They stretched and flexed, but held.

Elysia sat up, looking in confusion at Kallara. "Who are you?" she asked.

Kallara kept staring at Aktar with her jaw set, ignoring the question.

"Kallara," Simon said. "A friend. One of us. Who is this guy?"

"The singer?" Aktar said, squinting. "But she's a redhead."

Simon embraced Elysia. "We looked for you all over Xeros' house. They told me you were dead!"

She looked like she was remembering something. Her eyes turned hard, and she leveled a finger at Aktar's forehead.

"This one rescued me. But why? Who really sent you?"

Aktar grinned at her. "Forgotten Simon already? Aren't you going to introduce me to your new friend?"

"More important things are happening tonight," Simon said.

"I know," Elysia said. "But he knows me. And Simon, I want to know how."

"You know Simon?" Aktar asked, his eyes showing more interest. "And he's okay with you being so close to this guy..." Aktar looked from Kallara to Simon to Elysia again, his eyes mistrustful, bordering on fear. "Simon? Kallara? Changing your faces? You're all witches?"

Elysia kicked him in the shin, and he spat at her.

"I'm the one asking the questions."

"How did he find you?" Simon asked.

"I was locked away at Xelos' house. I didn't even realize. There was this great block of Jeppo marble, and I was in my old room, discovering what was inside… this one got me out. Warned me I was in danger there. Brought me here… to keep me safe. Or so he said." She kicked him again, and he winced.

"Bitch. Should have just taken you to bed first, then bought you breakfast."

She leveled her carving knife at his throat. He didn't flinch, and almost looked impressed.

"He was right, you do have spirit. Oh, I would have liked to see how that worked out in my bed."

She drew the knife along Aktar's collarbone and beads of blood welled up. "I'm the one asking the questions. Who do you work for?" Simon recoiled from the cold venom in her voice.

Aktar laughed. "Someone who was looking for you."

"Why me?"

"To find Simon. I don't know why. He's not very impressive. He'd be dead if it weren't for—" He strained to look around, spotting a severed piece of creature. "What is that thing?"

Elysia gasped softly and picked up her dead creation, cradling it in her arms. She put the knife to his throat again.

"I don't think he's going to talk," Simon said.

"You killed my friend," Elysia hissed. "I'm not afraid to do the same to you." Simon put his hand on her arm and slowly pulled the blade away.

"He might know something useful. Let me try…"

"No," Kallara said from behind them. "Let me."

"You? But…" He covered his ears and looked to her for approval.

"No, I have an idea. I think I know how to control it."

For the first time, concern showed through on Aktar's face. "Don't let her do that to me again."

"Then talk," Elysia said.

Aktar looked from one woman to the other, but kept his mouth shut.

Kallara started to sing, again in her native tongue. But this time the song didn't move Simon in the same way, though he felt it's pulling, drawing sincerity. If it was directed at him, he'd tell her whatever she wanted to know, and…

Golden wisps floated from her mouth and around Aktar's head. She walked behind him, leaning close to sing softly into his ear. Aktar shone with rapture, pure enchantment. She stopped.

It was as if a knife were twisted in his side; his face contorted with such pain and anguish. "More, please!"

She resumed the song and he smiled with a pure, almost child-like joy. Until she stopped again. "No, please… I beg you."

"Then answer her questions," Kallara said. She leaned over his shoulder to smile at him, and Aktar started breathing heavily. She nodded to Elysia.

"Aktar, who sent you?"

"Please, sing for me, please!"

"Answer, and I will," Kallara said.

"The Lokuta. Persei Lokuta!"

The name cut through Simon like a cold knife, and Elysia's eyes betrayed a fury bordering on madness. Her muscles tensed and it took all his remaining strength to hold her back.

"Did you attack Xelos' house?" she asked through clenched teeth.

"Yes, yes… I did. Just please, please sing for me again."

"Should I?" Kallara asked.

"Not yet," Elysia said. "Did you kill my father? The baker?"

He shook his head. "No. I roughed him up a bit. Used him to try to get in the door. But it was my man who cut him down. I don't even know why. Someone killed my man before I could ask. Now please, please!" He wailed like he was in actual, physical pain.

Elysia was shaking now, murder in her eyes. Still Simon stayed her hand.

"One more," Simon said. "Did you kill Xelos?"

"That old fool? When he wouldn't give up you or Simon, and went to destroy some statues? He turned to fight me in the end. That sword right there drank the last of his blood."

Simon let go of her arm, the shock of the casual admission overcoming him.

"Then you'll pay," Elysia said, and brought her knife down onto his hand.

Aktar grunted through clenched teeth.

"Sing for him again," Elysia said.

"But you got what you wanted," Kallara said.

"Sing!"

Kallara's voice faltered at first, and the song had a more somber flow, but still Aktar's expression changed back to elation despite the blood gushing from his hand.

"Does he know we're alive?" Elysia asked. Kallara stopped and Aktar started talking immediately.

"I don't know. Persei and Daymar stopped here on the way back to Pazh. Said Simon had appeared in Tamar but then was lost, presumed dead. They even met Glebric."

"Did they know of his power?"

Aktar spat weakly. He was losing color.

Simon tried to interject, but her questions were good. "Elysia, he's—"

"Answer me!"

"No! They only wanted Simon. And Daymar was interested in some of the sculptures. Bought them from Glebric with a pile of gold. Helped him finance his revolution."

"Did they know what he planned?"

"No. The last letter I sent for Persei got a response back from Daymar. Did you know he was elected President?"

President?

"He said Persei is in Marutha and—"

"Marutha?" Elysia asked.

"Apparently he's in charge of a legion there." He gritted his teeth. "You know, I should have nabbed both of you when I had the chance." He spat again.

"What chance?" Elysia asked.

"When we met before. In the temple of Attarso. You have a good sense of timing, Simon, I'll give you that. I was going to grab her there and use her as the bait. Looks like it would have worked too. Got you to come after all." The calm bravado started seeping away again, and Aktar bit his lip. "Would have been much easier than dragging that old man around. And then when he sounded the alarm... that was you again, wasn't it? You killed my man and wounded the other. You're the reason the old man was shouting! Then it's all your fault they're dead, that crazy old master and the baker both. Their blood is on your hands."

"That's enough!" Simon said, feeling the words twist in his soul.

"Did you enjoy killing him?" Elysia asked, without a trace of emotion.

"Xelos?" Aktar laughed. "He made me angry. I wished afterward that I'd given him a slower death, so he could feel the pain he caused me. But that's nothing compared to what I'd do to you, Simon. And I would have done the same to your father. I bet he would have died screaming like a girl, like your brother. Alexander, was it? Instead my man just clubbed him on the head and he dropped like a stone."

"You won't be so lucky," Elysia said. "Simon, give me his sword."

"Elysia, he's talking…"

"Simon!"

He grimaced and handed it to her, too weak to protest. She strained to lift it over her head.

"Persei will pay you well if you release me!"

"I don't want his money. I want your blood." The sword crashed down on Aktar's sandal, severing three toes. He squealed for the first time, but Kallara's shriek was even louder. She backed away with her hands over her mouth.

Simon tried to get in front of her. "Elysia, we don't have to—" The fire in her eyes burned away his reproach.

"Out of my way," she said with a cold finality. Simon stepped aside, at least trying to block Kallara's view from where she cowered in the corner, shuddering. "That was for my father. This is for Xelos." She put the flat of the blade to the side of his head, and his thrashing stilled for a moment. With a quick jerk she sliced off his ear, sending a fresh fountain of blood spurting from the wound. His keening shook the walls with its mad intensity. There was so much terror in those hard eyes that Simon almost pitied him, this murderer. But he did deserve such a fate. Simon just never wanted to be the one administering it, and to see Elysia doing that…

"Come on Elysia, it's done."

"Not until I say so. One more, for what he tried to do to me." She stared Simon down, and he retreated to where Kallara sat blubbering.

Simon's stomach wouldn't let him watch, but he would have nightmares about Aktar's final inhuman wail before he went silent for good.

Elysia tapped him on the shoulder. "Aliata help me when I get my chance at Persei."

"Haven't you shed enough blood?"

"You're a monster!" Kallara shouted, shrinking from Elysia's look. "Simon, how can you love someone capable of... of that!"

Elysia shook a finger at her. "What would you do to the man who killed everyone who mattered to you?"

"But you butchered him!"

"He deserved worse."

Simon tried to be the peacemaker. "Kallara has been through a lot too, Elysia. She's never seen any... anything like this.

"Let's get out of here. We still need to find Remeth. We can just go back through..." Simon looked around for the telltale shimmer of his magical gate, but there was none. "Kallara, do you remember where you came through?"

"I... it was such a strange feeling. I lost track. Can't you find it?"

He shook his head. "It's like it's not even there. But it worked for you, so it must..." Her stricken look stopped him.

"After you went through, the scroll curled closed. I had to unfurl it just to follow you. Once I left—"

"The gate closed." Simon frowned. "Do you know where we are, Elysia?"

"Near the port. I..." She looked down at her feet, clenching and unclenching one hand. "I came with him willingly. I thought he was trying to help. He had a sign from Xelos." She walked back to the body and rifled through his things while Simon averted his gaze. "Money and the key." She handed it to Simon, along with the sword. "Do you know where Remeth is? I saw him at the house."

"You did? When?"

"This afternoon, with Aktar. He looked like he was playing at being one of Glebric's soldiers."

"Then he must be out with them." The connections came together. "Glebric made an attack at the theater. Remeth must have gone with him. But that battle is over. Where else... maybe the port? Kallara, are you comfortable coming with us?"

"Is she going to slaughter them too?"

"If I see Persei, I will," Elysia said.

"But they didn't do anything to us," Simon said. "We're just looking to get Remeth and get out of here."

"But what about Glebric?" Kallara asked. "He killed Orna with his dark magic. Doesn't he deserve an even worse fate?"

Elysia's resolve faltered. "Killed who? Glebric? What?"

Simon put a hand on her shoulder. "You know how Shadash was channeling Zaliakara's power? Glebric apparently met Kashaka."

"Glebric?" Elysia said, incredulous. "But Glebric just wants to help free the slaves—"

"By giving himself to darkness!" Kallara said.

"Ventus was Kashaka," Simon said.

Elysia's face lit up with realization. "By Aliata... I sat with him. He's the one who gave me the marble. Wait... *was?*"

"We drove her blood right out of him. Sent it back to the temple where the ancients had imprisoned her. We hope it means Glebric's connection to her is gone, and he won't have that dark power... or its influence over him."

"But Simon, it's Glebric! He wouldn't hurt anyone."

"Tell that to Orna," Kallara said. "She's dead."

"You don't know that for sure," Simon said.

"Then where is she?" Kallara glared at both of them. "Once Glebric realized our Talent, he wanted to destroy us. Consume us."

"We have to deal with Glebric," Simon said.

Kallara crossed her arms. "We have to kill him. He released Kashaka, and knows where to find her again. He may still have the power."

Elysia shook her head. "I just can't believe Glebric... he's driven, and he wants to right these wrongs in our world, but he didn't do anything to harm me."

"Why are you defending him?" Simon asked, trying not to think of what Ventus had said.

"It's Glebric! He was always good to you."

"He followed you around like a little dog. I think he loved you." Elysia blushed. "What did you do with him?"

"What? He let me take the tools. Wanted me to stay but I said I had to go."

"Then why didn't you leave?"

"The Jeppo marble! Ventus proposed me doing a commission. I figured he'd pay well... and you're always saying we could use the money. And you know how I always wanted to try it. It was so beautiful!"

"Did Glebric know about your power?" Simon asked. She was so sincere, so excited about practicing her craft. He breathed a sigh of relief.

"Who, Glebric? He… well, I never used it in front of him. Not before, and not today. I know now that he cares about me, Simon, wanted me to stay for dinner. But then he left. One of Glebric's aides brought me to meet Ventus. I don't think Glebric even knew that I stayed. Ventus set me up in my room, and locked me in. I can't imagine Glebric ever meant to harm me. Maybe I can talk to him."

"I don't want to put you in danger again. There's been far too much today."

She crossed her arms. "Put me in danger? I was the one who saved you."

"But if I didn't—"

"And both of you should be thanking me," Kallara said.

Simon threw up his hands. "So what do you propose?"

"If what you're saying is true—"

"Of course it's true."

"Right, well… I think I'm the best one to sway him."

Simon's mouth formed a tight line. "I'm not going to be able to dissuade you, am I?"

She smiled. "I can take care of myself. You can stay nearby."

"Kallara, I understand if you don't want to come…"

"I don't want to be on my own. Not with people out there hunting for me."

"Right, then we'll search the port. If we're lucky we'll find both Remeth and Glebric."

As they passed through the door, Simon got close enough to whisper to Elysia. "Are you going to be all right?"

"I'm going to sleep better than I have in months, knowing that monster is dead." She smiled again, but it didn't put him at ease. It would take a while to forget the image of her as a gruesome avenging spirit.

XLI
ᎶᏋᎶᏋᎶᏋᎶ
Reunited

Glebric stood on the pier with Killeth, surveying the state of his fleet. After Azzam left he still had over thirty seaworthy ships under his direct control, including three he already owned, a dozen seized by his men or contributed to the cause by owners not wanting any trouble, and half again as many that would work with them, but more reluctantly. At least as many needed varying degrees of repairs. They'd only had to sink two more to get this level of co-operation. *I'll have to speak to Zustar and see if he knows anyone who can help us turn this into an actual navy. The Pazians will come, and without my power to face their ships, we need a new sea wall.* He stared off into the west. *How long until they come?*

"We stopped any more ships from leaving tonight," Killeth said. "So the Pazians won't get any report for a while yet. We'll have time to prepare."

Glebric nodded. "We need it. A few guards and the city watch are one thing, but the Senate will retaliate in force. And we can't count yet on the neighboring islands, but I hope we can win most of them over to our cause." He closed his eyes for a moment, letting out a great sigh. All these weeks of planning, but what he'd pictured as their great victory was only the first step. The weight of it all threatened to crush him.

"You should sleep," Killeth said. "Why don't we go back to the house?"

"But I have so much still to do."

"It will still be there after you sleep. You'll need rest to be able to deal with it."

"You're right, Killeth. And not for the first time on this night. I'm glad you joined our cause. I'll have need for many more good men in the days to come."

Killeth bowed his head in thanks. "I'd be more use if I could spend a few hours in a bed."

"So will the rest." Especially Zustar's men. A runner had come with news that they'd subdued the city watch, with more than half of them coming over to his side. But not before the rest had put up a good fight and there were too many wounded to handle.

Together they walked back to the shore, stopping several times so he could give instructions to his men. He'd gathered ten to accompany him back to the house first, with more to follow in groups soon afterward.

He was coordinating the schedule when Elysia appeared around a corner, flanked by two Izari; a man and a younger woman that could be his sister. They stopped and stared at Glebric.

"What are you doing here?" Glebric shouted. "It's not safe!"

When he rushed to take Elysia's arm, the man, who looked at least a decade her senior, leveled his sword at Glebric. His men drew their various weapons and pushed between them, with two seizing the girl, who fought against them.

"Let me go!" she shouted in Pazian, in a strong, clear voice that sounded familiar.

"Release her!" said the Izari man, also in Pazian, in a voice he'd heard so many times...

Glebric stared. "Simon? But how?" He gripped Elysia's arm tighter. "What is going on?"

"Glebric, I need to speak to you, alone," Elysia said, her hand gently covering his.

"Wouldn't you rather bring *Simon*?" He couldn't face her alone. Not with this new pain. "No. I'll bring one of my men. Killeth, come."

Elysia looked him over and nodded. When the strange Izari Simon tried to protest she silenced him with a look. Glebric led them away from the others.

She sighed. "Glebric—"

"How could you lie to me, Elysia? I don't know how this is Simon, how he looks like..." He opened his eyes wide. "Magic? Simon is another one..." His mind raced. *He is against me, just like the musicians, like that... Kallara!* That's where he knew the girl's voice. "How could you, Elysia? How could you move against me with these witches and sorcerers?"

"Glebric, listen to yourself! We're not here to oppose you and your vision. But what have you done?"

"What have I done?"

"Yes, Glebric. What dark forces did you align yourself with?"

Somehow her dark eyes pierced through his indignation and found something below. Shame. "But, I... how do you..."

"What did you offer Kashaka?"

"Who?"

"The dark water spirit."

"I don't know what you're talking about..."

"Glebric!"

He couldn't lie to her. Nor to himself anymore. "I only wanted to save my mother. And I was promised..."

"Promised what? Wealth and power? And in return you dedicated yourself to this darkness?"

"No!" *Did I?* "I only gave up Ventus."

"And who was he to you?"

"He owned my mother."

"But you're not a slave. You were a..." Her eyes narrowed. "Were you working for him? Even then? Against Master Xelos? Did you... did you conspire with his killers?"

"No! No, nothing like that. I was only to watch him."

"And Simon? And me? So you were a spy all this time? And then you had the gall to take Xelos' fortune for yourself?"

"No, Elysia, no! It wasn't like that at all. I had no choice! He threatened my mother. He owned us both! But all I did was report to him about what you were doing. Your art. I never wanted to harm you, or Xelos. He was so good to me. But then he was killed, while I was out—"

"Isn't that convenient."

"No! It wasn't my idea, I just welcomed a rest. I'd been with Simon every day since he arrived. Every day you spent with him." Could she see the hurt in his eyes? "Elysia, I always wanted the best for you. And I thought you were lost."

"So you gave yourself to darkness?"

"I was desperate. Trying to save my mother. I was getting rowed to Corus, to rescue her from Ventus' estate. But then I was drawn in... this being spoke to me. She promised me power if I would just stand up. I'd never stood up to anyone before. I'd always been a slave, a servant. I'd never gone after anything I wanted. Like you."

"So now you're confident, and take whatever you want? Are you going to take me too?" The disgust and anger in her eyes was too much for him. "Using your power? And don't tell me you haven't been using it. You should see yourself." She touched his hair, and even with all the anger he tingled at the contact.

"What?" He put his hand over hers, but she pulled it away.

"You've aged. I thought you looked older when we met today, but I didn't think anything of it then. But now, after whatever you've done tonight, you look ten years older, or more. Your hair is going gray at the temples. This darkness steals life from you."

She was trying to trick him. "Killeth, do I look any different?"

His new ally studied his face. "The lady is right. You do look more... distinguished. What you did with the ships and the water—"

"See Glebric! It's evil. She's evil. You're becoming like her. Evil."

"No! She doesn't control me. I just use the power for good. I can show you. But..." He leaned in close so that only she could hear. "But it's gone."

"Are you sure?"

He nodded weakly. "But don't tell them."

"Why not? Afraid they'll leave you?"

"They need me to be strong, for what is to come. We won this battle, but Pazh will strike back. They can't let us free any slaves. If only I had my power..."

Her expression changed as she evaluated his. "Glebric, you mean to get it back?"

"Think of what I can do!"

"It warps you, corrupts you. You may think you're the master, but she makes you a slave again."

"No!"

"Then why did she grant power to you. Did you dedicate yourself to her?"

"Only with words, I didn't mean it."

"Words have power. And this power bears a terrible price. She only supports you as far as you can help her, then she'll take it away again."

"But... why?"

"She is not a faithful mistress. What if she chose to grant that power to some new favorite?"

"No!"

"Maybe she already has?"

"No…" Kashaka, Elysia, Azzam… they'd all deserted him and his cause. For another man or another place. His eyes grew wet and he turned away from both of them.

But Elysia wouldn't let him. She touched his arm, more gently now, and looked into his face. "But you don't need this darkness to succeed. I heard how passionate you are about change. About helping people. About making sure no child has to grow up the property of another. All of us would support such a cause, if done with noble intent."

"You… you believe in me?"

"As do I," Killeth said. "And I think she speaks true. My people tell tales of spirits such as this, who grant favor in return for human sacrifice, twisting them to their ends. If she let you lead, it was only to serve her purpose. There is always a price."

Tears fell from his eyes. "I just wanted my mother to be free."

"And now she is," Killeth said. "You freed her, and so many others. It was you that did this, with your head, your good heart, and your vision. You can make more dreams become a reality. It will take hard work, but use your hands and your voice and an army will follow you to victory."

The words sparked life again in Glebric.

"Turn away from darkness, Glebric," Elysia said. "For good."

Her sincerity brought him to tears.

"But what if another finds her temple, and seizes that power?" Glebric asked. "They might use it against us!"

"With the help of my friends," Elysia said, looking back to Simon and Kallara, "we mean to make sure that doesn't happen again." Glebric saw the way her expression changed. He wished she'd look at him like that; he'd give the world for that. *But not to darkness.*

"So they're friends of yours. Simon, and that girl." He waved to the guards and called out: "Let them go, they're no threat."

Simon put away his sword, and the pair looked mistrustfully at Glebric, but Elysia's nod seemed to settle them.

"How do you intend to seal that temple?" he asked.

"I have ideas."

"After you finish, would you stay and work with us? We need all the help we can get."

"You say this Simon is in disguise," Killeth said. Glebric and
Elysia both nodded. "If he is so good with disguises, he could be a
great help to your cause."

"What do you mean? Tell us. Your ideas have been a great help
on this night."

"Attarsus cannot stand alone. But what if we reach out for support in the other provinces? There are many who chafe under
Pazian rule. If we are the only threat to the Senate, they'll squish us
like a bug. But if uprisings were to take place across the
Republic..."

"You sound like a diplomat," Elysia said. "If you could speak
on Glebric's behalf..."

Not another one gone? But Glebric knew she was right. "Killeth,
your silver tongue might be able to sway some to our side. And if
Simon can help you with disguises..." It just made sense. He
turned to Elysia. "I suppose you'll go with him too?"

"Yes," Elysia said. "This is a good idea. And Killeth will help
take care of us, won't you?"

If I'm going to be a leader, I have to make these tough choices. "I'll ready
a ship for you. You should leave right away. We've stopped any
ships from leaving tonight, but the news will get out, and the
Pazians will come."

"Thank you, Glebric," Elysia said, and kissed him on the cheek.

"Where do you suggest first, Killeth? To your people in
Marutha? Aren't they restive?"

"Egaras," Elysia said.

"Why Egaras?" Glebric asked.

"I know of some friends there, and if we can light another fire
right under the Republic's nose, it will draw their gaze away from
you. Or at least split their attention."

"I hate to lose both of you," Glebric said.

Killeth grasped his arm. "Just because we're out of sight doesn't
mean we're lost as allies, or friends." His smile was infectious, and
for at least a few moments everything seemed possible. "And you
still have Zustar."

"Is there anything else you need from the house, Elysia?"

She patted her pack. "No, I got it earlier, thanks again."

"It's what Xelos would have wanted."

Elysia thought for a moment. "There is a big stone there, green
marble, in my old room. Ventus had it brought to me. Can you

keep it there? I promise to come back and finish it someday."

"I'll have it kept for you." He walked them back to the others.

"Simon?" he asked, and the strange Izari version raised an eyebrow at him. "You take care of Elysia, on your mission."

"And Kallara," he said, drawing a wince from the dark-haired girl, "I'm still happy I was able to save you, even if you felt like you needed to run from me." He traded a look with Elysia. "I'm not that man anymore. Anyone on the side of freedom is a friend of mine." Kallara still didn't look convinced, but at least she wasn't spitting at him. "I'll make the arrangements for your ship. Would you like to leave in the morning?"

"As soon as we can," Elysia said, cutting off Simon before he could ask any questions. "Give us a chance to get our things together and we'll depart by noon."

"Thank you again, Killeth. And you too, Elysia." Glebric kissed her on the cheek and held her hand. Wishing again for more, but happy at least with himself.

He turned to leave, but remembered one more thing. He leaned close so his men wouldn't hear. "Do you know how to find the temple? *Her* temple?"

"Yes," Simon said. "We can get there on our own."

Glebric let out a breath, relieved he wouldn't have to face this... Kashaka again. "The world will be in your debt. The new world, not the Republic."

"Take care of our city," Elysia said, looking up at the acropolis.

"I mean to."

⚬⚬⚬⚬⚬⚬⚬

On their walk back to the bakery, Elysia imagined how she would thank Simon for both rescuing her and helping avenge Xelos' death. Even if Persei still walked free. Simon's hand felt the same, but she wasn't going to kiss him until he looked like himself again. It just seemed wrong. The first thing she'd have him do was wash all that off. Until she saw the front door and froze once again; the memory of Alexander's dead eyes inside keeping her out.

"What is it?" Simon asked.

"Is it... did you clean it up?"

"Completely," he said. "Before we even went out again. I was going to show you, but of course you'd already left."

She took a deep breath and let him lead her in. He lit up the room with his glowing coin, and everywhere she turned was clear and spotless, ready for the business of the day. Except for the counter, where his paints were spread out beside a scroll.

"I'm impressed. You two know how to clean up."

"I have to give Remeth a lot of the credit," Simon said.

"Don't worry, I'll put you to work. Now I'm curious about that picture, where is it?"

Remeth made sure everyone heard his yawn. "Where can I sleep?"

"Through there, first door on the left." Remeth disappeared through the doorway. "Did you clean the bedrooms?"

"Not yet," Simon said.

"At least it was just a mess, not…" She tried to shut that image out of her mind for the last time, and it was easier. Maybe killing Aktar did provide some real closure.

"What about me?" Kallara asked.

"Second door on the right."

She started through the doorway, but then turned back. "Shouldn't we close off that shrine, prison… whatever it was right away? What if Glebric changes his mind?"

"He won't," Elysia said.

"I'm too exhausted to take us there now," Simon said. "It's draining. I was only able to come to you because I was so worried. We should come up with a plan, and try sealing it from the boat."

"Then I'm going to sleep," Kallara said, in between yawns. "I don't sleep well on boats."

When she left, leaving them alone, Elysia slipped her arms around Simon, drawing him closer. "You're getting really good at these disguises. It could prove useful with where we're going."

He didn't hug her back, and when she looked up, he was very serious.

"I was going to ask, but didn't want to challenge you in front of the others. Why Egaras?"

"It needed to be plausible to Glebric, as a place that could distract the Pazians. But I wanted it to be far away from Persei and his Zaliakara, or whatever body she's inhabiting. If he's in Marutha, we shouldn't go back to Yalath…" Simon's face fell, and he looked to the doorway. "What's wrong?"

"Yalath. He's dead."

She stared at him. "How? You saw? Was it Persei?" When his face gave her confirmation, she felt the rage coming back. "And you didn't tell Remeth? How do you think he'll take it?"

Simon shuffled his feet. "It's complicated. But you know that. I know you didn't like him, but Yalath was a friend of Xelos, a mentor to Remeth. He still taught us a lot and helped us piece together more of this puzzle."

"That's another reason I was thinking Egaras. There's still so much we don't understand."

"Xelos' friend there? Nurra?"

"Exactly."

Simon frowned. "But she's nowhere near the coast. I checked a map at Yalath's. Laogas is way upriver. It will be quite a journey to get there."

"Then it will keep us far away from Persei. Hopefully we can learn more from her."

"The boat journey should give us some time to work on our Talents, and figure out how to use them together. You should have seen some of what Kallara and I did."

"Who is she anyway?"

"She was a slave, from north of Pazh. Valtari blood."

"Valtari? But she looks... oh, she's in disguise too? Can you wash that off? I don't want to kiss this other man I see in front of me. I want my Simon back."

His expression confused her. Was it this false face, or was he struggling with something?

"What is it?"

"Let me go wash up."

While he scrubbed away the beard and pale skin, she unfurled his scroll. The window in the picture framed Aktar's room, with his dead body lying in a pool of dried blood exactly how she'd left him, one ear missing, and his mouth open in a final agonized wail. *You deserved every moment of it.*

"Haven't we seen enough of that?" Simon asked, rolling it up with a dark hand.

She ran her fingers along his smooth bronze face. "I'd rather look at you, the real you. But I just wanted to see how it looked. All that came out of your head?"

"Yes. I could see you so clearly, but then the rest filled in, and when I saw him trying to grab you, trying to—" He shuddered.

She leaned up to kiss him, and when he put his arms around her, she felt so safe, melting against him.

Again he pulled away. "Elysia, I was so worried about you. I... I get so worried when you're away from me. It seems like every time I let you out of my sight, something bad happens."

"Yet I was able to protect myself? And that's twice now that *my* Talent helped save *you*, when you came to rescue me." She grinned. "But I know you love me and can't help but worry. Can I at least show you how grateful I am that you came for me?"

He looked around self-consciously. "But the others—"

She silenced him with a finger on his lips. There was something illicitly exciting about bringing him to her bed, the bed that had been hers since she was a child. Her heart beat faster as she led him into the darkness.

XLII

ᏮᏋᏮᏋᏮᏋᏮ

Sealed

After waking refreshed in Elysia's arms, Simon had asked them to push back their departure until later in the day. For once they weren't rushing away from a city and could put some time into planning, and he made the best of it.

Glebric had sent over more gold, likely feeling guilty for the trouble he'd caused them, and for what little Elysia had received from Xelos' estate. Kallara and Remeth had also retrieved the reward from Korg's warehouse. Numerius had apparently tried to convince her to come with him, but she'd declined in favor of staying with her new Talented friends.

They put the newfound resources to use, gathering supplies of food, paints and parchment for him, stone and wood for Elysia, cooking, survival and personal supplies, and a scabbard for his sword. Wherever this trip took them, at least they'd be prepared.

Simon wasn't sure what he would have done if Remeth and Kallara hadn't been such avid shoppers. A day in the markets was more draining to him than their night of searching and battles. They'd been overzealous in their purchases, and as a result had to store much of it in Elysia's workshop and the bakery. Although they put up a fight, defending the importance of every purchase, Simon had settled it by painting a picture of the workshop so they could come back if they needed to retrieve something. That had earned him a passionate kiss from Elysia, extremely happy that home was only a dive through a picture away.

He was still warring with himself a bit after last night. While he wasn't at all comfortable with how coldly Elysia tortured and killed Aktar, and initially felt the distance between them, once she'd been close and clear in her desire for him, his own urges took over and he succumbed to a wonderful night. But here in the clear of day it troubled him anew. They'd have to stop Persei somehow, but it hurt to see her do such things, even justified. If he could find another way, he would.

At the port they easily located the *Winter Breeze*, a fast merchant ship happy to be leaving Attarsus with its cargo intact after the battle the night before. The captain, a dark Egarasi, had been only too happy to give them free berths in order to avoid paying any new taxes Glebric and his new leadership might have decided to levy.

Zeno had been suspicious of the shifting deck of the ship, and only with some serious cajoling and a few apples had Elysia coaxed him down into the hold, where he'd spend the next week or more. The promise of a long rest and not having to carry four riders had finally convinced him.

Glebric had seen them off himself, with too long an embrace for Elysia. Simon held his tongue, but it gave him a chance for a better look at Xelos' former servant. She was right, the boy had aged and looked older than Remeth now, bearing a lasting reminder of the price of the dark magic.

It also troubled him to learn than Glebric had been spying on Xelos and Elysia before he even arrived. It long predated Aktar and Persei's interest, so who did Ventus and Numerius work for? Who was Tullus? Who were the Keepers? They apparently went to great lengths to keep an eye on potential Talent. Another of too many loose threads. If only he could go back and ask Numerius himself.

Simon didn't think this independent Attarsus would last very long. Remeth and Elysia had been supportive of Glebric and his ideas—and the ideas were noble enough—but they didn't know the Pazian legions like Simon did. A few squads would be enough to take the city, and with too much coastline and so many islands to defend, it was only a matter of time. He didn't know much about naval battles, but the sea was so vast and even the Pazian navy couldn't stamp out piracy, so how would a few merchant galleys under the leadership of former slaves be able to defend them? No, the sooner they were out of here, the better.

Elysia took his hand and they boarded the ship together. Leaving this port among friends was a new sensation, and Simon quite liked it. He stood at the bow with Elysia, watching as they sailed out of the harbor. "You know he'd be yours if you asked him,"

Simon said, indicating Glebric waving from the pier.

She scowled. "Well, the only one I'm asking is you." He shouldn't have forced it, but hearing her say it out loud did warm his heart. He leaned over and kissed her.

"What do you think of your city from this view?"

"It's like this is how it was meant to be seen, from sea level, with the acropolis towering above us."

"I only hope she'll weather this latest chapter."

"You don't think Glebric will succeed?"

"The enemies of Pazh don't have a history of success."

"But don't you feel this is something different? It's not just some isolated rebellion by restive provincials. Not just a slave revolt. It's a movement."

"Do you and Remeth really mean to do what you promised? To search out support for this cause in Egaras, and beyond?"

"I keep my promises. Speaking of which, did you tell Remeth yet about Yalath?" Simon looked down at his feet. "Simon!"

"He was out with Kallara shopping most of the day. I never got a chance. At least they're getting along great."

"I'm hoping it will help soften the blow... the fact that he's among friends. He's a good man, Remeth."

"Even better than you know."

"Now is as good a time as any." Elysia squeezed his hand and they walked over to the others.

"Isn't it beautiful?" Kallara asked as they approached. "I've only been on a boat once, to come here, and I was down below with a lot of smelly people. It was horrible. But this, is this how the wealthy travel?"

Elysia took her hand. "Come, I want to point out a few sites."

"I'd like to see too," Remeth said.

"They're of interest to... ladies," Elysia said. He still didn't demur, but Simon held him back.

"Let them go. They need some time together too. And I wanted to tell you something."

"What is it? Ideas for closing up that temple? I already told you, my Talent is not much use with no people involved."

"It's not that." He took a deep breath. "When Kallara and I went back to the bakery in the afternoon, and you went to look for Elysia..."

"Yes?"

He took another breath. "We… we contacted Yalath. I painted a picture of him, at his house, and we were going to tell him what we'd learned about Glebric and that we thought it was Kashaka and… but…" He put his hand on Remeth's shoulder, who looked at him nervously. "But he's… he's… I'm so sorry, Remeth. Your mentor, he's gone."

Remeth turned pale and clapped a hand over his mouth, his jaw quivering behind it. "Are… are you sure?"

Simon nodded.

Tears streamed down Remeth's face. "What am I to do, Simon? He meant so much to me. He showed me I was different. Showed me my Talent. Treated me tough, but fair… like a son." He broke down crying, head in his hands, which drew odd looks from passing crew members.

Awkwardly, Simon put his arm around him. "We're here for you, Remeth. All of us. We can't replace him, but I feel like you're my family now, and Elysia and I will support you like we support each other. Whatever you need." The words tasted like chalk in Simon's mouth, even if he meant them. He felt so sorry, even when it wasn't his fault at all. Except once again, he'd brought this darkness into the life of another…

Remeth peered through the fingers. "You're not very good at this, are you?" he asked.

"What?"

Remeth stood back up and grinned at him. "I should teach you a thing or two about delivery."

Bewildered, Simon could only stare at his friend.

"Kallara already told me, at the agora."

"She did? But then…"

"I really had you going there. Sometimes I impress even myself."

"This is serious."

"Hey, I'll take any chance to practice my craft. Stick around and maybe some of it will rub off on you."

"What, and I'll make you a painter?"

Remeth pursed his lips. "Maybe not."

"So you're… all right? But Yalath is dead." He was taking it far better than Simon expected.

"Yes, and that bastard Persei was behind it. Looks like I'll have to get in line behind Elysia with my grievance, though from what

Kallara said, I doubt there will be much left after she's done with him."

Simon winced. "But... do you need time to grieve... or?"

"I already told you. Yalath and I had a complicated relationship. He was a good man, but he was so hard to deal with. Even harder on me. I far prefer my present company. Speaking of which, Kallara is a doll! The little sister I never had. We're going to have so much fun traveling together."

"She's very Talented. A natural. And I think the proximity to Glebric and Kashaka really drew it out. I'm excited to see what we can learn from each other, sharing what we've been taught, and what we've learned on our own. Even if they're different disciplines, there's a lot of potential crossover. And I look forward to meeting this Nurra. Xelos and Yalath both had something different to offer."

"What do you know of Nurra?"

"Only her face, from Xelos' talking statues, that she lives in Laogas, and is a Talented friend. Did Yalath speak of her?"

"Not particularly kindly. But then again, you know his attitude toward women. Thought she was far too independent a spirit. Like him, she was looking through old ruins in her province. I always thought she sounded intriguing. Wondered if she'd be a better mentor than crusty old Yalath." He must have seen Simon's discomfort. "I know, my friend, I should respect the dead. I do. But he wasn't exactly nice to Elysia either. I have a feeling she and Kallara will quite like Nurra. And you seem to enjoy having strong women in your life."

Simon blushed.

"I do too." Remeth turned serious. "Simon, thanks for caring. It means a lot to me."

"Ready?" Simon asked. The four of them were in Simon and Elysia's cabin, with his picture of the temple laid out before them. He had no idea if the plan would work, but it was the best they'd been able to come up with, without understanding what was required to imprison a Damoz.

Remeth would watch the door and talk anyone out of coming in. Kallara would hold the scroll open, and the portal with it. Simon would have his paints and Elysia her carving tools to use their Talent in the temple.

It was Elysia's idea to seal the basin with clay, using her Talent to make it solid. Then he'd paint over it, to try to make a better seal. While he did that, she planned to start breaking through the walls, strategically, to fill the space with water from the outside. Either the temple would sink or at least be made less accessible.

Everyone nodded, and Simon, as planned, stepped through.

The damp of the air hit him first, followed closely by the smell of the sea. He turned back and reached out his hand just in time for Elysia's to pass through the shimmering glow. Seeing her appear out of nowhere gave him a thrill.

She shuddered. "Can you feel the evil?"

"Unfortunately, yes. The blood went in there," he said, pointing out the basin on top of the altar. "I'm going to take a quick walk up to the entrance. You have the clay?"

She nodded and walked it over to the basin. What had sounded like a good idea now seemed almost foolish.

Elysia's head whipped around, her eyes wide. "Did you hear that?"

All he'd heard was a low moaning, likely the wind over the tunnel entrance. "I think it's just the sea breeze."

She walked closer to the altar. "It's so beautiful. Coral. It's like a living stone. Some of our people make beautiful jewelry with it. I never tried, but it looks so intriguing." She pressed the clay into the basin, patting it down. Her back went rigid, her hands on the altar. It began to glow.

"Wait!" Simon shouted, some instinct screaming for caution.

"What did you say?" Elysia asked. "What kind of power?"

"Get away from there!" Simon said.

"Persei? I hate him more than anything. Deliver him?"

"Elysia, no!" He turned back to the portal, waving his arms around. "Kallara, help!"

Kallara's disembodied head appeared in the shimmering air and filled the room with a song of longing, pulling his mind back toward her. Elysia perked up and swayed with the sound as well, but when she took a step toward him she started shaking, as if torn between two forces.

Simon rushed to her side and peeled her hands away from the coral surface, then dragged her away from the altar.

Kallara sang right into Elysia's ear, and helped him push her back through the portal and into the cabin. Simon picked up her satchel where she'd dropped it.

"Simon," came a voice in his own head, soft and seductive. "Give her to me. I can give you everything you want. Wealth. Power. Security. Your father safe."

The prospect sounded so very appealing, and he felt himself considering it before shaking his head. "But what I want *is* her. And to be away from you." Even saying the words felt like swimming against a powerful current, and tiring quickly.

"You think you can stop me?" the voice asked, with a hard edge.

"I already did."

"You can't hold me here. I broke free once. I will do it again. And I'll be coming for you and your friends."

"And I'll stop you again."

"I'll enjoy devouring every last drop of your Talent."

"Never, Kashaka," he said, and stepped through the portal into the cabin.

He hunched over the table, totally drained. Passing there and back again was intense enough, but fighting against her offer was twice as difficult. After a moment of confusion, he rolled up the scroll to banish that voice from his head, and any connection it might have to Elysia.

Kallara sat with an arm around her, and Simon joined them.

"I... that voice..." Elysia said.

"It was Kashaka. She spoke to me too."

"She said that if I got you to work with her, that the power she'd give us, we could destroy Persei forever."

"If you gave me to her," he said.

"I'd never do that," she said, and he knew she was sincere. But he also knew how powerfully Kashaka had pulled his strings, and Elysia's desire for revenge was just too strong. He didn't want any of them to have to face that test again. "Now that I'm expecting it, should we go back, to seal it off?"

"It's not safe."

"But you were able to resist."

"Barely."

"What about Persei and Zaliakara?"

"I... I know we wanted to defend the prison, but we'll lose our minds, or worse. Though I think we'd all agree that it drew out more of our power."

"Could you seal it off in your painting?" Kallara asked.

"But I only know that room. Maybe a door or something… but I need to sleep first. And after I do that, I plan on destroying this scroll. Speak no more of that place to anyone else, until we find Nurra. Hopefully she can help us find a way to seal it for good.

"Thanks for your help, Kallara. I don't know if I could have brought Elysia back without you. Now if you two could leave us, we could all use some rest."

"I'm sorry," Elysia said, after the others had gone.

"We're dealing with forces we can't control, and barely understand."

"What did she promise you?" she asked.

"Nothing that could entice me. I have you, our Talent, good friends, and our freedom." He smiled at her, and she leaned up to kiss him.

"I think I'm going to enjoy this week alone with you."

"Consider it the next part of our vacation," he said, and carried her to their bed.

Epilogue

Numerius peered out the second story window of Korg's ware-house, the early morning light bathing the busy scene in a healthy glow. After the horror of two nights ago and his near-escape, seeing the light of another day was a wonder.

Glebric's men were more organized today in their task of searching everyone and everything moving to and from the ships. *Customs officials? Secret police?* Whatever they styled themselves, they were in complete control of the port, and that meant he had no chance of making his way out of this newly independent city by ship. He'd brooded as he ate his fill of his friend's food and slept better than he had since his initial confinement. The bill would go to the Keepers; they'd want all of his news. And they'd have it, hand-delivered, as soon as he returned to Pazh. Korg handed him Kallara's letter; it hadn't made it out before Glebric closed the port.

A knock on his door interrupted his reverie.

"Yes?"

Korg's face poked in. "Numerius, there's someone you should come and see."

Not one of these officials, or Glebric himself. Has someone sold me out?

Feeling naked and fat without a toga over his tunic, he followed his friend down the stairs and into his office.

Ventus, or a shabby imitation of his former informer, sat slumped in a chair. His face and hair were filthy, like he'd been rolling in a fireplace. Worse still was the smell. Had he not washed in days? The bewildered expression broke when he saw Numerius' face and his eyes lit up.

"Numerius! Thank Salar!"

"Thank Salar, indeed. No thanks to you."

The shock appeared genuine. "What do you mean? I haven't

401

seen you in months."

"Months?" *Has he lost his mind?* The eyes reached out to him, looking for a safe harbor.

"I... I..." Ventus' eyes flicked to Korg and back again.

"Korg, can you give us a few minutes alone?" His friend nodded and left. "Ventus, what happened to you?"

"It shames me to say this, but I woke in a strange place two nights ago. I was face down in someone's room, in a noble villa. My head hurt, like I'd drunk myself near to death, but I haven't been to parties like that in years. The house was empty but for a few guards that told me to hurry, that there was an attack and a fire. They didn't seem to find me out of place, so I didn't ask. When I got to the agora I could see the acropolis, and imagine my shock. I don't even know how I got to Attarsus!"

"So where did you go?"

"I had no money, so I begged... I actually begged for food! Slept on the street. My mind was such a haze. I thought of coming to the harbor, to see if I could find my way back to my house, to my servants. And that's when Korg saw me and brought me in here."

"You're lucky he recognized you. So before you woke up, what is the last thing you remember before that?"

Ventus sat still for a while, beads of sweat on his forehead and his lip quivering. "I... it seems... so long ago. A boat? A cave? Glebric! Yes, Glebric, one of my informants here, remember him?"

"Your slave you planted with Xelos?"

"Yes, that's the one. But, yes... Xelos is dead. Glebric had something to show me. By boat, a cave... the strangest place, like it was carved out of sea rock... a strange place, he took me there and I thought it was the kind of place you'd want to know about."

"Definitely."

"And then... an altar... a flash of silver... elation... that's all I remember."

Numerius looked at him for a long time, trying to find some loose thread to show this was an elaborate fabrication designed to trap him again. But Ventus was no actor, and his sincerity shone through. He felt pity for this broken man who had been so haughty and commanding last time he saw him. *Incredible. That force must have pushed out his mind completely while it was in control. The Keepers will want to question him.*

"Well, my dear Ventus. A lot has changed while you were... asleep. The city has fallen to powers hostile to Pazians like us." He pointed out the window. "They control the port, and would likely try us as traitors."

"What? But this is part of the Republic!"

"Was. Come, let's get you cleaned up. We leave tonight."

"Where? But you said they control the port?"

"A friend of Korg's will take us in his fishing boat tonight. We'll head to Corus, and from there on to Pazh."

"Pazh! Can't I just stay in my villa?"

"I am afraid it has been seized by those same hostile powers. No, you wouldn't be safe there. That must have been quite the blow to your head, if you've forgotten all this."

He rubbed his temples. "Numerius, it doesn't seem sore, like from a blow. Just a fog... a mist that I can't see through."

"Yes, a mist. Well, no matter. Food and water is what you need. It will be a long journey to Pazh."

This news must reach the ears that need to hear it.

ᎶᏍᎶᏍᎶᏍᎶ

Persei could hardly contain his excitement as he entered what appeared to be the central shrine of this strange watery temple. The blood had led them straight there, and his dark flames had made quick work of the wall that blocked off the passageway. Like someone was trying to keep someone out. Or something in.

At first he thought the blood was leading him back to Attarsus again, and that the gods had a good sense of humor. But then it had veered off slightly, closer to one of the other islands, Corus. They'd headed there to rest for the night before searching out the final location, which appeared to be due east, back toward Attarsus. He had found a room in a fine inn for him and Mirasha, and a buxom raven-haired beauty had shown them the way. She was so fetching that he'd entertained thoughts of bringing her to his bed, something he hadn't thought of in a while with Mirasha around. And had she somehow read his thoughts? Mirasha had invited the woman in, leading to a night he wouldn't soon forget.

Zosima was her name, and she was as entranced by them as he was by her. When Mirasha invited her to come into the employ of Persei, a *digniti* tribune, and come with them to Pazh, she had jumped at the chance. When she'd gone to pack her things and he questioned Mirasha, she said only that they should surround themselves with beauty if they were to visit the shrine of Kashaka with the intention of setting her free. She'd read much more about such things, so he deferred. And if more nights like the last were in the offing, he was looking forward to the extra company.

So here they stood, all three of them, Mirasha with the confident bearing of a queen, and Zosima on his right, shaking slightly. She'd never seen anything like this. Neither had he, but it was excitement, not fear that made his heart beat faster.

"Persei, you have come for me," said a woman's voice that felt like silk caressing his ears. Neither of the women had spoken. *The Damoz is here.* Persei took out the last of the blood and poured it out in front of him. The silver liquid did not fall straight to the floor, but curved toward the altar in the middle of the room. It rolled up the side and into a large basin carved inside the top, pooling inside.

"Thank you," the voice said again. "Open it."

He walked forward to the altar, and looked inside. Under the puddle of silver blood, the basin was half-full of something that looked like clay. He scooped it out, and the blood drained down into the depths of the basin. He tossed the clay to the floor.

"Now let me give you what you want."

"How do you know?" he said. Mirasha smiled knowingly at him, nodding to urge him on. Zosima looked confused.

"This place scares me," she said, and she leaned into him when he went to her side. Her soft breast touched his arm, awakening his desire.

"Yes, this one pleases me," came the seductive voice again. "And you. Take her, for me."

"How?" he asked.

"Persei, you're frightening me!" Zosima said again, turning to face him. And showing him all her glory. The soft lips, dark eyes, and abundant curves.

"Zosima, you're safe with me. But... your beauty drives me wild." He stroked his hand through her hair gently as he leaned forward to kiss her. She pouted at first, but when his hand found her breast a soft gasp betrayed how much she wanted him too. He untied the cords that bound her dress above her waist and unwrapped the cloth to reveal her perfect naked form beneath.

"But Persei, this looks like a temple," she said, looking around as he kissed her neck.

"What do you think they did down here?" he said. He lifted her up. For all her curves she was short and light, and with their lips united and her breasts pressed against him, he carried her to the altar. The soft, irregular stone pulsed with a faint glow.

"Take a look, isn't it beautiful?" he said, setting her down beside it. Her sly smile revealed a different interpretation of his instructions. She gave him another exquisite view, bending over and placing both hands on the surface of the altar, her hair cascading down her back.

His desire was throbbing in time with the pulsing light, the intensity of both growing by the moment. He lifted up his tunic, but paused, looking over to Mirasha with a pang of guilt. She bit her lip, and nodded.

The basin filled up with more of the shimmering blood, now almost up to Zosima's face. He didn't care, and she seemed not to notice as she panted, ready for him.

"Take her, and you will have everything, everything!" came the voice once more, husky and urgent.

So he did, plunging into ecstasy that glittered like silver.

Enjoyed the story?
Here's what you can do next.

Book Three:
Winds of Turmoil

Thank you for joining Simon and Elysia in the world of Pazh. Their story continues in **Kallara's Song**, a novella, and **Winds of Turmoil**, Book III of Arts Reborn, to be released in early 2015.

If you loved the book and have a moment to spare, I would really appreciate a short review at Amazon or on Goodreads. Drop me a note about it and you might make my day!

If you get on my pre-release notification list you'll be the first to hear when new books come out, as well as specials and giveaways. Sign up at:

http://www.jamiemaltman.com/newreleases/

More by Jamie Maltman:

Arts Reborn
She Had Eyes Only For What Could Be - a short story of Elysia
    - read for free at www.jamiemaltman.com
I: Brush With Darkness
II: Blood of the Water
Kallara's Song (novella, early 2015)
III: Winds of Turmoil (early 2015)

Short Stories
Dreaming Mountain, in the Beyond The Gate anthology

About the Author

Jamie writes from his home in Richmond Hill, Ontario, Canada, when he's not reading, traveling, watching or playing sports, or playing some kind of games with his wife and two young sons.

Jamie would love to hear from you:

Website: http://www.JamieMaltman.com
Facebook: http://www.facebook.com/byJamieMaltman
Twitter: http://www.twitter.com/jmaltman
Google+: https://plus.google.com/+JamieMaltman
E-mail: jamie.maltman@gmail.com

Glossary

PEOPLE

Pazian

SIMON BAROBA, legionary deserter and son of a *mundati*
      merchant, former aide to Garas Numeno
 - TYBERO BAROBA, Simon's father
PERSEI LOKUTA, *digniti* Legate, 7th Legion, younger son of a
      very wealth and storied family
 - BELLOS, digniti second son, Tribune, 7th Legion
 - CALLUS, *mercati* scout, 7th Legion
DAYMAR LOKUTA, Senator and older brother of Persei,
      General of the East
 - LOKILLA, his younger sister
 - MYSENA, a female Valtari slave
 - GALAX, Gathaki bodyguard
 - MYLAX, Gathaki bodyguard
 - AKTAR, Lokuta family agent

DARAS VANATRI MARASSANO, decorated *digniti* former
      General
GARAS NUMENO, former Camp Prefect, 7th Legion, veteran of
      30 years in the legions
GENARO MORICHEA, *digniti* Senator and former General,
      second to Daymar
HARRON, aide to DAYMAR LOKUTA
KYSO SCRIBORA, *suprati* Tribune, 7th Legion
LOKAS LEPILLA, *suprati* Senator and famed orator
 - POLAS LEPILLA, his uncle

Historical Figures

LUCAS MARCONA, former President and builder of the Basilica Marcona, 500 years prior

MARCOS LUKKEN, former President and builder of the Senate Hall 400 years prior

PORRUNA MACATOR, General and famous tactician who defeated the Western Macatri

POLLIAN, a famous *digniti* family

SUENAS VII, last King of Pazh, tyrant overthrown by the people when the Republic was established

Izar

AZZAM, Alkazy former noble and slave

ELYSIA, young sculptress from Attarsus
- her father, a baker
- ALEXANDER, her brother
- ZENO, her creation

GLEBRIC, Xelos' former servant
- his mother, slave of Ventus
- HECTOR, his friend

KALLARA, red-headed half-Valtari, half-Pazian slave girl and singer

LUKAS PORRUNA, *digniti* Pazian youth

ORNA, Borathi former slave girl and flutist

SOFIA, another former servant of Xelos

TADDASH, enslaved Scentari warrior

TELYS, a guard at Glebric's house

TYNOS, historical figure, leading artisan from Attarsus

VENTUS, wealthy Pazian merchant from Corus
- NUMERIUS ONTILLUS, his epicurean Pazian friend
 - TULLUS, his contact in Pazh

XELOS, master stonemason, from Attarsus
- NURRA, his Talented female colleague in Laogas, Egaras
- YCASTROS, his steward

ZOSIMA, Izari tavern server from Corus

ZONA, a female seller of fragrant oils, friend of Alexander

ZUSTAR, Borathi former gladiator turned trainer

Marutha

EPPETH, head of the archaeological dig in Gardisha

ILSON VANATRI, Pazian scholarly second cousin of the general Daras Vanatri, based in Jeppo

JUKARO, official at the office of the Prefect of Antiquities in Gardisha

URU-MARU, historical founder of New Maruthan empire and devotee of Kashaka

YALATH, Xelos' colleague in Jeppo
 - REMETH, actor and apprentice to Yalath
 - FALLAN, his first crush

Scentari

SHADUSH, Grand Thane, ruler of all the tribes
 - MIRASHA, his 16 year old daughter, now slave to Persei Lokuta

Aktiri

KALNEK, jailer

TIRIN, prisoner, sedition and treason

WARL, prisoner, murder and rapist

YUREK, Coinbrother

PLACES

PAZH (people or language: Pazian), can refer to
 - PAZIAN REPUBLIC (or REPUBLIC OF PAZH), dominant power in the Near Sea and surrounds
 - mainland PAZH, the peninsula containing the city of Pazh
 - PAZH, city of, capital of the Republic of Pazh
   - ARENIAL, hill and district of the city of Pazh, location of the Great Forum and home of most of *digniti* families
   - JANIAR, district of Pazh, home of some *digniti* and many *suprati* or wealthiest *mercati* families
   - MAZIAL, district of Pazh, north side of the main hills, out of the way and secluded
   - NARUNIS RIVER, main river running east-west through Pazh

- SALAMIS, busy southern neighborhood of the city of Pazh, home to Simon and many *mercati*
- VALLEY, district of Pazh along the Narunis river, home to the poorest of Pazh in large apartment complexes

MALAYUS, Pazian city on the southeast coast, originally established by Izari settlers

MELAXA, city on the northwest frontier of the Pazian peninsula, on the border with the Valtari

NAHUZ, Pazian city on the east coast, north of Pazh

PELARI, most famous wine region in Pazh

SAREA, city on the southwest coast, popular vacation town

Pazian Provinces

BOR (people or language: Borathi) - province in the East, ruled by local female elected governor, with men as warriors and main child-rearers, women in most administrative and government roles, known for men and women dressing in similar formless tunics. Generally dark-haired, skin like fresh cut oak.

EGARAS (Egarasi) - southwestern province, past home of several past great empires, including the oldest in the Near Sea region, natives have dark copper skin and dark hair
- LAOGAS, a city far upriver in the southwest of the province

IZAR (IZARI), people of the Izar Archipelago, light to olive skinned, with a variety of hair colors
- IZAR ARCHIPELAGO, a large number of islands in the middle of the Near Sea, previously ruled by local councils as individual city states, but now Protectorate of the Pazian Republic, reached their height around one thousand years ago. Individual city-states still have elected councils, but the Senate can override their decisions.
- ATTARSUS, leading mercantile city state of the Izar Archipelago, also famous for the arts
- CORUS, another significant city state in the Izar Archipelago
- NASOS, most northeasterly island of the Izar Archipelago

KAWAN (Kawanian), southern province famous for swift horses and capable riders, supplies most of the auxiliary cavalry to the legions. Natives have tawny skin, dark hair and slit-like eyes.

411

MARUTHA (Maruthan), southeastern province based around a
major river system, site of several great empires in pre-
Pazian times, home to many ancient ruin sites. People are
known for golden skin and often golden hair
 - GARDISHA, a city from the New Empire period
 - JEPPO, main mercantile city of Marutha, especially with the
Delta too silted up for seagoing ships
 - URAKA, provincial capital of Marutha
- MACATRI, tribesmen who previously held much of Marutha
until wiped out by the Pazian legions, the western Macatri
by Porruna Macator
MYRAK (Myraki), eastern province, generally swarthy and dark-
haired
PELUSIA (Pelusian), northeasternmost province, famous for
trading. Newest province in the Republic, the northern
half was carved out of what was once part of Scentar
before their defeat by the legions. People are typically
stocky, with tawny skin and hair
 - JAMAD, a frontier town on the north border, established after
Pelusia became a Pazian province
 - TAMAR, main mercantile city of Pelusia, famous for exporting
red dye called "The Blood of Tamar"
 - SAL DAR, provincial capital of Pelusia
 - SAL PRATTA, military port of Pelusia

Other places:

ALKAZY, (Alkazy), trading nation west of Egaras on the Great
Ocean, home to very dark-skinned natives and many
warring city-states that export captives as slaves.
BENJEA (Benjish), nation west across the Far Sea from Pazh,
followers of the Benjish religion. Now a subject province
of the Kingdom of Randesh
CHALETH, EMPIRE of (Chalethi), nation far south of Marutha,
across the desert. Source of trade in spices and exotic
goods
GANDARI (Gandari), nomadic desert people south of Kawan
GATHAK (Gathaki), barbarian people from northeast of Pazh,
often hire themselves as bodyguards and mercenaries
MARASSANO (Marassani), warlike people east of Myrak and Bor

SCENTAR (Scentari), nomadic horse people of steppe north of
    Pelusia, whose land formerly included most of the present
    province of Pelusia
  - SENTUSI RIVER, main river of Scentar and best winter forage
    grounds for their flocks
  - NAHAR HILLS, hilly country along the border between Scentar
    and Pelusia
VALTARI (Valtari), tribes hostile to Pazh northwest of the
    peninsula over the mountains

PAZIAN TERMS

Social Classes (highest to lowest)

DIGNITI, those of the original 200 Senatorial families of Pazh who
    still qualify for the Senate, going back to the founding of
    the Republic
SUPRATI, families who are eligible to be added to the Senate
    based on family success and financial qualification
MERCATI, merchant class of Pazh
MUNDATI, working class and laborers of Pazh
DISSATI, the poorest of Pazh, families who have fallen from
    higher classes, or freed slaves who haven't worked their
    way up
FREEDMEN, former slaves who have bought or earned their
    freedom, generally become clients to their former masters
PAZ, Pazian gold coin
SLAVES, slavery is legal throughout the Republic, and children of
    slaves are slaves by default
ZAL, Pazian silver coin

Military Terms

CAMP PREFECT, any army of one legion or more will have a
    camp prefect in charge of all logistical matters, including
    fortifications, supplies, and pay for the legionaries. Third in
    command to the legate and general.
CENTURY, a unit of 100 legionaries in a Pazian legion
CENTURION, commander of a Century. Elevated from the ranks

of the common soldiers, and receives 1.5 times pay.

COHORT, a unit of 600 men, 10 cohorts make one legion. The first cohort contains the best veteran troops.

GENERAL, the current head of one or more Pazian legions. A single legion can be commanded by a legate, but the Senate can name a General of a certain region or to prosecute a specific conflict, but a provincial governor can assume generalship over a legion stationed in his province

LEGATE, always from a senatorial family, assigned as commander of a single Pazian legion. Reports to a general.

LEGION, the main numbered unit of the Pazian army, made up of 6000 legionaries (at full strength) and auxiliary cavalry under the command of a single legate. Referred to by their number, ex. "The 7th" or "7th Legion"

SQUAD, group of 10 legionaries. 10 squads make one century. A squad shares a single large tent and their tools and supplies.

TRIBUNE, a junior officer in the Pazian legions, always from a senatorial family. They serve for 1-5 years, and are paid better than centurions

Political Offices

CENSOR, Senator elected for a five year term to review the financial position of current or future candidates for the Senate and other lower public offices. Also responsible for prosecuting illegal activities by previous officeholders.

GOVERNOR, Senator elected for a three year term to oversee one of the Pazian provinces.

PRESIDENT, Senator elected for one year with executive authority over the entire Republic. Has the right to veto any decision by the Senate, and to propose legislation. Can also assume generalship over any or all Pazian legions unless the Senate proposes an alternate by two thirds majority.

SENATOR, one of 500 men who serve in the Pazian Senate, subject to a minimum level of financial qualification. Any who are found short of that qualification can be suspended, and if not rectified within three years, can be expelled. New Senators are chosen by the Censor to replace any expelled, or who die without any male heirs, and they must prove their financial qualification and membership of the *digniti* or *suprati*.

VICE-PRESIDENT, Senator elected for a 1 year term, as second in command of the Republic. Automatically becomes President if the President should die or become incapacitated while in office. Can be sent as General by the President's executive order unless the Senate proposes an alternate by two thirds majority.

GODS

ATTARSO, Izari god with many forms
  - aka Father Attarso, patron god of Attarsus
  - aka Attarso the Hungry, patron of food-related merchants
  - ALIATA, his daughter, patron of young women and their coming of age
CHORON OF THE SECRETS, Pazian god of the hidden knowledge
DAMOZ, ancient evil beings that grant power to humans in return for devotion
GOD, Benjish single god
HARINA, Pazian queen of the gods, goddess of fertility and motherhood
HASUR, Pazian god of wisdom
KASHAKA, Maruthan goddess of water, main deity of the New Empire period
MELIAX, Pazian king of the gods
 - METRIA, a mortal dalliance in a famous myth
MIJA, Scentari goddess of fire
SALAR, THE IRON ONE, chief god of the city of Pazh, the army, and metalsmiths
SHYGAKAR, god of Aktiri
 - SHYGAKAR'S BLOOD, the high-quality iron of Aktiri
SUKKO, Maruthan minor fire goddess from new empire period
TAMLA, Pelusian god of weather, patron of Tamar
ZALIAKARA, female Damoz of flame, unseen for a thousand years
ZALIKKO, Maruthan fire goddess

Acknowledgements

The second time around is certainly a lot easier, if no less work. In fact, with the length, this one took more work. But I like it better, and I hope you did too.

Thank you to Amy Schubert for helping take this book from solidly good to great, with fantastic developmental editing input.

Thank you to my amazing readers Suzanne and Monica for various levels of review, copyediting, proofreading and sanity checking. And liking this book even more than the first.

Thank you to Keri Knutson of Alchemy Book Design for many rounds of experimentation to come up with an even more awesome cover in the end.

Thanks to my little boys for respecting that my office door was closed on many an afternoon. And interrupting anyway, especially when I felt like being interrupted.

This is too much fun, and I won't be stopping anytime soon.

— Jamie Maltman, Richmond Hill, August 2014